An outstanding first book for a number of reasons, of which the most important is the great freshness with which Mr Charteris handles words . . . all his writing is bright, new-minted, unexpected. The second reason for his success is the very original quality of his mind, which I should describe as being that of mastic with a sense of humour: a conjunction so rare as to be remarkable.

. . . it is impossible in a brief notice to do much more than assert that this is [an achievement]. Good books are like that: their incidental felicities are so frequent that one cannot hope to give chapter and verse. One can only say: read it for yourself and rejoice that a new star is rising.

John O'London's Weekly

It is the design of Hugo Charteris' first novel that sets it apart . . . a design almost cosmic in its implications. Mr Charteris has crystallized the evil of war into a philosophical framework . . . and has painted a future not ugly but filled with promise.

Montreal Gazette

The author's imagination, his observation is vivid. He can throw into words a mood and a character which make me feel that I would recognise exactly that type of situation and person if I encountered them in real life.

Manchester Daily Despatch

Mr Charteris brings off many arresting descriptions of things seen and felt. The characters of Bright and the girl, Jane - withdrawn, charitable, indifferent - are finely done, and the hopeless attachment of Grant for her is conveyed with great tenderness.

Times Literary Supplement

. . . the work of a real novelist . . . long, luminous and heartfelt. Though the theme is radical and gripping, it is unresolved. But the imagination, drama and creative power are something quite out of the way.

Illustrated London News

It is first rate - really exciting. Some of the scenes are superb. All the characters without exception are almost instantly alive. If I were a publisher, I should reckon I had got a real winner in Charteris.

Robert Henriques

... an exceedingly interesting and unusually promising first novel. Hugo Charteris is a naturally gifted novelist who, beside genuine descriptive skill, possesses the knack of evoking and explaining different types of character ... Hugo Charteris uses words not as conventional counters in a literary game but with a real feeling for the poetic and dramatic possibilities of the English language.

Peter Quennell, Daily Mail

Mr Charteris is a true novelist and his first novel not only pins down exactly certain aspects of English life during the first years after the war, but with great psychological subtlety considers such ageless concepts as "fear" and "love".

One recognizes the Matlock family immediately: bound together with uneasy love, feeling that first of many financial pinches, the once brilliant, charming son now, at twenty-three, a belligerent soak, and Jane herself - the "wonderful girl" - caged by family responsibilities, fearing the greatest curse of all, the inability to love. On this surface level Mr Charteris has caught them all to a "t", but he also makes us aware that they are doomed as Mr Eliot's Monchensey family or the house of Orestes.

Mr Charteris is clearly a novelist with his fingers subtly on the pulse of English life.

Michael Swan

Hugo Charteris has the temperament of the born writer ... He sees vividly, feels acutely, has a nervous dislike of the commonplace.

Evening Standard

The book has the distinction of living well up to the claims made for it. The writing is sensitive and, for a first novel, distinguished by a rare ability.

Johannesburg Sunday Express

This is one of the most impressive first novels I have read for a long time. Hugo Charteris seems to me to have a genuinely creative imagination - that is, an intense feeling for dramatic atmosphere, language and situation, as well as an ambitious psychological theme.

Rosamond Lehmann

A tour de force. Where physical action, straightforward narrative, psychological analysis and emotional atmosphere are welded in balanced proportions, he is brilliantly successful.

Truth

A SHARE OF THE WORLD

by the same author

A Share of the World (1953)
Marching with April (1956)
The Tide is Right (abandoned 1957, published 1991)
Picnic at Porokorro (1958)
The Lifeline (1961)
Pictures on the Wall (1963)
The River-Watcher (1965)
The Coat (1966)
The Indian Summer of Gabriel Murray (1968)

A SHARE OF THE WORLD

by

HUGO CHARTERIS

introduced by

JANE CHARTERIS

ADELAIDE
MICHAEL WALMER
2014

A Share of the World first published 1953
© The Estate of Hugo Charteris

Introduction first published in this edition
© Jane Charteris 2014

Published by

Michael Walmer
49 Second Street
Gawler South
South Australia 5118

ISBN 978-0-9925234-2-8 paperback
ISBN 978-0-9925234-3-5 ebook

INTRODUCTION

"I think your book is extremely well written and *riveting*, tho' I must say I can't imagine how you've managed to square your in-laws, if you have?..." So wrote my father's Aunt Mary to him on the publication of his first novel, *A Share of the World,* in 1953.

He hadn't squared his in-laws, as he wouldn't other people, again and again. Family legend has it that our maternal grandmother typed up the manuscript of her son-in-law's first novel with tears coursing down her cheeks, so upset was she by its portrayal of herself and her family. On re-reading it for the first time since adolescence, I imagine that the tears might have as likely been shed for the agonizingly painful depiction of the protagonist, a young man so wracked by self-doubt and low self-esteem, whose emotional responses are of such a destructive intensity that he stymies himself at every move, in both war and love. John Grant is a devastatingly critical, uncompromising self-portrait, even from a first-time novelist.

Aunt Mary notwithstanding, most people would have been unaware of the uncanny resemblance of the main characters to persons alive and related; the book was received and reviewed for what it was – a novel, albeit a highly, at times self-indulgently, autobiographical one. Some critics complained that its characters were hard to like (true enough); another that the re-appearance of a particular character from Part One (war) in Part Two (love, if not peace) was so 'convenient' that it stretched credulity. A quibble even then; coincidence happens and fiction has long used it as a plot device. For the most part, *A Share of the World* was hailed for its 'psychological subtlety', its 'true and curiously moving' account of a relationship struggling into existence, its 'freshness' of language, and the authenticity of the characters. (!) What only one or two picked up on is that it is often very funny.

The book is in my father's own words *"about a stricken moment. The pain, felt and inflicted, came from two young men deeply affected by war. At an irreligious moment of the western world they had come across something like the raw emotions of religion in destruction and chaos. They turned on a peace which denied them even this."* At the time, reviewers and readers seemed to prefer either one part or the other: war or love. To me, the two are inextricably linked. One reviewer, Francis Wyndham, caught this well when he memorably wrote in the *Times Literary Supplement: "[John Grant] decides to marry a girl called Jane Matlock and sets about it rather as if he were preparing to go over an assault course."* The mounting tension of the soldier's mission in Part One is mirrored movingly in the civilian's quest in Part Two.

That description comes from a sorrowful letter my father wrote in response to my grandmother's deep hurt. His distress at what he had done is palpable in his letters (written *after* publication in 1953 - see family legend, above!). *" Oh Irene –* darling *– please* understand *– that was a distorted shadow of you – and of me – and of all of us."* He brought Tolstoy to his defence, as the great copyist, who had *"space for immense detail – the whole of the contradictions, developments, influences, etc"*, but noting (with prophetic irony) that even Tolstoy had been ostracized *"by his own little world. Yet he wrote with compassion and love and no destructive purpose...I shall go on copying – I hope with love."* He cited his wife: *"Virginia has never been ruffled by a single line of Jane. Where true – she has said true, where untrue she has just laughed."*

There is nothing particularly remarkable about a writer drawing from life, but in my father's case the practice does seem to have generated a remarkable amount of hostility. As early as that 1953 letter to his 'belle-mere' he acknowledged that *"injustice is bound to be vast & inevitable because of restricted space"*; subsequent letters written over the years show he clearly considered the danger of upset an occupational hazard of the trade: *"I see no escape from this characterization business. Because no matter how you disguise a person's address, name, circumstances, if you catch their character they are still recognizable, like Big Ben, in fog. As easy as that."* (To a friend and neighbour, c.1964). He certainly easily skewered character with unusual psychological acuity: there are passages in *A Share of the World* that even now give a shiver of recognition, so exact is the telling detail.

What compelled him to go on, book after TV play after book, risking family and friends in this way? He wrote whereof and of whom he knew. In his case, this entailed reconciling himself to his early personal unhappiness; making sense of his 'birthright' in a rapidly changing, post-war world; and making good use of his long interest in the work of C. G. Jung to explore other selves – his own as much as those of his characters.

My father was born in 1922 into the Anglo-Scottish aristocracy, grandson of the 11th Earl of Wemyss. The death from cancer of his mother, Frances Tennant, when he was two, effectively orphaned him and his three older sisters; their father, Guy, a sweet but unworldly walnut-gatherer and amateur ornithologist, was barely capable of looking after himself, let alone four young children. Into the breach stepped the extended family of grandparents, aunts and uncles; the motherless siblings were shuttled between boarding schools (in my father's case; the girls had governesses) and various large country houses from Gloucestershire to Berwickshire.

Ann, Laura and Mary-Rose escaped this life of relative poverty and indebtedness to relations by marrying rich as soon as they could (with varying degrees of unhappiness). For my father, it ended practically if not permanently with the outbreak of war in 1939 and then again with his marriage to my mother in 1948. Whether it ever ended psychologically is a moot point.

This sense of peripheral belonging fostered in him a deeply ambivalent attitude towards his 'class' and stayed with him all his life. As he wrote to a Perthshire neighbour in the 1960s: *"Why do I hanker for aristocratic life when the aristocracy as a whole are about as endearing as shop-stewards? In childhood it seemed different. But then the trees touched the sky as we all know."*

For all that his privileged beginnings were not rosy, he missed something in that world. It wasn't wealth so much as custom, a connectedness between people, a rootedness in the land. Also, access to pheasant shoots and grouse moors, to tennis courts and well-supplied dining tables. In my parents' early married life when my father was making his way as a writer, these were supplied by the generosity of wealthier friends and acquaintances. He sang for his supper of course, being amusing company, an excellent raconteur, a competitive tennis-player and a first-class shot. His gratitude was huge and genuine; nonetheless, it did not prevent him from observing the

3

providers, both individually and as a class rapidly losing its relevance and influence, with the dispassionate eye of the novelist – and outsider. Lord Matlock in *A Share of the World* is described as being *"the dignified undertaker of the temporal power of his country and his class."* As my father snapped at the feeding hand, little wonder exception was taken.

Even so, more often than not he was dismayed and bewildered when anybody minded being 'put in' a novel; he felt his interest in them as *"a kind of love"*, as he later wrote to a friend. To another, who had been a model for a character in a different novel, he wrote: *"The curious thing about this terrible habit of mine – I never 'do it' to anyone I'm not rather fond of. I feel* they *might mind…"* More curiously, he apparently felt that those he was 'rather fond of' were inured from injury by his affection for them. Perhaps some were, many were not; only a few, the 'hysterical censors' as my father saw them, chose to make difficulties. And although the sins of the father were never, in my memory, directly visited on the heads of us children, his 'terrible habit' did drive us south, from Sutherland to Perthshire to Yorkshire, his final resting place. If he'd lived longer and continued writing, who knows where we'd have ended up.

In the end, what matters is whether *A Share of the World* and its characters have stood the test of time, as their real-life counterparts could not. I believe it has; after sixty years, the novel's energy, verve and passion have survived. The pain of the book, 'felt and inflicted', has, I hope, died.

JANE CHARTERIS
London, September 2014.

To
VIRGINIA

Contents

PART ONE

For strictly to separate from received and customary felicities, and to confine unto the rigour of realities, were to contract the consolation of our beings unto too uncomfortable circumscriptions. SIR THOMAS BROWNE

There never was a war that was Not inward. MARIANNE MOORE

1

THE shape of the bush in front was mainly conditioned by the winter which would have come anyway, but it owed something also to a shell, or rather the shell owed something unrepayable to the bush—the high bough hanging by a tendon and the low one messily amputated. At night the bush became a tree when there was a little light, and a subaqueous fern when the moon came, and sometimes it disappeared altogether until, at stand-to, it became first a man, then its same self, now familiar and forever, like childhood, with lichen on three boughs but not on the other. The piece of stuff on it suggested thorns and a tear in some far fugitive's clothing—or a picture of the first, previous war in which human beings had been so much closer together and the shells had apparently splashed bits of them about like water drops, into trees and roofs.

John Grant stood in a slit trench like a grave-digger who has broken his spade and is waiting blankly for another to be brought. He was wondering if one minded less, in time, or more—and whether his magnesium tablets would be get-at-able to-morrow and whether if he gave in to the mood, oh, stop my brothers in life, stop—walking up to the enemy and through his own lines feeling and saying this, it would have an effect.

A brand-new stocking-cap sat awry over his pale face and luminous eyes, suggesting the subject of an eighteenth-century cartoon captioned " Master Philip is to get some physic."

As a dream can dominate the following day with mental taste, more pervasive than reality, so the past forty-eight hours kept cropping into his mind, as though they lay before him for ever, with him now and behind him since birth. This valley of orange trees carpeted with mangled fruit and loud with the grief of a lost ass, with its smashed white wells, two burnt-out carriers, warrens of damp men, and periodic attention from out an impersonal void, crescendo shriek and cacophony of bangs in series, lulls and the same again, lulls and then a difference: the distant hammering apparently of a boy on tin, and then high in the air the music of the infernal spheres or the sighs in the sails of an invisible and devilish galleon as a graceful flotilla of mortar-bombs gathered way going straight down. This valley where every hour a drained face got separated from its boots by a supine lump of blanket, was a corner of a foreign field which was not forever England, but forever—and as ever—John Grant. That is to say, merely the hypo which had fixed now and here the perpetual negative of his fear. For John Grant was a connoisseur of fear.

For instance, only three days ago, off Sicily, during the last boat-drill he had still put on his life-jacket with dread—not of being torpedoed, but of tying the tapes wrong, and emerging from his cabin like a clown tangled in bolsters, as he had the first day out.

The futility of speculating about his magnesium tablets, and of waiting for the next raw rise, from stomach to mouth, drove his attention in the direction of the enemy-held village of Salturno, at sight of which his face became like a young Napoleon's. Now he thought what he thought last night, that the war was not, in fact, being fought at all. At nine—or 2100—the 2nd ——shires had occupied the hill in front; at ten the Germans were on it. Between nine and ten there had been one burst of Bren, two of spandau, and three or four miscellaneous noises. That was all. Yet the hill changed hands. "Jerry" took it. Then at two minutes past ten our twenty-five pounders turned the hill into a cone of orange flashes for twenty minutes. When the display ceased there were two long bursts of spandau, and silence: the 2nd ——shires' counter-attack, it was whispered, had been " seen off ": there was still " nothing " in front.

Ten men, thought the officer who had sweated in fear over his life-jacket tapes, could infiltrate at night into the enemy lines; so could one man. One man doing this with a machine-gun could kill twenty or more, as light broke, before being killed. One man could kill twenty, yet last night a hundred and twenty were moved back half a mile by two bursts of machine-gun fire and some miscellaneous bangs. The war was not really being fonght at all.

Hence the expression on his face—Napoleon waiting at Toulon; Napoleon foreseeing Arcola. The X-ray stare: inspiration from reason mixed with the excitement of a child who detected the king had really no clothes on at all in spite of the way the page behind him appeared to be holding something in raised white-gloved hands.

John was nearly beautiful. Not handsome because insufficiently masculine in the tobacco-advertisement sense, nor really beautiful. He was prevented from beauty by one eye, which unlike the other, at the same time as foreseeing Arcola seemed morbidly to confess to a murder, repenting under its higher brow with the objectivity of a corpse. The other was bright, " boyish," quickly smug when contented (which was seldom). His nose was a classical fragment such as lies about in an art-school cupboard. His lips and protrusive mouth alone seemed there for a driving, practical purpose.

This mouth was particularly to the fore when killing twenty by infiltrating one, but relaxed, and gave all to the higher eye at the thought of Corporal Meadow's cheek bared to the bone by an invisible knife which had sighed as it struck. As he stood there this mouth, and Arcola stare, became suddenly more pronounced. He had finally decided to tell Bright to stop talking now, and not —as he had at first planned—to let him talk a little louder first. Whether to back the command with reference to the Company Commander's wishes, and appeal to the man's own long experience, or to put it briefly and sharply from himself in spite of his new stocking-cap, was a problem which widened the Arcola eye to the limit of inhuman premonition. He decided to let Bright talk a little louder first and then give him hell off his own bat; not that he had ever given anyone hell, but daily jargon affected even thought.

Beside him on a ledge of mud and limestone fragments were Verey light cartridges arranged like ninepins to dry, a field-telephone, a bar of chocolate, some razor blades, " V " cigarettes, and a translation of the *Bhavagad Ghita* with mud on the pages. Letters, handed by torchlight before dawn, stuffed his greatcoat pocket. They were the accumulation of his four weeks on the sea, and whenever he thought of them a strange, almost gastric sense of appeasement and sweetness came over him, even though the letter from Susan was unsatisfactory. The one from his father was devoted to intrigued speculation on the future uses of airgraph, with an appendix of examples of how best to write legibly for photographic diminishing. It ended with seven different written lines of " The quick brown fox jumps over the lazy dog "; then a silhouette of a curlew, big; finally, lines getting smaller and smaller until illegible, and a large request to send the sheet back in its diminished form.

The mood of pencil-and-paper games had been hard to recapture by the muffled light of a torch, sitting in moist mud and limestone gravel, waiting for the next spasm of heartburn, and the next itinerant or the next visiting shell. But a tiny " God bless you " upside down in a spare space was like the grunt on the platform at parting, the grunt and the extra stress on the last syllable of " good-bye "—it compressed, just in time, some sort of affection— also an apology, as it were, for the inevitable distance of one human being from another, particularly of a father from a son. Only one letter was unopened—the fattest of three from Susan. John did not open it for the same reason that he had read the other two fast and superficially. He did not wish to think less of her, because to do so was to think less of himself. He had made so many promises and her letters undermined resolution to carry them out.

If they get a Bailey bridge over to-night the tablets would probably be available to-morrow. Bright was talking louder now. Three pairs of Spitfires crossed a gap in the clouds. There were probably more human beings in that valley mile than there had been since the world began, yet except for Bright, who was sentry, none were visible.

Bright.

How could you be sentry with your collar round your eyes, talking and hunched always in one direction. Perhaps you could.

A Share of the World

Perhaps after four years, from Alamein to the Volturno, you knew what you could do.

On the other hand, Desmond, his red-haired company commander, had introduced John to his men the night before last, going from shape to shape, whispering an occasional name and getting occasional grunts in reply, and wound up with the warning: "The worst survive." Back in lighted Company Headquarters, the second cottage after the dead ox, he said, "The battalion has been fighting for four years without rest or refit. It has had four complete turn-overs of officers. It has been used again and again when it has been promised rest—because the other mobs couldn't be trusted. By now it's almost entirely made up of emergency drafts from England—i.e., men not wanted there—plus the residue of the regulars who have been out four, five, six years; the dregs, only, because as I say—with few exceptions—the worst survive."

Desmond was happy in the six months' old discovery that he was good at war; he was a Norfolk squire who had been got rid of for obstinacy from the regiment's tank battalion.

He closed John's initiation with these words:

"Dregs or not it does no harm to remember there are no bad men; only bad officers. And training doesn't matter a f——. Given guts and common sense you can't go far wrong; without guts and common sense you might as well pack up."

Desmond had a large wooden face, flat except the nose, and pipe. He spoke slowly and each thought dawned upon him separately with the finality of a sun's appearance, and after that was there. What he thought, he thought.

Have I guts or common sense? John wondered. Can I make Bright good by being a good officer? Could I, for instance, have prevented him from going to sleep on sentry last night? Perhaps I should have shot him—so as not to be left with a "bad man." Was that what Desmond meant by "no bad men"—shoot the inadequate? To apply that principle, John calculated, would leave me Corporal Brown, also the man somewhere over there by the bottomless basket, and possibly myself. We three having been the only ones who stood ready during yesterday morning's "attack" which the artillery stopped. The others remained not only below ground, but also in some cases underneath gas-capes, where I found them when I went round afterwards. There was satisfaction in finding big men cowering, but not as much as in finding big men backing me up—like Corporal Brown and the man by the basket.

Perhaps I should have shot Bright when he opened his little pig eyes down there in his black deep hole, and said he had the squitters.

On the typed list (the only place where he had so far seen his men all together) Bright was catalogued as thirty-four, waiter, of no fixed address. John tried to picture him by the big ham and fruit basket, nursing the hors d'oeuvre trolley into place, or taking a fat woman's coat, but somehow the man doing these things was never Bright. But the face seen for an instant at the swing-door leading to the kitchen, or the face of the diner in the shadows, or of somebody in the street outside pausing under a lamp—these were Bright. And all were faces which he surprised in the act of looking at him, and which remained looking at him for an instant after their eye was caught, before looking away. Had he seen Bright before somewhere that the man should look at him like this? No, John had never met Bright; unless once when a train halted beside another train and faces were placed at an intimate distance, the one in front of John had been Bright's, smiling his particular smile, assuring him this was no coincidence.

John had read books about war in which men who went to sleep on sentry had been either shot, or nearly shot. On this occasion Bright had been fetched behind the broken wall during stand-to —at Desmond's orders—and there lectured by Desmond on what might have been the consequences. Bright had clearly expected nothing worse than the talk. His murmured contrition had mixed with the soft choiring of voyaging shells whose origin and arrival were faint like accidental bumps on a kettle-drum. Desmond mentioned the word " shot " in a way that identified it with his true feelings, and Bright ceased apologising as though touched for the first time by understanding.

John had stood at one side, and when Bright saluted and slouched into the damp dark-blue light which was not yet light, Desmond said: "You've got to keep after them the whole time. You can't sleep."

"I didn't," said John.

"It's your job to keep them awake. Your job," he said.

"Yes," said John.

"D'you know their names yet?"

"On paper."

"I'll try and change you with Peter so that you can move about by day. Meet them. You must know them. Unless you know them—and they know you—it's hopeless."

"Thanks."

"You'll have to watch Bright."

"Yes."

John now watched Bright—over ten yards of ground—which as it got nearer Bright became covered with shining empty tins. Bright had been told to bury them so that the flanged lids would not heliograph to the enemy the position of the platoon. Now, Bright's high voice was petulant and plaintive—the adult equivalent of an infant grizzling. Out of such a big man the sound was distressing, like a freak at a fair. He said, though John could not hear:

"Some people think their own piss doesn't smell."

"Bright," John said.

The man turned.

"You know we're responsible for from the well right round to the first house."

"Yes, sir."

"Well, watch it all."

"Yes, sir."

Two heads sprouted out of the slag to see what the talk was about. One had a tin hat, one nothing. The faces seemed to have wondered whether the officer said, Pack up, out to-night, Mondragone, Naples, and then that ship. When this hope died away, they subsided again into the earth.

As in an aquarium, time passed with the bubbles going up as the only event. That stone in that place, that claw just showing, the arrangement of the ground, the bubbles of thought, replacements of nothing, eternally arriving, dissipating, vanishing—the stare of one or two watchers—uncomprehending, seeing nothing, passing on.

Bright got out of his trench. John forgot his stomach to rap out a query in his too high-pitched voice. Hadn't the company commander said there was to be no movement by day? Bright's little eyes were intimately malicious. John had never seen all of him before. He was big; he looked like a gigantic tramp in his thick clothes and slack webbing. A wheedling piping voice came out of him as he put his hand indicatively behind him.

" I can't help myself, sir," he said. " I was thinking of my mate."

" Well, hurry up then."

The great figure shambled only a yard and began to fumble with his clothes.

" Since you've shown yourself, go right out of the area to do it."

Bright straightened interrogatively, as though such an order took time to be believed. Then he withdrew another five yards, and called:

" Will this do, sir? "

" That'll do," John said irritably. Bright squatted.

The sound of a boy hammering tin came five spaced times. Bright, mouthing, shambled back, tripping over loose trousers. High up the air became feathered with sound which, without crescendo, turned suddenly into crunching explosions and choiring fragments.

The field-telephone buzzed twice. John heard his Christian name—uttered reluctantly, as though this conventional familiarity of the regiment in his case did not come naturally. Would he please keep his men from moving about by day. Hadn't he understood the first time? Desmond's voice relented as though this were not the moment. Would he come to Company Headquarters at once with a map?

John crawled ten yards across slime and stones clasping a too-big map-case to his battledress top. A bare bough surprised him by being thorny, and caught his stocking-cap, and to free himself entailed an activity which was perhaps more conspicuous, he thought, than Bright's. Also it reminded him he should have put his tin helmet on, as the standing order required. He called to his sergeant's trench—three times. At the third call an eye appeared. The eye said, " What is it now? " The voice, " Yussah? "

" Take over, please. I'm going to Company H.Q."

The eye disappeared.

It had been a Sandhurst formality. One had to go by something. John got to dead ground and walked, listening back to see if his movement would bring a stonk down. At the corner of the first house in the village he was hailed sing-song from above. Billy Butler, the recce. officer, who had been sent on a draft from England for homosexuality, reclined with binoculars on top of a shed. He looked at ease and happy as he had never done in England—with his neck open and a beige scarf falling loosely over one shoulder. He, too, it was said, was good at war.

" You look happy," John said.

" And you look like an early German Christ in dark wood."

He always spoke in a deadly flat monotone as though he were the villain in a melodrama. " Anyhow, why shouldn't I be happy? It's going to clear up. I can make out two pairs of sailor's trousers over Salturno, which means that somewhere are two pairs of sailors without trousers. *A la bonheur.* But where, tell me—oh, tell me. Weren't the 2nd ——shires glamorous last night? Didn't you see them? Like a boatload of Armenians torpedoed off Gibraltar. They came through G Company and asked the way."

Bright, Billy Butler, and Desmond, a stranger, introducing shadows who grunted and couldn't be seen by day. Corporal Meadow's blood all over his right knee and the blessed man by the bottomless basket who stood up with a gun when told. It was all a little sudden. John looked at Billy and tried to switch to another mood.

" Mind the donkey by the church," said the flat deadly voice, " it's dangerously hungry."

At the church, glass tinkled at the donkey's hoofs. It wrinkled its lips over its yellow teeth, as though about to play a wind instrument, and then with harsh intakes of breath began to play its crescendo of bottomless dejection. Occasional faces looked up from ground level, in tin hats, stocking-caps, or dirty-haired. His appearance had broken their monotony, and—perhaps this was it

A Share of the World

—from Brigade, the order to pull out, back to Naples, that ship, and home. Only one man drying his socks before a smokeless fire of packing-case tinder, seated on a fallen saint and cutting his toenails carefully, did not pay any attention. For him the moment was enough.

Desmond and the Adjutant looked up.

"Oh, good, John." Their cheeriness and welcome, John at once realised, was a bedside manner: they were going to operate. They might even conceal from him the real nature of the illness.

John, unclipping his too-big map-case bought at the Army and Navy Stores five weeks ago, surprised the Adjutant in a doubtful and compassionate stare.

"John, Brigade wants to know if Massa Tre Ponti is occupied. I'm afraid it takes us—you, John—to find out."

So he had cancer. A cold stone came to rest in his foreskin. Once he had stood beside a girl playing sardines. He had found her first. He knew that she had given herself away as he passed, on purpose, with a slight movement, and yet when he joined her in the silent hot darkness and felt her arm against his, smelt her hair and wanted more than anything else to kiss her, that logical and obvious event would not come. Instead there was this cold stone lying in his stomach pit, and the nightmare paralysis which divided, not the will from the limbs, but the will from the wish. He did not get as far as willing. He could merely wish. But because he couldn't *see* himself doing it, he couldn't will it. Desmond's pipe-stem rested on a chinagraph circle round some italic print on a contour line. He could not move or speak. The moment was familiar—it had happened before. The woman, one of three in black, was on the spiral stairs, and the velvet ticks of the grandfather's clock in the hall were their feet coming nearer, and he could go no higher, there was no foothold on the sky.

He couldn't, he must. He couldn't.

He said, "That's the farm with the burnt-out Mk. IV., isn't it?"

He felt their surprise, and his own. There were many farms spattered like milk spots on the hill opposite, all with outlandish

20

names, of which after two weeks they only knew some. They became confiding, man to man. They planned the route with him as though it was to be theirs. Sometimes both fell silent in the strictest and most honest silence imaginable, weighing up which side of a building to pass, where to cross the track, what arms to take, and which three men.

"Though that's something," said Desmond after suggesting two, "you had better decide for yourself. You can't take five-year men—they're excused patrols—so you won't have much choice."

He ran his finger down a list. He said, "Bryant, Gallacher, Matthews, Corporal Murray, Macfadgean, Bright . . . Oh, ˜ don't know. You're better off than Peter Bolt-Ewing."

Better off than Peter Bolt-Ewing: he was better off than Peter Bolt-Ewing. The phrase stuck, perhaps because it meant nothing. A jingle: hey-nonny-nonny.

Bright! John wondered if Desmond would take Bright, and manage to have no bad men with him. He said, "I'll take Corporal Murray." They were dubious.

"Poor Corporal Murray! Try not to take him always. It's a compliment he's had a lot of. And he's one month short of five years."

His mind was sticking like a faulty gramophone. Always! He mustn't always take the miner with the jersey. Not next year nor the year after. Desmond said:

"What weapons will you take?"

It was up to him, their faces said. Up to him—up to him—up to him. He frowned. Was a Bren advisable—in case? Yes, they thought it was. Then a Bren and tommy-guns and grenades. Desmond ticked off points satisfied. Test weapons behind the church before dark, blacken faces here at ten, see Colonel Boy before leaving at eleven. Now the ground. We'd better go up to Harry's O.P.

A woman with jet lank hair, carrying one baby, leaning from it, and leading three, and bare feet like a monkey, her toes prehensile to the cobbles, met them at the baffle blanket.

"*Niente mangiare—quatro bambini* . . ." she turned after them whining, her hand outstretched.

A Share of the World

" I thought they'd all gone," said Desmond. " You'd think they'd go, wouldn't you? "

" *Allez,*" said the Adjutant; " *allez,* shoo, go away—*niente* cigarette."

At a corner they were hailed from the ground level. A lean face with a drooping moustache like a mandarin.

" You have to go round the back, Desmond. They've got a spandau on four-six-two." There was a noise like a near motor-bike travelling instantly at seventy for three seconds and then stopping abruptly.

" Rather close, isn't it? "

" Yes, I think the Queen's must have been pushed off."

The party looked blankly at a hill like any other hill—a jumble of white rock and scrub—towering close to the east above tiles like the waves in old charts.

The Adjutant said, " I think I'd better go back to Colonel Boy. You're O.K. on the patrol aren't you, Desmond? "

The lean face on the cobbles seemed possessed of much mysterious information for one who was level with the ground.

" The Kraut's putting airburst on the reverse slope now."

John heard wrenching explosions in series then the motor-bike again. Suddenly there was a swift, shrivelling, whispering overhead, followed by bang, bang, bangings, from all round; from out of the town itself, apparently, from under his feet, from out of the head on the pavement.

" That's us. Where are my glasses, Wright? " said the lean face, disappearing for an instant. " Thank you." It re-emerged with extensions to its eyes. The moustache suddenly taken out of its context, isolated by the glasses, looked stranger than ever—like a double-leafed plant an hour after transplanting; radically starved of all that it was used to.

The face abandoned the glasses for a sharp look downwards.

" Wright, don't waste those tablets. *One* will bring it to the boil."

" Och, ye need half another as well, surr."

In exasperation the lean face disappeared completely, and there was the sound of muffled altercation. " I boiled a full mess-tin with one yesterday," John heard. He felt like a child by a counter, taken shopping too young. Everything was over his head.

" Come on now," said Desmond.

The O.P. was a top-floor room on the village perimeter. An 88 had expanded the window to twice its normal size, blown out the back wall and revealed the street through the floor. A pale-faced youth sat hunched in the corner with earphones on, as though he were receiving electrical treatment for a serious illness. Kneeling in the middle of the floor, facing the gap, was a figure like a student rehearsing in a garret. He did not abandon a sort of tragic, starry-eyed concentration, just because people came in. All noises were louder here, and more numerous.

" Up fifty, same again," said the kneeler.

That over, then he became all the apologetic host. Gentle welcoming. If they had come ten minutes earlier they could have had tea.

" Hallo, John. Yes, we met on Blackcock, didn't we? Or was it Banshee? " There had been so many. A patrol? To Massa Tre Ponti? " Oh, dear; oh, dear; oh, dear—that, as I tell my men, is where we are lucky. No patrols. You know, I don't think I could do it."

This broad-faced, motherly Catholic at twenty-eight might have been fifty. The huge shadows under his eyes and the light in them reminded John of an aunt he once visited an hour after she had given birth. In the eyes of each—agony seemed relevant and fulfilling.

" Yes," said Harry, " you could not wish for a better view, and Massa Tre Ponti—*your* farm, John—your farm—is the hub of it all. But don't go too near the window. It has been enlarged three times already. That's why I moved here. Third time lucky has passed. There they go. Oh, lovely. Just where I wanted. Thank them, Corporal Smith."

An orderly grey line of six grey shrubs blossomed by a far house. Then an express train was suddenly upon them. John half-turned like a man on a platform too near the verge. Five times in rapid succession each brought plaster down and dust in showers, banged on the tin lids of their senses, and in the distance ended like a bus full of crockery crashing on rocks.

" All the same—thank our sharpshooters, Corporal Smith. We must have touched them on the quick. Unlucky. Perhaps you'd better go down for a smoke, Corporal Smith."

The pale youth had put off the phones and was sobbing.

Harry said, " We're rather on the promenade up here, on the sea front, as it were. Corporal Smith is always unlucky when he comes on. Aren't you, Corporal Smith? But you've done well."

Desmond brought John to the centre of the floor.

" That's the orchard," he said; " five o'clock from the grey outcrop."

John hardly heard him—but looked. He was a child before the cage of a tarantula. Where in that ominous and arid emptiness was IT. How many were there. What is that . . . that . . . that thing there? Is that anything to do with IT? Out there . . . himself. Again the feeling of impotence like nausea possessed him. It was not him out there to-night. South. Italy in winter monochrome.

From here the landscape looked wrecked and soiled more by gale and rain than war. The effect was of fantastic untidiness—as though a grimy infantile hand had splurged across it. The sky was smeared with smoke: grey and white ours, black theirs; windows of far houses were like mouths with hare-lips, outline lost from Sherman 75, or six-pounder. The eye went to buildings and felt tricked; went everywhere and felt tricked. Desertion—yet out of the desertion and dereliction came enormous ceaseless noise which the room magnified but deprived of origin. Harry's patter went on.

" I like the term ' leaning on the enemy,' don't you, Desmond? I see from the communiqué that that's what we're doing. Oh, I'm so sorry; I'm interrupting."

The olive orchard line of my arm, Desmond was saying; where the ground falls away, where the tree is, the tops of those cypresses is this cemetery called San Giovanni. Peter saw movement there on Tuesday; if you take that track, then. . . .

" Yes," John heard himself saying as though it were all clear,

A Share of the World

" yes, I think this side would be better, definitely this side. And when I get to the well, will that be near enough to hear them? "

" That's your look-out. You must be satisfied in your own mind that the place is empty—if you report it empty. There's only one way to be sure—go in and see."

Their voices sounded like a wireless left on in a burning room. Go in and see, John nodded. Yes, of course, he said, I'll have to go in.

" Lie up two hours first by the well, listening—and then if you hear nothing—well, check up. It's the only way. If you get fired on put up two red Verey lights and we'll bring down the D/F arranged. Have you got the ground fixed in your mind now? "

John's reply was drowned by the 88. Three times he started speaking, and was left looking inanely into the face of this man he met yesterday for the first time, in whose name he was not yet sure whether the "t" was double. He was trying to say Yes, but could not separate it completely from the shriek of metal's velocity, or the munching crash of destruction.

" Yes," he said finally. The look was behind both their eyes. Desmond filled his pipe, and said slowly enough for John to hate him:

" Distances at night—very deceiving. The only way—is to make landmarks. Preferably things you'll see against the sky. Skymarks you could call them. Now here, for instance—that mountain oak by the track—would be a good half-way check."

The 88 slammed five more shells into the top edge of the town.

" Harry must have done his stuff," said Desmond complacently, put away his matches, pressed his pipe bowl with a broad thumb, took another look at the ground through his glasses. Was the little act of self-discipline over? " Quite happy? " he said.

Desmond left him by the church. The donkey was standing at the foot of the steps worn into shallow curves by generations of worshippers, and perhaps a tourist or two off the beaten track. The face on the pavement lifted the drooping moustaches from a steaming mess-tin, and said, " Hallo there."

" Hallo," said John.

" I'm Peter Bolt-Ewing. Are you John Grant? "

" Yes."

" Average hell, isn't it? Have you got 23 Platoon? I had it at Mareth."

The man with the moustaches wanted to talk, and he talked. He missed the advantages, he said, of the desert war—civilised it was, few deaths, always a bed and marmalade, and none of this bloodiness. Was Corporal Brown still there? Splendid man. And Bright?

" Bright was my uncle's butler for a week. You can have Bright."

" Yes. I've got him."

" H'm. Well, have fun to-night. I won't say I wish I was coming with you."

" What about Bright? " John said.

" What do you mean? "

" Why did your uncle only keep him a week? "

" I don't think he liked his face. But you could correspond with my uncle if you like. Are you looking for a butler? "

" No."

" Well, tootle-oo."

" Good-bye."

John crawled out of the dead ground and saw his platoon's heads like coconut shies topping the slag of each slit trench, every face turned towards him. They knew. The sergeant called when he was ten feet away, " Patrol, surr? "

" Yes," said John.

" Well, f—— beat that," said the sergeant. " F—— B Company again. The only f—— company in the f—— battalion."

Who made this man a sergeant? John answered himself, The same man, perhaps, as made you an officer. What are we all doing here? How many of all the men in this valley ever aimed his expensive firearm at one of the enemy? He half expected a sort of master of ceremonies to appear, clap his hands, in the bottom of the valley, and shout to both slopes:

" All right, all right—that will do for to-day. Hot baths and

26

high tea is waiting. The wounded can pick up new limbs at the main entrance, and the dead can get back their lives on the first floor, second on left."

The play of it all, the appearance was still strong in him. Headlines, letters, aunts talking about war. Instead, there was Bright watching him over a layer of mud, cannily. John crawled towards Corporal Murray, whose slit was behind Bright's. When he was a few feet short of Bright's slit, the big man spoke suddenly, shrilly defiant, " Five-year men are excused patrols, sir. Five-year men have been f—— about enough, haven't they Tam? " Bright was not a five-year man.

Fine cold rain began to fall. Behind Bright's head, protruding from the earth, was the hill and the white farm called Massa Tre Ponti. Corporal Murray was " for it," Bright was not. Everywhere the same sieve was being applied to British males.

Corporal Murray was putting away an airgraph. The breech of his rifle was swaddled in rag, and he had undercut his trench wall to make a sort of neat cooking range for his mess-tins and methylated tablets. He looked up agreeably when John called his name.

" I've got to go and look at a farm to-night, Corporal Murray, and see if it's occupied. I'd like you to come."

John tried to make it sound valuable—" you to come "—as much as to say, others will come because numbers must be made up, but I ask you because you're the sort of person I would like to have with me.

A pinched look came into the man's eyes, a look which said, " Did someone tell you I enjoy it? "

" I'm sorry," said John. " You've had a lot, I believe. We're . . . a bit short of good men. You know better than I how it is."

" A job's a job," said Corporal Murray.

He began putting away his things, screwing up his pen and unbuckling his big pack, as though the train was coming in now. Bright, relieved, called to John as he crawled back:

" I suppose we five-year men have got something to be thankful for, sir, haven't we? " He was all smiles.

" Are you still on guard, Bright, or have you been relieved? "

27

" Just bein' relieved now, sir."

" Have you been relieved? "

" Yes, sir."

" Who by? "

Bright called behind him, " It's your shift now, Jimmy, innit? You're on now, aren't you? "

A ruddy-faced youth answered defensively to John, " It's no five o'clock yet, surr."

John said, " Bright, you've been watching me for the last ten minutes. Supposing during that time the Germans had attacked? "

He had never been in a real attack. Bright presumably had. Bright had three years of fighting, or if not fighting—then, three years of this sort of thing.

He felt like a pedantic ineffective schoolmaster who has surprised a boy with a paper dart: supposing we all threw paper darts. Bright watched him. The man's face was close: crafty eyes, small, small above the level of the brows, baby mouthed.

" Bright," he said.

" Sir? "

" You'll be for the patrol to-night. Take your stuff over to Company H.Q. Now . . ."

Bright said quickly, " Five-year men are off patrols, sir."

Faces sprouted and turned in their direction. John said:

" Yes, Bright, but you're not a five-year man. Are you? "

They looked at each other in silence. Bright's jaw clenched; then suddenly he smiled. Like a salesman, like a politician on the hustings, like a compère, like a managing director at a dinner speech or an organ-grinder offering a bashed top-hat, he smiled— yet only superficially like these people in excusable falseness. In another way he smiled as though John was someone he had known for a long time and had just done something so typical that a smile came of its own accord.

2

THREE pairs of lips and three pairs of eyes: all other features merged in the black equality of burnt cork. Emphasised eye-whites made the pupils shifty and fearful, though more mobile than usual; lips seemed pink and damp as though they were interior not exterior, privy not public parts of the body. The three men might and certainly might not have been waiting in the wings of a music hall, among ropes and strange dresses, props and beams. Time had stopped like a jammed cinema; this was the frame beyond which it would not go.

They ate slabs of processed cheese between biscuits like edible wood. John thought, " Something before you go, darling." They had left all letters, all belongings with the company clerk, in order that dead or alive they would give no clues. Desmond's back obscured the wedge of night which he looked out on, holding aside the blanket by the door. One star was over his head.

" Bright ? " he had said. " Rather a strange choice after last night."

" *Because* of last night," John had said, and Desmond had looked at him queerly: what sort of fish, fowl or herring are you?

" You'll have the moon after all," he said, and came back and began to walk round their backs as they sat. The slightly complacent expression on his face, John realised, would have been there even if he had been going himself. But that made it no less alien.

Desmond had " lost his name " in the MT park at Chalfont Magna but was now known as having " done awfully well " in Italy. " Doing well " in Italy—was that what they were there to do?

Desmond said, " Colonel Boy wants to see you before you go. But I shouldn't go yet."

A Share of the World

"What happened to the Queens," said John; "that hill?"
"I should think they're in Sicily by now."

Did it not matter what happened to the regiment on one's right? Apparently not. Nothing made sense. Everything was invisible. The heard had taken the place of the seen.

"The Coalies moved into the cemetery," said Desmond as though that explained.

John looked at the tommy-gun on his knees—a spectacular lie—and looked at it again; it had to be made true. Never before had appearance and reality so conflicted in his mind. On the one hand, This is John Grant leading a patrol; John's in Italy; he counted the Germans through a window, show Bridgett his letter but send it back. And on the other hand, this cold gun, black hand, Bright, Brown, and the white house which he didn't see himself going into.

"There's only one way to be sure. Go in."

Desmond had repeated it on his circuit of the table, chewing the cud on a phrase that tasted good.

Bright's head moved, looking at Desmond. Desmond did not notice when Bright's head moved. John noticed when Bright moved his little finger: perhaps that was why the man looked at him with almost a proprietor's stare.

Corporal Brown, like Desmond, was smoking a pipe, but the stem of it did not cut into a solid and secret complacency; it fitted into a coarse, broad mouth composed but not pleased.

"If anything makes you think you've been spotted—come back at once—and by a different route."

"Yes," said John. It was easier not to plan. What would happen was waiting for him like a stream full of capricious currents. Once afloat he would try and cope with them as they came. The village street in the dark had looked like a place never seen before and he had fallen into an empty slit, felt a fool as he was helped out by Corporal Brown. Where was the half-way oak and the white farm in that general metamorphosis?

Desmond clocked in another circuit. "Distances are deceptive," he said; "look backwards almost as much as you look forwards." He looked at his watch and went to the door.

" I should get across now," he said.

John said importantly, " Ready? " At the door Corporal Brown touched his shoulder with the Verey pistol which he had been fiddling with at the table and left behind.

" Oh, thanks," he said.

" Don't forget that," said Desmond.

Bright's mouth was open and he was feeling a back tooth with his tongue, looking at John, round Corporal Brown's shoulder, cheerful as though he wasn't going.

" I'll see you through the company lines," said Desmond. " Go out by the last house. I'll be there. You'll have the moon all the way."

John suddenly remembered he did not know where Battalion Headquarters were. " Colonel Boy's behind the church," someone had said.

" Which is my best way to Colonel Boy from here? " he said, as though it were a question of selection.

" I'll show you, sir," said Bright. He had fetched the platoon rations.

Ruins, trees, mountains over roofs near and far, cobbles, ruts and puddles lay in a mock day under a moon like a new shilling, with the sky near it like diluted ink.

" Lead on," said John.

The American patrol boots padded softly on the cobbles.

A sentry challenged, " Greta."

" Garbo," said Corporal Brown. Then, " here we are." John turned to his men as though they were a taxi.

" I won't be a moment." He parted the blankets. It was like going into a bright shrine. There before him by the light of many candles he saw the being who was known in the Signals code as Sunray—the commanding officer Colonel " Boy " Annesley. Like John, he had been in Italy three days. They had come out together.

" Oh, John; splendid," he said, and rose like a good host, advancing warmly, and even before John had finished saluting was walking him towards the table where a bottle of kümmel and two tooth-tumblers stood among maps and papers.

A Share of the World

Colonel Boy pronounced most " u's " as the French pronounce " en." Thus " must " became a rather nasal rendering of " mast."

" You mast have a drink, John. You're not in a hurry, are you? " Confusing. Nothing happened to help him to come to terms with reality—except Desmond—trudging round and giving advice with his secret smile, making even the advice seem part of the smile, something private. His own honey—doing well in Italy.

Colonel Boy was discussing the thing John and he had in common: seasickness. Hadn't it been " ghastly." Then Colonel Boy suddenly remembered, so to speak, the chauffeur.

" John," he said, " I'm awfully sorry, what about your men. Outside? Corporal Allen," he shouted, " give Mr. Grant's patrol some rum. Two, aren't there? Yes, two."

The Adjutant came in and was persuaded to accept a drink.

" I must say if John frightens Jerry half as much as he frightens me he'll do all right."

The Adjutant sipped, smiled politely. He had come on business. He had been out three years. He looked a bit like the school rugger captain at half-time ten points down: and a bit like a minor martyr in a religious picture. Fatigue and risk had charged his eyes with a spiritual quality not normally there.

As though now conscious of a critical audience, Colonel Boy switched to business. He had been learning from the Adjutant all day. Here at last was someone from the draft; someone about whom he knew and the Adjutant didn't.

" Now, are you quite happy, John? " He thrived on John. The Adjutant doodled.

" Got it all taped? " Colonel Boy put it differently.

" Yes—I think so, sir."

" Splendid! " he exploded, like an equerry who hears the scarlet pelmet is going to be ready after all.

Half a tooth-glass of kümmel took effect. John felt he was not going into strange moonlight full of Germans, but he was going to go on sitting here forever and ever. For, after all, was there not an early illuminated Bible lying open on the tin trunk, also a hand modelled beautifully in plaster of Paris, so hadn't they all been there since time began—himself too?

A Share of the World

The fabulous blue and the necks pouring blood like bilge, the two raised fingers of the gold prelate, blessing all, as well as the mob with the gross noses had surely slipped their context—it was he himself who was where he wasn't. Or did Colonel Boy's moustache instead of mouth, and cap-peak instead of eyes conceal the face of a man who carried illuminated Bibles on campaigns?

"Billy Butler put that Bible in the bag this afternoon."

Kümmel was fogging the outlines of mess vernacular, and John saw Billy putting that Bible into a sack this afternoon, hence its presence, unquestioned, as in a dream.

"Yes," said John.

"He went swanning and found an evacuated museum. Takes Billy, doesn't it?"

The Adjutant doodled, looked at his watch.

"Didn't he say there was a Venus wired to a tellermine Guy—didn't he?"

"So he said, sir."

John tilted his glass until two laggard syrupy drops reached his lips. The express train was upon them, muffled as it were, by the waiting-room door. It came five times, inflicting four crashes of masonry and once nothing.

"Rather rude," said Colonel Boy. The words were correct, like the peak of his hat, but the tone was not quite right—a little too blasé.

"I ought to be off, sir," said John.

"Splendid. I'm certain you're going to pin-point some krauts for us, John." He rose—tall—much taller than his adjutant—as tall as the five-year men chosen for height. For Colonel Boy also, height had been one of the deciding factors when he chose his career.

"Good luck," said the Adjutant, smiling at John. "It's mostly noise."

John thought, So my face needs that remark, does it? He blushed like an adolescent girl with spots. Colonel Boy lifted the blanket for John, and the light fell on Bright in the street, isolated, his face like a road-sign in a headlight. A cigarette glow quickened intensely, then hurtled into the night.

"Oh, Corporal Murray and Bright. Splendid."

33   C

A Share of the World

Two better men, Colonel Boy seemed to suggest, never stood behind a young officer on his first patrol.

Corporal Murray saluted. Bright shuffled.

Colonel Boy was like a man about to address a gathering—you could hear the mental patting and straightening out of his notes. He would like to say a few words—not only introduce himself, though that, too, was important, but also encourage, give new heart—which he had been told in Birdcage Walk was badly needed.

From what impenetrable layer of Splendids did he struggle to bring something up. John felt sympathy. It was a nightmare for two. This man also had forgotten his lines in the crowded silence, could not make contact, could not move the limb out of the slough of impotence. All day led, instructed with maps, army orders, customs, German tricks, by a tired stockbroker fifteen years his junior; all his virginal day walking about surrounded by unknown, mistrustful, exhausted faces—faces that wanted to go home, had been promised they would go home, after this and then again after just this last attack—until the new arrivals, the " new wine " imagined themselves more cruelly aggrieved, forgotten, imposed upon and mucked about than the old bottle. Colonel Boy had felt relieved to get out of their sight, as though he suffered from some deformity.

That way of saying " Splendid " was all John knew about the man—splendid; on the troopship he had worn his hat at breakfast as regimental tradition permitted. A tall man in a hat saying Splendid over cornflakes. Colonel Boy groped for words, upwards at the stars like a primitive pilot, down the street like a householder putting out his dog before going to bed, chafed his hands and, from this action, found inspiration. " Quite Christmassy," he said, and then conscious of inadequacy, effect still not obtained, he resorted to a valedictory command performance of his special phrase:

" Well, John," he said, " Splendid! "

3

THE night was quiet now. Desmond stood listening by the last house of the village. They padded to a standstill behind him and he did not bother to greet them, but continued listening and watching. John went to his elbow.

He said, " They sometimes put out a spandau team about now —blaze off a belt and go back."

They listened, and waited for the night to be seamed with tracer, silently, before the crackle came, as though it often happened.

Nothing. A dog howled and was answered. The mournful noise was taken up like cock-crow near and far.

Two layers of cloud. One silver, high up. The other, smoky and low, congested the moon, and promised to screen it but always proved ragged or transparent.

" It's going to be bloody light."

" Yes, it'll be light."

" Use the shadows. You'd better get off now. Happy? "

John smiled. " It's not the word I'd 've chosen." Desmond conveyed disapproval without sound or sign. John said:

" Yes. I'm O.K., thanks."

" Good."

The far hammer tapped tin five times—no flash in the night, but they knew mortar bombs had left on their niblick flight. Curiosity stilled them and they looked vaguely back towards the village, waiting, for where?

The feathery sigh crept into their understanding. Imminence. The first broad tuft of orange and sparks showed them stooping in various directions with heads turned from it. For the next they were flat and they smelt it close and bitter with shut eyes.

35

The next two seemed to lead up to them like footsteps leaving it to the fifth to tread on them—but the fifth made a noise like a sack of flour unshouldered to the floor. John got up, saw Desmond re-occupy his previous place against the night sky and say, " Anyone hurt? "

There was a noise like a man struggling with a weight which was too much for him, and then a stifled whisper in a voice nobody recognised, said:

" Christ it's ma leg—it's ma side."

" It's Corporal Murray," said Bright. " He's got it bad."

Desmond said, " Get the Company Headquarters' stretcher bearers."

Bright left.

In torchlight shafted and covered with two thicknesses of black paper, Corporal Murray looked like something at the bottom of a pond. One of his legs was back to front and his arms and upper half writhed slowly and tautly, as though he were enclosed in a thicker suffocating air.

Desmond said, " Bad luck, Corporal Murray," as though the man had been given out when he never touched it.

There were footsteps, hurrying, whispers, then the light on a stretcher handle. Hands from no body, and a voice like a mother's full of love and determination not to communicate panic.

" Och, we'll get you back to the M.O. as ye are, Geordie, will we not. There then. Hogmanay in Tarvit that's all ye've got."

John found himself on his knees holding the wounded man's hand. " Corporal Murray," he said; " Corporal Murray," like a girl in a ballad, putting his meaning into words which were merely an exclamation, a rank and a name.

All the tension and ache of his own impotence was now flooded away in a purge of pity. This he understood. This freed him, expanded him with a general affinity which went beyond the lines.

Not Germans, not human beings against us, around us, he thought. But IT. Behind everybody's face all the time. I met it first at B echelon on the way up; then it increased. Everywhere —by netted vehicles, in men sitting under hedges watching us pass, by low tents, and guns in stalls of earth poised for that un-catchable instant of concussion and departure, from the top of boulder-like turrets of metal, in spite of earphones and procedure —IT. And in the eyes of horses, mules and peasants moving slowly among rubble like ants, IT looked out—even from inanimate objects—from a patch of ground—signed by IT—with M and V tins, winey shit, and foul webbing. And in the sky IT whispered lusciously, hummed, intoned, moaned, whistled, crackled, sobbed, breathed, rushed, howled, shrieked, banged, erupted, rent, or with a little limited cough, underfoot, sufficed. And at night IT some-times had a look in an isolated lake of lapping yellow light under a falling star, hushed with eyes, wobbling to make the silhouettes frolic.

And then like this IT chose someone, dropped a pencil on the great telephone-book of stockbrokers and shopwalkers, adolescents and middle-aged regulars and miners—the Guys and Johns and Boys and Corporal Murrays—sent you away with your face covered with a rough blanket or with pulp for a joint, mauve, calling out mother Christ morphia or some stored obscenity for relief.

The stretcher had gone as awkward as a pantomime horse with a little group round it. And John got up.

" Where's Bright? " said Desmond, for the second time. John's behaviour at the stretcher had irritated him. He had explained to him the patrol was still " on," but the boy hadn't heard.

John stood with the shape of the tommy-gun jutting out of his stomach, saying nothing, as though he had lost his memory after one close shell.

" Find Bright and *start*."

Still the patrol? With Bright? Down there, where the waves were like the top of greasy soup and people the size of punctuation. From here to there, now, with one jump.

" Shall I get someone else as well? " said John. He did not wish to seem reluctant so he said it eagerly, as though it would only take a moment to fit someone up and nip off.

" No, find Bright and *start*."

John's presence reminded Desmond of what it was like to feel ineffective; he felt the contagion and revolted.

A Share of the World

"Start," he said roughly, and then relented. "He may have taken Murray's kit—gone to the R.A.P. I should look there."

"I'll look there. Near—near Battalion H.Q., isn't it?" Silence. Then, "Look, John—you know, you really must learn where these key places are. You were in the village this afternoon, weren't you?"

"Yes."

"Well, then!"

Some shells journeyed quietly overhead. John returned along the village road thinking I'm going back along it already—after ten minutes. What will have happened when I come back along it next time? Anything? The "idea of it" persisted. He could not even start on the reality.

The R.A.P. lacked only redcoats and a central clay-faced celebrity dying—to have been like a print of war. A carbide pressure-lamp hissed and threw jet shadows on stone-block walls, coops, barrels, and table made of the same thick stuff as the roof supports and rafters. Two men were in shirt-sleeves bending, moving, working round the red of two wounds, one Corporal Murray's leg and the other on the upper arm of a man whose pale face was turned in miserable interest, so that his chin almost obstructed the orderlies' hands. There were bystanders, holding things, one drinking tea and whimpering that he couldn't go on. The M.O. and the orderly occasionally spoke to each other in the unnaturally steady and quiet tones which the presence of the seriously hurt seems to evoke.

A spirit lamp bubbled cheerfully—a misleading murmur like everybody's kettle at home. The big figure with his back to the door bowing solicitously over Corporal Murray's feet was Bright.

"Bright," said John; "come on."

Silence. The M.O. said, "Too many people in here, please."

"Bright," said John.

"Yes, sir." The big face turned, surprised, eager to help. What was it. Was he wanted?

"Come on."

He did not understand.

"We've got to start now," said John. "Come on." And

he turned to avoid looking any longer at Bright's face—a great moon of deceitful amazement.

Desmond was at the last house. His irritation had gone, and he said:

" Two is really just as good as three for this sort of thing. You won't need anyone else."

" Yes," said John; " handier."

Why not one? Handier still.

Desmond, with the moon on his face, said gently, " Though . how d'you feel about it? "

He meant Bright. John understood. Behind him he heard Bright's breathing which was wheezy, as though the man's lungs had an uphill job to irrigate the blood of such an extensive frame.

He understood that he need not go after all. The sensation was familiar—from childhood after a temperature from tears. He could say he'd rather not and return the sort of look Desmond was giving him now, meaning Bright and that shell and my first patrol, d'you mind if I don't? He saw Bright's face in the R.A.P. and in his slit trench saying, Five-year men weren't for it. Saw himself going back along the village street for the second time in half an hour with a feeling of futility, and felt a sort of interest in Desmond he knew too well, and he said:

" Oh, quite all right. I feel all right. Not inspired," and added: " though."

" This business isn't inspiring. But you're quite happy."

Let it be. God knows it had a lure—the night down there below the village; the lure of the impossible and the cataclysm.

" Quite happy," said John.

" Well, off you go—and good luck. Wake me if I'm asleep when you get back."

" Right. I will."

The two men started. One small, in front; one big, behind. They passed through their own platoon's positions. Faces pale like large leaves on water looked up at them from the ground. There went Mr. Grant and Bright. Nobody uttered a Godspeed, a Keep-your-head-down. Nobody said anything.

John looked back once at the moonlit village above him: a

39

three-dimensional jumble of light in wedges, square planes and slivers divided by different densities of shadows, and behind it the precise two-dimensional black outline of mountains. A foreground El Greco Christ with its gibbon-like arms in an attitude of sharp agony might have stood close with an oval, ill face against flare-lit clouds. Instead, there with the moon on it, was Bright's black face —the white eyes looking at him with that unaccountable familiarity, that *affinity*, as though this were some obscure rendezvous they both had known about for a long time. Affinity, that was it. It was difficult to be sure but—did the man smile?

The nature of the fear felt in nightmares is hard to describe by relating it to other things and hard to remember except by chance. It is akin to hysteria, vertigo, impotence, and for those people like John who sometimes used the word Evil with a capital E, as though it existed outside the mind of man, it is akin to Evil. It seldom breaks through into waking life except in the elusive and transitory taste of a sudden association. In the natural world the commonest similar experience seems to be in the eyes of a rabbit fixed by a stoat, screaming with good reason before it's hurt, but not able to move easily away as it could.

In Bright's real or imagined smile John experienced a twinge of this feeling, sudden and piercing like a scream from a locked room. He turned, knowing the distance between him and the Germans was not a matter of yards.

Reason climbed back to its saddle on its huge and wayward mount, and John decided that at the first rise he would lie up and listen.

Behind him Bright's footsteps padded, sometimes inaudible because exactly in step, like a second self.

4

FROM the hospitable Catholic's " promenade " the way had seemed clear as the fixed road round the fixed pond with the movable ducks in a toy farm. Now, the game on the floor or the sand-table had gone and the real thing was this—the night, oceanic, and out of his power.

He had stood up in that O.P. aloft on a diving-board. Now, down here in moonlight, he was in the black and white confusion of broken water.

The parallel occurred to John in spite of the fact that he had never entered water head-first, although he had prayed to be able to do so beside a high bed standing on linoleum in a cold dormitory long ago. The memory of that and similar disabilities seemed close now to the surface of his mind as though they had come to gloat.

There they all were—as close as Bright—chattering, What's he going to do next, and like Bright looking as though they knew very well.

Moonlight made a world of the near and the far. The near was vast and black, split up by spaces of nothing, and the far was pale and precise. A bush beside him was a gigantic black, but a star, a remoter sun, was a pin-hole in a blind between shoals of cloud in the low tide of weather. Light was pale smoke which showed things best when it got behind them rather than on them.

Men in grey, krauts, Jerries, Huns, Germans, the Bosch, Fritz —what were they? John had met one, a woman on holiday, in Wales—an Anglophile from Dresden. He tried to imagine her, out there somewhere, with a Schmeizer dressed in grey. It would have helped had he succeeded. The trouble with fear was it was always a thing in its own right with little relation to real danger.

A Share of the World

He must dissociate the Germans from that ubiquitous IT which had infested sound, sight and smell, from the Volturna northwards; he must, at all events, dissociate the white house from IT, if he were to associate it instead with the woman in Wales. " Only one way to be sure—go in."

But his past, come to gloat, did not see him " going in ". Would they hear voices? John imagined German voices in the night, guttural cataclysmic consonants. Treading on the outside of his soles and heels and frequenting shadow, but not verges because of mines, John went up the first slope intending to listen at the top. Perhaps from there in the moon he might be given another chance to see the way clear.

" I must."

He actually whispered the words.

What was this compulsion—as strong in its way as the opposing " IT " of war. Like the old man of the sea in *Sinbad*, it bestrode his shoulders, and often, though a weight far above his capacity, he welcomed it in bitter-sweet pain. It was, of course, partly " you must " of an expensive public school and the opinion of tenants, nannies, and aunts; but partly also an " I must," a chaotic private concern influenced variously by the muddy translation of the *Bhagavad Gita*, and spurred by the contradiction of precedents, by those memories with their hateful certainty, chattering their smug prophecy of " no change." And also, perhaps, by that old nightmare, distilled into the moonlit smile of Bright, a face against which savages carry tapers at night, with their eyes wide.

A hollow on his left was clear, was nothing but a silt of night, a refuge of darkness from the moon—yet, when he looked back, there was a tiled shed there, its salmon tiles now like tarnished silver chasing.

The oversight bleakened him. He felt in the grip of the incalculable.

Then he froze as taught at Camberley.

Against the sky it looked like an elephant's huge head swinging on legs through which no light showed, but which might have been one single column.

A Share of the World

He sank away, faded into the ground, like the shadow of a mounting bird in meridian sun, wrapping his body, his petrified concentration round the shape of his gun and the object coming.

It was not distant but near upon him, his finger crooked—a near woman with a large bundle on her head. As she passed she said musically, " *Buona sera, Signori.*"

John smiled like a cancer patient at the doctor's joke. He had nearly fired.

The figure had loomed black, now it receded silver. He could make out the central rigidity under the weight and the speed of the legs downhill, scuttling to keep under the load. For one strange moment he was tempted to take the centre of the track, jolly along the middle of it without a weapon, breeze into the white house if he could find it, wish the occupants *Buona sera* and return. It would be such a simplification. He already found difficulty in imagining somebody shooting at him with intent to kill. Me? *Kill* me? To increase their compunction would have been the weapon one half of his nature favoured. To go openly. Indeed, even to walk among the Germans, and say, Oh, my friends. Oh, my brothers in life, Stop.

Corporal Murray's leg and the woman he nearly shot had taken the place of the king's clothes, the infiltrating one who could kill twenty.

From the crest he could see the olives—the perfect plants of the moon, the most natural thriving weed in that opaque sea of light.

He turned and put his face close to Bright's, avoiding the sight of it. " We'll listen here," he whispered.

To the east the sky was flickering incessantly—and silently. Cassino? Ortona? To the west the smooth sea lay like grey satin. By day to that side the pink stucco station lay in a tangle of fallen electric cable. One truck tilted at the back of another like the bored amorous pass of one bullock at another, going through a gate.

A dog howled, another answered. Like cocks announcing light, they announced their fear, passed it on from throat to throat. The land was awake.

A muffled gulping six times in front, silence and six reverberating

43

crashes like trams falling into a quarry behind the village. Some high shells journeyed, the whisper of rotation just disturbing their tuning-fork note.

Then eight red dots spurted from a point, parted and swung slower overhead, dawdled into nothing behind as their vicious, deafening crackle arrived. Then, last, like a distant motor-bike the explosions at the point of departure.

John felt seen. He saw faces in the night turned towards him, and in the rapid film of thought there was a close-up of the face that had fired.

" If you are seen," Desmond had said, " come back." Like Emergency Exit in a smell of fire, the possibility of having been seen grasped John's attention. Instead of listening he looked hopefully at that part of the night from which the bullets had come.

" We were fired on," he heard himself say, ruefully, admitting failure, pardonable failure, in the face of that fact.

" We were fired on; that's why we came back."

The lie was like going sick, full of false relief—avoidance of the white house which he knew so well already, the door he didn't go through, the thing he couldn't say.

Here would do. Here one could listen—listen till drugged and dreaming.

Soon you heard something—voices where no voices were— or into the room of the mind, cleared for any practical flesh-and-blood visitor from the present, there tiptoed instead a phantom from the past who never can have been far to have come so quickly.

This one stood at the head of the stairs in gym shoes without laces. There was blood on his head.

" And when I saw him," John thought, " I *couldn't move*."

5

THE curtains were drawn for sleep, but outside it was still day, making the rose a face in the middle fold. The door closed, tentatively.

" Don't," he shouted. " Don't shut the door."

The latch unclosed and a tall wand of pale daylight stood on the wall. A pause, and steps receded.

The big rose on the curtain was still a face and yawned when the breeze moved it, like a face in a fun-fair mirror. And behind the screen there were still whispers.

Of course there could not be whispers behind the screen because there was no one behind the screen. He had looked every night for weeks, and therefore, to-night he would not look. To-night he would go to sleep.

But first, just once, he would hold his breath, to make sure that there were no whispers. You had to hold your breath to hear them, hold your breath and stay rigidly still; otherwise, what might have been merely movement or breath became whispers, and you had to start again. Again and again. Just to make sure.

He drew in air to the full capacity of his lungs, and lay still—still as a fly on a ceiling. And he listened.

Nothing—nothing but far away a reassuring rhythm of clumping from the kitchen, and a drawer closing and another opening in Watty's room. Soon she would be going down, looking in as she passed. Saying, Good-night, John. He wanted a handkerchief. Yes. He couldn't find his. He lifted his pillow, but did not turn it; keep that ritual for later when it would be needed. When the head appeared, he said:

" I want a handkerchief, Watty."

A Share of the World

" Please! " she said. " Please."

She glimmered across in mauve sequins, stuffed one under his pillow. " Why, what's this? " she said. " Do you want a dozen handkerchiefs? "

When the passage light went out he called, " Watty, are you having savoury to-night? "

" How should I know that, John? Now tuck down and go to sleep."

He knew. They were having savoury.

If they had savoury Watty came at eleven because it meant an altogether longer sort of dinner, if not—at ten. Whether at ten or at eleven—she left the dining-room observed by, and preceded up the stairs by John.

He dreaded savoury. It meant he almost went to sleep on the stairs.

But to-night whether there was savoury or not did not matter, because he was going to sleep in his bed; the whispers being, as his sister Mary said, "imagination." He would test them once more and then if they were only imagination he would tell himself the story of how he led the Blackfeet to victory over the Sioux, or how he whipped Watty with a birch-rod after her bath, or how he made Mary Queen of the Cartagena pirates, and ruled ever after.

The screen had a flower design on a yellow background. The whole was heavily bordered with wood and it was low.

By standing up in bed and leaning carefully on its top he could look over it to the floor the other side. But this he had only done in the morning when everything was itself and harmless.

At night he would often put on the light and be surprised and reassured that the room looked the same, and then walk round the other side of the screen normally as though he were going to the dressing-table. But to-night he would not be doing that.

There was the short mutter of a gong. Watty's footsteps faded. Other footsteps came, and the rustle of silk from the floor below, and went down, with one pause. Then his uncle's footsteps, fast but heavy. Then slow old ones. Then an adolescent male, half-broken voice laughing, and his sister saying, " If you do, I'll, I will——" A scuffle and thunderous steps. Then silence.

46

A Share of the World

Now, I'll try, he whispered aloud, and he took in a great gulp of air as though he were seeing who could hold it longest. And he gave his whole self to his ears. He took away himself from his eyes, from his skin, from his taste, from his nose and gave himself up to his ears, listening to his ears.

Nothing—nothing until the split second before he exploded—that moment he could not be sure.

He tried again—and then there they were. Unmistakably. Chill anguish. And he listened without holding his breath. They came and went, mutterings. They were the quagmire, the ache of not being able to move.

He put on the light and looked at the silly screen standing there, and his untidy bed. The silly ordinary everyday screen. But he put on his dressing-gown facing the centre of the room, put out the light, and made for the stairs. It was no good staying and trying again. Second time the voices were always louder and once he had been touched.

They never bothered with the blind on the passage window, Watty said. Sun, moon and stars could look into the passage round the clock. John stopped by the opening to the sky and put his hands on the chill ledge. Behind the Forth Bridge the sun sinking had released black and green dragons. They leapt unleashed towards him through suds of rosy foam. The sun's rim shimmered without power to dazzle and a black wing was spreading, touching and killing the rosiness, and increasing itself by their death. It was cold.

The stair carpet was deep and warm, and ten steps above the dining-room door there was a curtain so long that its end could be used as a rug. There as usual John sat face to face with Robinetta in black and white, looking back over her shoulder, all in ovals—oval face, oval shoulders, oval fingers by oval mouth, oval frame and general impression of oval white on oval black

They had gone in. A voice he recognised would break above the general level murmur, then gracefully be reabsorbed. There were gusts of familiar laughter. Sudden silences for one quiet well-ordered voice; a clatter above the tapping of cutlery, a bell behind green baize, and whiffs that made him feel hungry.

A Share of the World

Security. Behind him stretched a chilly desert full of menace. He could look up the well of the stairs and see the huge dome skylight now black with night. And the face of the grandfather clock described indifferently how long he must wait. Inside it there might have been a gnome with a 'cello, condemned to play a perpetual velvet pizzicato in the dark.

Mac trotted into view. He had the wary manner of dogs by themselves. He sniffed at the curtain of the conservatory door, looked vaguely round, sniffed again and moved to the mat, where he had a scratch leaning his ear well towards his paw because he was getting old. John hoped he would stay.

" Mac," he whispered. " Maccy. Here."

The dog's ears sprouted like little black tents. He looked round, down towards the drawing-room, at the foot of the stairs.

" Mac," whispered John.

The hair on Mac's neck began to bristle, his ears went back, then forwards again. He growled. He stared at one spot on the cupboard as though there lay solution—then wildly, desperately, he began a panic-stricken bark, raucous carillons of doubt and anxiety which ended only to be repeated.

The dining-room door opened. A crummy napkin and a moustache appeared. John edged in behind the curtain.

" Mac . . . MAC. Come in or shut up."

The dog was doubtful. He let off a half-hearted parting protest and warning, and then took his time going in.

John heard a creak above him. Harris tidying up the rooms?

He looked round and up. A man stood at the top of the stairs. The sudden sight of him was the cold end and blank of thought. The sick wait for this to be different—the sick reluctance to have anything to do with his eyes.

The man had blue sandshoes on, a black overcoat with the collar up and a torch, and the bristles on his peel-coloured face looked some sort of patchy disease. No sound came from him. He seemed to be looking straight at John; then at his hand and sucked a finger. He put his foot on a lower stair and it was as noisy as nothing.

The pantry bell burred, and immediate steps. He leant away

48

from the banister in one smooth gradual movement like a tree in the wind.

The steps became muffled on the dining-room carpet, returned to the linoleum, went to and fro with clattering. There was a male mutter and a shrill response, then a door closing and a return to conversation which was now louder, and thicker.

The man came down ten steps as though he had slid down a wire on a velvet loop and his whole weight was above John, and his blue sandshoe by John's one naked toe which stuck from under the curtain.

John smelt wet straw and scent like the sample Watty gave him, and his heart was trying to knock itself out by irregular blows in the same place. His lungs were bursting to shout, to bring them there—down there with the napkins his uncle, Mac and Watty and Granny, all of them—at once now with one shout, which he could. Which he couldn't. The man's hand sucked his finger again. The knuckle was bloody. A drop fell on the white wood by the stair carpet.

Somebody rose in the dining-room, and Mac yelped. He heard his sister say, " You clumsy great brute. Say you're sorry to him." Laughter from another world. Heavy steps came near the door— to the sideboard or coming out. Why not coming out? John yearned for the handle to turn. The steps stopped and his cousin said, " Is it this? "

The sandshoes in front of John's face suddenly vanished, and it seemed at the same moment the conservatory door below was opening and a figure passing through it, with again the same noise as nothing. And long after he had disappeared, after the door had closed, the handle slowly righted itself without so much as a click.

John looked at the spot of blood on the white wood, gleaming, wet, red. He was trembling violently and stood up. Then he heard the chairs pushed back and firm steps came to the door—it opened slowly inwards. John looked at the gap. Quickly, quickly, he must tell them. A rustle of skirts made him, as always, pad upstairs —but not this time with the usual sense of liberation. This time chained.

When Watty looked in he was sitting up in bed.

" Watty," he whispered.

" Oh, John," she said. " Why aren't you asleep? "

" Watty," he said; " come in—please come in."

After a moment's indecision she put on the light. Seeing his face, she went to him. " What is it? " she said. And then again: " Well, what is it? What's the matter? "

" There was a man," he faltered; " a man on the stairs in blue sandhoes. And his finger was bleeding. He had a white face —absolutely white. And——"

" And? "

" And I didn't hear him. I couldn't hear him. I tried to hear him, but I couldn't. He was standing beside me, but I couldn't."

She looked into his face a long moment and put her hand on his brow. His eyes signed the statement—long, earnestly.

" You've had a nightmare, dear, that's all. We'll have to stop that fish for supper. I said so all along."

John's sister called across the landing below, " Why has Harris opened my window like the door of an elephant's hutch; she must think I smell."

A whisper answered, " Hugh, Mary darling, you'll wake John."

It was the routine world—just the same. And there was beside Watty's sequined knee the screen with the velvet design, the towel-horse, Watty's sequins, the spike he had got for hoiking crabs, and the spindly half-circle shrimp net which had never caught anything.

" Granny wants you to keep that in the conservatory," said Watty, passing the net as she verified that the window was open. The same world. The screen was just a screen; the stairs, when nobody was on them they were just stairs, silent stairs. Why should they make a noise when nobody was on them?

" He came in by Mary's window," said John; " he came in by Mary's window. Did you hear her then, Watty? She said someone opened it."

" Now, dear, you haven't woken up properly. I'll make you a little drink of something, then you'll get off."

" No—I want to see Mary's window. I must see it. I must. Come with me." He was out of bed.

The middle-aged woman in mauve sequins steadied her grey

head at him. Should he be humoured? If he made one of his scenes Mrs. Fletcher would come and say she wasn't good with them after they were eight. She brought his dressing-gown and accompanied him.

Mary's window was closed.

" She closed it," he said, and " he opened it." The floor, the dressing-table, the bed, white things that could lie so easily looked at him blankly like the screen did when he put out the light. " Well," they seemed to say; " what's it all about? "

At seven forty-five the next morning, Ella, the housemaid, had reached the stair on a level with the top of the grandfather clock by the curtain and under the picture of Robinetta, when she saw before her eyes two bare feet.

" Coo, Master John," she said. " Whatever are you doing? "

" It should be here," he said; " somewhere here. THERE. Leave it, Ella. Leave it. Please, please, please leave it."

His index finger darted to within an inch of a brownish stain on the paint by the stair carpet.

" That's you pipping them cherry-stones again. I told Miss Watford like I said I would. Now yer 'olding me up."

" Leave it, leave it, LEAVE IT."

He tore at her big red wrist.

" Coo, you little devil, whatever's the matter? Mr. Manders, Master John's off his head."

The always too hearty, ear-tweaking, teasing butler was glad to oblige.

" Here comes the fire brigade," he said. And John found himself struggling high off the ground, his fists occasionally striking bristly skin and hard collar.

" Leave it, leave it, leave it," he shouted.

At breakfast Mary said, " John's getting impossible. Why can't private schools take them before they're nine? "

" They do," said a voice behind *The Times*.

" Why hasn't John gone? "

Upstairs Mrs. Fletcher was giving John Bengers in bed. She had put something in it and was waiting for it to work.

" Dreams," she said, as she tidied his pillow, enjoying it

51

soothingly, " are nasty things. They get *into* you so, don't they, darling? Ah, your darling mother, how well I remember . . ." Mrs. Fletcher sat on the bed and her eyes assumed a far-off look, sideways and upwards. " At Selden once . . ."

John interrupted. His mouth was dry, his eyes large and luminous. " But Ella agreed it *was* there—didn't she, Granny? She said she saw it, didn't she? And I didn't have cherries yesterday, did I? Did I have cherries? And have you asked Harris about the window "

Ten minutes later Mrs. Fletcher was lowering the blind slowly, looking back at the bed. " Yes, darling," she said. " I promise to ask Harris. I promise."

He fell asleep—deeply asleep—beside the screen with the velvet relief, with a fist clenched.

On Saturday his father came from London and came straight up to say good-night. He sat unusually long, finally hovering round the door while John sat eagerly thinking of something detaining to say.

" They lie right under the ledges. You have to get right in with it. I got four. One huge one.

" I used to do it at Tenby," said Osbert; " when I was stationed there. I caught a denture once."

" I got a boot," said John.

" At Tenby we used to get them big enough to eat."

" I did," John said.

" Hmmmm," said Osbert, a cigarette stub was glowing, stuck to his upper lip, and the smoke of it narrowed his eyes. He turned his back to John, his face to the picture of Sir Galahad at a door, and surveyed it in silence.

" That's Sir Galahad," said John. He had been Sir Galahad some evenings . . . Sometimes Mordred.

" Yes, poor chap. He had his work cut out." Osbert dawdled. He was going to say something—so he opened the door and put one pump in it, as though to make sure of the way out before saying what he had dawdled to say.

" Watty says you have nightmares." He was looking at the passage outside.

" I don't," said John excitedly. " Watty has nightmares."

Osbert smiled in cunning, private amusement. Then he moved half out of the door and sideways preparing to shut it, so that only one eye and ear and a shoulder showed.

" You're not frightened of the dark are you? "

" Of course not."

" Good," said Osbert, and the door began to close. As the edge of it met the wall Osbert sang, " Good night " on two notes.

" Are you coming crabbing to-morrow? " shouted John.

Silence. Then Osbert immediately the other side of the door: " Yes. I'll have to see."

" ARE you? "

" Come and fetch me. Good night."

Steps receded, paused for two full minutes at the window with a view of the sea, and then went down sprightly, singing, " Who killed Cock Robin " in a high mock-mournful tenor loud enough for the people downstairs to hear.

He had left the light on.

6

TO get a rough bearing on his point of departure before moving forward John looked back and found Bright's eyes upon him, like two bits of egg-white stuck mysteriously in the dark. Being in shadow, the outline of the man's head was only obvious when it moved.

John got up and felt new patches of wet between his knees and thighs. He moved down the slope fast, profiting by a cloud across the moon and, as the grenades jolted up and down his high pouches, the plight of women athletes occurred to him; the idea, the appearance or headline of what he was doing—which he knew of of old to be the inoculation against its effectiveness—also occurred to him, with the women athletes.

An hour in this moonlit limbo without worse shock than a sudden peasant with a bundle, began to engender a feeling of safety. The appearance of it all became stronger.

Then the moon seemed to focus a magnifying-glass correctly on stems, branches, trunks and grass. They became black and clear, on the ground. As John chose an adequate shadow he saw a notice like a signpost blown down, " *Achtung Feindsicht*," in squat, impacted sans print, more German than the language.

All appearance of John Grant on a fighting patrol vanished and the physical thrill of the archæologist by the petrified claw-mark of a monster bigger than a London bus was his, only stronger by the fact that the claw-mark was, so to speak, warm.

Here was IT—here IT had been. No, he told himself, Germans —frightened citizens of Hamburg easily surprised in the dark. Reluctant clerks and half-hearted Czechs.

Achtung Feindsicht—here IT had been.

A Share of the World

A dried-up watercourse obliged him to touch Bright, help and be helped. Why did he notice touching him there in the dark as though the man were the opposite of an attractive girl provoking a physical repulsion as strong as lust? The butt of Bright's gun struck a rock.

They stood still in the water's empty bed and looking up at the band of sky like people fearing a storm. We must wait now, thought John; wait twenty minutes—but not here, blind, in a gutter for grenades. He inched up the far side like a reptile and lay watching on the verge. Bright joined him.

Mist and silence, olives, white rocks split and the dark earth; the in-growing angular pattern of fig-tree branches and a stone structure which might hold a painted Mother of God, tilted by blast. Silence and mist. A dead world in the cold sweat of the moon's miasma.

Had they heard? Were they just over there—those fantastically magnified beings, the priests, deacons, and bishops of death, the grey hierarchy of IT called Hans and Rudolph and Gustav.

Like a car passing on a wet street in the small hours of London, a lower shell went over.

If the white house was there—by that stone thing—could he go in? Supposing that was it, and the moment to move was now. John tried his limbs; they responded.

The past is on our backs, he thought, like a snail's shell. It is what we come out of. It holds up to certain speeds, certain ways of behaving.

He saw a penholder quivering in parquet, an interlocking pattern of normal and back to front, 'L's like in the border of a Jaeger rug.

7

THEY were discussing in whispers, propped on elbows, what weapons they, the Rhodians, should use. Water-pistols loaded with diluted ammonia, it had been agreed, would only be used in the " gravest emergency." Then someone said, " Tsst," and they stopped like the arm lifted off a record.

John held his breath as though Mathers gave six of the best for breathing. Silence. He relaxed enough to look at the door. Mathers would be there suddenly with the light on, in boating-jacket and grey flannels, and he would come into the middle of the linoleum without saying a word, looking over the top of each boy in turn, holding the signet ring on one hand with the thumb and forefinger of the other. Then he'd say, " You're having a high old time, aren't you? Aren't you? My good Grant, do you honestly think I say things to amuse myself? Do you? If you do you've got another think coming."

John held his breath; did not move a finger, a muscle. Nobody moved.

Six of the best. What were six of the best? John had never had them but he had seen people afterwards—MacDonald in particular. Everybody in the changing-room said, Show us, go on, show us. And MacDonald did, with a magnificent inclination looking backwards to enjoy their faces. There had been a hush and someone at last got out, " Phew! He must have been in a bait! " John had not really believed his eyes. *Blood!* It was his first term and he had pestered for information anyone he dared speak to. " With his hand? But does he really do that with his hand? But how? " Mathers had long nails and long black hair over the backs of his hands and, when he straightened the rugger scrum, he thrashed at the tiny yoked backsides and shouted, " Shove, you

56

stinking little idiots, shove!" In the washroom he used to show good humour by smacking backs until they shouted, " Ow, sir, sir," and sometimes when he was really genial he would hold their heads down by the hair till gratitude for attention turned to tears in the eyes and " Sir, oh, sir, you're hurting." He gave people six of the best after prayers in the gym—by electric light in winter—first rolling the mats from under the parallel bars, and then going to the main schoolroom and calling the name of the victim, looking as he did so one inch above everybody's heads, stooping forward slightly and fiddling with his ring.

He showed favour by adding " y " to a Christian name, or if the favoured person's name was, say, Scott, making it into a noun. Thus " So-and-so has done a Scott."

It was more revulsion than reflex when Grant squirmed under Mathers's smacks or tickles in the washroom, and he never said, " Oh, sir; ow, sir; please, sir, ow." He hated in silence as his hair was pulled, but also feared—feared to the point of going pale and being unable to move his hands on the desk as the black-haired man approached, looking one inch above his head and saying, " Look here, Grant—are you trying to be funny? ARE YOU? Are you? Can't you speak? "

No, he could not speak. Once Mathers had shouted," You stinking little snob," while John was merely looking at him.

The stair creaked again, then again loudly. Too loudly—for a heavy step went off downstairs with a jingle of coins and a cough. Then the front door shook the house.

" Go on," said an eager voice. " Lassos."

" The thing is to keep the noose open," said John, seeing himself with a huge spinning O above his head. " We must all learn before we amalgamate."

After the walk, two by two along chalk cliffs, talking of amalgamation beside cabbage fields and waste building sites, there was competition in the changing-room.

" I'm going to put Grant's coat away."

" No, *I* got it first."

" It's Magnall's turn." John spoke wearily. He was interested in justice, but he had to decide so many issues—so many, so much.

A Share of the World

Magnall took the raincoat. Before leaving for the cupboard with the twenty-two numbered hooks, he said, " May I be on your bodyguard when we amalgamate, Grant? Now I'm a Rhodian."

Although only ten, Magnall used the word amalgamate with confidence. It had become as common as " prep " or " locker," since Mathers had announced after prayers that St. John's twenty-two boys were to be added to the forty of Clumpton House.

" We, Thine unworthy servants," he had said as usual, kneeling at the frayed card-table, " do give Thee most humble and hearty thanks . . ." And the boys had put, alternately, their elbows on the seats, their foreheads against the tops of the desks all down the room and waited to whisper the known Our Father. After the last Amen Mathers had chilled them by having something to add. Usually this meant a name and then the euphemism " I want a word with you, young man." Instead it had been the announcement about amalgamation. Mathers had seemed fond of the word as though it were a " good thing," and he used it often.

" The bodyguard's full," said John. " Besides, you don't know the ju-jitsu holds."

" Squits aren't wanted," said Dick, chief of John's bodyguard, who could make a noise like a gun with his tongue, and jump to the goal crossbar and hang on by one brown arm.

" Everyone's needed," said John.

" Then we might find a sentry job for you," said Dick. Magnall had one more request.

" May I be in the first fight, please? "

Fight! Would there be a fight? John went cold inside. He affected disdain. Dick said, " Don't be a squit, Magnall."

End of term was near. John held manœuvres indoors and out. He equipped each Rhodian with a length of blind cord which, noosed, could be slipped over a person's head from behind—a much bigger person's head. When they amalgamated, he explained, they would be outnumbered two to one.

" Unity is strength " was adopted as the Rhodian slogan. And everyone had to swear on the Holy Bible to obey the Rhodian rules, because when they amalgamated there was bound to be " controversy, and ye old hammer and tongs," said the manifesto.

A Share of the World

On the last Sunday walk, plans were polished and certain Rhodians ordered to buy small weapons, invisible ink and boomerangs if Hamley's still had them, during the holidays. Discussion was carried on from pair to pair down the crocodile, boys turning back and shouting forward. It continued in the changing-room when they got back until interrupted by Mr. Hackett, the undermaster, saying:

" Let Grant hang up his own coat, good heavens."

Three struggling aspirants gave way and the coat fell on the floor. John, standing by No. 1 locker, went pale. Some strange ebbing reversal of his circulation took place, affecting the pit of his stomach with at winge a twinge and weakness. Mr. Hackett didn't understand. They *liked* hanging his coat up—and if they liked it, why shouldn't they be allowed to? *He* didn't make them.

The coat lay on the floor. Mr. Hackett remained at the changing-room door and looked at John—with an adult stare of resentment and dislike.

John felt many eyes upon him as he went through the act of stooping, picking up his coat, and then, as Mr. Hackett disappeared, handing it to Magnall.

At tea, as Dick described the wizard virtues of a boomerang, John thought Mr. Hackett did not understand.

He had no zest for cake and scarcely heard when people spoke to him. He cancelled the examinination in code after lights out, also the trial of someone who had been overheard, in the bogs, saying, " Grant puts on side."

" We'll let him off," said John. His hands were just covered by tepid water at the bottom of a yellow basin, two feet in diameter and eight inches deep.

In the dark he thought of why Mr. Hackett didn't understand. He explained to Mr. Hackett and finally imagined Mr. Hackett becoming his friend, asking him to play nap and rummy with him, when it rained, as he asked Crowley and Jakes.

Next day after lunch, before the twenty minutes' sit-down and shut-up, when several had said, " Please, sir, may I be excused," John, sitting nearest Mr. Hackett said quietly and humbly, " May I have a side, please, sir? "

" No, they're all gone."

" May I have an outside then, please, sir."

Unlike that of Abu Ben Adhem, this moderate request was not successful. An " outside " was when Mr. Hackett allowed a third boy to walk with him—on the far side of the boy to the right or left—according to the traffic. Usually this " outside " was reserved for a lonely new boy. Only when they went on the Maidstone road was there no " outside."

" No outsides to-day," said Mr. Hackett. He had a way of suddenly looking up, clearing his throat, sweeping his eyes round the room in an instantaneous roll call and verification of behaviour, clearing his throat again and loosening his book by briskly bending the read and unread portions back and forth. This he now did without looking at Grant.

John led the walk, thinking, God, let it be the Maidstone Road.

" Maidstone Road, sir? " he called, with a weak sickly smile at the first turning.

" No, Foreland Lane." Mr. Hackett indicated with his arm out like a signaller. Foreland Lane, no " outside." It had never happened before.

He had promised to tell Dick how his father shot five pigeons with a five-shooter pump-gun so that all five were dead in the air at the same time. But the story seemed a lie now, although he had seen it with his own eyes.

Dick said, " I'm glad Hack's not coming to Clumpton."

" I'm not," said John fervently. " I like him best of all the masters here. I wish he were coming with us."

He spoke with a fierce desire for what he said to be known. Let everybody know that he thought Hackett the best.

" Matron says he's looking for a place."

" I hope he gets a really good place," said John.

St. John's broke up for the last time. The Rhodians gave each other the Rhodian double hanclasp, meaning comradeship. The next time they met would be incognito among the enemy.

During the holidays John wrote seven or eight letters to Mr. Hackett, the last of which he posted.

A Share of the World

It said:

Dear Mr. Hackett,

I'm just writing a line to say how sorry I am you aren't coming to Clumpton. I'm sure we'll miss you more than you'll miss us.

Jakes said you were looking for a new place. I do hope you'll find one. Thank you for all the sums you taught me. It won't be your fault if I don't pass common entrance.

Yours sincerely,
John Grant

His father, surprising him at the letter and looking over his shoulder, said, " You'll be thrown in a pond one day."

However, the reply was immediate and kindly. It thanked John for " keeping St. John's keen."

John showed it to his father, who said, " Hmmmm." Then John put it away in a box where he kept a lump of amber and a Mauser cartridge. What, he wondered, had his father meant?

John did not think of the Rhodians when he stood in a vast oak-panelled hall, filling up with play-boxes and strange big boys who greeted each other extra heartily because of the newcomers. He had the drained hungry feeling which follows many tears.

One stocky boy with close-together eyes was louder than any. He said to John, " You can't wear caps like that here, can he? "

John grinned amiably, looked at his cap, and said, " It's rather a rotten cap, isn't it "

" It certainly is."

John was relieved when a master shouted, " Gannet One," and the boy went.

Magnall appeared, bewildered, by a corded trunk. Had they been back in the old small school John would have been telling Magnall that he couldn't have that desk because he, Grant, had bagged it for Dick. Now he went over and stood by Magnall.

" Isn't it big," said John. He wanted to be seen talking, confident. He was longing for Dick. Then a matron appeared and led off the tens and under to cocoa and biscuits, Magnall amongst them.

A Share of the World

Gannet had got somebody's cap. " Horsefall, Horsefall," he shouted. Just as the capless boy reached him, Gannet skimmed it to a big boy who caught it high. " Pass Horsefall, pass Horsefall."

" With you when you're tackled." Gannet had the cap again, and this time let the capless boy get up to him. " Do you want it ? " he said. " There it is. Why don't you take it, Chubb ? "

The boy put a hand out in a way that was not to be interpreted as violence. Gannet let him touch the peak—then tossed it to Horsefall.

Dick came in. John was just going up to him when Gannet did. Then Horsefall. They were *welcoming* him. Clumpton needed, they said, a hot goalkeeper.

Dick spoke with one hand in front of his mouth, as always, in case his breath, which was pure, should be smelt. And he looked over their shoulders for John.

John looked away.

When Dick came up they talked about shooting rabbits with a .22, which they'd both done. And Dick said he'd been 110 in a supercharged Bentley. He made the noise of it changing gear, punctuating each change with the noise like a gun which his tongue could make.

It did not take long—about three weeks. After prep one evening John was reading *The Old Curiosity Shop*, taking in ten words in every hundred, but his eyes going along the lines at a regulated and even speed while he asked himself, " How was I to know? "

He had worn the crowned singlet because he saw the pile and thought that was what the team wore. He had not noticed some singlets were without the crown. He had thought getting your colours meant just getting the crown on the ordinary school cap. When he took off his overcoat on the field's edge Gannet had come up to him, and said, " Since when? " Gannet had called Horsefall. " Come and congratulate Grant." Then Gannet who was not even a " second " in the school patrol hierarchy, which Grant was, said, " You've got a nerve." Gannet was the best centre half since Black left.

John had been passed the ball once. It was covered with wet mud and would hardly come with him. " Pass," shouted several voices. He would show them, he suddenly decided, and he set off. " Pass, Grant." The voice this time was Mathers'. " Behind you," screamed Gannet. He was suddenly on the ground, ooze coming up between his fingers and not able to drag from his lungs a breath.

There was a spattering of handclaps and then a cheer. Dick was lying flat in goal and the ball lolling in the corner of the net.

Clumpton lost by a goal. In the changing-room, Mathers came through. " Well, done, Dick," he said. " You stopped some snorters." Then opposite John, he stopped. Horsefall was towelling himself, naked at the next locker. John had his trousers half on and half off, gently stooped over them in modesty, and prevented himself from overbalancing by taking hold of the locker door.

" Can't you even pass," said Mathers, " when Horsefall tells you to? Or do you think you can take the ball on better than Horsefall? Do you? Well, then, I should think you had better brace up, hadn't you? And why were you wearing colours? . . . Bring me your order-card after tea."

Mathers had spoken for Horsefall's benefit, for the amalgamation's benefit as well as Grant's.

No talking was allowed in the changing-room, but when Mathers had gone Gannet stepped across to Grant and whispered, " I hope you get *two* minuses, *and* something else."

All this got mixed up with flashes of Little Nell and her gambling father and Quilp's tobacco smoke. Grant would have liked to have climbed into the story, out of his desk at Clumpton House and into the story. In a sense he managed to do so. The story was a cloche for self-pity. Quilp became more real, Gannet less, until a voice said at his elbow, " The great chief of the Rhodians! "

He wanted to read, that was all he wanted—to be allowed to do, read. His head left his hands.

Gannet One was standing very close. His little close-set eyes were gleaming with enjoyment. Behind him was a group of curious boys. Others joined them.

" Are you going to lasso me? " said Gannet.

The paralysis which John knew in nightmares was seeping into him. The women in black were on the turret-stair and he could go no higher. Their steps were imminently loud, but their noses never broke the edge of the circular stone from which the steps fanned out.

He said, " It was a game."

" The plan said you'd let Clumpton boys be Rhodians if they did what they were told, didn't it, Jackson? Where's Magnall? Bring him along."

Gannet One came closer. He was smaller than John and a year younger. He looked at John's book like a crow after a hop nearer a carcase. Then his hand shot out and he took John's pen.

" Can I be a Rhodian? New nib."

He held the penholder by its extreme end between finger and thumb at the level of his mouth. Then he selected a line between two floorboards, adjusted his hand a bit and let go.

The penholder stuck like a dart and Gannet looked at John brightly. Silence. Then the sound of running and a voice shouted:

" It's Magnall's bath night, Gannet. He's gone up."

All I want to do is read my book, all I want to do is read my book. They won't even let me read a book *The Old Curiosity Shop* by Dickens. And all I want to do is stamp on Gannet's face with running-shoes and grind my heel into his eyes with football boots.

Gannet picked up the penholder and inspected it. " Oh, I say, Grant, I'm awfully sorry, I've bust your nib. Oh, blast, I've dropped it again."

There were a few titters as the penholder quivered again in the parquet floor. Gannet took a piece of paper out of his pocket. " If a Rhodian gets ragged he must shout ' Boojums,' then others will come to his assistance and abolish them." It was the third rule.

Jackson behind him bellowed, " Boojums," and a master shouted from the next room, " Less noise in there." No one took any notice. Dick came in to fetch something from his desk.

" Hallo, Dick," said Gannet.

Dick answered with his head in his desk, found what he wanted, and went out walking almost sideways so as to have his back to the group.

" Boojums," said Gannet in a normal voice. Dick made the noise like a gun with his tongue and began being a Bentley.

64

A Share of the World

John was very pale. For a moment it seemed as if Gannet were going to do what he was always doing to the small boys, flipping their ties out, or catching the hairs on their temples, then he turned away down an aisle of desks and said, " Oh, leave him there; don't speak to him."

Horsefall came in.

Gannet said, " Grant's in Coventry, Horse—tell everyone."

Later, the captain of the school came to his desk behind Grant's. Jameson was often on his own and had lent Grant *A Tale of Two Cities*.

" What time is it? " John asked him. " Is it nearly prayers? " He affected a casual voice. Not even turning round fully but just half looking up from his book and leaning a bit back.

Silence.

" What time is it Jameson, please? " In his voice now there was a beginning of a plea. Please, God, he prayed, let him say something, anything.

Jameson said, " About seven."

" Seven "—it had been just, just better than nothing. Someone was being an aeroplane with machine-guns firing through the propeller. Pooley was practising scales. " Eighteen-ten " and the hollow ping-pong bounce resumed.

Blunt, the French master came in. He was tall, in a boating-jacket, and his cuffs came right out of his sleeves, and sometimes one of them had a handkerchief in it. He had asked John where he lived and given him *Hassan* by Flecker to read. He kept order by indifference and by, generally speaking, the most thorough dislike of his boys. Sometimes he leant over John and touched him so he noticed it—prolonged a correction with a red chalk. And sometimes he made jokes to him which he did not understand, and looked at him with kindly mockery, or smiled at him as the class sat down.

John turned his eyes back to the print which became weirdly magnified, diminished, distorted, liquidated. He blinked and there, pat, was a shallow, rough blister swelling a word.

Mr. Blunt put a list on the notice-board and then came straight to John.

A Share of the World

" I want to beat you at chess, Grant," he said coldly.

John looked at him with a wet straight face—then closed his book, put it under the desk lid and followed.

In the quiet room the tall man dabbed his nose briefly, sniffed, and returned the bright handkerchief to his cuff.

" Have you noticed the frieze here? " he said.

John gaped with a black queen suspended.

Mr. Blunt waved a long hand at the band of carved oak round the top of the walls.

" Crossed ostrich feathers interspersed with diamonds," he said. " How the man Crate minted enough to build this eyesore. Of its kind, exhibit A, is it not? "

Ostrich feathers? Eyesore? Crate? He had a feeling of false salvation—such as he had drawn from his book—only stronger. Then Mr. Blunt said, carefully looking at the pieces, " What's the matter John? " The use of his Christian name was more powerful than Little Nell.

It was a minute before he could say:

" Nothing."

" Good. Then start. We'll make this the first of a series."

Mr. Blunt's eyes lay long on his opponent.

" You should brush your hair once in a while." John touched his head without looking and moved a pawn to Q3. Mr. Blunt put out his hand and touched John's head, let his hand fall on to his shoulder. Something strange, a vast uneasiness was coming. What was this hand? What was it doing? What wrong language was in it? John would like to have shaken it off. But gratitude won.

In Number 2 dormitory the moonlight lay in a wedge on the linoleum and under the high beds the chamber-pots looked like huge water-lilies protruding from a completely still pond. A.P.C. mingled with fresh urine in the air. A star or two showed beside the gleam of a fire-escape drum. Someone turned over and the springs made a noise like a brown-paper parcel being unwrapped. Matron said she would give him a minus for the way he folded his clothes. Why did the night have to end? From time to time he would come back to the thought of his real pain—the spectacle of

66

himself sitting still while Gannet dropped his pen from head height into the floor.

He had not been able to move. He couldn't . . . couldn't . . . That image was coupled with another. Himself standing over Gannet One saying, " I could give you worse, but I won't because you're only a poor fish."

The sweetness of this prevailed at last and he went to sleep.

8

THE moon stood clear now and the only clouds might have been behind and above it, for they were motionless reflectors of light on to ground which must be crossed.

The white house had for John a field of resistance which intensified the closer he got. This listening point was harder to leave than the last.

He left it crawling with Bright behind, straight out into the light because no shadow was going their way.

Less and less shells, explosions and flickers interrupted the night—as though everywhere a time was approaching when all but a very few would be asleep. All but sentries and the inspectors of sentries; and supply troops.

The intervals of silence had the completeness which in England goes with midwinter midnight frost. John felt like a boat rowing noisily across a calm lake of light; there was no sound, no blackness anywhere except himself and Bright, and their two shadows which were a shade shorter and less dark than themselves.

An angular excrescence like a wreck turned from grey to black ahead, something definite, something not growing, nor built, something recently added—a tank?

No baby-grand was ever stalked more conscientiously or fearfully. When close, John desired some community of relief, turned to Bright and found the two eyes already upon him. Was the man smiling with relief—or was he . . .?

The twinge of fear recurred and was put aside by a merely rational feeling of intense loneliness.

Black-and-white notes lay open in a line, losing nothing by moonlight. Squirly, ornate writing was visible above them and two candle-holders stuck out convivially, musical arms to embrace a family of singing faces.

It lay on the verge of a track, lop-sided because of a drainage ditch, with a motor tyre and what looked like a mattress.

The track; the half-way oak should be in sight soon.

When he saw it his reaction was less of surprise and thankfulness than of dread; it confirmed proximity to the white house. Yes, it said, you're going there. To have got lost would have been an absorbing solution. The task would then have been merely to get back.

As he settled to listen at the roots of the oak with a new confusion of moonlight to watch, the sweet smell of a corpse came fitfully. Some breaths took it in close, others not at all. But the sickly sweetness clung, so that in the stomach it was always there.

Over there the white house would soon emerge, as they approached, like a face out of fog. Only one way to be sure—go in.

The red seam, one stitch languidly chasing the next, came over. Then the crackle, finally the burrr. Sooner than the last time. Nearer.

Was it at them? "The third burst came so close I decided we had been spotted. So I came back."

Fare forward. Storms in so many tea-cups, now the true storm.

"I am not lenient to boys who won't go in," the gowned man said, with a face like a skull and two white tabs hanging from his collar, an inverted white V, below a skin-covered skull.

9

HIS father's hands clasped, unclasped, slowly rubbed, kneaded, and manipulated each other—finally were straightened to be looked at. They were black from old walnut juice and the nails gaped dirtily at the end of each spatulate, knotchy finger. Osbert often looked at them in his many free moments, as he looked at them now, with satisfaction as though they were his justification. When particularly scarred, more than usually black or grimily wounded he would show them to friends with a complacent smile.

His green-jointed lamp flooded forty impaled butterflies, their corpses still vivid after years as though the pin through each body had magically paralysed them in sleep, not death. A skull, found when looking for chrysalises, and a cat carved in the first Thebes protruded from layers of paper, notepaper with a previous address, letters, bills, books, receipts, doodles and unusual postcards.

" I suppose," he said, looking along the backs of his hands like a pianist waiting for the last cough; " I suppose to-day I ought to tell you the facts of life."

And a little disruption of a nervous smile came to his thin lips, obliging him to look out of the window, then reach for a pencil and touch up a face drawn among sprawled letters of an anagram in *The Times* margin.

John, with equal speed, turned a page of the *Illustrated London News* and then another.

" I know all about that," he said.

Osbert's smile turned to relief and mockery.

" Oh, do you, indeed. And who told you? "

" Malcolm."

" And what did he tell you? "

A Share of the World

" Everything."

" To that there's little I can add."

Certain words, certain looks, certain points at which conversations had ended, certain sniggers and Malcolm talking about
his bitch—these made up for John that " everything " which
was an aching, admitted total ignorance. He prayed the conversation would, wouldn't end.

Osbert changed the pencil for a mapping-pen and added a
parenthesis on a small white card. " Aurinia," he wrote. The
lettering was minute but not spidery, each letter a tiny entity
composed of several pressures—and it lapsed into the next as
inevitably as a petal into its neighbour. Osbert knew some Latin
names, others he copied out of books. He enjoyed their sound and
the feeling of writing them like this—slowly and beautifully.

Then he had to push himself back to cough—like splintering
timber—again and again, while ash fell down his front like bird-
dropping down a rock. In the squall of spasms he groped at his
mouth for the stub stuck to his top lip and salvaged it till it
burnt his fingers, then, while still convulsed, threw it over the
top of the electric fire, to join others.

In restored calm he added the last " a " of " Aurinia " peering
through tears. " The groom told me when I was six," he said.
His smile suggested he would have liked a more comprehensive
audience for what was to follow. Had he been in a railway carriage
he would have included everyone with a look and with the loudness
of his voice, and then he would have gone on.

John swept over another page indifferently:

" What did the groom say? "

" I was so surprised that I went straight to the summer-house
and asked old Lady Warminster for a second opinion. She fainted."

John said, " Was it so dreadful? "

The cough came again, paper blew about and in the middle of
it Osbert, bowed and rent as he was, began looking for something.

" What time's your train? " His black hand moved among the
papers as though there was no light in the room. Occasionally it
turned something over, once it chanced on an open game-book.
He began reading an entry for 1910.

71

A Share of the World

" I hope you'll profit by my disastrous example," he said, " and be tidy."

" There," he said taking a dusty square box from the litter. " You'd better have that. Some boys wore them in my day. I'd let a week pass at least before you appear fobbed. Depends if you're liked or not. If you're what George Townhaven was, then you'd better not carry anything breakable."

John unwrapped from jeweller's tissue-paper a large gold watch, His grey flannel trousers ended four inches above his shoes and the sleeves of his tweed coat reached to his palms. He placed the watch against his ear.

" You might be able to get a cheap chain somewhere," Osbert said.

John opened it. It was ticking and the time was about right.

" Your mother gave it me." Osbert was doodling; he thickened the nostril on a bullet-type Polish head, framed in a heart upside down, walking on legs like a millipede's fringe.

What strange flower of nameless emotion bloomed in John when he heard that remote, formal " your mother." Had Osbert been separated from her by something more serious than death? Then Osbert said:

" I'll send you the *Khamasutra* and Burton's *Arabian Nights*. They might contain something foreign to Malcolm. And to you."

The names became stamped instantly on John's mind. His dark, soft eyes lit with a fierce diffident hunger. Would his father go on? He made a conspicuous show of being about to leave the room to fetch his luggage.

" Are you coming to the station," he said, " at four? "

" At four! " Osbert's voice changed from bass to falsetto. " You told me it was two-thirty." His hands began to revolve round each other again and he looked to them in vain for comfort, saying contritely, miserably, " I told Minnie I'd look in, but I could ring up, I suppose . . . I've put it off twice already."

" No, lord, no," said John. " I only asked out of interest."

" We went down there together last week," said Osbert as though he were explaining to a large number of invisible people, " didn't we? "

A Share of the World

" Of course," said John.

" We could go to a news film until three-thirty." At three-fifteen they watched bi-planes bomb the Alcazar, men signing a treaty and cricketers reacting sharply to an invisible ball.

Three weeks after the beginning of his new life John was cleaning his teeth and spitting in a basin half-full of soapy water when his housemaster unlatched the door, tapped it open the rest of the way with the toe of one patent-leather shoe, while holding a printed list in one hand and pencilling a mark on it in the other.

" Any complaints? " he said.

John's grin was often obsequious with masters he liked. It was that now, though he did not know what this question meant even though it came every other night.

" No, sir," he said.

C. V. Ransome—or C.V.R.—as he was always called, walked as though his duties would be unpopular but, by God, let no boy think he wasn't going to do them. He had a square jaw, a man's face, but a womanish body. He always looked tired, pale and remorseless, and his smile when it came only exposed his lower teeth. The upper lip remained still. And he stared straight and full, and his voice rasped. His laugh (it was often preceded by a shout " frightfully good " or " yes, we like that ") was a full-mouthed, leaning-back guffaw which often ended before anybody expected. And his eyes never, even on these occasions, changed expression. At night he ran through prayers like an officer carrying out the pardonable idiosyncrasy of a religious superior before battle. Indeed, he came limping in with an army Prayer Book, and having prayed, walked out as though beyond the door lay another wound and another war. All " his year " in the eleven had been killed. Reliability, he used to say, was the first virtue. And indeed it was easy to understand his selection—for in circumstances of danger, or manners towards woman, or fair play within the *status quo*, his behaviour could be predicted as certainly as a tide; or a dawn or a season. But why— all these things considered—did he often look as if he might suddenly start screaming and then be unable to stop?

" No complaints? " he said.

73

A Share of the World

" No, sir.' "

His expression was more than usually pinched and remorseless, and he had the colour of a stomach patient. His lower lip was down on one side, but he was not smiling. It was unusual for him to go to the fireplace and put an elbow on the mantelpiece and look back at John, just as it was unusual to have said " No complaints " after " Any complaints." Usually he left it at " Any complaints."

John's mouth was full of toothpaste and he wondered if he should spit at a time when the air was so charged with the unusual.

Ransome searched John's pale and round-the-mouth, spotty face. He might have been a professional examining the lie of his golf ball. Which club here?

" Boy Grant," he grated, " what do you know about this miserable business? "

John's toothbrush remained on a level with his chest, turned upwards in order to save the foaming remains of the paste from falling. His face remained obliging, almost ingratiating but blank and a little frightened.

Ransome almost smiled. He had taken the wrong club. His trapped look lessened. He lowered his eyes and swung the toe of one pump skilfully at a loose edge of carpet by the grate.

" Apparently nothing," he said and thought, visibly. " There's been a bit of a haroosh." His voice had changed, relaxed but remained tentative. " I'm asking everyone a few questions. I'm going to ask you a few questions. Just answer them simply."

C.V.R.'s trapped look returned and the wryness of his mouth amounted to a silent snarl. " Has Peters-Douglas . . . Peters-Douglas been paying any attention to you? "

Into John's ignorance crept fear and uneasiness. What was this language of omission. This desperate circuitousness. It was strangely familiar, like the old dream and the daylight reminder. Peters-Douglas had the room next door. John had once seen him in the passage before he got German measles and was shut away behind a notice: " Staying Out ".

" Or Jameson? "

His other neighbour also behind a notice isolated with 'flu.

74

A Share of the World

" Have they? "

Had they been paying him any *attention . . . attention . . .*

" No," said John; " no." He licked at some paste which had dried on his lips and his toothbrush remained poised. He felt a sort of what-a-good-boy-am-I and looked it—a small personification of vacant, astonished, unimportant innocence but with something overripe, cryptically dark and fearful about his eyes which made Ransome wonder. They reminded him a bit of Crowther's who had been a prime mover, and who had at first protested innocence in a way which could have instructed an actor.

But Ransome did not wonder long. He got a sort of wireless wave from John—a radiation. The boy didn't even know what he was talking about. Something about the toothbrush, about the general newness and amazement, something craven in his face and manner—disqualified him. He was not the type. And physically . . . . Ransome knew he was not the type—knew very well.

Attack went out of his voice. " They never . . . called to you . . . or anything . . . through the walls." A pump strayed now half-heartedly at the far wall.

" No, sir. Never once."

Ransome flinched a bit at the " once "—he didn't like it. Affected, but it decided him. He made a dot on his list, and then moved off the fender. In mid-room he paused. He must close on another note.

" How's the fives going? " On such a night at the end of such a week (his third as a housemaster) it was almost impossible in the light of " the miserable business " to concentrate on the fives of a new boy who wasn't good at fives, but he tried.

Even less than Ransome was John now capable of concentrating on fives. " Yes, sir," he said, not knowing what he had answered.

Behind him C.V.R. left a smell of clean clothes and tobacco. John heard him in the passage, in front of one of those many doors, and he imagined him looking at his list, making a dot. Would he go to Peters-Douglas or Jameson? The pumps wheezed. Then the limp receded, reached the stairs and faded. Duty done for another night in this " miserable week."

John was like a foreigner in a crowd of natives. What were

they all looking at? What were the police saying? What did that procession mean, the great swaying dragon secret and the priest shouting? He felt the very expression on his face and the feeling inside him to be an affront to the crowd.

Any moment they might all turn, all point at him.

Two trunks appeared in the passage next morning. The odd man, Jenkins, brought them up dispassionately as though they were buckets of coal and put them on end outside the doors marked "Staying Out." Boys gathered in knots guiltily as though grouping were illegal since yesterday and, as on the verge of Hyde Park, individuals drifted from group to group to see what he was saying— the loud one, the quiet one, the one who questioned as much as talked. Duff-Reynoldson, they said Duff-Reynoldson was with Rasper now.

At breakfast the noise of eating sounded louder than usual. the clatter of cutlery and footsteps of maids dominated.

The "slab" or two adjoining oak tables on which were strewn letters, parcels, *Daily Mirrors* and *Expresses* and occasional *Times* and *Telegraphs*, pressed suits, tails and jackets, cooked pheasants at five, and books in tiers or strapped together, stamped in gold names past and present, was a gossip centre because it was also the ante-room to the lavatories. Here, too, were the notice-board, the football boots and the "Library" where the five senior boys sat among coloured caps, ping-pong equipment, ten-feet coloured scarves, canes knobbled and smooth, and books of which the only set was the Badminton Sporting Library c. 1900.

John lingered there, to find out. Elbows straddling *The Times*, bottom out. There was no one he dared ask—therefore he must overhear. Five boys were discussing spots. The fact that John's face had measles round the mouth did not modify their zest for their subject. The morose, earnest face peering at Eden's speech as though he expected to find his name there with "is a fool" added, did not attract their notice.

The conversation on spots, with its special relevance to-day, was conducted by a fat boy—Goldsmith—who sat swinging his legs. He had originally come down to see what had happened to Belinda in somebody else's *Mirror*. Now he had an audience. His stutter never stopped him.

" G-G-Girton! " he said. " If he doesn't take a pull he won't be able to stand up."

The others egged him on by contradiction.

" His m-m-money fell out of his trouser leg in ch-ch-chapel." They writhed laughing, accusing, agreeing, contradicting. Goldsmith went too far.

" G-G-Girton's spots are no exaggeration! " Goldsmith went too far, they swung mock kicks at him, roaring with belly laughter in voices not yet settled in the new, bass register.

Goldsmith went on about spots. They meant four times a week, Girton's spots.

Someone said, " Let's see if Goldsmith's got a hole in his pocket."

Three bent low and went for Goldsmith who shot off the table, plunged one hand into his trouser pocket, bent low and fended with the other. The attackers adopted the same position and closed. The table squawked, hands interlocked. Goldsmith bellowed, " Damn you," and turned into a corner.

John glimpsed a white shirt in a flopping V of fly-buttons ripped open. And then Goldsmith with his hands finishing the last repair was staring at him, saying, " Christ! What's the matter with you? "

The others were indifferent, refused to follow Goldsmith's lead. The group turned off with squares of books as though they were bricks under one arm, loading them lop-sided.

John heard the word " Shagpots " and went cold inside. A bell was tolling. He picked up three books stamped " J. Grant C.V.R." in gold lettering, in two cases across the titles.

Standing on fragments of winter mud he returned his eyes to the notice-board to see if there were anything new. " Boys are reminded . . ." A hole in his pocket—change came out at the leg; spots and holes in the pocket. Spots. " It has come to my notice that boys crossing Arnolds Weir on the Lyttleton Touches side are in the habit, in the habit, in the habit." Habit. John put his hand to his face and touched the area round his mouth. It was gathered in sore lumps under the skin. Some he had squeezed into rose blotches which showed clear against his white face. One on the bridge of his nose seemed to link his eyes. It even had lashes—a fringe of spiney hair. Spots. What had they called them? He hardly dared utter the word to himself. It was the priest, the swaying dragon, and the linked secret in the crowd's eyes. Spots. He had them. They meant he might be getting attention from Peters-Douglas. He felt a revulsion that shrivelled the pit of his stomach. This afternoon, this very afternoon he would get Styles alone and get him to talk about the whole thing. It would be easy. He would say, " I can guess roughly, but how do they go about it—here? " as though he knew how they went about it in Suez, in Australia and Vladivostock, and was therefore all the more interested to know how they went about it here. " The following will represent m'tutors . . ." he read. Duff-Reynoldson's name was crossed off.

A noise like two men hitting wood with sledge-hammers, getting louder and louder, materialised into a figure with flying tails, top-hat in hand for greater speed on the last flight, took the mat in a bound, wrenched the swing-door and was gone with a curse.

The racing receding steps left a silence into which suddenly came a hectic tolling of a distant bell.

A surrounding desert, absence of everyone, silence, dawned on John and the first twinge of panic merely petrified him. He knew he should be racing off. There might yet be time. Instead he stood there and fumbled with his gold watch, which he produced from his trouser pocket. Then he ran, feeling a little sick.

The loiter of a Roman Catholic, not concerned, on the other pavement, seemed as unnatural as a still tree in a high wind. Then three choir-boys in scarlet and lawn like toy soldiers outside the distant chapel made him burst his lungs with effort, for as long as they were outside there was hope. When he was still a hundred yards away they went in, and a black verger came to the great studded doors and swung them shut. There was a time for him to do this, and he did it then even if there were ten boys with ten yards to go.

" If ever you should be late for Chapel," the tall man, called the lower man, with a face like a skin-covered skull had said, " face it and come in. I'll always give a smaller poena to the boy who comes in—even if it's only a minute before the end."

Perhaps the verger shut the doors to make coming in a bigger test. The cast-iron handles were on a level with John's face. He took both hands to them and levered and high above him and all down the edge the great doors parted.

The verger stood in the shadows. His face, like a tin at the bottom of a pond showed surprise. Every day surprise—twice on Sundays. For forty years, surprise at boys who were late.

Timber was shuddering, buzzing under the organ—as the majestic diapason provided an almost obliterating background to airy runs, and cascades of middle and upper harmony. A fractional pause and then there was a crash of vigorous and toneless singing.

" Oh, come let us sing unto the Lord . . ."

John's feet slowed. From the shadows he looked up a pathway, up to a bright altar between six hundred faces in tiers on either side holding red Psalters. Under carved awnings and wooden valances gowned old men sat sifting lists of those present. " Let us heartily rejoice . . ." the broken voices bellowed and on higher notes were cut through, utterly dominated by the trebles and altos.

John saw the bowed figures of the past week coming in late. Hurried, chetif, sometimes with a nervous smile, the old hands cold and only hurrying enough to save themselves the extra " lines " which would accrue from an insolent manner.

He had stared at them, everyone stared at them—every inch of the way, up the aisle, up the stairs to their seats, then afterwards a bit perhaps to see how long they knelt before joining us. What looks they got from their neighbours, from the men in the valanced seats, from the Lower Man who took things personally—everything personally from a dropped Hymnal to being late.

The six hundred faces he didn't know would be fastened on his face. His spotty face. His . . . John already felt the eyes of the verger on his back. A voice behind him from the shadows said:

" They make it easier if you go in, sir."

He could say he forgot. His first week. One more chance. Forgot completely. Never came to the doors, even. Otherwise would have gone in. Went in. I went in thought John, as he stood on the outer edge of the curtain. I went in and they all stopped singing and said, " Christ, what's the matter with him. Has he got holes in his trousers? Hasn't he got a trunk outside his door with all those spots? "

The Psalm Books were snapping shut like musketry, and a mellow voice from nowhere was followed by a shuffling and rumbling. The faces now looked over or through their hands— some into. And a great concerted sibilance rose:

" Our Father . . ."

If he could move his legs in that direction he would go in now. He would. He really would.

John went back down the deserted street. The Roman Catholic was still there, kicking a stone.

A day later the man with the face like skin stretched over a skull sat in a square desk high above. He lolled out like a gigantic jack-in-the-box after the surprise.

He was trying not to frighten John, but enjoying the fact that he was doing so. It happened so seldom that even a twelve-year-old was frightened of him, that it was a pleasure.

" If you'd gone in," he said, " it would have been less."

10

WILL I ever come back to this corpse-smelling oak by daylight, he thought, and see that it is like any other oak—not a tree different from all other trees, as the loved girl is different from all other girls?

Feathery feelings of sleepiness from time to time penetrated his too-long sustained excitement and vigilance. A light-headedness which he could always place chronologically told him it was after two. Perhaps sentries would be nodding. He left the oak and crawled towards a blur of white which might be the cupola of the well, seen in the toy view from the OP.

It emerged more and more clearly as the well he expected. He knelt by the stone rim and heard Bright come behind. What was the square shadow in the ground on the far side of the rim? There—six feet away.

It was a German slit-trench and within reach of John's hand the glint was a cartridge—an empty. He touched it: warm. No, cold. Warm, so that's enough. Cold.

Voices clamoured in his head, I can't go on, I must go on. They're there, just in front, they'll wait till you're on top of them and the shots will go through and through you like the needle of a sewing-machine through linen. You've found a warm bullet—that's enough information.

Bright leant his head over. "They're here," he said. "That's all, isn't it?"

The spandau teams roved everywhere, came sometimes within a hundred yards of our lines, didn't they? This slit proved nothing.

"We must go on," he whispered.

"There's mucking Jerries in the farm," whispered Bright; "if they're here they're there."

A Share of the World

His whisper was a curse, a plea, and a taunt for stupidity. Proved nothing. Must, must go on. To go back now would be like always. Bright's smile, the affinity. Bright's shoulder touched him and he felt loathing like a dull, weak electric shock. He separated the contact—then got up.

The mood carried him fifty yards in good shadow of poplars; then he flattened as a spandau fired on the right.

No crackle this time. Just the flickering tongues at the muzzle, immediate current explosions, and the tracers floating *away* from them, chasing each other into extinction.

Perhaps the gun was a hundred yards away. Level with them.

John lay as he fell, listening, watching. He listened, listened, listened until he heard his blood, his heart, and his breathing in each separate hair of his nostrils. Nothing—and still nothing. One moment he saw himself going into the white farm that night; because of Bright; to take Bright up the stairs. The next he saw the stairs—but they were these stone ones in Half Moon Street, and he couldn't go up one of them.

11

H E could not, he had finally decided, stay in doubt another day.
Yet he now said reluctantly:

" After *lunch?* After lunch *to-day?* "

" Yes, why not? " Jimmy was more interested in *Life.*

" I don't know . . . after lunch. It hadn't occurred to me."

John looked out of his window. It was about here one caught
sight of the Crystal Palace, though through glued gauze one
wouldn't. After lunch . . . He felt less like it than ever.

If a baby didn't breath when it came out of the womb a midwife
slapped it. He was sometimes surprised that he had managed that
essential breath even assisted by a jolt. He had possessed a camera
two years before changing the film himself.

" And don't drink too much or you'll be looking a bloody ass?
when nothing happens. Some of them have a gadget to put you
straight—but you feel a bloody ass."

A gadget! John felt sick—felt the falsity of his position growing
by bounds. Gadgets. As though he hadn't already got gadgets in
his case. Powdered limp balloons a year old.

Jimmy was all spectacles, cigarette smoke, signet ring (since
last week), and he sat crouched and cross-legged over *Life* intent
like a dog over a burrow. He swayed loosely in the electric train's
rhythm.

Jimmy filled his battledress, whereas John emerged from his,
sprouted from the collar and sleeves as though there had been
some mistake.

Jimmy looked up, peered, recognised the diminishing distance
and returned to *Life* with satisfaction. His cigarette might have
been the chimney for a group of buildings in full production. Big

83

nose which he occasionally excavated, squashed, pinched and straightened in one unconscious, unsensual smother from a big hand; cushiony lips under a thicket of new black hair; eyes intensely on the spot.

" It's a pity *Life* don't get a photographer to Kharkov. Make an issue, wouldn't it? " He was always smacking his lips over something—women, food, speeds, drink, hunting, a photograph, a piece of music, jazz or " classical," anything with some go in it. " Go " was without date, nationality or class.

Kharkov! John was wondering whether he would be a virgin for the eight-thirty parade on Monday. It took him for Company Commander and he would have to form up the parade, shouting many strange words to many strange people, all in a certain order and with a certain emphasis on certain syllables. If he were still a virgin it seemed to him probable that he would not remember the long pause in the new " Fix . . . (pause) Baynitts," though Barnes who, so he said, had an AT in the pines ever half-day, never remembered that or any other pause. Yet nobody ever said to Barnes, " It won't bite you in the tank-park " or, " Ever worna horse-hair round it? " in the showers.

Tarts, Jimmy had said on the night scheme, are mostly a nice lot. They have to deal with the most forlorn swine imaginable—all sorts—types you wouldn't believe. Elsie now had a Swiss company director who before the war flew yearly to Half-Moon Street, there to climb naked into a washing basket and be prodded through the wicker chinks with an umbrella by a tall, naked woman: his sensual *summum bonum*. She had to be tall. It had to be an umbrella. Probably, said Jimmy, apart from this annual treat miles from neighbours, this man was a pillar of a community and handed the velvet bag on Sundays, and perhaps was an influence in local education.

The story had encouraged John. They might then not laugh at him, might laugh away his fear that he was impotent, which he carried like a fairy-tale box growing heavier with every step of time.

In soutane instead of battledress, his cropped head and lustrous eyes might have seemed the prey to doubts that he was really called or in a state of grace. Indeed the brilliance and earnestness of the hunger in his expression would have suited a more exalted problem than whether to accompany Jimmy to Half-Moon Street after lunch.

The train passed high over dun-coloured figures about their business, suburban shops, black bark, plots, and roofs flecked with new tiles.

Jimmy hauled down his greatcoat.

" Cheer up," he said, " you're not going to the dentist."

John smiled wanly and doubted whether they would still be friends by dark.

When Jimmy left him on the platform, to telephone to his mother he said, " I'll tell her to put Susan to bed before you arrive."

Susan was fifteen. Whenever John went to the house she behaved strangely, or, as her mother told Jimmy, " became impossible." John had treated her as an equal in age, which was what he did with everybody except his contemporaries. As a result she had spent long stares on him and took away his plate at breakfast the moment he finished. When he sat next to her he felt down the side of him nearest her, a mild sweet ache. After his last two visits she had broken out in rosy heat-lumps, which according to Jimmy, she had never had before.

John had been deeply grateful for this disfigurement and for the " impossible " behaviour he never witnessed. He admitted the sweet ache when near her, but beyond that his thoughts did not go any more than Susan's clothes went beyond the black and white required by her school. Now without any sweet ache his thoughts besieged that other she in Half-Moon Street. " Quite ordinary," Jimmy promised. As ordinary as a long plank across a ninety-foot drop.

If only he had saved her on the pavement verge from a taxi's wing, retrieved her scarf from the wind, met her in a train ten years ago. If only she had waited for him to finish a kipper before seizing his plate, or had had heat-lumps when he went. Anything. He would have called any of these links love, and gone gladly.

Without love, he knew, impotence would win. Was his blood, he wondered, so geared to his affections that its natural reflex

85

would fail without their consent? Not in theory. In theory he would have liked a different sort of beautiful girl for every day, after every lunch of the year, and with them he would have put into practice the million and one varieties of his fancy, done the things which were never spoken, never written, but which were presumably widely done, in spite of appearance sternly to the contrary. For he judged other people's desires by his own and wondered their faces were not more indicative of delight which they, unlike himself, must surely have the means, the will to realise.

Look, says the child on the scooter to the other child; look at me, I'm going a million miles an hour—and it makes a noise to suit.

The disparity between theory and practice was not greater in the pale candidate for His Majesty's Commission as he stood by the lighted tabloids while a man leaning out of the walls of them, adjusted with a censorious expression on his bored face.

" My mother expects I'm going to be killed," said Jimmy, joining him. " When I tell her I'll be there for dinner she gets so pleased that she talks with a hushed religious voice: one more rite before the end. Come on now—lunch and then Elsie. Does your father think you're going to be killed? "

John saw his father taking a telegram from a boy. Dribbling ash over it, getting it mixed in the straps of his field-glasses, shaking himself with his cough like crashing timber—opening it, reading, and then looking round vaguely as though there should have been someone older, responsible, to whom he ought to show it and then, seeing no one, stuffing it into his pocket, walking off looking at high branches with tears that might have been the wind making their way down unaltered features, wetting a face that remained wise, weak and a little anxious.

" He'd be rather impressed if I were," said John. " He would think it . . . surprisingly definite . . . effective. I doubt if he'd believe it."

The black iron spears that flanked the plane trees and grimy grass of Green Park had gone, and groups of American soldiers in sleek civilian trousers and garish breastwork walked or sat looking through cigarette smoke with roving predatory eyes. Sometimes they spoke to each other in unnaturally loud voices as though people were listening. Some followed a girl out of sight with flat eyes and then said something over their out-thrown legs, and looked in the direction for which she had merged.

" I once risked one of those," said Jimmy; " but I'd never do it again. When I see a reproduction of a Picasso on the wall, a white wool rug, a bidet and an intestinal carving in wood, and an electric fire I begin to feel safe. But gas like a trellis-work of old bones, wrapping and a Prayer Book, scent over stink and paint over dirt—no thank you."

John stopped. The theory he realised had not been a first cousin of the practice. He told Jimmy he could not go through with it. The big florid boy with a man's ring and a man's moustache was amused, delighted.

" Just *see* her first," he said. " She'll lead you over the jumps." John said he couldn't.

Jimmy said, " It's like bathing. Once you're in there's no problem."

They stood facing each other in Piccadilly's new bareness and scanty traffic, down which passed the pedestrian parade of Allied uniforms and badges. A leaf began its twirl towards the ground and John remembered how years ago his father in a black Homburg hat had gadded and dodged after them on his way to the office. Twelve caught before the first of November was the minimum for good luck. And from week-ends he came back with a whole wood of them, screened behind armfuls which reached to the ceiling. Four gaudy pheasants lay on his luggage in the hall. To think of it all was reassuring. Why was the only permanence long ago?

Now here he stood offending his friend by fearing a tart. Yes —indeed he had wanted to—to lay down his fairy-tale box—his rolling snowball of fear. But this was hard to explain. His pale face seemed more than ever meagre under the Octu haircut, and he looked more than ever the novice in the middle harshness of training; and from a military point of view, a little ridiculous— as though the white tabs on his shoulders designated him for at most a clerk's job with the searchlights or evacuees. He was the sort to look at, whom majors in Bond Street dared pull up for not saluting.

Jimmy asked, was it the fifteen quid that was worrying him?

"That's another thing," said John; "one really ought to be able to find someone who would do it for love. Oughtn't one?"

He wanted to get out of it all—with a headache, with a scruple, a joke, a missed train or a stopped watch. He would have made use of anything. Jimmy ate a hearty lunch.

"You know what," he said. "I believe you're in love with Susan. Waiter—bill, please. I must be off. No. 18 *is* getting a little like the dentist. One must respect one's appointment. When we "stood alone" it was less crowded."

Jimmy went, taking the last gulp of coffee on his feet.

John passed number eighteen as though looking for number twenty-eight, peering at it as though it might have been number twenty-eight with the two defaced, but not stopping.

At the end of the street he crossed the road and came back, counting the numbers, looking up—puzzled.

Opposite the house he stopped. The street was empty. A cat loped, finally broke into a chetif canter across the road and vanished into an area.

No. 18 was different from its neighbours—parts of it were freshly painted. Two windows on the rop floor had pink curtains with frilly dados—like underclothes, John thought. Behind them he imagined Jimmy lying under a Picasso, asking Elsie to turn the electric heater off—now. And the gadget in the cupboard. A light was burning in one ceiling. A still light—as though left on by mistake. That light described them together.

By now he only wanted to go in because he was afraid to. But that, for him, was gradually becoming the greatest incentive of all.

Later he was looking in at a tobacconist at the corner, at a great blue "Players" sailor in a pier, a gold-locked tar in his ruddy prime looking out at the sea he was not afraid of. An ink note below said "No Cigarettes" in front of cartons meant to look as if they were full. He had passed uncounted times and he was pale, exhausted by the weight of the nothing that had happened.

It might have eased him to have kicked in the tobacconist's window; inside him, there was an equivalent activity taking place.

He left the street eventually for fear that Jimmy would find him there—looking at a notice—" No Cigarettes."

And a colonel in a coat like a tailored blanket stopped him for not saluting, pointed a leather stick at his stomach, asking him whether he expected to become an officer.

" Well, then." The whole episode was like the arrival of the milk bill for a bankrupt magnate.

John waited for him to stop, then saluted.

In the blacked-out station—like a circus tent closed and lit for a few repairs—Jimmy's face welled into a patch of yellowy light looking pleased. John said:

" Well, was it glorious? "

The carriage enclosed them in its blue penumbra. A sailor came in and looked at them, sat down, breathed at them conversationally, seemed on the point of saying something, then saw a mate go into another carriage and joined him instead. A woman with a black bag subsided into a corner and stared into a side window in which apparently there was neither reflection nor view, but just the jet rectangle glued with torn gauze.

" Did I tell you that bastard Williams only gave me a B for D and M? "

" Yes," said John.

The idea of it could not be dismissed. Jimmy stared at the tip of his cigarette. He had wanted an A in D and M to wipe out his C for Wireless. His whole zest was in the thought of it. He had been eased of his previous zest.

" Williams doesn't like the Brigade."

John thought, " Why couldn't I go in? Why couldn't I move? "

Their battledress and shorn hair looked surprising in the gigantic gilded mirror of Jimmy's London home (in Sunningdale). They might have been looters lucky to be there first. Seven black overcoats and two British warms lay on green marble all folded similarly like sleeping seals, showing silk linings, and at the end of a long corridor several voices talked in competition against muted jazz.

Jimmy's mother came from a door at the side and said, "Darling," as though the word were a sort of punctuation mark in time, a full stop to the last period of waiting. Having put one arm round him (the other held a file), she offered her cheek gracefully, as though the rest were up to him.

"And John," she said, holding out her hand. Then, "I'll join you presently." Her life in war and peace, Jimmy said, was devoted to justifying riches. She went.

A fat officer in the Horse Guards with his leg stuck into the middle of a stool full of American and British periodicals went on talking when they came in.

"All I know," he claimed in a loud voice, "was that Winston came in at two that morning and told Bikki that we'd had it."

He spoke with the strenuous emphasis of one who is not always taken seriously.

A girl warming her back against leaping, yellow flames, pulling her skirt decorously against the back of her legs, thinking of something gratifying, said:

"But you *can't* believe Bikki." She gave a bit more attention to the subject and appealed to the rest of the room:

"I think I'd believe Haw Haw before I believed Bikki." And she laughed a sort of decoy laugh which was joined by others.

"Oh, lord, Jimmy, must they do that to your hair?"

"Hallo, Jim," said one of the men. Another said, "Idle brasses."

John was introduced. "Ring for some more ice, will you, Jim?" And the patchwork conversation resumed.

When Susan came in she kept to the wall as though there lay security. She was wearing a black-and-white school uniform. The girl by the fire, Jimmy's elder sister Diana, said:

"To what do we owe this pleasure?"

A Share of the World

And one of the men said, " Susan—Susie come and kiss Uncle Jake while it's still permissible."

Two of the men looked at her with a sort of amused appreciation. Susan said to the curtains, " Mummy said I could have dinner down to-night. And I needn't change."

Diana said, " When I was your age I had a tall glass of tepid milk on the top floor in a dressing-gown."

Susan appeared not to hear. Avoiding the middle of the room, she arrived within reach of a corner of the long stool littered with periodicals. She dragged *Esquire* on to her lap. She seemed to regret the combination of her breasts with a school tunic. Diana's eyes remained on her, fed and went fat with amusement on her, and then took a fleeting look at John.

" Does anybody want to powder their nose? " she said, a little reluctantly as though it would have been fun not to have changed the subject, fun to have gone into why Susan was there.

In Jimmy's room, disused, but central-heated till it smelt, he said with relish as he inclined to brush his hair:

" I feel like some shampers, don't you? Just to round things off. You know why Susan's eating with us, don't you? " He laughed. " To stave off the old heat-lumps."

" Is that it ? "

" I wonder what she'll get this time. A twitch, I should think."

John's feeling for Susan was a physical kind of gratitude, and he thought of Diana's eyes trying to X-ray for the company the amusing gaucheness of a girl in a hockey tunic, down to dinner years younger than anyone else, in love like a thrush in a strawberry net; as dignified. John saw the gesture with which Diana smoothed her skirt at the back of her legs, her confidently acquisitive eyes as she made people laugh. He hated her.

" I can't love your sister, Diana," he said. He always had to pin-point his position.

Gratuitous and priggishly phrased. Jimmy said, " I doubt if she'd ask you to. Come on, let's go."

On the stairs John wanted to explain, but Jimmy did for him.

" She does make people feel a bit wormlike, I'm told. Not endearing. But not her fault."

A Share of the World

" No. That's not it."

Diana pointed people to their places. She ended, " And Susan next to John, that's right, isn't it? "

She added a delicate little smile—the most delicate, instantly effaced smile imaginable.

Anything that John and Susan said to each other was not the point, and since the point was the only thing they had in common, they said very little.

John caught sight of her eyes in the candlelight as she looked up the table towards her sister. They gave him a sort of glee. There was nothing anybody could ever do about such eyes: people could implore, lecture, threaten and hurt them, but they would take their course, a hot, merciful, pugnacious course through the world. If necessary, murdering. Or is it, he wondered, just that she's fourteen?

Jimmy was exuberant. Already he had got a new edge. " Why isn't Enid here? " he kept on complaining. " You might have asked Enid. Didn't you tell her I was coming? "

Diana said, " She said she had a cold."

Jimmy tore his hair and rolled in his seat. " But Christ, is that *all* she said? "

People teased him. He luxuriated. He was at home. His mother came in, kissed him, helped herself from the sideboard and from a footman in the act of serving someone else. She went out sighing, " Female brigadiers! "

Picture lights curled over uniform, wig scroll, ruff and lace.

Diana was doing a maintenance course. She described what she was learning and got it all delicately, deliciously, hopelessly muddled, shook her head and lay back in laughter. Why she ever arrived anywhere she simply couldn't understand. Somehow John did not imagine she would ever break down or ever forget to check carefully petrol, oil and water even before taking her general a a hundred yards.

She said, " Caroline has her General in front. Mine *never* sits in front. I'm dying for the day. He's the spit of Gary Cooper."

The Horse Guards major listened to her with satisfaction.

Susan said, " He's in the Pay Corps."

A Share of the World

" Yes, darling," said Diana. " Hadn't you better run up now or are you going to have coffee? "

The black scorn which lived in Susan's eyes was particularly pronounced whenever Diana opened her mouth. It would not allow the skirt-smoother to be a girlish giggler in front of an empty petrol gauge she didn't understand and a madly glamorous general; it seemed to insist she be judged as a glittering athlete in feminine self-interest.

" Won't you have one of your things to-morrow if you don't go up? " said Diana. " H'm? Shouldn't you, darling? "

" Not yet."

Diana smiled sweetly. " Susan's a little like the poor. She's ever with us."

" And what could be nicer? " said the Horse Guards major stoutly.

" In fact," said John, " someone else's departure would be easier to bear."

Silence. Susan negotiated a crumb with her knife tip towards the verge of her plate, giving it all her attention. Diana looked incredulously at the Horse Guards major; at everybody, with a little shake of her head, with a giggle seeking company.

" Well! " she said, but her eyes said, " I've met him once—perhaps twice."

Jimmy stared straight at John with hostility, amazement and amusement equally mingled.

" D'you mean your own? " he said.

John was blushing. He had spoken from his stomach, from too much blood in the head which Diana's manner suddenly provoked.

" I might even mean my own," he said.

The Horse Guards major leant forward, picked up a pat of butter and threw it at Jimmy's head, and in a voice imitating a child in a temper, said. " Yah! you howwid, howwid thing! " And thus, so to speak, the waters of the conversation closed over the corpses of John and Susan.

" Well, *you* were in smashing form this evening! " Jimmy said. They were on the landing outside John's room. Down the well of the stairs Diana's voice could be heard in the hall saying, " Good night," then shouting at a closed car window:

" Yes—Friday. 'Bye now." And the solid slam of the front door.

" I'm sorry," said John, " my goat—was suddenly got."

Jimmy was, retrospectively, fascinated. What had happened had a sort of " go."

" But d'you run around like that, swinging social haymakers —because if so, I must travel with you more."

John fell asleep. He woke strangely. There was something wrong. His panic was gradual. Something was on his face— hair. It trailed across his skin and he couldn't move, as in a nightmare.

" I must get away," he thought. Then was able to calculate. He smelt childhood, warm flannel, fresh hair, and unsoured breath. The hair moved and he smelt it, and was able to sit up and away from it.

" It's Susan," said a whisper.

" Susan! "

" Yes. I . . . I had to ask you something."

She had to ask him something. Susan. A trapeze of moonlight lay under the open window, and he realised he had felt blindness. He could see her black hair on the shoulders of pale pyjamas.

" Susan," he said, stabilising, extricating, calling the roll of reason, turning on the lights of the mind and driving back to the wainscot the dream-rats already vanishing, leaving the shadow, the feeling of their invisible population.

" Susan." This time the name sounded correct. She said, " I'm so sorry. Did I frighten you? "

" It was your hair," he said.

" I wanted to ask you something."

He noticed now a craven anxiety in her voice, or was it squeezed, shuddering with cold—his own shoulders were already chilled. He touched her wrist and pushed the sleeve up a little. He said:

" You're freezing." He had copied her conspiratorial whisper. " Hadn't you better go back. What is it? "

94

A Share of the World

" Listen, I must know——but I must know . . . . now . . .
are you coming for Christmas? "

" Coming for Christmas? "

" You said last time you might come for Christmas."

" But . . ."

" Don't you *see*," she whispered. " *Now* they might not ask you.
Diana runs everything. Mummy's too busy. So . . ." She looked
over her shoulder as though there was no time to lose.

" Please," she said. " Are you? "

" But Christmas—Susan. I don't even know where I'll be—or
if I'll get leave—or . . ."

" For Christmas," she said dully. Her teeth chattered and her
hand moved on the bedclothes.

He tried to make out her face.

" Just say," she said.

" Susan—I'll come if I can. Of course. But . . ."

" No, no—not like that. Do you really *want* to come here.
More than anywhere else in the world? "

What would happen if someone came in? Poor child. Dear
child. Dear Susan.

He said tenderly: " Of course, Susan. Of course I want to
come here very badly. Your brother's my friend and—I love
everybody here."

" No, you don't."

Silence. Then she drew in breath through a wet nose and he
suddenly realised his face was damp from her tears.

" Susan." The outward movement of his hand was paternal,
consolatory, and had no forethought of any kind attached to it.
Only when his fingers were caught frantically by a chilled hand did
he question where his hand had gone.

Her outline lowered and he felt the bed take on another weight.

" You're ice," he said, " you'll catch cold. You must go back
to bed."

" *Who* do you love here? " she said.

" You must go, Susan," he said frantically. " Please go back."

The words were not his. They were dead wood without sap of
feeling: palings round the tiger of longing. Her head fell forward

on his shoulder and her tears were warm on his neck. He lay back and held her in his arms, looking over her at the moonlit gable, and thinking this is happening to me. How lovely; oh, how lovely her hair smells. What should I do?

If only she wasn't cold. Her coldness became the most important facet of the whole situation. He knew he must look beyond it, but he couldn't. He made one more impoverished effort.

"You must go back you know." And then cancelled it with, "Darling, you must." The word was a new dish to his mouth and he savoured it, even at that moment amazed at its nourishment. He said, "Darling, darling, darling—you know you must go back."

She lay still now as though she were listening to someone coming.

"Darling," she whispered, not to him, but trying out what he had said to see if the sound were the same. One thinness of wool and one of silk separated her breasts from his chest, and her hair was invading him through his nose. As inevitably as he stood tongue-tied on the steps of No. 18 he now took her weight on his right shoulder and dragged the bedclothes from under her and covered her. "You're so cold," he explained—to her, to himself, and to an invisible and perpetual audience.

There was, he now knew, happiness on earth: not the usual retrospective happiness, the sweet selections of nostalgia—but present heaven which interrupted itself to look amazed at the moment and say, "How—oh, how beautiful this is."

But that first flower was fear's gradual opportunity; he must, he must pick this flower.

Then how instantly it died, leaving nothing but the malsain fragrance of pity and remorse.

"Rather a good week-end," said Jimmy in the train, "though probably your last *chez nous*. Susan'll have smallpox after what you said at dinner."

John's book was on his lap shut and he had not bothered to undo the clasps of his webbing belt. He had hardly spoken since leaving the house. He said nothing now. Jimmy was intrigued,

fished a bit in his face, made an interrogative grunt. Then he said:
" There's no need to look as if you'd put the baby in the hot
oven. What's the matter? Diana can take worse than that."

Even if it takes years. If she wants I'll marry her, after the war.
Meanwhile she shall know that if she has lost something then she
has given something incomparably greater. Whatever happens—
I must make what happened good.

The names of stations on green hoardings flashed by, familiar
series—Croydon, Purley. . . .

A girl of fourteen or fifteen whom he had met twice, a girl of
fourteen who was not allowed to go to Peter Pan till she was ten
—because " the least thing " upset her. The least thing. I will
never, never, never allow what happened to become squalid, he
swore. I will make that blood like the mention of blood on war
memorials. I will turn it back, with love, into love. And she
shall know in the most careful detail that it was not for nothing
that my fear was a killing growth she cut out. " I will." His lips
had moved under his dilated eyes. She shall feel the earth under
her.

That was how he saw it: putting the earth under her. He had
a vision of Susan standing on a globe not so vast that it looked flat,
but enough curved to show she stood four-square still on the element
to which she was born.

He formed up the eight-thirty parade dressed in a white sash
and when it came to Fix (long pause) Baynitts—he forgot the
pause and much else besides. But he scarcely noticed.

After supper, instead of remedying military ignorance which the
next day would throw into relief, he wrote to Susan.

Familiarity was impossible: they scarcely knew each other,
had not exchanged more than a few commonplace words. He
wrote in a mood of passionate friendliness—passionately to insist
on the lasting value of what had happened, friendly because he
wanted to start at once on what he called the " porridge " of their
acquaintance. It was the first step in placing " the earth beneath
her feet," or to put it more medically, less metaphysically, of rushing
an ambulance to the expression in her face as he had last seen her,
on the doorstep.

A Share of the World

He said, " I love you—will always love you, and while you grow older, will be waiting for you, for as long as you wish."

Then altered this to " will always be waiting for you."

This letter, he felt, was the first step of putting " the earth beneath her feet."

Only by being thus to her, and to himself swearing violent oaths and praying for strength to observe them—could he bear to live inside himself, inhabit that particular house of flesh with two predominant pictures on the wall of memory—himself hanging about the door of No. 18 and himself . . . with Susan.

He expected the expression with which Jimmy came towards him two days later.

John was by the notice-board. He still had the white sash for the week about his body and he held a sheaf of detail, lists of names and points to remember, untidily arranged and written.

" Susan's ill . . . " Jimmy said. " I thought you might like to know."

" I'm sorry." John looked straight at the angry eyes. Men came and went, hobnails on stone, shouting, after breakfast preparing for the day. John had the Guard detail on top, and someone came and peered at his sheaf.

" I've done corporal once," said the person grieved.

" I did corporal last month."

" It's round to you again," John said.

Jimmy waited till the cadet went. Then he seemed at a loss what to say, groping, suddenly anxious for everything to be different, for there to be an explanation, a contradiction, from John.

John said nothing. Jimmy's hostility returned.

" Well? " he said.

John said, " I hope it's nothing bad."

Jimmy said, " My mother asks me to tell you not to write letters. If you do . . . they'll be sent back."

He added quietly, " And I should go and drown myself."

John thought—this must make no difference—the whole world knowing or not knowing. I shall love her—and for as long as she wishes—I shall wait. Meanwhile, I shall " put the earth beneath her feet."

A Share of the World

Warm effusions of remorse and high-minded resolution later, by their very relief and agreeableness, began to stink in his nostrils. It was too easy. There was only one way that he could respect: to be different, and to put, not write, the earth beneath her feet.

He developed a conversational hobby horse. Only what is difficult is of value; and weakness, just as much as power, corrupts.

12

THE white house did not emerge gradually from the ink and broken glass of moonlight, but was there suddenly like a face at a window, pale against the night, motionless, watching, saying, Here—no, not over there—here I am.

And it stopped John in the middle of a damp crawl between the shadow of scrub and the shadow of a shallow terrace. He turned looking towards the shadow where Bright waited as though he had known all the time the f—— house was there, just as he knew the f—— Jerries were inside it.

Their bodies touched alongside and John adjusted his position so that this was no longer the case.

No noise anywhere. One owl hoot gave another illusion of English country night. And a dog howled close. Had the shaly rush of a train, growing, diminishing, and a glimpse of moving fire passed in the distance it might have seemed correct by the first reflex of the mind, and only corrected by entrenched fear. That was why the sudden plight of war wrought such havoc. One part of " second nature " refused to take it in: would not bend to it and therefore often snapped. Only the deepest part of second nature admitted it, perhaps had been waiting for it, knew it of old as that IT which John tried vainly to see in terms of Hamburg clerks with wives, velocity of metal, flesh wound or painless death, but which remained IT, as vivid as though painted on the faces of the men in grey—not with the obliteration and night camouflage of modern burnt cork, but the bright leer and circle eyes and nodding head of the witch doctor's mask. IT under the whispering shells and the wobbling demoniac dancing shadows from a green flare falling at an indeterminable spot in an unknown land. " IT " was familiar as an old dream.

A Share of the World

The mask now was the white farm. Perhaps John Grant, this off-centre product of upper-class England in the twentieth century, could have faced it better if he himself had been wearing some lurid regalia of death, been accompanied by drums and shrill instruments. Did he not always feel more like prayer beneath a pealing organ and a roof that mounted in shell-shaped arch and counter arch until the detail was merged in the final harmony of obscurity?

But no such aid in music, dress, or community of movement was available for John—indeed he even shunned the leg that had touched his by chance in the dark. The only companionship available made him feel more than ever alone.

His imagination supplied the IT for the enemy—but could do nothing to supply the same profound force for himself. Up to his intellect to make a case for going on, and up to his will to execute it.

Was "John Grant has done frightfully well in the third battalion" enough? The bubble reputation?

It was, perhaps, more than was immediately available for "the men." John spurned it, chiefly because it had bad company. It was a soft, field-rank-and-over currency; thriving among regular soldiers, some parents, and the popular press.

Was saving Slough or High Wycombe enough? It seemed indistinguishable from saving Düsseldorf. A basic human ugliness and bleakness was strong in each case. Perhaps the only sweetness available to this thin introvert, lying flat in Italian moonlight was his longing for something satisfying to come out of himself for its own sake.

Incentive? Pride or love, he had often asked himself in less penultimate moments than this, hoping to ease by understanding the root of tensions growing savage with the yearning of their opposite demands. On the one hand, to despise Bright more sweetly and completely than ever and, on the other hand, to lose himself, belong, offer no home to Bright's stare, hate no one, float in the sympathy which he had felt by Corporal Murray's stretcher and extend it to the Germans opposite, whom he did not know. And like that Catholic called sometimes an "old woman" in the O.P. on the "promenade" in the highest winds of war, take the ex-

perience in sweetness with no political or national context, but only
a private honey of suffering changed. Suffering changed: would
that do as a definition of love?

All this in a camp bed, of course, by candlelight under the
quiet stars, and on board ship, and after the *Bhagavad Gita*—and
a fill of food, drink and warmth. On the ground it was otherwise.
Now the problem was constricted to a familiar misery—as controllable
as nausea or a sudden sneeze. The grip escaped from that dream
part of him, not colony or even dominon but self-ruling, acknowledging no influence of any kind—the grip of nightmare impotence
making sensitive lead of his limbs and taking away from him the
power of moving towards the white house or even of seeing himself
do so.

It would be wrong to say that his mind moved here and there
desperately seeking to negotiate this impediment. It did not. Like
a saw in a notch it slowed and stuck—was held by the lure and
repulsion of the farm, showing white like a face in front.

The men in grey, that is to say IT, were inside the buildings and
perhaps in slits in front of them and the night waited, and Bright
waited—and the past waited with its blasé smile of foreknowledge
and the future waited bleakly waiting to be joined by a self still
unbearable to self.

The moon behind a film of cloud X-rayed its thickness and
thinness, its ribs and flesh.

"The third time the spandau opened up it fired well wide of
us, but I'm certain they knew we were somewhere there, certain
they had seen us—the first burst was straight at us. I reckoned the
slit with the warm rounds had been evacuated because they knew
we were coming and had made other preparations. So I thought
it best to return—at once and by a different route. The white farm
can, in my opinion, be taken as occupied."

There is only one way to be sure—Go In. The moonlight faded.

An old hinge wheezed into a loud knock and a smaller, like
something unlatched banging in a wind.

The white face of the farm re-emerged, surfaced in light, and
at the same instant gave tongue wildly, a dog touched on the quick
panic, again and again, harsh carillon of falsetto barking.

A Share of the World

Then silence. Uneasy growling. Silence. Did sentries look out on the familiar nothing in front? John saw the wide, pale beaten-zone of their eyes across his path.

The dog snuffled. Dogs did not live alone. Farmer or enemy. Dogs stayed behind alone. High and low clouds combined across the moon's face and the imitation of day seemed finished. Now would be the time—to move . . .

How long was that "Now?" How long did John stand an auctioneer of decision with the "going, going" always poised on her lips. Minutes, hours? Time like shapes—was distorted, difficult to judge. He couldn't move—and the sea-shells were scattered round the base of the stove, but still he couldn't move.

13

JOHN held a tiny pink fan-shell in the delicate clutch of a pair of stamp tweezers. The rim was sticky with a line of seccotine like an irregular yellow hair. Very carefully he laid it on a wooden box lid, where it became part of Susan's monogram.

In his last few letters (which he addressed to the house of one of her school friends as instructed by her) he had stressed that for two people so young as themselves to swear eternal fidelity was imposing upon themselves too rigid a vow. He, he said, would always be there for her; but she should let herself think in terms of life with someone else " one day—perhaps."

Meanwhile, to contradict any impression of backsliding, and to fulfil an emotional need, to provide her with something lasting and symbolic (the earth under her feet) he was sticking these sea-shells on a box specially made and stained by the camp carpenter.

In the act of transferring a larger, mottled brown and yellow fan-shell, he paused with the thing in mid-air, and looked over his shoulder: a waft of stale petrol had reminded him of the autocycle.

It—and its engine in pieces—on the other table—belonged to his hut-mate, Titch Bentley. Also the air rifle, the old *Sunday Pictorial*, suède shoes, Tiger Tim, alkaseltzer, detonators and primers among loose change, Court barbers' hair mixture and a photograph of a luxurious girl looking sideways and down against wavy light and shadow, suggesting she was in a house on fire and didn't know it, but kept on looking down and sideways and interested. A mound of used third-class railway tickets were also Titch's. " I collect them." " Why? " Titch's smile would expand into a capital U saying, " Well, have you guessed? Rather slow, aren't you? " The regimental battle-school, it was said, had never had a better commander for its demonstration platoon than Titch—even if the Commandos *had* turned him down as " unsuitable."

The autocycle stood on its bracket by the stove, a small pool of oil under its chain-box.

Titch was six months his junior—he would ask him to move it. Titch was an unusual officer in this regiment. Though bigger and stronger than most of the men, and even freer with four-letter variations, he yet had the social qualifications which, even in war time, the regiment warmed to. Sitting in restaurants he did not make people wonder how a regiment officered by conceited children could be so celebrated.

His hair was colourless so that his eyebrows were nearly invisible. He had sloping shoulders and was muscled in a way that is commoner in middle age—biceps without definition, tapering like a horse's upper leg, straight from shoulder to joint. Colourless down grew all over him, among orange freckles and (on his face) grog-blossoms; it was thick on his cheekbones under small pale-blue eyes, which twinkled, sharing other people's joy and belly-laughs at " Titch's latest." He was proud that he had not learnt to read till he was ten, and since then very little. One necessary examination he had passed by a feat of cat burglary the night before. Even from that there had been kudos.

So when John said over his shoulder, " You're not going to keep that thing in here, are you? " Titch's mouth became the capital U of Cheshire cat confidence that here was someone else who thought him a one, someone who would say in the Mess:

" He goes to bed with the spare parts."

" Are you? "

Titch said, " Why not? " And was still smiling.

" Because it stinks."

Titch understood now this was an objection. " I'll see if I can find somewhere."

The autocycle remained. Once he used it in the rain and it sweated and reeked of cooked mud. Pools stood under each wheel.

John said, " Did you find anywhere for it? "

" No, there's nowhere for it."

" What about the back of the Mess? "

" I may need it quickly. Before the pub shuts."

Titch's smile was still confident, saying, " Isn't that like me? "

" Or to go and get cigaretttes from the village."

" Yes—to go and get cigarettes from the village."

" No, really, Titch. Please put it somewhere else."

" Oh, I'll see."

" I'm not asking you to ' see '—but to *put it somewhere else*."

And Titch put his broad back at John's face like a tongue stuck out. The autocycle remained.

A court of appeal existed in the shape of a major with a stutter who " lived out " in all senses. He was a regular, looking forward to the day when he could again roll up at Wellington Barracks in a bowler at eleven and leave at one. When sergeants shouted, " Permission to carry on, sir? " he answered their salute with a perfectly crooked finger and " D-do, please, sergeant." About the autocycle he would, so to speak, have sent for a bowl of water with more conviction than usual.

" S-such a childish m-m-matter m-m-must be arranged amongst yourselves."

The huts were on dunes. Sand blew under the doors. The regimental flag flew high between the sea and the barren slopes on which daily they did platoon attacks with " live." White stones flanked clinker paths and Italian prisoners in green trousers, brown patched, made hard-standings for transport. John taught wireless in a Nissen hut.

Titch began to overhaul his autocycle, decoke and clean it with pink tinted petrol so that it gleamed and smelt stronger.

The real organiser and commander of the camp was a small, sad-looking captain whom no officer had known " before." He shunned intimacy which may have been the cause, or the result, of his recent divorce. Men charged at company orders each morning found him difficult to lie to. Not that he said much. He just sat there looking sadly at the pens on the blanket before him, emitting an atmosphere which hatched the truth out of the closed egg of silence, or made it painfully egg-bound.

John promised himself that he would not mention such a futile affair as the autocycle to a man so busy and whom he respected so much. One day the Captain and he drove back from the foothills together, through the slate quarries, the derelict cottages, and the dead grey lakes, and the Captain said:

" Titch is really remarkable over those obstacles."

John said, " I suppose only a chimpanzee could do it better."

" Oh, come. Is it as bad as that? "

John said, " Have you ever shared a hut with a hot autocycle? "

The Captain smiled. " Can't he keep it somewhere else? "

" He says he can't."

" I should tell him to move it. Why don't you? "

There was an order put out by this captain that officers should not keep explosives in their rooms. John said, in cocktail party, couldn't-matter-less tones:

" And somehow the sight of ten detonators, and forty primers mixed with hairbrushes, cigarettes, whistles and matches gets me down."

The little man looked suddenly tired. His brows contracted almost imperceptibly, as though he had seen a milestone which dashed a small and unimportant hope that they were half-way. He said nothing. John waited, watched the black-faced sheep in the oozey grass with their dewey valance of wool. Everywhere the grey scars of disused quarries, rotting beams and antiquated tackle, rust and weeds. " Why do I? " he thought, and said:

" Titch is just the person for this war. I can't understand why the Commandos turned him down."

He could pretty well imagine why and so could the captain, who made some noise of vague assent, but said nothing.

Titch's refusal by the Commandos left its mark. The week after his interview he dismantled a mine washed up on the beach, and gave a lonely and purposeless demonstration of how to throw the Mills grenade after holding it for two seconds. He now always (instead of often) got drunk when he fetched the recreational transport.

On these occasions, he came into the hut after midnight, turned on both lights, because he could not select exactly the switch which dealt with the bulb over his own bed. He smeared down the switches and stood getting his bearings. John could always follow movement by movement, the spectacle of Titch thinking—even when he was sober. When he was drunk he thought like a tortoise put down in a new place. At the door he always had a long think. Eventually his small eyes in which pupil and white had got liquidly mixed with blood would rove round, at last reach John's bed, his sea-shells and kit, and then the mouth would try and get something out—word, was it, saliva, or groan?—be fed up with the effort, fed up with the pain which movement aggravated, fed up with standing there. And so the boots would start towards the bed uncertainly, as though against an irregular gale, loud on the plank floor.

Sometimes he undressed, sometimes he didn't. Almost always he was sick within an hour, sometimes in the light, zinc, general-issue basin, sometimes not. If in it, then his head would moon and loll over the brim like a beast of burden over its manger, gazing with a sort of glazed expectation of what was to happen next. The exclamation " Christ! " wiped away with the back of the hand meant he had finished. Asleep, he often cried out, " I can, I f—— can," or variation.

The autocycle remained and to it he added a small wireless in a frame like ivory. " From Zara," he said in the Mess, with his oafish, humble grin, expecting and getting, hearty teasing.

When he came in he turned on the Forces programme loud, and when he went out he sometimes turned it off. To John, it seemed that there was always a man in the ivory box saying something short very loud, which was followed by a short multitudinous baying which ended with unnatural unanimity and abruptness. Then the man's voice again—high with a sort of would-be infectious verve for verve's sake. Then finally a crescendo of howls over which the voice soared, whipping it, jabbing it, perhaps drawing breath to shout, " Come on then, Luton," or, " Once again and all together." And while it went on Titch was not listening, doing something—engrossed in something—or even out of the hut.

Sometimes John felt like praying, as in childhood, by his bedside. It provided an agreeable and perhaps beneficial clearance of the mind. At such moments he would remind himself that he would one day die, or he would put out feelers for that peace which the world cannot give by trying to "outflank," intuitively, all discord. Kneeling had become important since sharing a hut with Titch. In fact, he prayed more often than usual because he was afraid to.

Titch sometimes twiddled with the wireless knob, passed and re-passed the station he wanted, while John added another minute shell to the nascent monogram composed of Susan's and his initials; or while he knelt in pyjamas, his bare toes beside bright black boots.

They lived as close as brothers and now never spoke. The sand continued to blow in under the door, they came in wet and exhausted, their ears singing from the passage of bullets a yard over their heads. The shell box grew, and Titch came back from a week-end in London with bloodshot eyes, and telling his friends.

He had taken Sue to the Four Hundred and there met Zara. Wasn't it his bloody luck? And Ella, the maid he had told them about, had left, which mattered most of all. She had had the right idea, and the right everything else. Does he lie? John wondered. Then admitted—probably not much.

He spent more time on his shell box, or writing to Susan at a school friend's address, reassuring long letters often saying in so many different vague ways, " No, *it can't come to an end.* What has happened goes on for ever whatever happens—whoever we marry." Sometimes he wrote two pages about her body.

Then one day—he was duty officer—he entered the demonstration platoons' hut to inspect beds and kits. He came in by the door at one end and saw the other one open.

" Shut that door, please," he said to the duty sergeant. " The sand's getting in everywhere." At the same moment he heard the ranting, blustering voice of Titch's sergeant, Mathieson.

" Well ! I'm waiting! " just outside the open door.

John said, " Never mind. No, never mind; leave it open."

The duty sergeant hardly understood.

" The sand gets in, anyhow." John was looking at a kit with his walking stick clutched behind him like an elderly connoisseur at a sale. " They probably left it open to air the hut. That's a good kit. Excuse him next time."

" Sir. McGilroy excused."

A Share of the World

John moved to the next, listening. He drew a mental line through a cotton reel, a comb, and the centre of a tin hat chin strap, and found the cotton reel a shade to the left: he was listening all the time.

" Well," Sergeant Mathieson ranted, " have you lost your tongues? "

John strayed to a kitbag by a window, checked the number on it, looked out. Titch was behind Mathieson flicking at a weed with his stick. Mathieson was as big as Titch. In front of the two big men the young demonstration platoon was standing easy in the drab lumpy shabbiness of battle order and denims. Their faces, in three ranks, were mostly blank, like people in a queue, one or two obliging, but nonplussed.

John stood back and surveyed the kit from a distance like a portrait painter. " Excuse him."

" Sir," said the sergeant, and copied the man's name from the locker.

" Well, then," Mathieson's voice dropped to a motherly gentleness, " if you want it that way, you can have it that way. But I'd like to tell you all this much—I'm going to find out. If it takes me a f—— month I'm going to find out."

Silence. Then a soft reiteration:

" I'm going to find out." Then crescendo. " And if I find out before the man who did it comes and owns up, I shall take him into the hut *before* he goes on a charge, and I'll lock both doors of the hut. D'you hear? I'll lock both doors, and he'll spend twenty minutes in there with me." Sergeant Mathieson ended very quietly, " And he'll wish he'd never been born."

" No anti-dim here," said John. " Macdonald. Wasn't he the one who was back-squadded? "

" Yes, sir," said the sergeant, writing again. " Macdonald. Show anti-dim.

" Squad. Squa-a-a-d shun," bellowed Sergeant Mathieson.

" I see there's a pane cracked there," said John, pointing his ash-plant walking stick at one of the windows.

" I think that's what Sergeant Mathieson was talking about just now, sir."

A Share of the World

At lunch John addressed Titch for the first time that week
—in a would-be friendly way, loud enough for everyone to hear:

" I was an unwitting eavesdropper on Sergeant Mathieson
to-day, Titch. I think you'd have had a fit if you'd heard him."

Titch groped. What was all this. What a bloody silly word,
" unwitting."

" Well ? " he said.

The small, sad-looking captain, eating and writing at the same
time now put down the pencil and gave up both his hands to the
meal.

Someone said, " What did the man say, John—f——? "

John mimicked Sergeant Mathieson's speech, adding:

" At that rate it doesn't really matter who wins the war. That's
how the Hitler Youth are brought up."

People ate, thought about it.

Someone said, " I shouldn't care to be closeted with Sergeant
Mathieson for twenty minutes."

The captain said paternally, " You know, Titch, you'll have to
watch Sergeant Mathieson. There was trouble like that before
with him. If ever he says anything on those lines in front of you jump
on him,"

There was silence. John looked straight at Titch, and Titch
said:

" I was there this morning." He spoke sheepishly with his
humble, oafish smile. " I thought it was a good way of finding out
who'd smashed the window."

His expression, so to speak, passed the hat round for Titch:
let everyone contribute according to their means. They did.
Encouraged, he said:

" That twirp, Corporal Sandby, cracked the pane and if he
can't say so then a good bruising will be just the job, wouldn't
it ? "

" No," said the Captain. " We can't have rough justice. If
McKinley cracked a pane Sergeant Mathieson wouldn't take
him into the hut and shut both doors. Would he ? "

Later John expanded the allusion to the Hitler Youth—to
everybody except Titch. He did it carelessly, skilfully and as it

seemed—objectively. To one or two suitable ears he said: "That was all I meant the other day when I said I'd sooner have Titch against me than with me. I do like an *incentive*—a *complete* incentive."

That evening Titch repaired his auto-cycle, and tried it out on its stand inside the hut. John heard it running as he came down the clinker path from the Mess. He turned back and wrote a letter. When he went to bed Titch was asleep—on the side of his face with his mouth open, as though he had been shot in the back. John opened all windows and the door wide. But the fumes clung.

The following day Titch took the P.U. to the town to lead back the recreational three-tonners at midnight.

The question of background for Susan's monogram had vexed John. He was not happy about the almost orange satin of the wood, and as he became more and more pleased with the design of the interlocking letters he became less and less with the stain. He had an idea. Below the seaweed line on the beach there was a silt of minute grey shells, each a perfect miniature whelk half the size of a match head. By coating the whole blank stained surface with a film of secotine and applying a layer of the grey-blue shells a good neutral, enhancing background resulted. But it was a long job as the shells could not be sprinkled on as at first seemed likely.

While Titch was fetching the three-tonners John coveyed with his stamp-tweezers, small clusters of miniature whelks to fill the upper and lower loops of Susan's S. The employment soon became mechanical, leaving his mind prey to the smell of Titch's auto-cycle.

When the lower loop was all but complete and the whelklets expanding towards the border mosaic of crushed oyster shell, John suddenly got up and put the auto-cycle roughly out of the door on to the clinker path.

The box was coming right now. So simple—and then to Titch's face he'd say, "Yes, and every time that I find it here I'll put it out on the path." Skies within shells. Pink cirrus, ribbed pale green. Brown fan-shell flecked as in human eyes with black rifts, yellow spots. Cowries thumbless fist. Whelklets—quadrillions of deserted homes. Hot wood in the dry dunes. Bleached antler of driftwood; white pebbles to make your fingernails on edge.

A Share of the World

Spirit lamp and picnic of long ago. Ampères. Only four clocks. I'm steering. Granny, I steered. Susan's eyes, black, scornful and sullenly lit for impossible rebellion. Sulky, bellicose mouth and flared nostrils like a charger. Her body . . . John looked up at the wall and a sweetness and tenderness like a blush suffused his blood and altered his saliva. He went on with the box. Each shell a love, an atonement.

Titch came in as usual. He stood at the door getting his bearings, but had no need to smear down the light switches since they were already down. John's back and the array of shells seemed a sight harder than usual to focus. He said, " Jesus wept," and began his progress against the irregular gale and bed. To-night he undressed but was sick soon. He fell asleep half uncovered. After the last retch he said, " F—— sea-shells." John opened all the windows and the door, and put out the light.

After five minutes he got up and covered Titch. Titch said, " I f——g can."

In the morning Titch had his trousers half on and was cursing what his clock said when his eyes lighted on the floor space. " Where the f—— hell . . .? " he said, and went to the door.

There had been a wind in the night. He brought it in, looking down through his arms at it. The handlebars were slightly crooked and the lamp glass was cracked. The silver grip of one brake was clotted with fine damp clinker-dust, and the side of the petrol tank was drossed where petrol had dribbled out and dried.

" Did you put it there? " he said.

" Yes," said John. He was tying his tie, leaning over his shells to catch the reflecting angle of his small mirror.

" I put it there."

Titch's stockinged feet came close.

" The lamp's smashed; you've b—— up the handlebars."

" Then I'm sorry, but it wouldn't have happened if you'd kept it out of here."

" I'll keep it where I f—— well like."

John said nothing. He reached for his battledress allowing his face to reflect the proximity of a dog's mess in human shape. Titch said quietly, " I'll fight you. I'll fight you now behind the hut."

And it was not out of this moment he spoke but out of the accumulation of weeks.

John put on his battledress. He had turned pale. He went for his belt on his bed, disregarding Titch.

He was a head taller than John and four stone heavier. He lowered over him as he passed to get his belt. When the distance between them was six feet, John said:

"You're brave, aren't you? Really heroic. No wonder they won't take you into the Commandos."

Titch picked up John's shell box and threw it at the stove. Newspaper stuck to its bottom and a heap of shells were dragged after it. It was a noise like a drawer, full of small coins, falling.

Nightmare's mild, permeating ache instead of movement; he could do nothing, say nothing—because the only thing he wanted to do was to take Titch's life slowly with his bare hands, and instead he stood there, fearing him.

At last he stepped forward and picked up the lid: the monogram which had not been completely set was partly missing; two shells were broken. The small whelks had mostly come off. The dovetailing in one of the frail joints was smashed. Something about the way John examined it held Titch's attention, for he stood there watching.

"For my lamp," he said.

John was pale. He picked any shell with a tacky rim from the floor and put it inside the box. He settled down to search as though alone.

Titch said, "Oh, for Christ's sake," dressed and went to breakfast.

John would not have gone to breakfast if he could have avoided it, but he could not avoid it because the thing he now wanted most in the world, and at once, was a letter from Susan; and that would be behind the lattice of tapes across the green baize in the dining-room.

Normally he did not look forward to her letters because they reminded him unpleasantly of his own. Only accounts of hockey bore the stamp of herself—a self which he had found hard to identify with the girl who came to his room in the small hours. To-day, however, a letter from her seemed the thing he could not do without.

There was one.

He opened it while Titch was teased for not knowing that a rifle bullet revolved in the air. Titch said:

" I thought that squirly line in the barrel was bullshit."

Susan wrote: "Yes, I think you're right. We should get accustomed to the idea of a future one day perhaps without each other. So much may happen before we can even meet again.

" My cousin Peter Clarke is staying. He kissed me by the lake and I rather enjoyed it though it wasn't the same. I tell you because you made me promise to tell and because I wanted to see if it was true what you said—that we will find we are not indispensable to each other. Since I enjoyed the kiss I suppose it is true. I was in the tennis six last . . ."

He answered before first parade: " Did I ever say we were not indispensable to each other? If I did, please forget that I did because it isn't true." And, " Now you have given me this kiss to think of I can't rest." He implored her not to let herself be kissed again, and asked her to send a telegram saying simply " Yes " if she would be " his " for life.

He was due at the tommy-gun range for firing at life-sized figures from the hip, shoulder and snap-shooting, and it was away from the camp, so he did not read the letter through and in the customary final paragraph devoted to her body, more extravagant than usual, he left out a word or two which made erotic gibberish of the last words before his signature.

In two days a wire came, " Yes." He stuffed it into his pocket, embarrassed, because by then happier. He had realised that he would have fought Titch with weapons which killed. Survival defeated was what he would not face.

But the auto-cycle remained.

He returned to the shell box and planned another to follow it. The telegram " Yes " never looked at but always there made him long to celebrate the relationship in a shape far, far fairer than that in which it sometimes appeared. The mosaic of crushed shell became finer and the blues blended.

115

14

THE beginning of the night was long ago and the white house waited.

A warm round by the well and an L.M.G. level with Massa Treponti on the left, which fired at us so we came back. Grant got back, sir. Oh, splendid; that's most frightfully good.

Yes the warm round would be splendid and also the fact that they were fired on . . . Boy here, sir. Yes, they just got in now. The krauts are using that farm . . . warm rounds at the well just short of it and fire from an outhouse on the left. Oh, capital, Boy, capital. Our patrols were active.

Splendid was so easy.

Was that a searchlight behind the mountain?

Dawn.

Bright brought his head near John's and obliterating consonants in his desire to approximate silence, breathed rather than whispered, " S'cone a be f—— tayligh' soon."

I could have moved towards it, I could have. He got up crouching and his clothes felt like air after a tepid bath, staring at the unchanged face of the white house.

He turned.

The hammer of decision had fallen and the night's lot had gone for a few pence.

You could hold the enemy in their places with your eyes, and you could keep the dawn slow by looking at it, but when you moved away the enemy scrambled after you and light leapt up in the sky.

John took a different route. A back-to-front view of the country in a changed light produced new deceptions. But it didn't matter.

A Share of the World

Over there—somewhere over there in that direction and from sea to sea, was safety, the letters he hadn't finished reading, and that slimy, gritty grave with a field telephone and a bar of chocolate in a niche; home.

On this rise, until the top of it, precautions, after that briskly and upright without listening—towards the ridge, the village, ready with Garbo at his lips.

All night the fingers of his right hand had never left the pistol-grip of his tommy-gun. Perhaps a long education with a shotgun influenced not only this position, this *qui vive* way of walking—but also equipped him with one reflex which fear could not affect— the reflex before a sudden target.

Therefore, when he put his weight on a wet root, and slithered back a foot and saw at the same time a silhouette rear up in front of him like a jack-in-the-box, he fired as soon as he could get a grip of the forward handhold.

The toy spattering sound of the fat slow velocity bullets and the orange flashes finished and the figure heeled back into shadow and solid night, the medium from which it had upthrust like a wave in the sea.

Silence—a silence which hung by a thread of boundless amaze-ment and fear and which a sudden smooth King's English voice tried at once to reinforce by talking as usual.

" Corporal Bowen? " The voice was almost at John's elbow. " What are you firing at? "

The lack of answer made the silence a monster sinking slowly on its hackles, a wide-eyed thing before it sprang all claws, all yells.

John said nothing. Bright's voice began. But it was executed after one hoarse syllable by a Bren, firing into the valley behind. The Bren sound was pedestrian, English, moderate, but thorough after the harsh fanatic rip of the spandau. One by one the tracer floated out over the valley, languid until the ground by deflection seemed to double their velocity.

Near shouts: from Bright—a hysterical cadenza of four-lettered words round Jesus and Christ and B Company and Garbo, and stop, stop, stop—merging with that rarefied voice by John's elbow, saying a different sort of stop, stop. Then a nearer Bren, in precise staccato iambics, t'tac t'tac t'tac, metallically deafening, affirming matchwood, bones and flesh like soggy cotton wool. John stood up. A flare caught its breath—upward, expanded in light which dawn made silly and the King's English yelled, " Corporal Brennan, I said, Stop Firing ! "

John remained standing looking at where he'd fired. Let the tracer come again and dip down to where he stood. That was what he wanted. Not much. He did not want anything much now. But it wouldn't matter. It would be less tiring, simpler.

A lull. Bright and the King's English said, " Stop " together. Then the King's English, " Who are you? "

The farthest Bren took up again, a private war and lonely search.

" B. Company," said Bright. " Recce patrol from B Company. Mr. Grant."

John went to where he had shot. He saw the head and shoulders first. He had already seen the silly impossible positions of death, people in bed yet not in bed—running, crouched, reaching for something, counting stars on the back, voluptuous face-down sprawl, a pile fallen in a hanging-cupboard or spilt rubbish, old clothes, face the colour of a vein, and boots so ordinary with laces neatly tied but in the body something white showing, surprising inside or out.

This man still stood on his legs but lay sideways. In him already was the inertia of stones, the mountain scrub and damp earth. That quiet harmony with the inanimate was communicated in a swift and certain impression but it did not prevent John from sinking on his knees and looking for signs of life.

Mortar bombs were exploding in the valley behind—like mines because they arrived without noise. " Mister who? " said the King's English, the impalpable B.B.C. voice level with the ground.

" Grant," said Bright. " B Company."

" Well, stand up—all of you. Let's look at you."

John stood again and, looking down, said, " I've shot someone." The Bren on the spur still fired in short bursts across the slope behind them.

A Share of the World

The King's English bawled, "Henry, for Christ's sake stop your Bren."

The figure that rose seemed to be wearing some head-gear, but it was only hair.

"What the f—— hell's happening?" it said in petulant pure accents.

The relief with which officer usually met officer in the firing line was not here. The man with the long hair looked from John to the figure at his feet and then shouted over his shoulder, "Stretcher bearers." He pulled the man's shoulder gently and said quietly, "Poor old Corporal Bowen."

Then he looked at John—incredulous, hostile.

"What on earth happened?"

"I came back by a different route . . . I thought he was a German."

John could never say "Jerries" or "Boche." The man with long hair had an angry little face which a moustache made military but not virile. He had the proprietary manner of those who had been through the desert.

"You thought he was a 'German!'" he said and then, as though to prevent himself saying what *he* thought, he went to find out, to shout what the f—— hell had happened to the stretcher bearers.

Light was increasing. Blades of coarse grass, stones, and scrub emerged, an entrenching tool and a slit which John hadn't seen immediately behind him on his left. A stocking-cap face looked up at him like a horse out of a shed, in a blizzard—blank, wretched, but now with something to look at.

John knelt again beside the dead man.

The enormous experiences of life are at first like the least. Their very size shuts them out. There is no room for them at a moment's notice.

The extent of war's chaos, touching everybody a little, some a lot, might have prompted many who found themselves in John's position, to say there and then: "Such things happen in war," and even excused themselves of any outstanding failure or incompetence.

A Share of the World

But John had at once to say, He lies there dead because I wanted to tell a more polished lie.

The thought kept him there on his knees—and if there was anything in his own definition of prayer—the reaching out towards understanding and harmony with what one is, what one has done, and what one desires—then he was praying.

The officer who had gone so noisily for the stretcher bearers must have returned quietly, John imagined, to stand beside him. Two legs and boots were there, the boots nearly touching his hand. John looked up—into the the blackened face of Bright.

And then Bright smiled.

He smiled like a man who had known all the time what the card was, and to the whites of his eyes was added the white of teeth.

15

DESMOND'S face jutted its pipe against the sky behind Company Headquarters, savoured the smoke, the situation, in which he was at home, knew what to do. Behind the gravity as always was the private smile, the complacence which lingered because the taste of it was sweet. The connoisseur who knew the vintage, the vintner, the village of every bottle of war.

"It's no good, John," he said. "You'll have to go."

John was silent. The mud was drying on his clothes, and his face had the double etiolation of scrubbing and fatigue.

Sergeant Allen and Bright had "marched themselves in" to complain they had no confidence in their platoon commander. Desmond said he knew them both. They were survivors, left-overs, after many battles. And they were not left over by chance. But he would say no more about that. The point was—John must go. There would be other opportunities, he said and his smile almost, declared itself openly (perhaps to hide it he turned and tapped his pipe on a lop-sided grindstone behind him)—other opportunities with other men. This battalion would soon be going; after what happened in G Company at Astuno and after two years of promises —there could be no two ways about it. It would be going—and he offered the fact to John as a comfort—even added "breaking up," as though thereby a record would be effaced.

He said, "I don't want you to go. I hardly know you. I don't think you've had a fair chance and when I say you've got to go, I don't want to suggest you're a coward."

"I should bloody well hope not." The interruption was too keen, too high-pitched. It was more hysterical than righteously indignant. "Bloody-well-hope" was a stranger to his tongue until

that moment sounded it. Desmond let his smile out for a moment
—on a leash.

" But that doesn't alter anything. When they do that—the
officer must be changed."

Oh, yes—John understood.

" These things happen in war," said Desmond. He was feeling
towards the bouquet of this particular bottle, knowing its history,
its year, how much rain there had been. And he added, " But
you've got a clear conscience—that's all that matters."

John was silent.

Desmond would have gone on to say, " Perhaps I shouldn't
have let you go after Corporal Murray was wounded," but he didn't
because he knew from the Adjutant's face when he put his report in,
that the opinion was already held. So he said:

" A job's a job. That shell was unlucky but you had to go."

John suddenly said, " Bright! "

The steady float of Desmond's mastery of the right thing to do
was punctured by the intensity of this monosyllable, spoken quietly
at his side. But it was not for him. The unlucky newcomer,
green in all senses, had spoken to himself and was looking with
unfocused dilated eyes beyond the battered houses, the sky soiled
with airburst, and mountains decapitated by cloud. Unsuitable
type, thought Desmond, probably graded A and passed out top
in one of these new Octu's. Good at morse.

" Yes—I think you made a mistake to take Bright."

" I took him in case we all got killed."

Desmond thought, Yes—he had indeed better go, and because
the expression on the young man's face was the opposite of receptive,
in fact full of a luminous haughtiness and private interest, Desmond
said, " You'd better get your things out and go with the carrier."

Bright watched John collect his kit—over ten yards of tins and
refuse, over earth wet with rain, urine, and tea-slops. He alone
of the platoon stuck up out of the ground with his back to the
enemy and his collar round his ears. He lured John to look at him
once; then he got in a smile.

16

AT Monticelli, the Infantry Reserve Training Camp straggled along a road between mountains. The wind blew from snow-covered summits, and the oblique rain was colder than snow. Surrounded by tents and M.T. parks the villagers carried on as usual—the men played cards in doorways in short black cloaks when it was fine and indoors when it wasn't. And the women in all weathers carried logs down the mountain on their heads, walking rigidly straight and fast as though it were a race to keep their thick necks under the load. The white oxen plodded with mournful, patient eyes, as though the bloody groove across their shoulders, and the whip across where their genitals had been, and the urge of those strange cries, that musical and perpetual petulance was all they could expect.

From a military point of view the camp was two things: half-way house between the U.K. and the Italian front; and a human junk heap—for " empties." Of this latter *raison d'être* John became a part. Temporarily, of course, and with a good excuse. Everyone there had an excuse and everyone would soon be going—even though they were there this time last year. Like patients in a sanatorium the " empties " could not refrain, especially in their cups, from touching on the main subject.

" It was quite simple, I suppose—Sydney just didn't like me," or, " They gave me this truth drug to see why I was being sick. Damn silly." Or very rarely, " I'm afraid I'm not the warrior type."

The senior regulars who read old *Tatlers* with a drink beside the huge smoky stoves, like water-butts, were for the most part silent about why they were there. For them even alcohol could not introduce them to the facts. On the notice-board they read the typed tailpiece—wounds, promotion, death and decorations of people they knew. There were exceptions, one, who had a reputation as a wit, had wept a whole day at Cassino as though bereaved. Now he was wittier, better company than he had ever been before. But for the most part the regulars were like understudies who, having waited years for a chance, forgot the words.

Lacrima Christi, Strega, Kummel, milk chocolate and V cigarettes, paper napkins, local pig and eggs were the material consolations. Sometimes a visit to the officers' club in Naples and a box at the gold and scarlet opera, where the leading lady cost 50,000 lire afterwards—a price which suggested some soldiers made money.

John wrote letters by one of the huge tin-barrel stoves. He applied to join the parachutists, the Commandos, the S.A.S., the cloak-and-dagger people in Cairo. And at other desks similar letters were occasionally written.

The possibility of his being accepted for the parachutists kept him awake at night but, like a dice player, he waited to see what he had thrown—very little. The first reply from Regimental Headquarters (after weeks) suggested that before making such applications he should take the trouble to learn the traditional formula—which started, " Sir, thanking you for permission to speak."

Those three weeks were a long time and by their end, a form of mild jaundice joined with nervous exhaustion had given him the mental aspirin—apathy. The letter from R.H.Q. lay on a tin ammunition box beside his camp bed, and Orange, the servant he shared with Middy, knocked it off with his leg, discovered it with his hand—and disposed of it as rubbish which perhaps, John thought, it was—rubbish answering rubbish.

On certain mornings when it would not have been noticed if he had not got up till eleven the temptation to lie with his knees to his chin overcame him. Then he watched Middy's boots go by his face to parade.

Jack Middy had shot himself through the foot ten minutes before an attack—his tommy-gun had gone off in his hand. Although medically down-graded and exempt from fighting, he insisted on making himself available to his battalion and waiting.

A Share of the World

He had waited two months and was still waiting. Always available.

The idea that people thought he had done it on purpose haunted him. He was sure they spoke of it, thought of it, laughed at it. He imagined it rivalled Anzio as a topic. He would have liked to have been everywhere at once to have stopped this general conversation. If one of a group, he could not walk away alone, he had to stay till it broke up. If circumstances compelled him to leave then he dallied at the door on the fringe, trying to make the last words friendlier and friendlier, until he felt he could leave with impunity. But he never could. Once or twice his whipped look, his endless scavenging for respect—just a little respect—earned him some crushing abuse which turned him white after the first few syllables—the proof, the proof—he had known it all the time: he was a sort of leper.

In this hospital of human pride—John was perhaps as serious a case as any—but his symptoms took the outward form of sustained indifference; he was, so to speak, in a private ward, a room to himself. His struggle was domestic, internal. " They " could think what they liked; if he satisfied *himself* that would be enough. And in the end, he vowed coldly, he would satisfy himself; not in order to " do well in Italy," but to be different—prove some sort of free-will.

He wrote long letters to Susan but never told her what had happened. Sometimes his whole letter would be three pages, as it were, of erotic wishful thinking. And sometimes in reply he got an enthusiastic description of a hockey match and two stilted paragraphs of love in his own style. He felt she was changing. Her letters were shorter.

Anzio happened. Rumour of swift success was followed by rumour of extermination. Drafts came through. Young men with new walking-sticks and second pips conspicuously brighter than the first. They asked questions, and listened to the answers speculative and entranced.

Each morning people looked out to see if air support would be possible to-day.

Sometimes aircraft blundered north through the cloud and mountain, echoing moaning, now sharp, now mat. And the people who had come back read old *Tatlers* beside the ever-changing faces of those going up. The best jokes were about fear—about the man who ran a quarter of a mile in front of a lame Czech who followed him trying to surrender.

Underneath was no joke. In idleness the things that were wrong fermented and became worse—so that when a tall general came and talked out of a jeep, like Monty, breezily in corduroys, about morale, the phalanxes listened like convicts to a chaplain. Most of the men, like most of the officers, were there for no good reason.

Perhaps the tall general's own feelings were only revealed when he lost his temper with the microphone and the engineer officer responsible. A flushed A.D.C. with a yellow jersey peeping by his tie, suggesting the meet at the big house, ran from C.O. to C.O. and the phalanxes were rearranged on the slimy grass, closer to the jeep, the sociable, man-to-man, no-nonsense jeep; like Monty's.

Far away, it was said, "General Alex" had walked about on the worst day of Anzio and said nothing. For saying nothing even more than for walking about on the worst day, he provoked twinges of general respect. Confidence almost.

In the spring it would be different.

In April . . . in May the break would come. Rome, Florence, Genoa, Austria—the soft underbelly . . . Once they cracked, would they dissolve? That was the public problem—the private ones, more complicated, also took a slow course. John's thus: on Tuesdays the duty officer superintended the issue of mixed slops and left-overs, that is to say, swill to villagers who wanted it, which was all of them. The bitterness and competition between those who wanted it for their animals and those who wanted it at once on the spot for themselves made necessary a few soldiers, an N.C.O. and an officer to keep the queue.

The officer came from the Mess seven minutes before time and stood beside the man with the ladle while the N.C.O. quelled rivalry.

Sometimes to justify his presence, his existence at the I.R.T.D. and at the queue, an officer would suggest to the N.C.O. that a frail child or a crone should have precedence or a bigger scoop, but such matters usually settled themselves or were being carried out even while suggested. Therefore, the officer was left free to look at the extreme misery of the villagers and the noise and morality of seagulls which resulted, and to look as if he were necessary, which he was, but not obviously.

John was doing this one Tuesday, smelling drains, smouldering charcoal and the meaty swill, and examining the ferocity in the eyes of a girl clasping a Spam tin on wire, behind a woman who must have got in front of her with an elbow, wondering whether to do anything, act on the mere evidence of the girl's eyes, when he decided no, looked at his watch and thought time to start, and turned to say so to the man with the ladle.

It was Bright.

The queerly-shaped head on the huge body behind steam was turned towards John, watching him. Their eyes met and Bright smiled—in affinity.

Instead of saying " Start " John turned away, pretending to check the orderliness of the queue, this side and that, and only then shouted " Right—start now."

When he took his place at Bright's elbow and watched the stuff like boiling vomit splashing into American Spam tins, German mess-tins, British jam tins, and one Italian helmet—Bright said, " Better here than up there isn't it, sir? "

John said, " Don't fill the big tins to the top."

John had come to terms with what had happened on the patrol as a patient comes to terms with an illness. Perhaps his surroundings, the other rejects, the news of Anzio, where any shell hit someone, blizzards on a penurious village—all combined to make an atmosphere which belittled his private misery and reconciled him to it.

But after Bright came, this improvement ended.

The man was everywhere John went, greeting him with a salute —and a smile.

Just as Bright's features did not belong to one another, nor his head to his body, so there was no integration in his activities. In two weeks he was officer's servant, armourer's help, sanitary man, ordinary guardsman, mess waiter and finally sat in the stores among the black blankets and white mugs, drinking tea with a bed at the back.

Once when John was alone in the company office, he looked into Bright's dossier and found he was awaiting a medical discharge certificate for—gastric ulcers.

When, as duty officer, he had to censor the outgoing company mail—a hundred letters to read and seal—he picked up each as though it might be from Bright—and was both relieved and disappointed when it was not. There was never a letter from Bright. This made sense. The parents, wife or children of Bright were somehow unimaginable.

If there had been a letter from Bright to be censored John would probably have felt sick as he handled it and expected—what? . . . Something written *to* him—all for him like the smile.

Inspecting " employed " personnel John looked up from a second-rank belt brass with green stain on the side and found the head of Bright held high at attention, but the little eyes slanting down at him and even without a smile communicating acquaintance, partnership.

" Look to your front," bawled a voice behind John. Someone else, thought John gratefully, hates his guts.

John said: " That's a filthy belt, sergeant major," as though he wished to state the crime before the punishment so that the sergeant major might give his opinion also before more was said.

" Yer in shit," whispered the sergeant major to Bright. The little eyes looked out and away over the mountains. The fat lips remained closed.

" Can't yer clean a belt yet, Bright? "

" Put him in the book," said John.

" SIR." The yell drifted over the village startling hens and cadaverous dogs. " Guardsman Bright, dirty brasses."

When he had dismissed the parade John sat on a chair near the door of the company office, took his hat off and let the air meet his forehead like liquid. He was feeling sick and his hands were shaking.

" 'Flu, sir," said the clerk, who had just had it.

A Share of the World

" No, thank you," said John, and wondered why he had said thank you.

It had felt as if the man was offering him something.

Then Middy was posted to a battalion " holding " on the southern edge of Cassino. The night before he left he was garrulous going through his packs.

Days came suggesting spring. The harsh cries and the drag of wooden shoes in the street became more numerous, also the shouted nagging " Ma-Rɪ-a—Pep-Iᴛ-a," and the slow, gentle lurch and creak of the ox-carts.

Crocuses appeared on the mountain and, soon afterwards, primroses where the tall general had said from his jeep that he welcomed a slogging match if that was what the Hun wanted.

Cherry and almond blossomed on the airfields before Caserta and the negroes played softball beside acres of new lorries, cranes, tanks, and bulldozers, and dark-green tents.

John lived, as it were, in the prison cell of what had happened —and instead of a window, looking out on other things, there was the face of Bright in the one street, among the tents, in the mess-room when he shouted any complaints (among the few that answered that formality as though seizing every opportunity to communicate); and there even when not there, so that John left letters unfinished, mistook doors and sometimes left table before the last course, thinking he had finished.

The thought of what Bright might be saying to the other guardsmen occurred occasionally but academically, and was of slight importance.

It was the smile—the man's personality expressed in it—the predatory familiarity, debasing affinity which walked into John's mind confidently and made itself at home. Like a murderer visiting his mother.

Why? What nonsense. Yes. What nonsense.

John wrestled with the intruder and tried to find out how he always got in. The parasite, he said, is only made possible by a weakness. The sucker-fish would get nowhere if a shark had hands.

Such quaint and remote citations from nature did not apply.

A Share of the World

If he was a shark and Bright a sucker-fish—then indeed—he had no hands, and was, anyhow, a funny sort of shark.

The day came when Bright went—quickly—not discharged into safety by a medical certificate but in a military police fifteen cwt. after a summary appearance before the commanding officer, charged with selling W.D. blankets to the Italians.

After that riddance there was a new air as though everything were taking a turn for the better—a different past and a new future. And John was suddenly sent to Cassino to take the place of Middy who had been killed.

Poor Middy, people said in the Mess—how?

And the people who knew what had happened, tried to control their faces, wipe them clear of laughter, embarrassment, incredulity, leave only the pity which they did—yes, did—feel in varying degrees, before saying, " He fell downstairs." Then it was the others' turn to be unable not to laugh.

" DownSTAIRS! "

" But there aren't any stairs at Cassino."

" There is apparently one flight left—and Middy fell down it."

" And——?"

" Broke his neck."

They looked at each other in pitiful incredulous amusement. Only Middy, only Middy—it was no exaggeration to say " only Middy."

Somebody had to say to John as he left, " Mind the stairs."

He smiled, exhilarated—almost optimistic. The first flamingo-pink blossoms of spring had never seemed so full of promise—and pathos. Cassino and spring. Tears stood in his eyes while the driver described how much nicer Jerry was in the desert. His head was full of the reassuring drone of the *Bhavagad Gita* which he had read the whole of the previous evening. He was certain that now at last he was going up to some desired consummation.

In Caserta recuperating Indians sat in night-shirts and turbans on a low wall. Some squatted. Without their uniforms they conjured up India.

Highway Six was the first met of the names which brewed the vivid nostalgia of war. Like a thermometer it graded the proximity of danger, had a red line almost, after which vehicles were parked behind things, and men looked out of things and people had IT in their faces.

At B echelon—fifty bivouacs and two marquees among olives —Peter Bolt-Ewing now a captain, sat in a deck-chair reading *Put Out More Flags*, and an angelus ting-ed from a village below as though everyone must hurry. Over the top of the book Peter said he would be " going up with the food to-night." John thanked him and looked around as though for a place to put " his stuff."

" Are you all right? " said the sad moustached man whose small body John had never seen before. " Or can I do anything? " And then as though it were a minor point, " You *are* Grant, aren't you? Yes." He considered the situation and added wearily— pointing out an explanation: " We met, didn't we? I'm L.O.B. to-day."

The conversation was on weak legs and gave up when the captain looked sadly down the slope where a gunner was washing, lobster shoulders and earth-coloured face in the sun.

" Does anybody know when this f—— war's going to end? What about the second front? "

John climbed a hill and on top he sat down and looked at the farthest ridge, blue, beyond a conical hill bright grey in the sun, grained with white razor rocks, like protective scales on a monster. Lizards crossed his path like shadows of birds flying overhead, and out of the breeze the sun burnt.

His platoon headquarters at Cassino, he had been told, were in a house (with stairs), but his forward sections were in earshot of the enemy, lying in rubble bastions. They were fed at night, and ammonia went up in kegs to be spilled—sometimes directly on corpses, sometimes down gaps in fallen concrete, over the rubble, between charred beams or across an uneven pulp of bricks— everywhere the nauseating sweet stench was underfoot.

John went into Cassino that bright afternoon on the hill. The lure of it was immense and he went into it, purged himself there of the death which he had caused by wishing to lie convincingly. And he purged himself there in imagination of the past, and of Bright's stare.

A Share of the World

To do which it was among other things, necessary to kill a German. Looking towards the blue horizon, he realised that he wanted more than anything else in the world to kill a German—not remotely, but closely, so that the proof of it might lie at his feet. He pictured various ways in which this might happen—by day, by night, in a shattered room with a window for a door and a bomb hole for light, from one crater to another. His limbs became tense with what he pictured. It seemed the kiss which could free him—this infliction of death on a German.

The 25-pounders below the tents banged in series and he thought of death, what it must be like to die. Death is a wedding, he said, I do believe that. You go to it and there religiously you are joined by the White Bride whose face you cannot see, but whom you know. You are made one flesh. You return. It's a going home. I do believe that.

He took out his small green translation of Arjuna's talk with Krishna—how inappropriately did not occur to him—and read of a man who longed not to have to kill. The problem seemed the same. The desire for purity.

And although desiring above all else to kill a German he now felt the phrase " bowels of mercy " to be full of meaning, a physical melting which he then and there experienced, pitying the German as he killed him, like a priest doing a god's will, Abraham and his son—God and His Son. The thing that must be done—without hatred—on the contrary, with love, towards purity and no fear.

The 25-pounders banged again—savage explosions down there in the field suggesting accidents rather than something intended. And a German heavy hit the conical hill so that a tuft of black smoke dawdled away from it.

John hardly noticed these earnests. If anything, they increased his internal sweetness. Death was a wedding—the bells were ringing. He would write a letter to Susan—no, to his father—about cherry blossom and Cassino, pollen and ammonia—the chord of life.

Nay, but as when one layeth
His worn out robes away
And taking new ones sayeth

A Share of the World

" These will I wear today "
So putteth by the spirit
Lightly its garb of flesh.

He watched a lizard on a stone, believing itself unseen. Palpitation, almost imperceptible, in its throat's undersurface, showed life in all its fragility.

Full of a double misery, a double sweetness—ready to kill or be killed, go to the wedding or officiate. He came down quickly, loosely—as though the truck for Cassino were waiting at the bottom.

Peter, the sad, dry captain with the forlorn moustaches, was in the same position. But beside John's kit was a pile of suitcases, packs, holdalls, and greatcoats stencilled with serial numbers and a green triangle.

Peter said, " I'm afraid it's a case of sorry you were bothered."

John did not understand.

" Fodder from the Four Hundred." Peter considered his own words with a gleam of enthusiasm and felt they could do with some embroidery.

" And a little more L.O.B. for yours truly, pray God." Then he muttered, " Fertiliser," looking moodily at the olive trees.

" So——? "

" You're to go back—with the truck that brought them. I don't know. You'd better ask. Nobody ever tells me anything. I just listen. Now and again I glean something."

To go back. Yes, of course. John stood there foolishly, of course. The past never changed and the future took its colour from the past. The past went on happening.

The ramblings of the morose Bolt-Ewing went on like machine-music at a fair after someone had been crushed under a coloured car.

" I wish *I* was going back," he said. Then wistfully, " Some people have cousins in Naples. Female cousins—young gold women on the hill of oranges who would exchange themselves for a tin of spam in spite of handles to their names like Victorian chamber-pots."

Again he got sad consolation from his own words as though they were a sunbeam in a cell.

A Share of the World

" Golden girls and rooms looking out on the sea—and no need to go to bed because you're already there. Bed in the loggia, bed in the orchard among the swallows and wistaria. Bed upstairs and looking at Vesuvius along the gold barrel of her body, niche in the V-foresight of her toes, or the backsight of her buttocks. Bed and peaches and shade, bare feet on marble and a song any time you like—for a song. A song for a song. And coarse, jolly, meaty servants with religious names who don't mind being servants. Bambini flocking to my Spam and caramellos. Oh, Jesus. I'd give my gratuity, when it comes, for cousins in Naples now."

" It would be a help," said John, " of a kind."

" What d'you mean of a kind? Can you suggest anything better? "

" No, I suppose not."

" Cousins in Naples and peace," said the captain, and returned to his book, correcting himself once without raising his eyes. " No —not peace—truce. An endless truce with armies maintained, and cousins in Naples."

After meeting and talking with a major holding papers and maps, a fly-whisk and a parasol John went down the hill with his things.

" Monticelli, sir? " said the driver.

" Yes," said John.

" And the right direction, if you ask me."

A heavy shell pitched in the olives a hundred yards above the tents. The smoke, like dirty exhaust, lazed away with the breeze. The angelus added a perfunctory tang-tang-tang as though marking a new phase of priestly movement. And the gunner began scrubbing his teeth, spitting brilliant white in the sun.

John watched a lizard tranced in a shallow crater already weedy—life was here where it was in danger. To leave it was nearly unbearable. The wheel moved under the high pining note of first gear and where the lizard had been was nothing.

PART TWO

Oh my share of the world; oh yellow hair

W. B. YEATS

1

" THE campaign in Italy," said the small old don, curving a hand and laying it twice on his silver hair, gently and firmly, as though it were a wig and slipping, " The campaign in Italy, I believe, was extremely arduous." His voice had the purity and sweetness of a child's and his old eyes looked at the scarlet Virginia creeper on the Bell Tower quad, wanly as though the attempt to visualise the campaign in Italy was perhaps a piece of futility—even hypocrisy—on his part.

John said the mountains had favoured defenders.

" Ah, yes, they would have done, wouldn't they? " The humble old eyes opened a bit wider. The creeper became a mountain and up it went attackers—arduously and on top were defenders—favoured. Mr. Webb blinked and, abandoning the attempt, turned with a comfortable " Well, now " to the list of freshmen.

Outside autumn had scattered the streets with its damp gold and brown; young men with used faces stood in their corduroys and tweed jackets, talking by bicycles. Country cars stood in rank and waited till women in W.V.S. or other badges drove them away, leaving between the white lines only a few brightly coloured vehicles which might have been for sale second or third hand. Some negroes and Indians in western dress, like drake ducks in eclipse, mixed in the bright bookstalls with bare-legged men refulgent in loud school blazers smelling of camphor. And from old walls in dark archways, and Gothic porches, in sheafs hung the week's matches, concerts, meetings, lectures, debates and recitals—with superimposed one photograph of an undergraduate headed WANTED, and soon taken down.

Who would go so far to say that John had committed a murder, who, of course, but himself. And who would then assert with arrogant finality that he hadn't, and that, furthermore, he was as good as any, perhaps far, far better? Who on earth would have bothered—but himself?

The faces of undergraduates at this time were broken up into many forms of similar internal argument as a glance at the photographs will show. Some, of course, had not been to the wars and were five or six years younger. These were like a few unused stamps mixed with used. Many of the used faces were wizened without being mature, worn without seeming experienced—and some—like John—fierce without being bold. Compared to the groups of nineteen-ten—before either great war—they looked small, uncertain and most surprising of all—less developed even though they were considerably older and far more " experienced." Confidence, shading off into complacence, had given place to doubt and greed.

But if these latest comers did look worn without seeming experienced—is it surprising? Fighting in any of the three elements never afforded much practice. Most of the time nothing happened —then suddenly " everything." And if you were lucky you lived through three or four occasions when everything happened. But three or four times each utterly different from the last and making you feel you knew nothing, still knew nothing, merely wore people out without making them experienced. Perhaps this accounts for the tone and expression of many generals—an altogether artificial down-rightness, cut-and-driedness emphasised with a stick or a hand. They know deep down that they do not know and are perhaps even powerless to affect the course of war because every one of them has felt a twig in the current, seen his plans taken like a hat in the wind. The only hope, was faith and the capacity to impart it but they talk as if they had actually controlled thousands of men through fire and terror because if they merely talked as if they had waited by a telephone to hear what happened, like distant followers of a steeplechase in which they had stakes—people would think, " I could do that," so they don't.

It was more than three years since the confusion of war joined with John's innate weakness of character had brought him to that moment when he looked down into the face of Corporal Bowen, a man of about thirty from Manchester with two children, whom he had killed.

Three years—yet still—when he was walking in a street, sitting in his chair or in front of his tutor—his fist, or his thigh and his face muscle would gradually tighten. And he would be approaching step by step the white farm he never entered, or consumed by curiosity to know if there had been any Germans in it; or more often had missed Corporal Bowen, or hadn't, and was on his knees under Bright's smile.

That smile remained. It was a mirror which gave him back an image of himself—the image he refused to accept—and yet, somehow, a faithful mirror. Its certainty was absolute. The man might have been a familiar spirit who had followed him invisibly all his life, noting a series, a pattern of behaviour, and then at a certain moment become flesh, and appeared at his elbow under the moonlit village, smiled prophetically then, and at dawn in confirmation.

A pattern of behaviour—he asked himself—a series that would continue? All his life? The leopard's spots?

The idea took root. He was, he told himself, caught in a web— the web of himself. His energies, his hopes, had always been devoted to escaping from it. To the " I am what I am " of the poem and the " You are what you are " of à Kempis his instinct was to reply, " No, I am my desires as well as my practice."

Bright! Who was Bright? he would ask, looking out of his window at the college pigeons. An ordinary soldier with a bad record, a strikingly big man with a freakish skull and an insolent smile for those who were easily insulted? . . . Why do I feel as though he were more?

Many young men returning from the war went through their belongings, tangible and intangible, to see what they possessed. John found himself on several such pilgrimages of assessment.

The first was to Susan. Their correspondence had petered out two years ago like an engine running on wrong fuel. The break had occurred shortly after she had left school. She had taken a voluntary job washing dishes with a Lady Heatherlake at the Owl Combined Forces Club in Wigmore Street. Her handwriting had changed and she had ceased to copy him in style or sentiment. " Sometimes, John," she had written, " I wonder who I'm writing to I knew you so little—and so long ago and at a time when everything seemed different."

The letter met him after his return from south of Cassino to Monticelli. It had provoked him to his last zeal. He at once imagined he had been happy in the receipt of lacrosse scores and laborious imitation of his own fanatical endearments. He implored her to continue. But her capital letters had developed strange tails like birds of paradise, and the p's and t's had revolutionary uprights like tacks among stitches. Her reply was short, affectionate but gave the impression of someone downstairs waiting for her to finish. And to his reference to their past correspondence—" which had meant so much," she replied, " we neither of us had met anybody then and you were very sweet about what happened, which was probably my fault." " What happened? " " My fault! " Was that all?

He had let go eventually with relief. The taste of ashes he discovered had been stronger than he had known. The relationship had become habit; a lie in a very vacant niche.

Who was she? Child courtesan, lacrosse enthusiast, jet-black eyes with too much of the pupil's perimeter showing. Her letters had revealed nothing—invited nothing—they had possessed no antennae. Could he, for instance, have told her about Bright? The attempt would have increased the smile and added another strand to the web.

Although she was sixteen and in Kent, and he at leisure, if not at ease, by golden campanile, wistaria, and bees like black wrens booming in blossom, far from danger he had reviled her for being insensitive to what war was. And she had said, " Yes, it must be dreadful," dutifully, like a child copying its parents' movements in church.

So the correspondence died without ever having lived.

Yet now after four years John, back in England, looked for her. Why?—he asked himself.

On a certain level—a level that mattered—she was *all there had ever been.*

A Share of the World

He wrote to her suggesting they meet. She replied with impersonal enthusiasm—as though what fun—he too was going to join in—the fun. Her lettering had abandoned experiment for pace and size. The freak tails of the fs and gs had apparently been frozen at an intermediate stage. Only in a P.S. she rustled the dead leaves of the past.

" It will feel odd, won't it? "

He invited himself to tea—an initiative which did not strike him as peculiar till he arrived and found himself with her and two girl friends. Then he sat in their company and for a few seconds abandoned himself to thought, piecing together the bits of this surprise.

Had there been room the three girls would all seemingly have sat on the carpet in front of the fire. They were expensively dressed, in league and effervescent as though—don't look round now—wife-buyers were listening. Two of them had only half a face like the cover of *Behold this Dreamer*—the other half blacked out by hair.

Susan was one of these.

He looked at her despondently, with half an ear on the conversation and half a mind for his contributions to it. She was pretty. Long limbed, relaxed and direct. But she clung to general conversation. One of her friends sometimes laughed, when an opportunity occurred—with relief as though she would have liked to have laughed, much, much more. He felt a gulf between them and himself which he could not plumb or place.

They vied with each other in adoring Danny Kaye. Behind the talk the airs of *Annie Get Your Gun* subsided, one after another with a soft clink in the cabinet and were audible as from a deep velvety distance. He got muddled until he realised that *both* the friends were called Caroline; and both also were employed by a florist. Susan was learning typing.

" With a view to what," he said in an aggressively personal tone.

He tried, when she looked at him, to engage her eyes on another level—to remind her—but her directness fled: she answered into her hair and to the others. A twinge of jealousy and contempt of their tight little league subsided into a feeling that he was older

141

A Share of the World

by another life and another dimension; and perhaps could never now be young.

This was her grandmother's house. *The Gathering Storm* lay under a huge arrangement of beech leaves, michaelmas daisies and dahlias; a magnifying glass by the cigarette box, a Corot above the little clustered shrine of photographs—one of royalty conspicuously signed.

Let her have her anonymity. He would not pursue her into the crowd. Presumably he was unusual in never letting the past rest; presumably other people divided their life into bulkheads between which they demanded no connection—though it struck him strange she had not wished to meet him alone and together lay the ghost of what had passed between them.

Of course—she might almost imagine she dreamt it. Indeed— it had marked her subsequent letters no more than a dream. He began to feel his visit to be an irrelevance which had escaped nobody's notice but his own.

And when he touched Susan's hand saying Good-bye and looking her in the eyes, he had a sudden faltering of confidence that she had ever lain in his arms at all.

She said: " Good-bye—I'm afraid it was rather a ghastly hen-party but if you care to hang on Billy Rushton's coming for a drink." On the stairs she inquired after his plans, movements and address.

At the door he said: " What's Jimmy doing now,"

She said: " Oh . . . didn't you know—he was killed."

John looked up with swift contrition and the feeling he had known it.

" Right at the end," she said, " after the surrender."

He stared down into the empty area murmuring condolence; then glanced at her almost furtively—to see if this were a bridge— back—and away again, because it wasn't. Silence. He went down a step.

Without having intended to he suddenly said: " That week-end . . . seems rather like a dream now, doesn't it? " He looked at her.

" Yes," she said, " it does." And she smiled—nervously, without meaning.

Had he met her that day for the first time, she would have seemed less alien.

" Good-bye."

" Good-bye."

There followed, as he walked away, one of those moments when he came face to face with his life. And he experienced the vacuum which at that time Sartes extolled, with international success, to his juniors, but which Nature allegedly abhors; he experienced *nausée* and the only joy left seemed to kick it all down—the sweet-tasting " No," of a child asked nicely.

2

HE was standing on the fringe of a crowd, a rather typical position for him, looking into the middle of it—when the thing happened.

Couples were dancing in a confined space and a girl called Jane Matlock whom he had heard of, moved into the floor and waited for the man who had asked her to dance to disengage himself from the crush through which she had fared faster than he.

John knew it was Jane Matlock because he had met her in childhood. Most people in that room knew each other from childhood or schooldays, as for instance, John had known Christopher, Jane's brother, at Eton. It was a drawing-room in Hyde Park Gardens and the people in it had grown up in the country and London palaces which were now, for the most part, totally or half deserted, converted, or presented to the nation. Those not so privileged by birth were there on account of professional, cultural, or financial eminence. Perhaps one because he was witty, which people said was nowadays rare.

It was, in a word, " Society "—the worse for wear, more than usually infused with foreign and business blood, but still feeling itself " at the top."

Self-respecting miners of the thirties had hung about in doorways, at street corners in the rain, when all attempts to get work had failed, and had often managed a clean shirt and a brushed suit on Sundays, but the real state of affairs had spoken out of their faces and manner in spite of a get-up which recalled other Sundays in God-fearing sufficiency, if not prosperity.

So, many now in that room, particularly among the middle-aged and elderly, were dressed in deceiving splendour suggesting ladies' maids and household staffs in the ratio of ten, twenty, thirty to one.

A Share of the World

But somehow from their faces and their manner one knew that this was not so—with the exception of a very few whose extreme riches had now even separated them from the people who had formerly been, so to speak, the next layer of the pyramid. In other words, the very rich had changed their status from firmly base pinnacle to disembodied cloud. They segregated even here, because even here they felt partly cut off.

In spite of such fissures emerging and exercising sometimes subtle, sometimes obvious disruptive pressures, everybody still knew everybody and labels therefore abounded. It was to some of these labels that John referred as he watched Jane.

To the over fifties, friends of her mother, she was " rather a wonderful person." She had kept on with her nursing—" No, darling, not a V.A.D."—to the end, which some had not. (And for these girls there had, on the whole, been no officers' messes, M.C.s extensions of previous life.)

People said of Jane, " I don't know what Neenie would do at Edgby without her."

To some contemporaries who knew what the word " prig " means, and were in the habit of using such drastic and intellectual terminology she was that—a prig; to most contemporary girl acquaintances she was " Jane? " with a shrug and a titter and where-shall-we-go-now change of subject. Her ceaseless emotional struggle to be perfect, to *be*—not merely *be called*—wonderful, was for them irritating. To seven or eight she was the " sweetest person I know " without meaning anything but that and to her brother Christopher she was that, but satirically. To contemporary young men who knew her and gave her face its exceptional due, the undeniable warmth and gusto of her body was aggravating because it was reserved for dancing—even dancing *her* as opposed to their steps. And the warmth of her mind was also aggravating because it was reserved for love of her family, love of doing things, riding and going to the theatre, etc., and for indignation and censure of divorce, pre-war Conservative Government, post-war Labour Government, sins of parental omission, filial ingratitude, and the material motive; in fact, for many things but not for them, the young men.

A Share of the World

By her brother's label she didn't " really exist." She " loved " Christmas, sunsets, flowers with an exclamation of adoration, kittens, parents and her laughter he thought was nerves not mirth.

To certain middle-aged men of professional ability and small vanity she was an ethical anachronism which they esteemed because it somehow added an underrated sauce to sex appeal which they had almost forgotten, like a reach-me-down flannel nightgown.

And to some, she had cheerful courage in the grand style of *The Pilgrim's Progress*—and if she was censorious then that did not matter much because she was boldly, bluntly, merrily and sometimes almost obscenely so. Her " quite unforgivable " would be followed by " I hope he loses the whole lot. *Bloody* man! "

These labels had at one time or other been available to John. They had, of course, amalgamated into an impression of the unknown which was weak beside the impact of first sight; weak, too, beside her skin like firelight on snow above a scarlet velvet dress and bare shoulders brushed by cendré curls, stubborn mouth, blue eyes, soldierly eyes, far apart and at the moment conspicuously innocent of enthusiasm. When her partner appeared she smiled agreeably at her better progress, adjusted a gold bracelet and accepted his dancing attitude gracefully. Immediately her face was settled, looking over his shoulder, it abandoned animation, and remained pent up all round the room. She looked—and danced—as if she would have preferred dancing by herself. Then even the air might have proved a hindrance.

John decided to marry her. It seemed to him afterwards that the decision came like that—instantly, and out of the blue. But why? He thought he knew why. It cannot be unusual for bankrupts on the edge of gambling tables to throw everything that remains to them not on the evens but on the thirty-to-one chance or for people who have had many small operations to welcome one to kill or cure; or for all-but-conquered armies to attack. And the more completely the bankrupt is bankrupt, the armies conquered or the invalid chronically afflicted—the greater must be the ease with which they come to some drastic theoretical decision. What counts is not the adequacy of the theory; the hope is really in the drasticness; in this case in the enormous pent force of nothing loved.

A Share of the World

Probably, if he had known her he would never have come to such a decision: she would not have appeared in such a kill-or-cure light; there might indeed have been nothing drastic in the design: she might have seemed neither wonderful nor unavailable. As it was, he knew her only by the hearsay labels and the label he decided to believe was that nebulous and easily ridiculed "wonderful person" of the over fifties. It was ratified by his eyes. For "wonderful" she was in the sense that his mouth thickened when he looked at her body, which would have thrived in the ugly event of public and national nakedness, and wonderful she now immediately became as the elect of his sick and desperate theory.

As she danced she looked almost pugilistically virginal, and this increased her "un-availability."

Indeed her remoteness left nothing to be desired; for she was remote by the fact that he did not know her; that she might already be engaged; that he had three hundred and ten pound a year from the government for three years, then nothing and no job; that he would have no link with her except occasional meetings such as this and she was remote by her beauty as all beauty is remote. But most of all, she was remote by virtue of the sort of husband she would certainly have—a man, in other words, not himself.

For neither by the ethical standards of " IF," nor the pictorial standards of four-square tobacco, nor in common-room, changing-room, brothel, passing the port clockwise or any other activity had John ever succeeded in seeing himself as a " man." Nor even by the calendar—since he had never believed he would reach the age of twenty.

By becoming her husband he would become " a man," and by becoming " a man " he would become the thing that he could never be and so break the pattern, the web of himself.

His first move in that drawing-room was towards the only link—her brother.

Christopher was by the white-clothed table where a packed crowd of men and a few women faced four active waiters. He was on the fringe listening to a man who conducted what he was saying

147

as though it were a piece of music. Christopher held two champagne glasses—one empty, the other full. The full one he stared into as though it were prophetic tea-leaves. His head moved regularly and slowly like a mobile in a shop window.

"Yes, YES," he drawled, "that's exactly it—*exactly*."

"C——" said a loud voice, loud enough to bring some heads up and some heads round, "C——, take your empty what? Take your empty?"

A burly baby-faced man with spots, holding five empty glasses by their stems in one hand and putting his other out like a fieldsman wanting a practice catch after a wicket has fallen, stood ten foot away with a girl looking more terrified than she was.

Christopher prepared to throw. The burly one said:

"Not too hard for Christ's sake."

Christopher threw the glass. It went wide, hit the gilded claw-arm of a high-back chair and broke.

"Oh, C——! I didn't mean *throw* it."

Christopher's face grinned, worked, swayed and then a little grey-headed figure with a length of sari round her shoulders, went nimbly up to him and John saw wide, supplicating eyes as she spoke to him. Her small hand came up and was about to alight, but was unable to, as though he were an animal that bit.

He passed his hand through his hair, corrugated his features, took his lower lip in his teeth and groaned, all like a schoolmaster affecting despair at the same old mistake.

And then, like a person overacting, he shot out a hand and John heard, "But how *can* I apologise—I don't know what Lady More-land looks like."

This loud mention of the hostess's name, and the word "apologise" when people were, anyhow, looking in their direction made the little woman gnaw a knuckle, look intensely at the floor, praying God to tell her what to do, where to go, what to say—now or ever again, and finally look for someone behind John and walk in his direction.

John turned. Jane was approaching, her face taut with indignation and anger. Mother and daughter met beside him. But Lady Matlock spoke as though she were saying, "What a heavenly dance it was." She even disguised her expression by smiling at the far door.

" I should very much like Christopher to go home," she said. " Could *you* persuade him, darling? "

Jane looked past her mother as though at a foreigner maltreating his ass, tears not far off.

" I think," said her mother doubtfully, " if we said we had a taxi at the door he might come."

She didn't really think so. She hoped Jane might. Then it would be feasible—if someone else thought so.

" Why? " said Jane.

Lady Matlock did not know. She said, " He's with Paul again," as though that might help towards a solution. She raised an index finger, gnawed the edge of it delicately, remembered herself, stopped and said, " I do mind, you see. I just *do*. I can't help it."

Her thoughtful, worried eyes waited for Jane.

" I'll try," Jane said. " See if you can get a taxi."

Mother and daughter went on their separate errands.

Getting taxis in London at this date was not easy. John followed Lady Matlock. She said to the butler by the coats, " Could you *possibly* tell me where I might telephone for a taxi? "

John said, " I'll fetch you a taxi if you like."

Lady Matlock's face lit up as it always did when a good-looking young man jumped forward to help. So rare nowadays.

Then it all came out. " Of course, Osbert's son John. Dear Osbert. We never see him. Where *is* he now? "

John eventually provided the taxi and rejoined Lady Matlock at the door. " Christopher has ' gone on ' with Paul," she said, looking at John as though she expected him to know what *that* meant. Then she introduced her daughter with the agitation of a small farmer who in spite of the appearance of himself and his sheds, owns the country's prize heifer.

" My daughter Jane—and Osbert's son, darling, Osbert Grant's." Their hands touched. Lady Matlock stood like a referee behind them, warning them. She was entranced at the past uniting again. Osbert's son and Jane. She forgot Christopher. But Jane had not forgotten. She did not know Osbert except as someone she had heard too much of or his son; she knew it was cold standing there, practically naked under a fur coat, after being baked inside, and she knew her brother had behaved abominably as usual, and they had to catch the eight-thirty to-morrow which meant another short night, end of another mad dash south for what? For the last five hours, meeting Osbert's son and now soothing Mummy from Euston to Hatchford with assurances that Christopher would get over it. In a way she had not felt so fed up with it all since her mother made her use a night off from night duty in 1943 to attend a dance at Hatchford because the Horse Guards were stationed there. Four hours in the train each way—to be fumbled with by a marquis in a dust-sheeted library. The Horse Guards. One worse than the Guards—socially; militarily she wouldn't know.

She said, " Thank you so much for getting a taxi. Can we take you anywhere? "

Lady Matlock said, " John will be staying till the end. Why don't you stay a little longer, darling? "

" Oh, Mummy . . . one can't *go back*."

Jane had an air of firmness with her mother which suggested it was the only possible way of dealing with her. She smiled at John as though he were one more face, and the taxi drove off with Lady Matlock promising he should hear from her that week and how lovely it would be if (the taxi changed gear) . . . Edgeby.

The taxi receded and the empty street was there in front of him. A constable looked up at the lighted windows as he turned on a pavement edge, his movement strikingly separate from the drums' beat. What I got you got. Dooda, dooda, day. The band sounded stifled by shuffling, and voices were merged into one dead-level, continuous noise, as distant waves become the noises of the sea.

John looked at the decision he had taken, like a drunk waking up with the only indication of where he has been, in his hand —a water-lily. Why, how? Absurd. Yet somehow he could not throw it away.

3

THE small card bearing his name in a handwriting accustomed to plenty of room, even for grace-strokes, seemed a mistake because it placed him three from her. For forty-eight hours he had imagined himself in her company in a variety of situations of which the only common denominators were proximity, and the absence of a third person. He had proposed to her indoors and out of doors, with and without preliminary; he had undressed her, and watched her dress; he had lain with her and imagined an intimacy which dispensed with speech.

Then they placed him—*she* placed him, three from herself.

He heard very little of what his neighbours said but broke bits of bread and converted them to crumbs, smiling at his right elbow if conversation came from his right, and at his left if it came from the left.

She laughed too easily. She made use of the whole armoury of fashionable superlatives—" extraordinary " and " absolutely " were ubiquitous, also the construction " couldn't be " couldn't have been, duller, sweeter, more tired, prettier, more fun. And her hands were seldom still, as though they each had an independent life. Sometimes her thumbs sought the complete shelter of her curved fingers as she threw back her head to laugh. When drinking she brought her head half-way to the glass and obtained the necessary tilt by placing her lips lower than the rim. And sometimes she obscured what she was saying by intruding food before the last word. He had imagined, being wonderful, she would be less affected by nerves.

He heard her describe Ascot as " absolute hell," and all politicians as " the bottom."

A Share of the World

These sweeping statements required her thumbs to take complete shelter. And she followed them with an interrogative laugh to mollify her neighbour's face who loved racing and was going to stand as a Conservative.

Above the low-cut line of her dress she had beginnings of breasts such as eighteenth-century portrait painters must often have supplied where wanting. On either side of her were men regarded as potential catches. Lady Matlock glanced frequently in her daughter's direction with a smile that went from Jane to the young men and back, quickly, like a boy whipping three tops, and laughing in appreciation although the length of the table (and what her neighbour was saying to her) prevented her hearing what had been said.

When the girls went to " get their coats," Christopher approached the wine waiter with light in his deep-sunk, bespectacled eyes. Liqueurs. Lots of them. Conscious that eyes were upon him he made a spacious gesture, a little wrong, like a ham actor. " Everything you've got," he said, and came back limping. He had been wounded three years ago, but his limp varied. Public places made it pronounced.

He said, " Artificial stimulants are about the only hope for this sort of thing, aren't they? "

He emphasised one or two words as though to make up for the inaudibility, the half-heartedness of the other. It made his speech like a broadcast from America on a bad day.

He was host, but he put his head near his plate and waited for the men, congregated around him at one end, to find their own feet in conversation. They were none of them his choice.

John asked her to dance as she came leading her group of girls carrying their brocade, gold, black-and-silver bags, some already acknowledging thankfully people they knew—and liked far better than anyone in the dinner from which they came. (All " dinners " were breaking up in the same way.) She seemed grateful as though he had offered her his seat in a bus.

The little ritual of where to put her bag was got through without his assistance, without his notice. He was emptied of all but apprehension of being against her, touching her, as though she were dangerous and could injure physically without violence. This feeling was an ache, and so strong that it could be called antipathy. To *lessen* it he thought of her weak and ugly points—her nervous laugh, her fidgety hands, her ungainly way of drinking, and garrulous generalisations; in a word—how un-wonderful.

Some reversal of blood and annihilation of thought took place as the covered prominence of her breasts pressed on the front of his dinner-jacket. His mouth at this moment had it been a dog's, would have made a mother draw her child away.

And after two rounds of the room he had, so to speak, snapped, " You've a will of your own at corners."

Her face, which till then had looked mathematically over his shoulder seeing who was there, seeing if it was going to be fun or hell or something in between, reckoning, taking Christopher into account, his state now as indicator to his final state—her face came back and confronted him.

" What? "

" You have a will of your own at corners."

Now he laughed to mitigate the statement in face of her hostile " what "—which she seemed to have given him merely as a chance to say something else. She always had been led (and she had never resisted such guidance) to suppose that she danced well.

She said, " It's your job to supply the will."

" Yes. But there shouldn't be any competition—in dancing." They completed a round.

He told himself he had only said what he had said in order to establish a real basis for language. Like a savage meeting another savage he had pointed at a lily and made the noise " white."

She had replied with a different noise.

By so doing she had anchored conversation to the level which he had hoped to leave at once.

" Two wills at one corner might be spectacular," he said. " Two spills . . ."

She was not intrigued. Young men who tried to make themselves interesting by making short personal remarks, then Christmas cracker conversation.

" Did you once learn ballet dancing? " he asked.

" Yes," faint and altered because interested.

" I feel it. Your dancing is a branch of gymnastics."

" People haven't found much fault with my dancing. You're not exactly fleet of foot yourself."

" I'm sometimes in the way, aren't I? Particularly at corners."

" Yes."

" Feeling your partner in the way must be usual for you."

When the music stopped she dawdled only a token instant before excusing herself on the artificial pretext of having " people to look after," as though she were in charge of a tour.

He watched her from doorways, from little gold chairs and over the shoulders of other men. Someone said to him:

" Cheer up, John, it's not as bad as that."

And he danced with her mother.

She was a light and airy dancer and he, she said, reminded her so of Osbert. Her small bright eyes looked up at him with the eagerness of eighteen years. She had had such fun, she said, with Osbert in the " old days "—a figure of speech he thought, because, for her, all days were still new days, and always had been and always would be. Now, *he* was Osbert and the time of Life was youth. Time was so short—up to the last minute Time would be short for the things there were to be done, seen and enjoyed.

They twirled and she said, " I *am* enjoying this." Another twirl and she said, " You must come to Edgeby—soon."

Did he know Christopher? Oh, did he? Her face clouded. How interesting. Christopher was so strange now—she looked up at him as though he were a doctor suddenly standing by Christopher's bed, a famous specialist who seldom went wrong. " Drink," she said, throwing herself on his mercy, on his experience, with a look and then exploding into a pathetic little laugh.

" I'd be silly to try and hide it."

Then serious again, lying back in a twirl of waltz, a bit too jumpy, a bit too purposefully young, she said sadly, " Wilfred says it's the war," as though she were quoting *The Times* against a host of popular dailies. She assumed he knew Wilfred; that " everyone " knew " everyone."

" It happens every time—*every* time—and . . ."

A Share of the World

Then suddenly, " I don't think I can stand it much longer."
And although she had only met him once before, tears gathered in
her eyes with the speed, the ease with which she had accepted his
offer to dance. She was all longing, all honesty, in conscious
matters, emotional and physical alacrity. Christopher now, as a
topic, was tears—nothing but tears. Why hide it? Why for that
matter hide anything?

" You didn't know him *well* before, did you? " she asked as
though she were talking of her son's face before a plastic operation.

" *So* funny. *So* sweet. The *most* perfect mimic." Sensing some
sort of general flat echo of all mothers on all sons, she at once
insisted, " No, I mean *really* unusual. Wilfred used to say, ' he was
the best he'd ever known.' "

Still flat, so she said, " I wish you'd seen him. And now—
nothing. *Nothing*. A sort of disease of nothing."

John sympathised.

" He swears by ' Family Reunion,' " said Lady Matlock, her
body still bounding jovially in sharp contrast to her tone and
subject. " Have you read it? He marks it heavily and leaves it
about—Wilfred thinks, on purpose."

They did another round, Lady Matlock's eyes widely submissive
to the mysteries of Family Reunion—the obstacles it presented to a
sincere mind—hers, perhaps understandably—but Wilfred's!
Brilliant Wilfred who couldn't see anything in T. S. Eliot. Though
she wouldn't go so far as that: it *had* a power. Didn't it?

" You are all people to whom nothing has ever happened,"
quoted Lady Matlock, with a nervous laugh as though it should
not be funny, as though ten years ago if someone told her she would
worry over that line she would not have believed them.

She explained, " ' You ' is Wilfred, Jane and I. Christopher
marked that with four lines along the side. His pencil went through
the page." Again she gave him that flattering stare as though he
were the specialist, the expert. Then she saw Christopher. He was
with a knot of six or seven people who were peering at the dancers
as though in search of one person like themselves. They were
clearly " going on "—or, as they might put it, getting out.

" He *can't* go already," said Lady Matlock, " it's too rude."

A Share of the World

And she relinquished John in mid-floor and went to her son. He did not look at her as she came, nor even when she spoke at his side. But he said something without change of expression; and she went past him into the crowd as though suddenly ill.

John found Jane. He asked her to dance, and she said, " Let me see—one, two, three, four . . . five from now. Will that do? I seem to be rather in demand to-night."

Her eyes were bright. She was looking past him explaining, so to speak, what had happened in the film so far; but to be asked the thing that was happening now somehow dried up the words on her lips. Then interest flagged and she looked at him and said, " Five from now," as though not sure whether she had said it yet.

His exacting hectic stare was wasted; she refused it admission. Smiled into it.

" Five! " he said. " That's an incalculable period and I can't wait. It's like the millennium. I shall be a foolish virgin by the bar."

He must talk like a pedagogue in a pub, spikily, cleverly, to get a grip on a surface that eluded him.

She admitted sweetly now, looking past him, with fulfilled expectation, that five from now was " hell to remember." Then, " Be round if you can—about then." She moved past smiling, glad for the chance to be indefinite.

John watched her. She crossed the room and a man with black floppy hair, " blue" chin and long tapering hands buckled his knees, opened his mouth into a huge O of surprise and accusation, and pointed at her with an index finger like an old-fashioned pistol. " So THERE you are," he roared.

When they closed they laughed so much that it was many steps before they picked up the beat of the music. Corners were of no account to them.

John left.

To pass the cabbage when you are asked for the potatoes is not necessarily a proof of profound passion and many undergraduates at that time walked about as if they were hosts to a matter of life and death. Therefore John's face and behaviour passed in a crowd. Only perhaps his daily leaning to the Ninth Symphony of Beethoven—before breakfast and after tea, which were the hours of service in the chapel opposite—drew comment by the loudness and persistency with which it was played.

Outgoing communicants with the stale taste of a little wine in their mouths and the doubt of validity in their minds looked up sometimes and saw his face at the window looking out over the chapel roof like an anaemic general waiting for momentous news. And after tea on a mild day, permitting windows to be wide, the Song of Joy outroared the organ voluntary in the ears of the people equidistant from each.

Then the letter came. " Mummy would love it if you came for Christmas." *Mummy* would . . . So, he thought, she puts honesty —on occasions—before manners, wonderful manners.

4

JOHN went to a party in a basement in Wellington Square and the first person he saw was Christopher—listening to a man in purple corduroys as though he hated him and his silvery hair, and might soon say so if the man went on talking so close and enthusiastically about nothing. Christopher looked as if he was there for the drink—and, God willing, a little violence.

For John, Christopher was immediately all that mattered in the room. He was the link with Jane, the girl he was going to marry but to whom for weeks he had not written or spoken.

John went to Christopher's side and heard the man with silvery hair say, " He says he's going to do it in something *diaphanous*, and Mike Lodyar's going to play a *search*light on him from Tun Turret as he goes up."

" How *wonder*ful," Christopher said with succulent, deliberate rudeness. And he turned to John. The silver-haired man laughed in agony at the story he had told in order that it should not go without laughter. He turned away drinking and hunting for a face with his eyes, all in one movement.

Christopher and John stood together for a moment without saying anything. Christopher's head hung and moved in the way which gave his drunkenness its own particular stamp and individuality. " Are you really coming to Edgeby for Christmas? " he said.

John said he was.

The contempt with which Christopher had suffered the silvery-haired man returned to his face. He even began to look about him as though John were no longer beside him. But at the moment when he seemed most distracted by other things he said, " Why? "

A Share of the World

So this was the way.

John said, " Well, since you put it like that—I find your sister attractive."

" Jane? " Christopher seemed uncertain whether John might not have made a mistake and be talking of some girl who was not in fact his sister, but did on occasions come to Edgeby.

" Yes, Jane."

Christopher thought, looked at John, then made a noise in his throat like a professor who sees down a microscope, the thing he had not expected.

" Will you be there? " John said.

" Have you ever been to Edgeby? " John said he hadn't.

Christopher said, " I may be there, I don't know . . . I suppose if you've never been there——"

" What? "

Christopher signified by a shrug, a manner, a stare at the far wall that words were inadequate when it came to some sorts of experience.

John said, " You don't like Christmas at Edgeby? "

" No. I don't like Christmas at Edgeby."

The contrasting attributes of sixteen and sixty were strong in Christopher's face when he was drunk. Only his deep-sunk eyes seemed to have a sort of—to him—painful honesty: they avoided other people's eyes as though to save them having to share such honesty as well might make them feel their own selves intolerable to themselves. Indeed these two deep-set eyes of Christopher even travelled over inanimate objects as though they, too, might come under a blight which he would spare them if he could.

" They ' want ' me," he said suddenly, " and ' the tree ' this year will be ' too pretty.' And it'll be the first year ' we can be together ' again."

The inverted commas were his. He set apart with a drawled emphasis the words he wished to taste of dust and ashes. " And Jane," he said, " I don't think I can face Jane. Not yet."

John felt suddenly afraid. He said, " Why Jane particularly? "

Christopher allowed his eyes once to meet John's; furtive,

159

destructive—yet humble eyes, oppressed by the same weight which had made gathering lines in the forehead above them. " She doesn't exist," he said. " She's not herself."

John said nothing.

" She's a stencil of what my parents want. She's a ' rather wonderful person.' She could have been a person. She doesn't exist."

Christopher had been a successful and graceful athlete at Eton. He had also had a reputation for gentleness and modesty. He had been president of a society privileged to wear tiger-skin waistcoats, and sealing-wax stamped on their top-hats.

It should have been strange for an Eton contemporary to see the new Christopher—traces of modesty hanging about him, or if you like, increased a thousandfold in his miserable eyes; grace still in his drunken stances.

But John was thinking about Jane.

Christopher said, " She needs to be *really unhappy;* to get away from Edgeby soon or it'll be too late. What she is now isn't her."

Jane, yet not Jane. Ever more remote.

Christopher said, " Isn't Bergheim in rather an expendable, category ?" He stared at a man talking with many listeners. Christopher laid down his glass and went towards him, stationing himself insolently and pugilistically close. Bergheim, a very young don, was trying to sell someone a chain letter, assuring him with astute prolixity that such letters were the answer to their poverty and the country's inflation. His brilliance was a complete cover for the bazaar avidity which drove him on. And for those who should see this, he kept a twinkle which in the last resort could say it was " only a joke."

" Oh, Bergheim," Christopher said softly but effecting complete interruption. " Oh, Bergheim."

As John left and mounted the stairs he heard obscene hysterical language, in the same high-pitched voice which had a moment ago proclaimed the Keynsian analysis of a monetary spiral. Then a crash, short and sharp, followed by the lighter sound of breaking glass.

So Christopher had had his drink—and his violence.

A Share of the World

As John heard the crash of Bergheim's fall, all Christopher's own work, he thought how seemingly irreconcilable it was with the poem which Christopher had published in one of the university magazines the previous week. The poem went thus:

The solution came
Contrary to expectation
From a child
Playing in Madison Square.

" Who's that man there, Nanna
Who's that man
Under the ' Daily News ' ?

" Come now Franklyn Arbor, come at once
Dawdling by a dead drunk hobo
Wasting half my morning
Playing me up.

" That is GOD there Nanna
Under the tree, under the sun,
Will you be there to-morrow man
At about the same time? "

And the man said
" Always have I, always will I ;
Been, be, am I here

" Mamma he was staying still there
in the centre of the city
in the rush hour of the world
I am near or nowhere
He said, Mamma, he said that.

" Frankie I've been meaning
Right now I'll do it
To show you to Hueffner
Who'll help you contribute
More happily to the group.

161   L

A Share of the World

" Can I take Ma-Polar, Mummy
Can I take my bear? "

When Hueffner came in quietly
From behind-like the sound of his name
And said
               Relax, reveal, rely
               Resign, recall, remind
               Yourself of how it started
               (Put your bear down)
               And if necessary cry
Ma-Polar seemed the only hope,
Among the files and files
The green light
And the profitable files
Of exacerbated care
Ma-Polar the only hope.

And Frankie said
               You might in time detach me
               From Ma-Polar my bear
               Though even then he'd become
               Other things
               But you will never wean me
               From the man there
               Under the tree, under the sun
               In the centre of the city
               Staying still
               In the rush hour of the World.

               And if I go there now
               Where I saw him
               And he is not there
               Or if I did invent him
               To suit desire, then
               Nothing is changed.

162

A Share of the World

Invention means discovery
Whether of the atom-bomb
The Yale-lock
Or GOD.

John's only memory of Christopher talking about religion was Christopher shouting in his cups that the most important incident in the New Testament was Christ's physical ejection of the money-lenders. Otherwise the nature of Christ got overlaid, he said, by such ditties as " Every Christian child should be meek, obedient, good as he " when the only recorded instance of Christ's childhood was absence without leave. Indeed, he had said, it was not surprising the authorities—the priests and governors—had made Christ God. To have left him man would have left an unsettling precedent. A Pope had to be installed at once as Lord High Keeper of the Dam against Christ the Anarchist, the Sea.

Christopher: at Eton the loved and envied: such a boy as had once died young and had a book written about him by his parents so that someone so Homeric—boxing, versing, flying—should not go forgotten. Christopher who now described this book as " the ultimate crap."

The germ of truth in this valuation, John thought, had to be stated—by Christopher, at any rate—violently, because Christopher was so close to it all. Rupert Brookery, Raymond Ashquithary, which some strange nausea obliged him to regurgitate with incoherent noise.

" Unreality "—Christopher's favourite word—at once the beam and blight of his eyes.

It had lain on Jane, " She doesn't exist."

5

IN an age when many people try to explain all behaviour economically or not at all, it should be perhaps noted that John, though brought up under the capitalist system, had only become aware of how it worked on the same day as he discovered that it would not work for him. Perhaps the Edwardian convention of never referring to money, as though it were a matter more privy than bowels (because by then the aristocracy thought it *was* the bowels)—had done something in his home life to retard understanding of such an important subject. Or perhaps money had never interested him except as a means of freedom, and even in that way not much, freedom seeming often as available to tramps as to millionaires. Somehow he would have freedom, just as he would have breath. If he failed to get either the result would be the same, and he would not be there to feel the misery. His political self was still second nature. The big house had stood in the village and both had stood in and were harmonious outcrop of countryside. He belonged in the big house and the villagers belonged in the village, and together they had made a whole of which the content of mutual respect had been strong. He had, in short, experienced a political harmony and the feel of it was still second nature. This, in 1947, made him among his fellow-undergraduates as the crocodile is among other animals; the reminder of a previous type of earth-life less specialised, centred on marshes.

The question, therefore, of how he would support Jane if she agreed to marry him, hardly occurred to him. Somehow he would be free—even if in a ditch. No. It was the other freedom that was in doubt—the freedom within himself, the freedom which seemed to be denied to him by that series of behaviour which he had christened "the web of himself." Only she, he told himself, could save him from that; only she could break the series by being the thing that never could happen, happening. At Oxford this far-fetched idea became the pearl disease of his oyster-like, shut personality.

At night on linoleum in the narrow bedroom where once undoubtedly hunting-boots had stood in a row, and hangovers endured, he knelt and prayed, encouraging in himself a vacancy, excluding thought by effort until he felt a sense of distance, of ever-increasing space and into that he would let fall the only unspoken words which did not jar him into thought or objection, but which soporifically and rhythmically deepened his mood: O Lord, have mercy upon us, have mercy upon us, have mercy upon us.

Prayer was one of his hobby-horses over long glasses of coffee until two.

He would ask his listeners to notice the surge of the old prayers, how they contained the double emphasis of diminution and expansion, humility and eternity for each self, "We thine unworthy servants . . ." on the one hand, and "for ever and ever, amen," on the other. Didn't we all want to unload the burden of pretence about ourselves, be dust now, but didn't we also want to feel "for ever and ever," feel we belong more than momentarily to an elusive essence which can never be dust.

And on war, in which he had played such a striking role, he would say, "It destroys life prematurely, but it puts in the way of millions a chance to show love as they might never otherwise have done. Those that volunteer to do jobs in which they may die may experience a feeling of sublime generosity which elevates life and differs them from Christ only in degree. Not all who were brave were in search of the bubble reputation. There are other struggles," he said, with his eyes glowing in his pale face, "which are the only important ones. And they are not international—they are internal. And now it is the curse of the atom bomb that it has promoted war to a false position, promoted it to the place of the greatest collective evil imaginable. It is not that. Indeed it may soon prove a device of nature to restore harmony which we have lost because we can analyse more than we can love. You must never, never analyse more than you love."

And when he heard people talking on every side—about how to dispense with conflict once and for all—conflict between nations, conflict between children and parents, conflict between classes and, above all and most often, conflicts within themselves—buying books on integration and visiting middle-Europeans with the same object in view—something revolted within him and he would make a case for conflict, implore them to accept conflict (in his usually embarrassing, over-wrought, way), accept it as the only road to and *sine qua non* of peace, of harmony—pointing out that a chord was conflict accepted, not conflict abolished.

He found a translation from the Anglo-Saxon of *The dream of the Holy Rood* and was excited to hear of Christ as the Warrior rather than the Lamb of God. The *internal* Warrior, the " shoulder-companion " of whom the most hard-pressed for survival could be gently proud. Somehow the harshness of the language was suitable for 1947. A bleakness, yet a sense of voyage had returned—if for no other reason than that no land was in sight.

" There he lay, after the victory."

Tears sprang to his eyes at that idea of Christ taken from the cross as conqueror. And with one of those facile associations which made sense to him, that victory, and all important victories seemed victories of people who escaped from " the web " of themselves. Jane, he told himself, was his Jerusalem. To which he was going up.

The abject haughtiness, the lofty diffidence of his face—relaxing sometimes into a sudden soft fastidious stare—was the concern of one of his friends who asked if he were ill or in love.

He smiled away from the man—as though he had been funny in another way than he knew. " Perhaps you're right," he said. " Perhaps I'm both—a sort of mixture."

" Or perhaps the war gave me a taste for tension, made crisis an emotional food, since it had to be that or poison. Perhaps now I'm just pining for dons and débutantes to feed me with the same exalted misery as I got from *Nebelwerfers* and *Panzergrenadiers:*

A Share of the World

For we on bloody dew have fed
And drunk the gall of paradise

Doesn't the whole of Britain hale from Porlock now? "

If John found in Jane the tension necessary to complete " the chord " of his feelings (by virtue of her very remoteness, " wonderfulness, full womanliness, unknownness ")—then, before he saw her, a meeting occurred, with his father and sister, which somehow put her further, too far from him—so that " the chord " became discord and he finally left for Edgeby ill, with a mild attack of shingles. (A doctor gave an opinion which he listened to with a maddening smile of unruffled other knowledge.)

The meeting went thus.

6

THEY were in Osbert's Knightsbridge flat—Mary, John and Osbert.

"John's in love," Mary said, and she laughed satirically and raucously at the same time as glancing at him with sincere apology and guilt.

This was Mary. Everything had to be funny. She had no forehead but a long jaw. Her words were always pressing to debunk; but her brown eyes were sympathetic to all feelings, beginning with those of animals and therefore reverend. She was naturally " in touch." Her oral verve accumulated guilt until every few months she had a crisis and ceased to " operate " as though the two forces at work inside her—like tug-of-war teams—were immobile from parity of strength. Because of John's face she said, " Jane—why not. Priddy girl, priddy place."

Osbert usually listened to Mary with a perpetual smile, but to-day the smile was either faint or absent because he knew that his son and daughter had conspired to visit him on the same day to make him do something about " his things " at Stiley.

Mary said, " But what are you going to live on? "

Osbert looked away up into the Knightsbridge sky as though in painful anticipation of such bluntness being applied to him.

John's smile faded. He looked at his sister with a gleam of contempt.

Mary said, " Not bread alone? " And then, laughing toughly, the guilt in her eyes so thickened that she looked at her father for less opposition. He was now smiling faintly, far off into the freakish battalions of chimneys and cowls.

She said soberly, flatly, like a professional confiding a trick of the trade, " Seriously—you must have nine hundred. Jake could get you more." And she enforced the suddenness of the switch with a long look from her sympathetic, powerful eyes.

" Could get me . . .? " John said. " What d'you mean? "

" A job with more."

" A job? "

" Yes—a job."

Osbert stole a look at his son and then retreated back to the sky. Mary had got him this flat.

John was wondering why Jane said " nine hundred "— arbitrarily like that. Was it like nineteen and six—much, much less than a pound?

" Why *nine*-hundred? " he said.

She said, " Priddy girls who've been accustomed to servants don't like marrying gloomy paupers."

" You know them all, do you? "

She said nothing, sitting there on the floor. He thought she looked like a male comedian dressed up as a rich woman. Her cossacks hat, if anything, looked genuinely military, and her ill-assorted jewellery like loot. Yet, as a female, she had chosen the men she wanted.

" If you must know," he said, " I've never even spoken to Jane Matlock." This sounded truer than the truth.

Mary was delighted. She rocked back and exulted.

" You're quite a boy," she said. " Isn't he? He ought to advertise in the *Matrimonial Times*."

Then she caught sight of a clock and said, " Jesus—now what about these things, Papa? "

Osbert's face contracted. The flat bell rang—and rang again. Mary looked suddenly lifeless and frightened—her jewels like manacles. " Another time," she said vaguely. Osbert looked relieved.

Hmmm," he said as his daughter kissed him. And when she said, " Good-bye," from the door, he said " Good-bye," with a sudden strange stress—as though to catch the post of affection before it left, as it had so often, before he was ready.

Mary's eyes now full of an immense diffidence, established the fact that somehow she had upset John. "Good-bye, darling," she said. "Bring Jane to lunch at Claridges, hm?"

"Thanks," he said. "Good-bye."

"And you'll go with Papa for the things, then?"

"Yes."

The door closed and Osbert said, "I've got to go out now." And then as though someone had contradicted him, "Hm? . . . What?"

John looked at his father as though he were looking at himself.

Osbert Grant had never lived in a house bought, rented, or even found by himself. These three rooms in a fifth floor in Knightsbridge Mary got before she flew to Nassau with Jake last Christmas. In them Osbert had awoken to the fact that he was poor, old and alone, conditions he had never envisaged or appreciated. They had come suddenly, stalking up behind the war, during which he had plenty of everything—even, it seemed, of youth and health. Down there by the Severn he had paid for his keep with his presence, which his hosts had found comforting like that of a friendly animal whose behaviour remained unaffected by the fall of Paris or Singapore. Indeed, against the perspective of suffering, war, and political theory, brought home each nine o'clock news, his insistence on how best to shell peas or pick raspberries without squashing them, his personal feud with the ginger cat (carefully planning inconveniences for it) took on a moving quality. The "Ah! Is this not happiness?" of the Chinese poet, the delight in the moment was his, and it emanated from him, infecting others on summer evenings, top and tailing currants while Caen stank.

When he went away, his mess, the bark, cocoons, skins, shells, fossils and butterfly net went with him, and his hosts from parents to children felt somehow less permanent, which was strange since Osbert had neither money nor "character," in the schoolmaster's solid sense.

Now John stood in his father's flat because his aunt had written, all underlined. "If he doesn't get his things from Stiley soon there won't be anything left. Do go down with him."

Osbert sat at a large flat writing-desk. The inkstand just broke the disordered surface of papers like a rock at high tide. Some directorships had recently been ended in letters he scarcely understood from people he had never met. Unanswered the hard words lay with jottings for anagrams and profiles of gulls. He bowed his tall long skull improved by baldness, and watched his hands as he rubbed them, massaged one with the other sensitively, varying the movements, sometimes taking pleasure in a position, or in their blackness.

They were as black as though he had gloves on because last year's walnut season had been in his own words " killing work." Scratching under the sooted bark of London trees had kept the skin used, and here and there broken.

He looked down at his hands, as usual, as though they were the symbol of, at any rate, one devotion—one justification; and also as a refuge from the impending subject.

John said, " Well, what about your things? "

" I suppose I can go on here," Osbert said, making an effort.

John, standing by a window, watched a pigeon glide with reflex wings, settle and strut pompously along a ledge. The traffic was like distant surf and as big as dice. Women were sewing furs in a level with him; their life-size surprising across the gap.

" Or I could live in the lodge at Stiley. Bridgett said I could have the lodge."

Osbert liked to enumerate alternatives. Each additional alternative weakened the reality of any one.

He isolated a finger for particular inspection. Spatulate, worsted with earth, and possessing a blood-blister like a black tick. His face lit complacently as he scrutinised it.

Osbert's problem—or rather the problem which relations had decided was his problem—was whether to live in London and " see people " or at Stiley lodge, and " have " the country and " see no one." He could not have both company and country. He must choose.

" And your things? " said John. No reply, " What about your things? '

" My things," said Osbert. He put away the particular finger. " They're there. Where else do you think they are? "

" I know. But are you going to fetch them? "

" It's no good fetching them here if I'm going to live down there."

" But I thought we'd decided you'd better live here."

Osbert selected a pencil and inspected its point as though it had to be just not sharp but a certain sharpness.

" Did Mary say anything to you? " he said, and tried the point. Since she had found him this flat, he wanted to know what she might do next.

" She thinks—and I agree—you ought to bring your things here."

" Does she, indeed! " He was grateful for the suggestion from a dynamic source; it gave him an opportunity of objecting and so, of giving John—and himself—the feeling that he had thought the matter over, and things weren't as easy as that.

" That's all very well. I can't bring everything."

" Bring what you want."

" You don't know how difficult things are—moving things."

He selected from the layered chaos of his writing-table a piece of paper, which he perused over the top of his spectacles—as though it were the latest report on prices and time-tables and terms of moving things nowadays.

" We could hire a pantechnicon. Spend a day down there. Do it together."

Osbert got up coughing his cough of tearing, crashing timber, putting the back of his hand up, bowing forward, and at the same time whitening himself suddenly with ash the length of which a moment earlier had been three times the length of the button of cigarette adhering to his top lip.

He walked to the mantelpiece over the gas and took up a sooted notch of wood with two prongs and two swellings and a tapered end. It might have been a submarine monstrosity, or the magnified model of some insect nature never evolved. He turned it this way and that and smiled—moved it to the foot of a stone madonna.

" A better dignity, a better impudence," he said.

" Good and evil," said John.

" Hm-m-m," said his father, and moving aimlessly across the room, suddenly broke into a bowler's run and as his arm came up checked himself with a groan, put his hand on the back of his hip as though he had been struck there, and remained petrified with pain.

But it passed.

And he came back to his desk. " Betty was asking after you," he said. " You ought to go and see her."

" My train goes soon."

" Oh."

A long oh and a sad oh—studied, suggesting that as a father this was a moment to feel sorry. The hands began to revolve, he considered them, searching perhaps for an expression of the feeling which always came too late.

" Then we'll go down to Stiley? " said John.

His father again selected a paper from his desk, and this time after a glance, laid it aside as if for the attention of an invisible secretary on his left.

" You don't know they'll let you in."

" Aunt Bridgett said there was no difficulty."

" I dare say she did. Have the boys arrived? "

(Stiley was to be a Borstal Institution.)

" They're waiting for the barbed wire."

" I thought it was to be for the good boys only."

" I suppose that's relative. They're putting old army barbed wire round the house."

Osbert reached for a half-finished *Times* crossword and doodled on the border. Five years ago his " things " had gone into the blue, packed and loaded by other people, arranged and stored by other people without instruction or supervision, and every year he had had a letter from Bridgett saying, " I think you ought to go and look at your things."

The last had said, " You *must*."

John felt an old familiar rage rising as the worn hand had tweaked little expert lines under the slinky eyes of a fleshy face, a Slav Shylock emerging from the scattered wherewithal of an anagram. Yet, at the same time, he felt, " That's me sitting there."

" Monday, then? " he said sharply and coarsely.

A Share of the World

" Hm-m . . . Monday! " Could it be fitted in?

The Knightsbridge sky suggested no objection—even to eyes that sought one.

" Monday," said John.

They went down by the three-fifty.

In the thirties Osbert used to cover the *Strand* with ash and pinion his spectacles in it; now he stuffed *Lilliput* in his pocket. His walk—airy—as though he trod from cloud to cloud irregularly spaced. It seemed miraculous that the ground was under his feet after each step. For sixty years he had looked, not where he was stepping, but where he was going and where other creatures were going, flying, swimming, crawling, hopping, looping and alighting.

The porter was touched to the quick of class-consciousness.

" D'you wannit here? "

But Osbert with his coat open was on his way to the bookstall and when half-way took a tango step, a long, low, lunge forward to avoid a mechanical barrow without breaking the rhythm of his movement. Once in safety he raised his hat to a woman in a mink coat, with a bulb-planting instrument and twin Sealyhams in flashy harness. Then he watched her recede as though she were a dog with five legs.

" I ain't got all noight, y'know."

John said, " Yes, put it there, please."

" We can't all afford to play around, y'know."

John gave him sixpence, fining him one and sixpence.

The man looked at it and went.

Osbert bought *Lilliput* and read it on the verge of the platform before the wrong door. He made courteous apologies to people trying to get by, but always returned to the same spot. Finally, he mounted and disappeared, only reappearing—coming down the corridor petulant and anxious—two minutes after the train had left the station.

" Did you move? "

" No."

" I left you opposite the bookstall."

" Not quite."

A Share of the World

Osbert was too often mistaken ever to contradict confidently and flatly. He merely maintained his own opinion with a sceptical noise behind a shut mouth.

They were alone in the compartment.

When the houses gave place to fields John said, " Why don't you come to Edgeby for Christmas? "

" Hm-m-m. Neenie. I haven't seen Neenie since the first war."

" D'you know her daughter—Jane? "

" No."

John watched a river and a pack of tied punts, deserted terraces, and mock Tudor sweep under him.

" I'm going to marry her."

His father's eyes were in *Lilliput* and remained there.

" Neenie used to fidget so much that my father refused to be in the same room with her."

John waited. Trees, houses, two children waving, cart horses, rusting barbed wire, concrete pipes, pre-fab and bomb-gap, advertisement, allotment and wired-off pitch—that piece of England went by and John wondered why he still minded his father's indifference. Why he still had to say, " I'm going to . . ."

Five minutes passed.

" Does she fidget? " said his father.

" Who? "

" The daughter."

" Jane? Yes, I suppose you could say her hands fidgeted."

Osbert put away *Lilliput*, took off his spectacles, and looked out of the window thoroughly. They passed a farm and a pond, bordered with the slush of ducks and cattle, and one oak breaking a line of hedge thrusting up its black branches into the white sky, like a diagram of nerves. A rook flopped off, fell aslant the wind and bore away, obliquely.

" One notices the change of the seasons more as one grows older," said Osbert.

A cigarette stub, dead and smokeless, adhered to his upper lip, and he revolved his hands about each other and looked out of the window. There was something purposeful about his interest—as though to-day he must hang on to it at all costs, as though for once the beauty and the companionship of all that, out there, might not be effortless like breathing.

The park wall dropped from twelve to six feet on either side of the front lodge. This lapse was now made good by triple coils of concertina wire out of which sprouted two newly painted notices:

STILEY HALL
BORSTAL INSTITUTION
No entrance except on business

Bates, the lodge-keeper, had apparently made good; he had a field of chickens and outhouses newly tarred, and before his door stood a Hillman Minx van. Rooks in the bunched tops of seven elms overlooking the rubbish dump were the same.

Bates remarked cheerfully and a shade apologetically—that things had changed. He heard that only good boys were coming here but what with all this wire they couldn't be that good. Chickens were that silly and slow.

How was Mr. Osbert keeping?

Osbert revolved on his heels with his back to Bates, then facing him looking high over his head, then at his potatoes, then at the coverts in the distance, at the lake where there was a gap which shouldn't have been there. He murmured shortly. His health was a topic which could become boring if he told the extensive truth.

" Are they cutting down the lake trees? " he said, loud, because he wished to interrupt Bates who was just about to say something to John.

" It's all coming down, sir. German prisoners on it now."

" Oh. I wonder who's got my nesting-boxes."

He did not really wonder that. He was claiming the significance of having put nesting-boxes up in that wood.

And Mr. John had come through all right.

" John was in Italy," Osbert said—and it was like the nesting-boxes. He appropriated it with a sudden extra resonance of the voice.

Bates himself had come through the first time, and as he saw it there were the lucky ones and the unlucky ones. If your number was down then no matter what you did, you caught it.

They inquired after the Bates family, the chickens, the village hall bought to become a roadhouse, and then they started down the drive which was as full of holes as a thrown-away sock. Light made scattered mirrors of the puddles all down its winding length—till after a bend there stood an immense edifice in dark-coloured sandstone blocks, built a hundred and twenty years previously. It was sort of magnified and symmetrical mock-Elizabethan—an architectural curiosity—not ugly except for the colour. A Palladian ruin, one quarter the size, stood roofless in weeds by the lake. It had been so damp down there and they had been so rich. . . .

Osbert deviated from the road as certainly as a retriever, went straight to a bracken and bramble-bush thicket, trod down its fringe and a cock pheasant exploded outwards.

" The Army left something." He took off his black " Anthony Eden " to the departing bird. " God speed, old friend," he said, " you may now fare worse than formerly."

Mud covered Osbert's town shoes, his overcoat swung open, and *Lilliput* protruded with the frayed edge of *The Times*, and another dead cigarette adhered to his upper lip going this way and that as his head turned this way and that like an erratic lighthouse, pricking out the beam of his observation, near and far. From here you could see whether mallard were sitting at the top end. Now you could see the whole surface.

" Sad," he said suddenly. " *Labuntur anni* . . ."

A group of big men in brown-and-green patched clothes, grouped round the fresh yellow boles of newly-cut pine watched them pass.

" Germans," John thought. " How close they are."

Osbert looked from the Germans to his son, relatively.

" A pity the Army never taught you to walk."

The headmaster was away, but the housemaster, officiating, said the boys were having their dinner, that it was a lovely place for them, that they would look after it, make it happy again, learn from it, and that one of the houses had been called Grant, after the family, with Lady Bridgett's permission.

M

A Share of the World

" Indeed," said Osbert. " I'm afraid that may not be a suitable banner for reform."

The housemaster, by his tie, was a Wykehamist with piercing blue eyes and one shoulder lower than the other. He nailed Osbert with a long blank look and then tapped out his pipe on his heel. The blankness of the look, with its complete lack of disapproval, was an attempt to believe that Osbert had not really meant what he said, or perhaps even that he had not spoken. The pipe was replaced at an optimistic, upward, between bared teeth, jutted angle. Improvement was a matter of faith—you could improve a boy by believing him better than he was, and improve a man's remark by believing he hadn't made it, and giving him time to say something else. But Osbert was looking at scoured floorboards which he had stood on but never seen till now.

" A ripping place," the Wykehamist said. " It must be painful to come back like this, sir, painful to see the trees cut down. I feel for you, sir."

When Osbert was called sir by a man of education he immediately tried to live up to the dignity which he felt had been conferred. He asked questions of a serious nature regarding Borstal. They were fully answered, and Osbert spaced his attentive listening with noises of grave understanding, sometimes watching a bird through a window or trying to remember which picture had occupied that particular rectangle of etiolation on the wall.

The housemaster took them to the old laundry, down denuded corridors, through green baize doors, and smells that had remained —pantry smells, kitchen smells, polished stair smells—all fainter, damper, but certainly lingering there, fighting disinfectant. In the distance, they heard the noise of many people eating.

And they reached the chillness and dampness of the outbuilding called the Old Laundry which John remembered once having used as a " fort " with his cousins.

" Er—thank you," said Osbert.

The Old Wykehamist wanted to help. Osbert became agitated. No, indeed, he could not take up such a busy man's time—as a matter of fact—there was so much, so scattered, that he himself did not know where to begin. And the Wykehamist went away with the assurance that he would be " on tap " if needed—also boys for lifting things, anything. They liked helping. " It's one of the things we concentrate on," with his stare of blue penetrating hope.

Before the dust-sheeted mound of his belongings Osbert Grant now stood like a tramp in front of a snowdrift; no comfort there.

" Well," said John. " Here we are."

But Osbert was looking up at a huge cupboard from the top of which some wisps of straw trailed down.

" Sparrows are untidy builders," he said. " Lecherous drabs. I'd've put Thomas here. Without gloves. That would have taught them."

Thomas was a ginger cat he used to put gloves on during the nesting season.

Osbert lingered—towards the cupboard, turning his side, finally his back to the white mound.

Then he suddenly looked over his shoulder at the corner of a dust-sheet and considered it as though it had spoken.

Still standing sideways he plucked it back.

It was a collector's cabinet. The glass door was smashed, and the stained wood patched with damp.

Osbert took hold of the slim key, half rusted, and pulled. He knelt clumsily. His mouth was open and he put up the back of his hand to his dentures. He fiddled and wrenched and sighs mixed with the stertorous breath of exertion. His hat fell off and lay among dust and glass splinters. Then he was suddenly still.

" Ruined! " The word was a shouted whisper. Apparently from no feeling at all, he had rushed to the extreme feeling. " They might have told me—what? "

John turned from that falsetto " What." He could not bear to look or hear, because suddenly he felt—There, that's me.

John loathed him, loved him. The violence of his resentment and the violence of his pity rent him with their contradictory claims. He trembled—and saw himself there: face to face with another strand of the web, another dead face, a new occasion for the smile of Bright.

Osbert might now have been a man hunting for his own reprieve. Although the outer door would certainly prevent him, he tried to pull out the butterfly drawers by taking hold of the knobs through the broken glass. The whole cabinet trembled, but was too heavy to tip forward.

He got up, pulled off a whole dust-sheet, part of which tore off in his hand—a clammy, rotten, noiseless tear. He found another cabinet. The door resisted—then came open. He recovered his balance and tried the drawers. Three were solid with the cabinet and two knobs came off in his hands. The fourth opened and for a moment he was startled, then mollified, by the bright expanse of brilliant wings—as though secretly he had not expected to find anything. The neat Latin names, shut in darkness for five years, were reassuring with their formal statement of identity—*Cyaniris Semiargus, Carterocephalus Palaemon, Damaus*—the syllables he loved to write exquisitely and sound on his palate. They had a bedside manner for him, but it did not work long.

A small cabinet lay on its back with one drawer missing like a mouth in it. " My slides! " he gasped as though someone had that moment carelessly toppled it backward.

Even the drawers that remained were empty. His slides were gone; he had lectured with them at Oxford, and in London.

" Oh, God," he said, crouching there; " why—why didn't they . . . John . . . what? " And he turned on one knee and let fall his left arm downwards and outwards, the palm open like a Shakespearean actor saying my liege. The resonant male voice with which he told stories at dinner-tables was now compressed into a something querulous and sibilant, at times falsetto. And his long, noble face with the high bland brow was now given over to the little eyes looking out like condemned prisoners.

" What? " he said. " John . . . what? "

And as if to prove something still questionable, Osbert got up and went to the highest dust-sheet under which would be the Sheraton bookcase. He tore it off, unveiling as he did so the lovely bride—with smallpox.

" You see," he said. " What? "

All the defaced furniture, the dog-eared bound books, and the ransacked cabinet seemed to listen to the word indifferently as though it were the latest drop of damp.

A Share of the World

John looked at his father holding a corner of dust-sheet and knew—he had known. For five years he had known, and that was why at that moment he could only be like an excitable schoolboy who has broken a lace when already late for a game.

"Mmm?" No noise could have been more desperately, pleadingly interrogative than Osbert's grunt.

"This is not him, this is us," John thought.

"The rain must have got in," John said at last. "How else . . ."

He suddenly remembered his grandmother telling him that his mother used to buy his father's railway ticket when they travelled together. He bent down to pick up his father's hat—he felt a tear sliding the wrong way, up instead of down his nose, and he took note of the fact.

Then Osbert said, "Where's the silver?" John knew then that it would probably not be anywhere, that his father had been keeping the thought of it bound and gagged.

John helped to look for the silver. They half took things out, half moved arm-chairs to look half behind them; they half took off the dust-sheets and looked at half the parcels. It was not there.

The housemaster appeared at the door with his pipe, and behind him were three boys in grey flannel trousers looking good.

The Wykehamist said, "We'd like to help awfully, sir, if we may."

"Oh—er—thank you . . . no." Then the thought got the better of him. "Have you seen the slides—er—lantern slides of butterflies—and the silver—the whole silver canteen. Gone. Stolen I suppose . . ."

The staunch, stocky figure gazed directly at Osbert, giving everybody time to consider what had been said—and the speaker time to reconsider, correct or amplify. Was Mr. Grant suggesting the boys had taken the silver. If so, let him say so. His boys had arrived last week: the Army had been in possession five years (he had been led to believe), and in between there had been a period of possibly eighteen weeks (he thought he was not wrong in thinking) during which the considerable amount of store furniture and what-have-you, had been consigned to the care of an elderly (at least elderly) couple. People were and always would be quick to suggest his boys were at the root of local mischief, but it was an attitude he was prepared to fight with a strong marriage of common sense and probity, the only marriage he would ever know.

All things considered, he waited for Osbert to speak again, staring at him meantime in the confidence that he would not speak lightly.

" I stored my things here during the war," said Osbert vaguely, looking round him as though these were not his things.

" I stored them here and now some have disappeared. I just wondered . . . if you could help, if you would know." The stocky figure moved its banner-like pipe.

" Sanderson! "

One of the boys signified hearing.

" Go—to—Mrs.—Mason (the Wykehamist enunciated each word like a person teaching a child to read) who—lives—in—the room—at—the—end—of—the—row—of—hooks—where YOU HANG YOUR COATS . . . And ask—her—very—nicely—if—she—will—kindly—come—here."

" With the funny nose," said the boy.

" Mrs. Mason," said the Wykehamist, transfixing him with a blue stare. The boy went.

And then the Wykehamist came and stood over the empty drawers, the warped cabinets. He sewed on his own name-tapes, this man, and he looked at the condition of the bookcase, which he dated and appraised with a knowledgeable eye, and tilting his head backwards very slightly so that he had to look down, as it were, to look level, he said firmly, and quickly, " I'm most awfully sorry, sir."

He had taken it all in. And he was sorry—sorry also perhaps for some failure in education which it was not for him to judge or condemn, but only deplore here in the victim, perhaps also author, of a really bad show.

Mrs. Mason thought when she saw Mr. Osbert, as she called him, that it was for a chat and she went on and on about Lady Bridgett and, about how she'd been keeping poorly, and wasn't the war terrible and Mr. John, fancy, in it, and only yesterday bothering the chauffeur with them water-pistols, and the chauffeur's daughter with slugs.

The élan with which she evoked the past was not to be interrupted, and Osbert stood beside her as though he were at a November 11th service, waiting, and at last he said:

" Macey—my butterflies—you remember I . . ."

She minded the time he caught one on the parson's hat at the cricket match. Wasn't it Mr. Bennet now? Her memory wasn't what it was. Hadn't there been a laugh? That fluttery animal and him all in the net together and the tea everywhere.

A smile got mixed up in the pain on Osbert's face.

" Macey," he said; " look at this." And he went to the cabinet with the empty drawers. Winter dusk was falling and the Borstal boys gathered curiously, like savages round a camera, while Macey groped for her specs.

But she didn't know, she didn't remember, except as 'ow she was told to touch nothing, but the Army, them searchlight men— and she threw up her arms—indeed she dared say that them as were getting killed should sometimes just have seen the carry-on of them that weren't.

Osbert said nothing as he walked down the drive, away from the noise of a bell and the roaring rumble of feet. He had murmured thanks with his back to the Wykehamist, revolving, following rooks with his eyes, looking across to a white smudge in the dusk— the pavilion beside which he had ensnared the Vicar and an orange— tip all in one movement when he was nine—local moribund lore. He had murmured as the Wykehamist spoke—murmured assent, gratitude, leave-taking, hope, yes he was quite right, there was always hope, and again leave-taking.

And John thought, He is my father, out of whose body I first came, of whom I am part for ever as my son will be part of me forever. I am his immortality, but I am also his nature's continuation—that web of myself did not start with me. Will it be handed down to my son with only the chance of modification of my wife's character. Are we all beyond the help of ourselves?

And he saw his father kneeling before the empty drawers in

which he had arranged and precisely labelled the brilliant and beautiful specimens of far countries, and he saw himself kneeling beside Corporal Bowen, the man he had never known, and he thought of the white house into which he could not see himself going, and now at last and all the time of Jane, whom he was " going to marry."

Before they got to the lodge it was dark. Once John put his hand out to his father and touched him, but it felt wrong, like touching himself, so after prolonging the touch an instant he brought his hand back.

They were each of them alone.

7

JOHN sat in a third-class carriage moving at sixty miles an hour towards Jane. " Nine hundred at least, hundred at least," said the wheels. And before a mildewed blotched cabinet he saw kneeling—not his father, but himself.

The left half of his face with its bright, boyish, normal eye might—nevertheless—have been looking forward to good shooting, good cooking, and perhaps bed with Jane; only the right half possessing the too-voluptuous part of the a-symmetrical mouth, and the rounder eye under a higher brow dulled—or was it brightened? —with the impartiality of a corpse, seemed ready to live up to any extreme of theory compatible with the vague and unearthly tensions upon which it was nourished.

Indeed, there in the smell of stale smoke, frost, and carriage dust he decided that the qualities with which we are born, or into which we are conditioned, are unimportant, being beyond our responsibility—they are the " web " of each self. But afterwards it is possible for the true individual to break free from his web, having understood it, then—shape himself and his life. In this was the only meaning of " freedom " still valid.

He looked out on the bare hedgerows and upon a man standing still with a gun, watching the bottom of an oak, and upon a hoarding for pills, and he wondered how the mind cured shingles—and how it gave them.

Yes, he had an extraordinary incentive for finding that freedom. Hadn't he looked into his life and felt like a child in the Hall of Distorting Mirrors—from event to event—a wide yell, a cringing grin, a swollen panic, or a narrow canniness—and in the war his own face merging, because of that smile of affinity, into Bright's,

185

into Corporal Bowen's and back to Bright's—from the smile of affinity to the aimless gape of death?

Was it the wild optimism of insanity to have chosen one other mirror in the distance—a mirror in the same hall—and run to it, to Jane whom he didn't know, believing she would give him back the promised likeness?

" Promised? " Why had he said " Promised? " It seemed as if there was something promised. As far back as he could remember this had been so. Something complete, harmonious, and if the word would do, beautiful, had always been promised.

If she loved him—or if he loved her.

Was that the point—if he loved her, or more largely speaking, if he loved?

He did hear the unsensational murmur of this alternative. But it was a river below the level of his gaze. He was looking defiantly upwards on arid peaks of performance where he imagined himself free not only of that " web of himself " (and of his father's bequeathed qualities), but also of doubts arising from the stare of Freud and Marx who waited like undertakers with separate coffins for the body of his desire—such simple though contradictory explanations dressed in black, both smiling—each with Bright's face.

Jaws so clenched are not common in third-class carriages, and an old woman lent forward thinking the boy in the corner might have been badly wounded in the war, and was unhappy because afterwards without uniform it was worse, when nobody cared. She offered a sandwich.

" It's only that pork stuff which isn't pork," she said. " My sister's hens will be getting it if you don't."

Jane was crossing from the house to the stables as John's taxi appeared. She turned back.

The taxi came in between the brick columns surmounted by tiered tiles, diminishing upwards, the last and smallest supporting a stone ball, and John saw her face. He had been unable to remember it even approximately in the past weeks, and the beauty of it estranged him almost to the point of dislike, though at the same time, he experienced an abdominal thrilling weakness.

A Share of the World

He was about to get out of the door nearest her, when the door nearest the house was opened, a hand grasped the suitcase at his feet, and he turned to help, perhaps glad of the postponement of touching Jane's hand, pressing her fingers, or being shaken—whatever she practised. And as he turned a voice that he had heard before said, " Hallo, sir."

The suitcase had caught on one of the little collapsible seats which the old-fashioned taxi had, and John was leaning forward to disengage it so that when he looked up and into the man's face their eyes were only a few inches apart.

It was Bright.

" Small world, isn't it, sir? "

As vividly as the smell of a remembered house the face brought fear and revulsion, a sharp twinge of old experience.

The face John felt would now smile with familiarity, affinity—just to establish their common past. It did, and while the smile was there Bright stood quite still for an instant as though he were having his photograph taken. Then the suitcase slid out and John turned to the other door and to Jane.

All wonder about how she would shake hands and what she would say first went unsatisfied—because he never noticed.

She led him upstairs only a few steps behind Bright—walking lop-sided, leaning away from the heavier suitcase—" because dinner's in half an hour," she was saying, and Bright's trousers were scrupulously pressed, though the stripe in them suggested a flashy bridegroom more than a butler.

He would probably like to wash and not bother to change unless he felt like a bath, wouldn't he?

He didn't hear.

She added, " Have you met Bright before somewhere? "

" In the army," he said.

" Italy, miss," said Bright.

" What a coincidence," said Jane.

" Yes," John said. But he did not feel it so.

This was his room. She hoped he would be all right. The loo was there and the bathroom there.

In simpler circumstances the names of these intimate essentials

on her lips would have faintly excited him. As it was, he saw
Bright briskly unclicking the latches of his suitcase.

" Did Christopher tell you about my father? "

" No."

Bright passed close carrying a suit to a drawer; came back and
said, " Excuse me, will you be changing, sir? "

John looked vaguely at his open case.

" I shouldn't bother," said Jane; " there's only us. Unless you
want to."

Bright wanted an answer from John. John gave the answer to the
case. " No. I won't change."

Bright was touching his pyjamas, laying them in a drawer,
breathing hard and sibilantly.

" He's ill—ulcer. The house is rather a hospital, I'm afraid.
But he gets up now and then."

John commiserated—so vaguely, so absent-mindedly, that Jane
thought both his manners and his manner, " atrocious."

She went—with a few final considerations of his needs. Bright
crossed the room with shoes and John went to the dressing-table
and took things out of his pocket—silver and coppers, pencils and
paper as though it were something he always did before dinner, and
not just a thing to do in order to do something, mitigate the moment
of being alone with Bright.

Bright's footsteps crossed again and back, then halted, behind
John, whose eyes on the tilted mirror saw the man's face appear
behind his.

" You do remember me, don't you, sir? "

" Yes, I remember you."

John pulled out two dirty handkerchiefs and a shiny theatre
programme. Looked at them. He affected indifference, disdain,
but perhaps could not have looked back into the mirror even if
he had tried. Bright had a butler's voice now. One day it would
be a priest's—or a bus conductor's.

" I thought you did, sir. There was just one thing I wanted to
mention—seeing as how you remember me—the little matter of the
blankets. My spot of trouble."

" Well? "

A Share of the World

" Well, sir, I thought I'd ask it as a favour that you wouldn't mention it to Lady Matlock or Miss Jane. You know what it is, sir, trying to live a thing down. People won't let you make a new start."

" Lady Matlock "—" Miss Jane," the creased trousers, assiduous unpacking. Only the smile at the car door . . .

It was on his lips to make some reassuring answer when Bright added, " If we really started digging things up there'd be no end to the things that got about, would there, Mr. Grant? "

John experienced a phenomenon of the blood—a blushing or paling which did not show in his skin but which he felt from the back of his neck to the pit of his stomach. The sudden sense it brought, of being unable to move, was like the pure essence of fear in nightmares.

His lips were now thrust out in a pout of imperial haughtiness and his eyes shone. He went to the bed and began to take off a shoe. Laces flicked. Bright's footsteps sounded again and a drawer bawled. In the passage Lady Matlock called Tutti on two notes, exquisitely, like noises off a stage.

" Excuse me having mentioned the matter, sir," said Bright. Then in a new tone like a businessman taking the pen from the person who has signed, " Nice place this, isn't it, sir? "

John did not reply.

Bright had finished and was at the door, not out of it, but stationary in it. He was going to say something else. John took his time with the other shoe, charging his face as he did so with the extremity of disdain.

And Bright said, " Miss Matlock's a smasher, isn't she, sir? " Having spoken he didn't move.

John fiddled with a knot. The silence and stillness of that huge presence was as perceptible to his nerve endings as a draught. John resisted until he thought, " I am afraid even to look." Then he looked—and as he looked, knew what he would see.

Bright was smiling as he had smiled below the village in the moonlight. With derisive foreknowledge. With affinity. John looked away. The web of himself trembled; the spider was still there.

8

LADY MATLOCK lay all mentally Danaë to T. S. Eliot (and to lesser slim volumes as well) but she was granite obstinacy to her husband even when he couselled her with poetic profundity.

" I *can't*, you see darling, I just *can't* "—meaning something *here* (in the stomach)—a sensation which Sir Wilfred had always dispersed in himself by silence before speaking.

The present bit in her teeth was the Christmas tree: was it or wasn't it prettier than last year? She champed over the doubt roving round the glittering cone with a sort of hostile surmise.

Then John came in. He too was ridden—with a bit in his teeth: Did Bright think he had been successfully intimidated? Did he?

Salutation. Drinks. " We *are* a funny little trio," said Lady Matlock taking a sipping of gin and orange. There was a gleam of hard-won glee in her bright little eyes: Osbert's son, Christmas, gin and dinner time. Christopher might yet come: Wilfred's X-rays have exaggerated. Her eyes returned to the tree, haunted by something a-symmetrical.

" You've got a funny butler," said John.

It was one of Lady Matlock's excessive sincerities—that she could not be insulted or offended at the moment of insult or offence. If somebody had said to her out of the blue, " You're a hypocrite," she would at once have felt—ah, yes, yes—that's possible —and she would have raised her nails and given herself over to pained interest in why the person thought so, even though she might never have met him before.

Thus when John, whom she hardly knew, opened his visit with a mildly boorish remark—a gratuitous wrenching of the conversation from its context in order to criticise the butler, she was immediately all ears to hear why Bright was " funny."

She even went closer to John and laid her hand on his arm because his face was so serious.

She said, " His breathing, you mean. He steams rather, doesn't he?" She laughed, became guilty, thinking, " Perhaps one shouldn't laugh at people's infirmities. But what," she said, " what . . . ?"

" No," said John. " Not his breathing."

He realised he had never spoken of the man before. It was difficult as though he had an impediment in his speech, a near stutter.

" He was court-martialled for selling army blankets to the Italians."

Lady Matlock was distressed; also amazed. The man was new, but so good. If it wasn't for his breathing while serving (and his inability to mix distemper into imitation hoar frost like Baxter), he would be better than dear, dear Baxter who had never remembered anything.

John looked at his shoes. It was said. Now he wanted to moderate it. With a nervous laugh, " He's probably quite honest here in his own country."

Lady Matlock sighed, " Right—a thief. It only needed that didn't it, darling." She thought about it, finally giggled at Jane with a note of hysteria. " Wasn't that all that was needed to fill the cup of this Christmas, darling?" Jane was knitting with such grave interest that Lady Matlock pulled herself together and said, " Tell us more, John. *So* interesting."

Then a branch which needed another bauble, caught her eye.

" Go on, dear," she said, getting up and going keenly to the tree. " I don't know *what* I shall do. It took me a month to find him." She rattled and hunted in a box of left-overs, absorbed, while John said, " That's all."

Realising he had spoken, Lady Matlock repeated in tones suddenly made flat by interest in something else, " No, I don't know what I shall do."

A Share of the World

Before they went into dinner she restored her attention to the subject.

"Blankets!" she said. "As long as he only takes the utility ones it won't matter. Now, how shall we sit? Dear me, I wish there were more alternatives."

Jane expostulated. Neenie explained—ardently and repentantly; she only meant . . . other Christmasses . . . . so many people, so many ways of sitting; arranging had been fun.

And from the side of the door Bright emerged with the soup as John broke bread.

After dinner, sitting separated from Jane by three empty feet of chintz and a cushion, and remote from her by the preoccupation in her face which went far beyond the exigencies of knitting, and had nothing to do with him, John listened with half an ear to Lady Matlock talking about "Osbert as King John in the Braxton Pageant—*so* funny," unpacking the past now without melancholy as though all could be used again—to-morrow perhaps.

Jane's feet were crossed at the ankles. She had taken no particular care with her face or clothes. The dress she wore was an exalted dressing-gown with zips on the side. By her ankles a frilly rim suggested a nightgown underneath. For her it was clearly an evening like any other. She referred to her pattern book, counted, and occasionally deserted her thoughts for a laugh at something her mother said.

There she was. Jane—and the emanations from her presence were like the emanations from the audience in that nightmare where he had the leading role and had not learned his part. She knitted solidly, implacably, and thoughtfully, and was clearly pleased to be exempted from conversational effort by the natural run-on of her mother. She even seemed to feel exempted from listening to John; her mother did that, also, earnestly enough for two.

He found himself looking at his hand with surprise. That's me. I'm sitting on a sofa next to the girl I decided to marry. I decided to marry her only when I saw her, and before I spoke to her, and because she was labelled as "wonderful" and looked after pilots with burnt-away faces till " the end." Because she would have a man for a husband, not me, and was therefore the ordeal and the answer—because the answer would have to be an ordeal.

It had all seemed so valid—back there in his room. Now the inhuman artificiality of the whole structure as revealed by her presence, made him sick with apprehension—like a man in a dangerous area with a bad map. Where was he? Had he merely gone round in a few insignificant mental circles close to home? Had he moved so slightly that going back would present no obstacles? No, that also was not true. Somehow what had happened was not as false as that.

Jane referred to a watch with a long red hand, and began putting away her knitting.

Neenie said, " Darling, love, couldn't I do Daddy's tray to-night. I know how to do it. Then you could stay and talk to John."

Jane gave the matter serious thought as though she wished to delegate the job for the reason suggested. But she decided against.

" I know where everything is."

Conversation between John and Lady Matlock soon died a natural death. Even Neenie came to an end of the things she had to say, and more than ever her eyes filmed with sleepiness like a parrot's, her lids lulled down and started up again as she laughed with a delight which had become mechanical, being cut off from any true source by Christopher's absence, Wilfred's illness, and the sad discovery that John was not as funny as Osbert.

9

WAKING, John saw Bright drawing the curtains on a garden he had never seen before. Memory made an effort, a conscious tracing of association dragging all the way an anchor of incredulity.

Deep sleep had only come late in the night after dreams so near the surface that he had exercised in them an element of control and tiring responsibility. He disentangled the real from the enormous claims of the unreal, put reason back in its usurped saddle and listened with loathing to the studied quietness of Bright's steps.

Good manners from Bright: hideous, like a song from a corpse.

Once the big man let fall his predatory gaze on John's head. Their eyes met and John felt free in that he had told Lady Matlock the thing that Bright did not want known. At the same time he noticed—as he looked away—that he now possessed a sense of guilt towards the man, and was more than ever . . . more than ever what?

Afraid of him? No. He told himself he was not afraid of Bright nor of anything that Bright could reveal about his part in the war. Nevertheless, there was personality in mere size. Bright was nearly a giant. That awe should go out from eleven to eighteen stone was natural.

That, he tried to assure himself, was all there was to the feeling which the man's physical proximity produced.

Bright went, shutting the door as quietly as though John were gravely ill.

The path below the window was a thermometer of decay. The first twenty yards was clean gravel and sheer black verge;

then short weeds started and battled with gravel for another thirty. Beyond that shrubs had closed the gracefuls spaces between them and creepers triumphed over a stone pretty, eight classical pillars in a circle and a roof to match.

In the passage a door was opened and a dog cajoled to come out. The door closed. Footsteps. Voices—Lady Matlock's high and penetrating—Jane's obscure, conscious they could be overheard. Lady Matlock talking about Daddy's injections.

" Then you can ride with John, darling."

A long murmur . . . and then Lady Matlock dropping, obediently it seemed to inaudibility.

Father and Mummy. Father *paterfamilias* and Mummy *mamouchka*. Jane was filial to one and maternal to the other. Yes, he thought, remembering her expression, as she knitted, with a twinge of jealousy—at least filial. More labels cropped into mind " Jane *adores* Wilfred "—" Wilfred *worships* Jane." Even the routine superlatives had in these utterances appeared at a loss, and one he seemed to remember had discovered a way out and said: " Janes loves her father." *Julia patrem amat:* loves, honours and obeys. All in Latin or in a catechism.

John looked at the ceiling and realised that only for him, of all the people in the house, the day that was breaking was exceptional. He sat among them like a man in a railway carriage nursing a bomb in his writing-case. The others, so to speak, read their papers, looked out of the window, knitted and referred to their watches, accepted him as one of themselves. But he was not. He sat among them with a resolution that would prove completely disturbing. He was not going to spare anyone because he was not going to spare himself.

The initial violence of this attitude perhaps shows to what extent he expected her to say " No." And since—lying there in bed he wondered whether he would propose that very day—it could be argued that he wished to receive that " No " as soon as possible.

The mirror, as he brushed his hair, reminded him of Bright's smile behind his left shoulder, and his face fell into the expresssion with which he had looked towards the German lines a young

A Share of the World

Napoleon elated with a pre-vision of Arcola—John Grant, an undergraduate who might get a second, going down to breakfast —and to propose.

And no reasonable objections from a friend could have affected him because reasonable objections existed nowhere so cogently as in himself. He was therefore inoculated against them.

10

JANE looked tense and tragic at breakfast, but she ate busily and with relish. She had not made up, and her face was a smooth grey which against her long cendré hair, made for a uniformity of colouring which her mother regretted. A heavy wool jersey accentuated the slimness of her neck, the curls that brushed the collar, the delicacy of her wrists and the comparative robustness of large breasts held full and high by a brassière.

When she got up for more coffee she pulled her jersey taut into her canvas belt, which had three buckles like a horse's girth—not with any wish to entice, but merely because the thing would work up.

They talked of Christopher at Oxford. Her pretty hands were never still. The fingers—deprived of knife and fork or any specific task—tied themselves into knots and then unknotted, fiddled with a ring, clasped and unclasped, clenched into fists with thumb unclosed, climbed on top of each other, wrestled, merged, disbanded and took no rest. Perhaps that was why she knitted so much. Movement to camouflage movement.

" People can't go on blaming the war all the time," she said, drinking loudly and putting down the cup not exactly in the saucer's centre.

" Does he blame the war? " John said.

" Mummy says all the time, ' It's the war.' No, I don't think he says anything. Not to me at any rate. He doesn't speak to me."

She collected four Christmas cards, an apple, and bustled to the door—a surprisingly ugly walk for someone who danced gracefully.

" Well, we'll ride at eleven then. Will you be all right till then? "

A Share of the World

She took him in sitting there with a piece of toast and marmalade, looking round with a look in his eye which made her dread the ride. Would he help her into the saddle and then kiss her knee on a level with her face? That was what happened the last time a man had had that look.

Next door her voice cropped up again on the telephone, ordering food, then getting on to a chemist, ordering medicine, specifying a certain size of hypodermic needle, finally throwing a log in the fire and knocking over the guard as she did so, adding, " B——! "

The way she straightened her jersey had been like a duck standing up in the water, briskly flapping its wings, trimming itself for flight; and she ate and swore with gusto. In the ugliness with which she walked there was ominous independence; a taste for enough room.

She interrupted his thoughts by coming back for something, stooping to look under a chair beside him. He watched her and at that moment the long-beleaguered garrison of his theory sighted at last the first true forces of feeling—the outriders of desire. As she bent a sudden faintness sent sweetness to his nostrils, his saliva, and to the pit of his stomach.

He now told himself he not merely " would " but " could " propose to her that day.

Lady Matlock burst in. " Darling! " The word was a heraldic fanfare and she held up a telegram.

" Christopher's coming! " Her face was radiant.

" That's very decent of him," Jane said.

" Oh, I know—don't I know all that—but I don't care. He's coming. That's all that matters. The telegram comes from Paul—I don't even mind that."

" *From Paul ?* "

" I wouldn't mind if it came from the devil."

Neenie moved towards the kitchen. She had tears in her eyes. " I must tell Helen. We must have champagne."

11

IT was a day so dark it might have been always evening. The crudded plough was powdered along each ridge with white frost, and grass was crisp round the now-indelible hoof and shoe-prints of the last softness. The symmetrical copses of fir in that flat land loomed black like ships in a convoy—black and low, low down, rooted deep between grass, winter greens and plough, without fences—a sea of arable.

" We'll have to walk them all the time," said Jane.

The air found out the insides of nostrils, killed smell and the horses chucked their heads down in bellowing sneezes, plodded with redundant energy, as though to keep every inch of themselves moving.

Jane's face became brightly coloured in the iron-grey weather just as in the bright rooms it had been an unredeemed grey.

And her attention which indoors had seemed devoted to Father, was now turned with equal concentration on natural scenery. She rode ahead on a narrow path, looking to right and left, upward and downward with enthusiasm, in spite of the extreme monotony, even desolation, of what there was to see.

And once, stopping short of a fir copse, a black formless hulk in which no detail was visible though only a hundred yards distant, she said, " I love these dark days."

John drew abreast and saw in her eyes, watering from the cold, a wideness and stillness, which was not for his benefit.

The frost-fog had put them, as it were, in a moving room, so that the way they had come was always closed a few feet behind them.

The stillness waited for them to do something, watched them, listened to them—the breakers in, the movers.

A Share of the World

Their breath smoked and the horses breathed, switched their heads and rotated their ears, and champed at the steel in their mouths, their eyes swollen in perpetual apprehension.

Jane looked suddenly sad.

John said, " I'm afraid it's rather a grim Christmas for you." He had not expected to say it; an impulse of sympathy had snatched him from the sterile resolution to which he had been screwing himself up, watching her back for a mile.

Her face softened. They rode on—very much together. Then he said, " I suppose Christopher will feel less strongly soon, won't he? "

The softness fled. " *Christopher* feel less strongly! "

She heeled her horse forward. He caught up with her, feeling as irritated as apologetic.

" You surely see what I mean."

" I don't," she said. " You seem to think *he* has a grievance."

The completeness of her censure was provoking. The suddenness with which she had taken offence was altogether disproportionate—almost " psychological."

And the tone of her voice was suited to life-shaking tragedy—the gradual paralysis of someone loved or an air crash with best friends on board—not suited, as he saw it, to a storm in a drawing-room teacup. The very high-pitchedness of her tone was irritating, particularly because it betrayed preoccupation with domestic affairs, which shut him out.

He said, " All I meant is—you, none of you, seem to make any sincere effort to investigate his nausea. Perhaps there's something in it."

At first rage kept her silent. Then suddenly under the fringe of her front teeth and her eyes became injected with tears.

She said, " I think you're quite incredible."

She increased the pace of her horse. No actor playing Orpheus looked away more consistently than she did for the next two hundred yards—to hide tears.

These tears were sweet to him. Until now he had felt as if he had never affected her—her movements in dance, words in the one letter, speech since he arrived or thoughts at any time. He relished the tears for that and he relished them because they provoked in him pity, which like the twinge of desire as she stooped to pick something from under his chair, was a step towards love.

He drew level with her, looked discreetly at his horse's head and made his silence sound contrite.

She said, " You don't realise how Father *worshipped* Christopher. And perhaps you don't realise that Father may . . ." She loosened some strands of mane from under the saddle-bow and leant forward to pat and smooth her horse's neck, looking as she did so into its face as though it had interrupted her by a sudden limp or wrong cough. " How seriously ill he is," she went on carefully, and then very carefully and quietly, " And Christopher chooses this moment to . . . I don't see how you *can*." She could not finish but resumed her stare away from him.

He let two fields pass, potato clamps go by like barges in an embankment fog, one copse with bare-limbed deciduous trees thrusting up from the fringe of packed evergreens but all one colour, like a derelict hulk loom, and fade. To become intimate with her, get to grips with her, involved an effort of concentration even during silence. When it faltered from failure, he looked about him like a person at a bad play.

What was this note in her voice when she talked of Christopher?

He stated the opposite of what he expected in order to make her reply stand out—get leverage on her mind.

" You were never, I suppose, really ' close ' to Christopher? "

Her eyes, now caring nothing for tears in their lashes, turned towards him, marked him down for a person who went from one absurd misunderstanding to another.

" Never ' close! ' We were . . . he was . . . we shared everything, *everything*. He was my greatest friend, my *only* friend . . ."

She looked away and felt that what she had said was such a miserable understatement to an obtuse stranger whom it didn't concern that she took refuge in physical exertion and change of subject. " Let's trot," she said, " it's getting late."

A family, John thought, full of lovers and broken hearts— a whirlpool with currents and counter-currents and undertows, eddies and misleading calms—a little tucked-away whirlpool now

A Share of the World

spate from outside influences, from illness, war, social revolution, and with addition soon—unless I am a branch of illness—from me. Unless (and he took in the vigorous independent figure fading ahead in the fog, going back to Father), unless, even as a branch of illness, I fail to infect—or as a force of love, am not received.

Lady Matlock wanted to know about the ride (from the top of a step-ladder); every little detail, where they went and what they saw.

She would ask Jane later what they said to each other.

They had to hold the holly up while she questioned them.

" Is this your room? " John said at Jane's door.

And she said, " Yes. Nice, isn't it? "

Had she faced him he would have gone. But she didn't. She walked to a window and he followed her, smelling her room, his legs tired, his stomach strangely stirred by the movement of the horse, now strikingly absent.

She turned to the bed, undid her jacket and took it off. And suddenly he knew. She knew. She went about her business which was compliance. He moved round the room.

" You were a bonny child," he said, peering at a photograph.

" When I was eight."

It was Grandmother's steps. They could both move towards it but they mustn't be seen.

He strayed by the bed. She was taking off her shoes. There was a smell of cooking and her father coughed in the distance.

" Christopher was right," he said as he stood by her bedside table.

" What? "

" The *Oxford Book of English Verse* and the Bible."

" Oh, he minds them, does he? "

She was undoing her shoe knowing exactly where he was.

If it had not been for Susan he would not have crossed the threshold. The thought struck him strangely out of the blue of the past that was never done with; the past that went on and on.

He sat down on the bed behind her and put his hand on the plump of her upper arms and drew her backwards till her head was against his chest and then he moved his hand on to her breasts, lifted and gently compressed them while he kissed her neck below her ear where curls and collar met. And at every stage, at each new touch, he was amazed to have got so far.

She was compliant, impersonally compliant without being welcoming. This was not disagreeable, her body seemed to say, and it was none of her doing; it meant absolutely nothing. A nice back-rest after a long ride was not unpleasant. But her breathing became altered, also her colouring, and a heavy relaxation thickened her face.

" Darling Jane," he said, " I love you."

It might have passed had it not been for the finality with which it was said—" Check-mate " instead of common or garden " Check." The finality—for Jane—altered the whole emphasis of the episode. A fashionable duellist who suddenly discovers his opponent is shooting to kill could scarcely have been more disturbed.

She got up—unclasping his hands from her body firmly and easily as though she were taking off ornaments, and putting them aside.

" It'll be lunch in a minute," she said.

She went to the dressing-table and began tearing a comb through her hair with the bleak and uninterested regularity of a char scrubbing a floor. Her eyes were bright.

He stood behind her. Jane—at home in her shell.

The *Oxford Book of English Verse* and the Bible, *Black Beauty*, a brush mounted and an old pony-club certificate, *Diseases of Infancy and Childhood*, *The Treatment of Third Degree Burns* by Dwyer, a woolly rabbit and Thomas à Kempis—and a *Common Place Book* with probably at least one excerpt from Charles Morgan.

A print of Paris and some miniature painted skis and musical chalet, and lace curtains from the high head of the almost double bed—he saw her suddenly as a hygienic and long-sequestered dressing, white and clean and fresh, to which he was going to apply himself, like a stale wound. And at this he had an inkling of pity. Already the thin red line of her upbringing and " classical " behaviour was pressed at several points, her benevolence used, her correctness hysterically undermined and mocked by the brother she was sure had been " closest."

He saw her breasts moving under the wool jersey as her arm worked at her hair, and laid a flower on Susan's memory for having come to his room when she was fourteen, without which breasts might now have seemed untouchable.

" I shall have to take off my things," she said, getting up. She would have to take off her things. The common-place words, like a phrase in an oratorio, could have been repeated a hundred times and for each repetition his imagination would have supplied a sweet variety of association.

He went to his room and changed, thinking it has started—and it has started well. Now that his hands had held her breasts, they seemed still to hold them, and now that he had told her that he loved her, his theory, by which she was to be the solution of the " web of himself," seemed, strangely enough, not on the way to solution—but as though it had never been.

Indeed he felt surprised—as though only in the last few minutes had he ever had anything to do with Jane.

That afternoon John looked out of the drawing-room window towards the drive and saw a big man in camel-hair coat which reached nearly to his ankles, and a green pork-pie hat. Jane was wrapping presents.

" Who's that? " said John.

" Bright," she said; " it's his day off. A woman in a mauve Vanguard comes to fetch him. Is she there to-day? "

" Yes," said John.

He returned to his book, and the noise of Jane's holly and candle paper, and the hiss of fire getting the better of new logs were the only noises. All round them sofas and chairs and tables waited, congested with Lady Matlock's preparations for Christmas.

And one blackbird, puffed out till it was round, alighted athletically on the windowsill, looked in with a keen single-minded inquiry—and then fled.

She said, " Did you know Bright well? "

A Share of the World

" Yes. Quite well."

" He has a strange face."

" Strange? "

" Unpleasant, strangely unpleasant."

" Perhaps." John had folded his book over one finger, and was staring out of the window. He said, " I had the rare misfortune to go on a reconnaissance patrol with him alone."

Out of deceit; self-consciousness, and out of self-consciousness, verbosity; an old mixture.

" Did you? " There was no invitation in her voice.

He suddenly resented her. She *ought* to be interested. Wasn't any patrol, any extreme experience, interesting.

" What happened? " she said, and she had no sooner said it than he knew he had no intention of telling her. Not yet at any rate.

" Nothing very glorious."

" Nothing very glorious ever did happen, did it? "

That annoyed him, too. A facile and fashionable commonplace about modern war—almost true—but by the little that it wasn't true, by that much the lowest lie imaginable.

He said, " Did you mind what I said this morning, in your room? "

She thought, writing, " What did you say? Oh, that! " She wrote then, " It's not a thing people often *resent*."

" ' Oh, that . . . ' You thought I didn't mean it? "

" I didn't think at all."

" What did you feel? "

She completed a parcel while he lent a finger for a knot. He repeated, " What did you feel? "

" Must we really talk about it now? "

" You thought I said it lightly."

" Well, since we've met twice before yesterday . . . for a few minutes . . . here and there . . ."

" Lightly! "

She licked a label, scrubbed over it with a clenched fist, all as though he had said, " I send New Year cards to the people I forget."

A Share of the World

" Will you marry me? " he said. " That's what I meant. And that's what I mean."

She thought—not of what to say, but how to say it.

" It's very sweet of you, but . . ."

" Sweet! I haven't offered you a lift into town. Will you . . . that's all."

" John, please! " she said. " Don't let's add to the difficulties of this Christmas."

She looked at her watch. " My father's injections," she announced. Then, in case there should be any misunderstanding, any imputation of flight, " I'm coming back."

He sat among the hothouse flowers and silk cushions, and after half an hour decided it was not necessary to take so long to finish injections.

The warm optimism of the morning had vanished. And now— the old sterile determination to affect her, wrench her, if necessary, destructively from that mood in which she did not take him into account, returned. He made no allowance for her " nerves " in the recent conversation.

12

SEXUAL relationships apart, it is seldom assumed that people
like or dislike each other for physical reasons; yet probably it
happens all the time.

There were two bodies for John at Edgeby—Bright's and Jane's.

One he had shrunk from touching in mud under enemy guns
and across the thickness of two uniforms; the other he longed to
lie with naked.

It was as simple as the two forces in a magnet; indeed, perhaps
if Bright had not been in the house, John would not have gravitated
so swiftly to Jane—proposed to her in such a way as ensured failure
of a humiliating kind.

On the other hand, he never had any patience; and never
respected " technique " which he believed was usually a substitute
for, or civilisation (i.e. death), of feeling. It is therefore probable
that under any conditions he would have offered marriage to Jane
in a hectic and gauche fashion, as though all wooing were deceit,
and not confirmed as it is, in the instinctual lives of animals.

Ever since he had decided to marry her, he had been worried
by not having made known to her his " intentions "—as though his
thoughts were things that really belonged to her; just as he felt
that all his thoughts about people were partly the property,
respectively, of each person concerned.

To those who regard a love affair like a card game or business
deal (" you must win ") he had played his ace and she had taken
it with a small trump. Or, militarily speaking, he had put all his
troops in front at once, while she still had all the room in which to
manoeuvre.

But such comparisons as might have sprung from his sister
Mary's wisdom he would have listened to with a smile of contempt.

A Share of the World

" DARLING! " was the commonest loud cry at Edgeby. It resounded from room to room, floor to floor, sometimes without sequence as though Lady Matlock merely wished to reassure herself that at least Jane, at least one darling, was still there—up and about. Jane also shouted conversations through a hundred foot of passage, starting with a peremptory yell, " Mummy! "

Wood fires hissed, hyacinths bloomed and satin cushions remained undented in three empty downstairs rooms. Every day Neenie and Jane were too busy to use, even though they helped to dust, them—keep them as they had always been.

John sometimes sat in one of them—reading—or more often listening. For him there were only two people in the house besides himself, and by listening carefully he was able to avoid one—and " chance " upon the other.

He expected to meet Bright everywhere; he never expected to meet Jane. He expected when he turned on the light at his room door in the evening to see Bright in the centre of the floor motionless, waiting for him; he expected to see him at the head of the stairs as he went up and at the end of the passage he was in. Always standing still, waiting.

Whenever he did see Bright the man was merely about his business—putting wood on a fire, laying or clearing the table, polishing or washing up. The big man would try, with a look, to establish a link, as though they were spies in an enemy country.

Once, approaching his room door, John heard Bright inside—brushing clothes. He turned back, to fetch something downstairs, actually did fetch something; and read a paper for a few minutes with the thing he had fetched in his hand, waiting to go back.

If ever he thought Bright was going to speak to him he turned or went away. And if the big man was close his nerves responded as they do to a dagger's point an inch from the forehead.

He ached for the distance to be greater—or much, much nearer, as it would one day be?

When Jane was near he ached differently. One moment reason told him she could only have replied to his proposal as she did; the next it reminded him their tongues had touched—which for him was the greatest—not the second greatest—physical intimacy

—and from this he felt able to accuse her of an inconsistency which could be used as a weapon against her hard ethical outer-shell; something with which he might in time affect her.

She was always working—sometimes on housework, or outside her father's door where a shelf was hinged on the wall, rapidly on letters, or helping her mother stick old Valentines on new trays, or going through attic cupboards in an overall. After dinner she nodded over her knitting, or knitted until it was time to " do " Father's tray. For many of her tasks—particularly those involving the maintenance of rooms seldom used—she showed neither enthusiasm nor rebellion. She just did them firmly.

" Are you paid anything? " he asked her.

She was not amused.

The boorishness with which he sometimes spoke to her was like nailed boots—to get a grip on her surface, make some progress.

Only her flesh gave him hope. That seemed weak.

When he touched her she continued neither to resist nor comply. Only—her mouth seemed to have a skill and a generosity of its own, opening warmly to his.

He began to measure the day by its opportunities for physical intimacy, and sitting with his books among the satin cushions and hyacinths, he listened till her footsteps went to her room. Then he joined her.

Once she tried to pass him when he came in.

" Why must you go? "

" I must."

" Why? "

" To wind Father's wool."

" Wind Father's wool! "

" I promised."

" You promised? "

" Yes, I promised."

He looked at her as though she would probably never have any idea how ridiculous she was. It intrigued her enough to delay her at the door. " Well——? "

" You're a wonderful person, aren't you? "

" What d'you mean? "

A Share of the World

" I mean you'll crack one day. I mean that one day the contortions of your fingers will not be enough relief for—for doing Father's wool—and then you'll crack."

She looked amazed—then hostile and left him alone in her bedroom.

Neenie's ceaseless preparations for Christmas brought them together more than John's contrivance.

On the deserted schoolroom passages Jane asked to be guided because she could not see through the holly she was carrying. He came behind her, unclasped her belt, slid his arms under her jersey and cupped her breasts inwards and upwards so that he had the weight of them in his hands. Then he kissed her under her curls, browsed there smelling and kissing, while he held her tight against him. " Don't you understand? " he said.

" I'll prick you," she said—but her voice was altered, and for the next half-hour as they stuck evergreen behind gilt and gold-leaf, the air between them was a conductor in the circuit of desire.

At such moments how remote, ill and academic had seemed that " web of himself." Life felt within his grasp: possible and triumphant. His mercurial nature responded like drought-stricken land to a storm and that evening the first bars of Beethoven's Fifth Symphony reduced him to tears as uncontrollable as a nose-bleed. Lady Matlock crowed with laughter, compared his to her own *larmes faciles* and her eyes watered a little in sympathy, as they always did when anyone near her wept.

" Dear John," she said, " I'm so glad someone else does that."

On the afternoon of Christmas Eve he sat in a deep sofa, looking down the deserted drawing-room, hearing a small clock tick against a silent house. Bright and the servants off duty, Lady Matlock gone into Hatchford, and Sir Wilfred in bed. He listened for Jane. She had said she would be ready at half-past three. At any moment he expected her steps to cross the floor overhead— into her room.

Half-past three. He was drowsy with food and drink and contemplated with satisfaction the arrival of his fingers at her skin after threading through layers of winter clothing. Then they could go out together.

At a quarter to four he got up and looked at the clock closely because the light was failing. Quarter to four. He listened, even looked at the ceiling as though he might read its lips if he could not hear it. No sound. Then he went to her room. Not there. He listened at her father's door and heard an old dry cough like a pebble falling on pebbles. Somehow it was the wrong sort of silence for two people. He went to the hall and there by the stand for wellington boots he found her discarded shoes.

She had gone. He went out and walked till the trees stood jet against one streak of yellow in the west. The only figure he saw— a woman in a mackintosh with a big basket in an unknown field— he pursued until close enough to look into her face, although he had known from the back that it was not Jane. The last moment was like a dream, the Jane that wasn't Jane.

She was alone in the drawing-room pouring out tea.

" I looked for you everywhere," he said.

" I had to pay some calls; I thought it would bore you."

" Was that what you thought? "

She faintly shrugged her shoulders. She behaved as if there were several other people present.

Footsteps sounded in the next room. " Bright," she shrieked. The footsteps paused and came to the door. The big man appeared.

" Could we have the other butter, please? "

John looked into the fire. When the door closed he said, " What did you really think? "

Jane was saved from having to reply by the return of her mother from Hatchford.

Neenie did not even take off her coat; she admitted she had only twenty minutes with them before she must again take the road to Hatchford—to meet Christopher's train. Jane wondered why she had bothered to come back.

" But darling! I'd hardly seen you all day."

Jane accepted this in silence; then said, " I really don't see what's the point of going to the station."

Lady Matlock seemed unable to believe her ears. " Not go! But, darling, I must be there when he arrives."

" Why d'you think he will? "

" But, darling—he *might*."

The mere possibility of a train containing Christopher would have drawn her barefoot across mountains. Her face affirmed this as she looked at her daughter—a little incredulously as though her question had verged on ugliness.

13

AS Neenie left for the station Sir Wilfred came down the stairs in time to receive from her a valedictory kiss and an inquiry as to how he felt " up." He was dressed in a dark velvet dinner-jacket with some sober-coloured silk round his neck, tied like a stock. His face was like that of a Chinese sage carved in leather-coloured ivory. Always in this, his home, he moved as if he were there on sufferance, with dignity, but as a visitor. This manner derived possibly from the hyper-conscientious attitude he had always held about " earning enough " in spite of being married to a rich woman, and from the belief that Neenie had an " artistic temperament " to which he must allow freedom. To-day the weakness of his legs somehow accentuated the sweetness, and the insubstantiality of his material relationship to this dwelling. Each slow pace he took was a voyage, and when he reached the fireside he looked at it with recognition but without familiarity. From that position he looked up to take John's hand with a radiant courtesy and kindness by which he apparently excused himself conversation for he soon settled to *The Times* crossword of which two words remained to be done. The peace in his face might have been due to the fact that anxiety could suck no more out of him, or it might have been due to the fact that recently certain things of which he had long been doubtful had become clearer in the twilight limbo of drugs and in the precognition (it had seemed that) of death. Only at Jane's mention of Christopher's train did he raise his head like an old professor overhearing the topic which was the field of his life's work. Then he looked into the fire over the two empty spaces for four-letter words and said nothing.

The latest development in his relationship with his son had as

A Share of the World

usual been at Christopher's initiative. He, Wilfred, had been careful not to practise even legitimate avoidance of estate-taxation—such as forming a company and making his family directors, or making it over to Christopher in order to avoid death duties.

Laws, he held, were made to be obeyed, not got round. Thus he rationalised it. But possibly he was gratifying the hunger for altruistic and " dutiful " behaviour into which he had been drilled in childhood. However, in spite of this moral fastidiousness about tax-evasion he was anxious, with an intensity worthy of the Old Testament, that this first-born should inherit and make a success of whatever should be left. He used to speak of " when Christopher *has* Edgeby." Now during his last relapse, Christopher had intimated, via his mother, that he would not, ever, *have* Edgeby, or the money which would go with it. In making this decision Christopher felt he had at one and the same time hurt his father to the maximum and also, so to speak, vomited up once and for all something about his father's character which to him was insidiously dreadful just because it seemed on almost all occasions, the very opposite of " dreadful," seemed " perfect," " ideal." Having made the decision Christopher told Jane, " Now, at last, I love my father." For Jane this remark had terminated once and for all her periodic attempts to make Christopher " see reason." She gave him up as, " merely bloody "; Neenie clung to him more than ever as, " derangé, darling, by the war."

And Sir Wilfred looked in the fire and thought there was never any coercion used with him. Only example. And love. Why had love failed? No, he must never believe it had failed, could ever fail. Indeed the only real pain, as he had told Neenie, was that for a time Christopher, by callousness, had made it impossible for him, Wilfred, to love him. Nothing personal. But just that. In his humility or—as it sometimes seemed—his broken-in-ness Sir Wilfred was not aware of death by platitude: God is love, he said to Neenie *à propos* how to treat his son. Who was he to improve on or give a personal slant to old truths?

Wilfred's comprehensive scholarship had amassed for him a library of wisdom—but to Christopher it seemed all burnt on three-ply wood. But Wilfred derived fortitude from precedence

—even a certain unfashionableness—as when he told Christopher that T. S. Eliot had no ear. Christopher had not answered. It had been their last conversation on a general subject.

Jane looked at the expression on her father's face and went to him. She put a footstool under his slippered feet, she took his hand, bent close to his face, and said cheerfully, " Are you all right? "

" I'm lovely." It had been the favourite expression of an outstandingly ugly parlourmaid they had once had, and occasionally he revived it. Then he said, " Why does Mummy think Christopher's coming on ' the last train before Christmas? ' Does she honestly suppose that he *knows* the last train before Christmas? "

" I know," said Jane.

" Or even that it's Christmas."

Wilfred smiled benignly at John inviting him to share in the humorous aspect of the world in which his son lived—ignorance of Christmas being but the smallest part of it.

" I'll give him an Easter Egg," said John.

" Oh, no presents," said Sir Wilfred. " I see you don't know the rules."

When Lady Matlock returned—alone—from Hatchford station, she said, " I only went in case. I didn't really expect him. Poor darling, he's so much more likely to come at the last moment and I suppose it isn't that yet, though heaven knows it feels like it."

And she giggled feebly at her husband's eyebrows which never missed an opportunity for affectionate irony.

Sir Wilfred, having abandoned *The Times* crossword for his knitting, counted stitches and vouchsafed no comment. Neenie looked at him; everything he did was poignant. Doubly poignant on account of his calm, his business-as-usual manner.

Jane said, " I'll ask Bright to find out about trains to-morrow."

John could never accustom himself to this everyday use of Bright's name. Whenever anyone said " Bright " it made him go hot, like overhearing something bad about himself.

Lady Matlock gnawed her nails and stared into the fire. Sir Wilfred loosened a length from the ball—resumed knitting, and said, " Perhaps we'll get a telegram from Paul saying, ' Christopher missed the train.' "

Lady Matlock laughed a shade too loud, a shade too gratefully. " Darling," she cried, " d'you think we might? Nothing would surprise me."

Sir Wilfred went on, " Arriving Boxing-Day—if I can get him off. Love, Paul."

They laughed.

A clock ticked, ticked, ticked.

" Isn't it an occasion for alcohol? " said Sir Wilfred still without looking up. " Or must I wait till you've all washed? "

" But, darling—should you? What did Doctor Vance say? "

" He knew better than to disappoint me further."

Sir Wilfred tried hard to combat a natural asceticism, be as other men. Camouflage was a branch of good manners; being like the next.

Neenie said, " *Would* you, John? Bright will give you the tray."

14

WOULD John go to Bright?

The room had six bells, but since the war they had been seldom used. ("If we go ourselves it saves them two journeys.") John looked at one of them and it was on his lips to suggest pressing it.

Then he went.

He remembered a character in Nostromo who had been tortured during a revolution by a big priest. In later life he met his torturer in the streets and at social occasions, and although by then he, the victim, had been reinstated, and was powerful in comparison with the big priest, he remained at sight of his torturer—the victim. The idea of revenge which had seemed sweet in theory turned to the ache of impotence at the first distant glimpse of the familiar, shambling, figure, in the street: the Big Priest coming towards him.

John had never been tortured by Bright, yet his reluctance amounted to physical faintness as he turned the pantry handle, and went in.

The emptiness of the room was a sweet relief, a sudden freedom.

The door of the silver cupboard was open showing glints in blackness. A saucer of what looked like pink milk, stinking of ammonia, lay on the corrugated wood by the sink. Bright had been there. John went to the cupboard to find the drinks. Then he saw them on a tray in the corner already prepared; the familiar five or six bottles, like a family, Noilly-Prat, Gordon's Dry and their children.

He had laid hold of the tray when he heard a sound and turned to see Bright come out of the silver cupboard with a grey rag and a platter.

A Share of the World

"Got everything you want, sir?" He came towards John polishing, and his question, like his clothes and like his assiduous polishing, were not what they seemed. They were the soft flutter of the great bird of prey, hopping with naked neck and enflamed eyes on the perch which was always waiting for it in the face of this beautiful wretch.

To-day there seemed to be a particular meal and the little eyes were sharp with anticipation.

John stepped to one side, saying, "Everything's here, I think," looking down at the tray.

Bright followed him—to check the things on the tray perhaps. John saw his feet—tiny feet—come close and smelt the ammonia of the rag; he stepped aside again, but quickly and silently Bright stepped in front of him. The leading edge of the tray touched his apron.

"Excuse me mentioning it, sir—but did you happen to mention the matter of the blankets to Lady Matlock?"

It was like when you forgot something you knew very well. The emptiness which is solid. At last he said, "Will you please let me pass?"

"Because," said Bright, "perhaps you didn't get to hear that I was acquitted at the court-martial? . . . Did you know that, sir."

Like a stutterer John found it easier to say what he had already said than to embark upon breaking the ice of a new word.

"Will you please let me pass."

Bright stayed in front of him long enough just to indicate that he would have stayed there as long as he liked—then he stepped aside.

Neenie said, "You look pale, dear. Won't you have one?"

He murmured something about a bath and went. On the stairs he raised his right hand and held it out. The fingers were trembling. He felt faintly sick. His head teemed with imaginary alternatives to what might have happened—he heard the noise of himself putting down the tray—confidently and quietly since Bright seemed anxious to talk. Violence was too far a flight into the improbable to be pursued. But it beckoned. Indeed he yearned to destroy Bright and did once say in his wild way, " I would not feel I had committed murder." And he remembered the German enemy with whom he had felt an affinity of suffering, human beings caught in one web of convention facing human beings caught in another. He had been licensed to kill them. Yet weren't the killing wars of individuals likely to be more " ethical," more justifiable than those of nations? Did numbers make morality? He imagined himself standing over Bright with a smoking weapon and—as though he was in fact that person—looked into his mind for remorse or any feeling that he had broken a natural law. No, he found none; only fear of the consequences. Fear again. How passionately he despised this ubiquitous fear; the cement of convention; the death of the individual. To be above it seemed the only nobility. And he lowered his hand still shaking not from the concussion of a firearm that had killed but from a few words with the butler.

Jane crossed him under the upstairs passage light. She was in nothing but a dressing-gown, and under it warm and bare from the bath, but he scarcely noticed her, and went past her door to his own room.

The table was set for five.

" Couldn't we have that taken away now? " said Sir Wilfred, indicating the vacant chair.

Neenie said, " It might as well remain now it's there. Mightn't it, darling? D'you remember the time he hitch-hiked and got here at eleven? Though . . . perhaps if we took it away he would be more likely to come."

She giggled appealingly, looking round. She knew she minded immoderately—and was superstitious and perhaps silly sometimes —but why pretend?

Sir Wilfred had special food put before him—pabulous and pale, with special anæmic condiments and two different sorts of pills, in tiny bottles labelled illegibly.

Jane sat beside the empty chair and opposite John. Lady Matlock, opposite Sir Wilfred, frequently peered round the silver candlesticks, to see if he was all right. In spite of this frequent concern Sir Wilfred felt a draught and asked John to close the door connecting with the drawing-room. At the noise of its shutting Neenie protested loudly. She liked it open and if John were in a draught she would change places with him.

Sir Wilfred said, " Darling." And then because she was not listening to him but still talking to John, he shouted, " DARLING— NEENIE—*I* asked John to shut the door, *I* am in a draught. And, Neenie . . . Neenie? "

Lady Matlock was laughing. " Yes, darling, what? I'm listening."

" And I DON'T want to change places. In fact, I *won't* change places with you."

Lady Matlock laughed away, thankful for the fun—because there wasn't such fun with Christopher's chair empty and Wilfred's face like that, hardly Wilfred at all, and in pain all the time.

She explained: an open window would have been *too much* air, but everything shut—doors and windows—was not *enough air.*

Sir Wilfred made a face like a French porter who hears the passenger has eight trunks and wants them all with him. Lady Matlock laughed again. Tears stood in her eyes. He was being like he used to be—deliciously funny without saying a word.

" Oh, make that face again," she pleaded; " darling, for me."

Sir Wilfred rose, picked up the wine, topped up everybody's glass, shakily, and when he reached his wife's chair he made the porter's face very close and then kissed her.

" Oh, darling," she said, and felt it was she who should have been cheering him up. " I do love that face. I had quite forgotten it."

The table with its hinted reflections of the things that stood on it, gave and took light, and so also in their way did the faces of father, mother and daughter, happy now for a moment in spite of the two miseries which might be without remedy—Christopher's " state " and Wilfred's illness, waiting for them there outside the rim of light of the present, tiny moment.

" I hope my daughter's giving you a good Christmas," said Sir Wilfred. " I'm afraid I've been on her hands a lot."

A Share of the World

"She's a devoted nurse," said John. "I have wished once or twice I was ill."

Since he was not a G.I., or in any way given to wisecracking, and since he said it quietly and with unaffected sincerity, the remark amounted to a statement of his position.

Jane ate with a little more concentration than usual and John, looking at her, saw another face in the darkness behind her. It was so separate from any visible body that for a fraction of a second he thought it was a mirror or a picture. Then it smiled; a little private message from Bright by the sideboard.

Neenie said, "Darling, I know you never have a moment—I *must* do more of the bedside drudgery."

At the word "drudgery" Sir Wilfred pulled the corners of his mouth even lower than for the French porter, peering round the candles and fixing his wife with a mask of dejection and injured feelings. He was at that moment in pain and had one hand inside his jacket, pressing and holding.

"Oh, darling," cried Lady Matlock, getting up with her mouth full and going round to him. "I didn't mean that. As though there had ever been drudgery with you in bed."

Now, Sir Wilfred signified with another face, the conversation had taken a turn which made it difficult for him to believe his ears.

Jane laughed. John smiled, and noticed Bright smiling, with a revolting discretion, fitting in and collecting plates. And in the middle of the tiny commotion, the smiles, John found Jane looking at him, and not looking away for a whole second, in which she said a silent, separate "Hallo!"

And at that happy moment the door opened, noisily—and slowly—and with no immediate entry, as though someone with a tray or a load were coming in. The handle crumped against the wall and a cold air came, suggesting the front door and all intervening doors were open—then Christopher—in a streaming gas-cape, swaying a little.

He seemed to have difficulty in recognising the room—or the people in it.

There was rain on his spectacles.

221

A Share of the World

" Is this the right house? " he said. Such a quiet voice—a gentle yearning drawl, and just the suggestion of a smile.

Lady Matlock turning from Sir Wilfred's neck, cried, " Darling! " One word, but in it a rushing, hectic escape of rapture and gratitude.

She ran to him, her arms out.

And he said, " Yes, this is it."

15

IF, as some of his relations said, Christopher only behaved as he did to make himself " felt " or " to be different " then he was, now on both counts, completely successful.

His father's attempt at good spirits collapsed, his sister ate and then knitted indignantly, his mother sat at his feet on a stool, craned upwards to him in a whole-hearted attempt to elicit details of his hitch-hike and his life in London. And John completely resented him for completely occupying Jane's thoughts and emotions, coming in as he had done, and taking from the only face he wanted the only look he desired—blowing it out like a feeble flame just lit.

At ten Sir Wilfred took the ears of his retriever and stretched them back till the dog had a sleek face and elongated eyes. Some intelligence seemed to pass between them as a result of this—for the dog, when its ears were released, made slowly for the door followed by its master, carrying its basket and *The Times*. They both moved like mourners—for Christopher, for the apparent failure of love.

At half-past ten Jane went up without having changed her expression—to do her father's tray. And at eleven the gold clock on the writing-table, with its visible works and swinging gold heart, tinged exquisitely. Neenie, sitting at her son's feet on a footstool, put a hand to the side of her face so that the little finger fringed the corner of her mouth and exclaimed:

" The stockings! " She had quite forgotten.

Christopher, till then monosyllabic and reluctant, sprang to life.

Stockings! He had masses. He fetched an armful from his room—shooting and football stockings—relics of his successful past, and spilled them at her feet, far more than she needed, as though preparing a bonfire.

" Oh, darling," she piped. " *Just* the thing. But do we need so many? Do we? "

When Jane came into his room with a stocking John shut the door behind her. " Stay a moment, won't you? "

He took her in his arms and lay back with her on the bed but she was taut, still had things to do, still preoccupied.

" A minute," he said, " let's rescue one minute from the wreck of this awful day."

" What on earth do you mean? " She looked angrily at the ceiling.

" Wasn't it a bit like hell? "

He meant several things including her family atmosphere, but he limited himself to one.

" This afternoon," he said, " I had no right, I suppose, to expect you to come. Have you any idea what it was like when you didn't? "

She said nothing. He went on, " You sit thinking of Christopher and Father, I sit thinking of the bit of sofa beside me which you could perfectly well have sat in. Your father thinks how he has failed with his son, your mother thinks Christopher is here, and Christopher thinks it's all dead . . . and when I say thinks, I mean in each case suffers. You surely see it's a little hell, with a background of carols and evergreens and hypodermic syringes."

The stubbornness of her mouth increased. While Father might die—his son came home drunk; his wife devoted the whole evening to hearing about a hitch-hike; and his guest said his house was hell.

John said, " It will need a lot of tears before you get free of your family. A lot of breakage."

A tear separated itself from her lashes and went a short way down her cheek.

He said. " Have you any idea what it's like to be in love with a girl who's in love with . . ."

" And have *you*," she exploded, " any idea what it's like when someone you love may die? I don't think you have. Because I

A Share of the World

don't think you have any idea what it's like to *love*. Now, please let me go." She raised herself. "I hardly know you," she added as though that fact had only just occurred to her. "You talk all the time as though I were under some obligation to you . . . it's the most extraordinary presumption and I don't understand."

He prevented her from going. "No," he said, "*You don't* understand; so please don't go till you do."

Because it was all wrong and artificial and he had no feeling he began thinking, calculating, as though someone had given him a sum, about the acreage of a field or the volume of a tank . . . the day mustn't end like this. If it did the wrongness would grow in the night. "I want to explain," he said, gaining time for more calculation which arrived nowhere and was so barren he abandoned it and blurted out, "I have no choice. Don't you see I have no choice. I want you too badly to be patient. I know the theory of how to woo; but I want you too badly to pretend I don't want you."

She said nothing but seemed to have gone farther from him at first sound of the rising note in his voice. He said, quietly again, "There is something I must ask you: you don't sit beside me and you choose to walk by yourself—but in my arms you seem happy, in my arms your hands stop fidgeting, getting their only rest. And your face becomes less like a fighter pilot before going up. Does all that mean you love me?"

She said nothing, so he added the words he loathed the sound of, the Hollywood echo of, uttering them contemptuously in order that this should be clear, "A little?" he said. "Do you love me a little?"

In her four or five experiences of being courted she had found men mainly inept and unsubtle, like fish floundering in limited water. This case seemed outstanding. At any other time, however, she would have risen to the occasion with the kindness and gratitude one always felt for the supreme gift. But the evening of this particular day, which had started at half-past six a.m., was different. She no longer trusted her senses and bed seemed the only reality. She reached for the stocking still to be hung—Christopher's—the last discipline and got up as though their conversation had come to a rounded finish. Only by a slight shake of her head as she loosened his hand on her arm, did she try and convey her feelings.

" Wait," he said, " there's one thing more. My Christmas present to you."

He took from the dressing-table drawer a small jewel-box and opened it. " There," he said.

It was an eighteenth-century diamond and ruby brooch, clipped into velvet the colour of night. It had been his mother's and was the only valuable he possessed of any kind. It was very valuable.

She made no move to take it—so he picked up her hand and put the blue box in the palm, and closed her fingers over it.

So the day would not let her go or give up. He had burrowed in her, as it were, and retrieved yet another unused feeling, fresh compassion—as much now by his face as by the jewel.

She said, " How lovely . . . Thank you for offering it to me. I must put it there, mustn't I? You do see, don't you? Perhaps later . . . or for someone else. You may want it later."

" Jane, wait," he said quietly. " Listen. No, don't go. If you take that you don't commit yourself at all. You can marry someone else and wear it at your wedding if you like."

She shook her head—because speech, any word seemed to inflame him, prolong everything.

He said, " Listen! Look! " He took up the brooch and threw the window open. The curtain flapped in his face and rain fell on a silk table-mat where it showed up like ink immediately it touched.

" If you don't want it—I'll throw it away. Because that's how it is. All or nothing."

With a look of pity but no responsibility she closed the door, hearing but not seeing the furious fling of his arm.

The jewel disappeared without a flash or a sound—as though he had thrown nothing. And indeed, he felt, suddenly, as if he had thrown nothing. He felt as if he had made a wild and idiotic gesture with an empty hand now already wet with the unseen rain. It was the thing he fired at in nightmares with the great white surface showing no mark and moving towards him, or in reality the war he had fought against his own side.

She had closed the door gently and normally, as though she

would leave the lights on in the passage and be there if he called, but he must try to go to sleep.

He sat down at the writing-table with the left shoulder of his dinner-jacket getting wet. He got up and shut the window. Nothing —he had thrown nothing. There had been no sound, yet there on the table the jewel-box was empty. He sat on the empty bed beside the depression where she had lain unwillingly in his arms.

The harsh though faint overhead light remained on and he made no attempt to put on the one beside his pillow. The *Week-End Book*, *Oddtaa*, *A Farwell to Arms*, and a paper-back by Gyp, bound specially. Pyjamas folded by Bright.

He heard a soft clinking outside Sir Wilfred's room. Jane and Neenie whispering. Lights put off. Footsteps shod, changed to the hushed lopping of bedroom slippers. The sound of a kiss and a coo, the musical equivalent of darling, my heart, and doors closing. Silence.

How long before a footstep, noisy but slow and irregular, like someone finding his way up the stairs in the dark, along the passage to John's door?

It was Christopher—standing there. He said, " How about a drink? "

If he stayed, the pillow would smell faintly of Jane, where the depression was. He would go round the trap which his mind had become and up and down it, always treading on the same spots, always pausing face to face with the same piece of wire, like the wolves at the Zoo; the rhythm, the tireless reflexes of hope, behind the pattern of the wire, of the web he couldn't affect.

" Yes," he said.

In the passage—on a ledge—her father's tray was covered with a beaded napkin. Ready.

On the bottom step Christopher stopped inexplicably. Facing away from John, he said, " The thing is—I can't find the key of the drink cupboard."

" Isn't there a cellar? "

" No, it was the first economy," he said sarcastically. " Now— ' a little ' is kept in a cupboard. With a key."

A Share of the World

" Well . . . *I* don't know. Where's the key kept—usually? "

" ' Usually '—' it's kept ' in the lock," said Christopher. He turned his head sideways and passed a hand through his hair with difficulty as though it were treacly stuff, and opened his lips showing a clenched line of uncleaned teeth. But he remained at the bottom of the stairs with his back to John.

" But when I'm here . . ."

His sudden silence re-put the question.

John repeated, " *I* don't know where it is."

Christopher gave him time to reconsider this—then said:

" They ' usually ' put it somewhere quite easy. Jane does. But this time it's not in the gramophone, or in the pantry drawer. I thought you might have seen them at it."

John suddenly noticed that all the lights were on downstairs, even table and picture lights. And at the same instant he saw Christopher for the last half-hour—looking in " easy " places, turning on ever more lights, walking about like an uncle playing hunt-the-thimble, among the photographs of himself, on a pony, in a boat, in Pop at Eton, in long clothes, as an officer, with a tennis cup—looking for the key of the drinks cupboard.

Now differently, as though to an accomplice who had proved loyalty, Christopher said, " Isn't it bloody? "

And he resumed his search—behind Christmas cards, in drawers, under ornaments, moving almost indifferently, languidly from place to place—without touching anything as though that was in the rules.

Only once he stood on the top of a chair and felt along the top of a picture frame parting holly and yew with his fingers.

" Christ," he said; " this stuff everywhere." He opened the baize door which led to the pantry. The lights were on there too—he had been everywhere. The door swept after him, excluding him and the sound of his quiet watchful tread. A clock faced John, ticked with the striking indifference and callousness clocks have in the small hours.

My window is wide, thought John, rain coming in, the bed disturbed. On the table lies an open jewel-box with royal-blue velvet getting damp. The cicatrice in the stuff shows where the double clasp has lain embedded for years. Somewhere in the grass is the jewel. Is Jane lying awake? If she is—has a gesture with diamonds done what nothing else has been able to do—affected her. Perhaps there should be many more diamonds where those came from. Could that lack be the trouble? Mary would have known. Three, four days . . . I must remember, of course, as she says, I must remember: it's only four days.

The *Tatler* man held up a miniature hoop. What was it meant to be? Was he going to eat it? And the old mill on the front of *Country Life* rained diamonds from its rim and the vista of leaves and stream water was full of careful contrast. To-morrow was Christmas. Last Christmas—Trieste. The dreadful forced jollity of Englishmen Christmas-ing abroad. The hell of " What's yours? " The rounds of beer. Would Christopher find the key. Voices.

Christopher kicked the green-baize door half-open and then stood in it, whisky bottle in one hand, two glasses in the other, looking back, saying:

" Why on earth not. Come on."

It was somehow no surprise to see Bright come up behind Christopher, take the strain of the door and walk in with him, dressed in a pale-blue and black dressing-gown of shiny material, scarlet slippers below plum-coloured pyjama legs.

Christopher said, " Splendid man. He knew at once."

Bright said, " It'll have to be a quick one, sir. You'll get me the sack."

" Why? " Christopher's drawl had become less pronounced. His limp had vanished. He sat in an arm-chair and put the whisky on the floor.

" You'll get me the sack. Won't he, Mr. Grant? "

John wondered whether to go. He looked at the bottom stair and thought of his room. Christopher had a tall, coloured, hock-glass and an ordinary wine-glass, the first his hands had come to in the cupboard. He filled both to the brim with neat whisky and gave one to John and one to Bright.

" Why don't you sit down? " he said to Bright.

Bright sat in a high-backed chair blotting out the heraldic dog-lion embroidered on the back. He looked like a magistrate in hell—sentencing people, as Christopher would have it, to heaven, to Edgeby.

" Christ! " said Christopher. " I hate drinking out of a bottle. Nothing ever comes."

He got up and moved to the green door. When it sagged to behind him Bright raised his glass to John.

John looked away into the dead fire.

"You don't want to be chums with Bright; do you, Mr. Grant?"

The black and white undersides of the logs, sectioned like mud in a drought, were without glow.

Bright's breathing was harsh, working the vast bellows of his chest, nourishing his little malignant eyes.

" Surely you're just like the rest of us," he wheezed. " Aren't you, Mr. Grant? Flesh and blood? Weren't there times when it showed? "

Who was Bright? Where was he born? What was the inside of his room like? Why did he not seem as other men. Why can't I bear to look at him, even be near him?

Christopher came back with a half-pint beer glass. His elbow knocked down a tall Christmas card which in falling laid low a whole line.

Bright finished his drink and said:

" Well, thank you, sir. Back to bed and a spot of kip before the festivities."

Christopher said, "Why on earth. For Christ's sake. You haven't even *had* a drink yet. Here."

He sounded petulant, concerned. Yet when the man went, he paid no attention and never answered his last good night from the green door.

Bright came back:

" And seeing the time, gentlemen, I should have wished you a Merry Christmas."

Christopher stared at John's knees, waited for Bright to go, put his hand through his hair, frowning as a substitute, it seemed, for cursing the man he had implored to remain.

" I've got a feeling *anything* might happen."

A Share of the World

His eyes, set away deep behind their spectacles and brow, looked at John strangely—with unusual directness: he clearly *wanted* " anything " to happen.

" Do you like Jane? " he said.

" Like is hardly the word."

Christopher had not listened.

John knew, and said, " I'm in love with Jane! " trying the sound of it on his lips, tried to believe it, tried to see how such a thing could be.

Christopher said, still—apparently—not having listened, " My mother says you're in love with Jane . . ."

" Well . . . supposing I am? "

The whisky was taking effect—removing ton by impalpable ton the weight which Christopher normally seemed to support with his eyes. Now there was no doubt. His facts—couldn't anyone see they were facts?—facts now came easily, lightly.

He said, " Jane! I don't see how anyone can be *in love* with Jane—unless they're really in love with Father, Mummy, Edgeby—all this." And he waved his hand at a small bookcase full of books bound in a special green chosen by his mother, and at a cardboard silhouette of himself in Pop at Eton in tigerskin waistcoat and daffodil buttonhole.

The gesture with the hand was exaggerated, the sort of thing Neenie said " he never used to do."

He added, " Or unless they're in love with themselves." And he looked brightly and destructively at John. Then, " What intimacy can there be with her? When she's not really there."

John said nothing.

" What do you feel *in contact with*? I mean—even your invitation to stay here probably came from my mother, didn't it? "

Is it not my fault, then, John thought, that I cannot affect her? Is what he says true? Is she not there to affect; is she " wonderful "; is she behaviour " personified," an adjustable embodiment of the desire to please the people she thinks it her duty to please?

" My father," said Christopher; " it's all my father. He thinks that to thrive—in the biological sense—is wicked, naughty. It's this f——, bloody duty, this endless guilt which he feels, which cripples him, and which he wants us all to feel. Guilt and the atonement by duty. The only chance for Jane—if you love her— is to break her shell. Let her out. She's got to be violently unhappy, she's got to shed—all this. In love with Jane! You must be in hell."

Hell is here and now, thought John. This minute is hell—but I must answer Christopher, and myself in Christopher.

" Aren't we all," he said, " mainly composed of characteristics which are not our doing? You may see Jane as second-hand; perhaps somebody may see you in your present mood as even more immediately and fashionably second-hand."

Christopher looked at the carpet wearily as though that were not the point.

" At least," he said, " I am nothing. That's at least a starting point." And he quoted, " In order to possess what you do not possess you must go by the way of dispossession."

He opened his eyes a little wider than usual, they seemed to come forward through his spectacles—and changed his voice to what John suspected had been his normal tones in the days when county mothers of county daughters had thought him the most suitable of the suitable.

> *And in order to arrive at what you are not*
> *You must go through the way in which you are not*
> *Wherein there is no ecstasy.*

" And is that what you're doing? " said John satirically—to protect Jane and his relationship with her.

" I really don't know what I'm doing. But I shall, in time. When I hear people ask my mother what is Christopher going to ' *do* ' —then more than ever I realise that for the minute I'm not going to ' *do* ' anything."

" And if you had no allowance? "

" I think I should starve rather than ' have Edgeby ' or ' *do* ' something . . . We have only one life as far as we know. One third sleep. Why make another third even more negative than sleep? ' Doing something in which we cannot express ourselves, deepen ourselves before death." He paused, drank and stared, then said, " It's this bloody feeling of guilt. That's what one's got to get rid of. Why should one feel guilty, WHY? It was imposed—blast them. Doing one's bit, pulling one's weight, playing the game. England was killed by the Public Schools—by schoolmasters. By people whose private lives were several sorts of mess including sexual. By the denial of the human being. And now the f—— Socialists. The desert."

He filled up and drank.

" My father . . . and my mother. ' The perfect marriage.' The perfect place. The perfect children. The perfect life. Edgeby! Jesus Christ, one dimension is dull."

Christopher's eyes seemed to have forsaken cover. They started forward accusing objects all round the room. Prints, pictures, colours, perfectly matched, symmetry; Regency this, Regency that; daffodils in December, exquisite vases, like lyres, like urns, like classical vases before them; the latest periodicals, the latest novels, the white telephone, the bound common-place books, scrap-albums, photographs of people, groomed and posed or dishevelled and natural. He made one of his incongruous gestures taking it all in.

" Dead," he said finally, and his eyes retired behind their protection, avoiding John's.

" Have another drink."

John wanted to go to bed. Christopher said, " It's only one o'clock." He was going to ring up Paul before he went to bed.

Christopher filled up John's glass against his will. Returning to his chair, he tripped over a light chord and a small standard lamp fell over, knocking a vase and many Christmas cards to the floor.

" Christ! " He stood over the debris with the whisky in his hand, wondering whether to pick it up. The focus of intelligence and intention fogged in his face. He swayed a moment longer over the debris and sat down.

A door at the top of the passage opened and footsteps came to the stairs and began to descend, slowly, carefully in bedroom slippers.

Sir Wilfred in a white dressing-gown made of material like a bath towel. Wasted and brown he looked like Gandhi about to

address a meeting. He stood at the head of the second flight where
the whole hall was in view. His high forehead gleamed as though
polished.

" Christopher, darling; if you want to sit up with John could
you please move to the library where you won't be under the
bedrooms."

Sir Wilfred turned like a herald who has fulfilled his function,
and mounted the stairs as though his slippers were red weights.
A stone-deaf person seeing only his eyes would have thought he
must have uttered words which Christopher would never forget,
a Day of Judgment, classic ire and pain of All-father, cursing
and utterly bleeding for such a sin so close; but a blind person
hearing only the gentle voice would never have believed the eyes
had been violent.

The door shut on the landing above their heads.

Christopher took a gulp of whisky. His face worked as though
it were seen through moving water. He began to smile—the smile
gathering way with conviction.

" The technique of it," he said, " you have to admire. ' Darling '
—the perfect move to put me in check, put me in guilt. And did
you notice ' under the bedrooms '—the buried ' I '—buried till
it stinks."

Christopher suddenly shouted, " MY, MY, MY bedroom." The
ceiling rang brazenly with his words.

" Oh, Christ! " he said. " Come on. Let's go and ' sit up ' in
the library."

John said he was going to bed. Christopher filled his beer glass
half full of whisky—some went over the edge.

" Good night," John said.

Christopher did not answer.

On the landing John paused in front of Jane's door.

It was white with four square and two rectangular panels. It
had a brass knob and made a brushing noise on the haircord carpet
when you opened it. He strained his ears, hoping to hear her breath.
He imagined she moved. Sir Wilfred coughed and up the stairs
came a clink from the hall.

A Share of the World

Sir Wilfred's cough came again but this time clearer—so much clearer that John turned, and saw his door open and Jane standing in it looking back and downwards into crepuscular light, solicitous and noiseless like a mother leaving a child that has just got off.

John was so surprised that he could not move from the almost eavesdropping position which he occupied at her door. He could only step back as she approached—approached and passed, without a word or a look, her face white and tense.

Only when half in her room, the door brushing the haircord, she stopped and said:

" Don't you think you might go to bed? " and closed the door in his face.

John's curtains were flung inwards by the wind as he entered his room. The writing-table was wet and the jewel-box was on the floor. An orange peeped at him out of his bulging stocking.

Before shutting the window he looked out, wondering whether to look for the jewel with a torch. No . . . He shut the window and, walking over to the pillow, picked it up, patted it into a full shape and turned it over. But his pyjamas had also been underneath her and as he put them on a smell that was her scent, half herself, and faint, ineffable as nostalgia came to him and, as it were, dragged velvet across his open wound.

" Don't you think you might go to bed now? "

He wanted her more and more every time he saw her.

He put out the light and remembered the years when he had never been able to sleep the night before Christmas. The hope and therefore the impatience had been too great. He could never trust that sun to rise by itself, but must track it across the dark far side of the world with a clock, until it showed the curtains weren't wall, and came again. He must do that even though he knew the quickest way to make it come was to sleep.

Then he unpacked Red Indians in electric light and wound a locomotive while his nurse grumbled.

On this eve of Christmas it was not hope which kept John awake. It was refusal to despair. And when he did sleep he could not even be an accepting spectator of shallow dreams. Responsibility—

the thing he desired above all things, the only thing which could free him from the " web of himself "—followed him into unconsciousness and tired him with lunatic but vital problems, of which the waking essence and distilled taste was failure.

16

FOR the adult villagers at Edgeby it was just another Christmas morning, for their children it was the morning of mornings, and for their livestock it was another dawn.

The cocks announced it before it came, and then again while it was coming, grey behind the birch and firs and without reflection in pools opaque with ice. The Vicar's notes for his sermon, freshly written, though similar to last year in their emphasis on *peace* and goodwill—to all men—lay in the leather shabbiness and stale-smelling cold of his study. The pensioned head keeper, angular with arthritis, lit his stove and threw his limp cat on to the ritual spot of the doorstep; chains rattled in the byre; miniature Christmas trees stood in the new council house windows white with fake snow behind utility curtains; and down some bullet-holes in the church door fired by Royalists at Roundheads, wood-wasps did not alter the position of their winter sleep. Above, from the roof, grey gargoyles grimaced out over the flat lands, their wide, lichened eyes undazzled by the rise of perhaps their three hundred thousandth day.

When John got out of bed he went to the window because (looking back this seemed the reason) Jane was on the lawn below walking this way and that with her head bent. Occasionally she looked up and about her, into the distance as though half-heartedly beginning to act the part of someone who had gone out before breakfast to admire the garden and take the air; then the exigencies of the search would compel her to be wholehearted about it and she went on slowly like a golfer combing the rough. Finally she stooped, and John came away from the window.

He was nearly dressed when he heard her steps and a knock on the door.

A Share of the World

She was methodical, doing what she had to do as no doubt she used to be when she had to tie up the jaws of the dead to prevent that outrageous lolling which was no help in a ward. She wished him a " Merry Christmas " and put the jewel on the nearest edge of the mantelpiece. " Here's this," she said, and suited her voice to the mention of something more than merely financially valuable. She laid the thing down with extreme gentleness and respect which- being so unlike her habitually jerky movements, was conspicuous. But after such perilous digression into the uncertain lanes of feeling she regained the high road with a rush, thanking him, as soon as everybody would be thanking everybody, for the stockings which were just what she wanted and too lovely.

" Oh," he said, " so you accept the stockings."

In her hospital days she had tried to cure herself of showing more sympathy to those who didn't complain or, more literally, cry out, than to those who did. She had argued the latter were doubly pitiful in that they had not even the comfort of self-control. Gradually she had succeeded.

But it seemed to him she only felt weariness and resentment for the self-indulgence with which he paraded his pain. And he suspected these feelings were increased—unconsciously—by the fact that she might have looked forward all her adolescence and during the war to " a romance "—sublime months of trysts, letters, aching absences, precious moments seized together as the leaf was unfurling, as the leaf was falling, months during which she would remain the still unravished bride, suspending in the name of delight, all she had to give—her beauty illuminated by love of the moment, every single instant. Now against all expectation, even against her will he was perhaps partly the fulfilment of that expectation; yet he would not allow it to be her way—he snatched and spoiled. The act of searching for, finding and giving back the jewel had animated Jane's face—perhaps with the feeling of gen- erosity which is so like love. Then he had spoken and blighted it.

" So you accept the stockings."

She turned to go, signifying as much of her feelings as she could with an oblique and stony stare to one side, and the slightest shake of the head meaning " you must be nearly mad."

A Share of the World

" No," he said, " don't go like that—with a dumb appeal to reason." He took her hand off the handle and closed the door. " I've got something reasonable to say."

His pontifical manner in his shirt sleeves, without shoes on beside the intimate untidiness of his slept-in bed, long words before breakfast and all on Christmas Day, completed the route of her tender feelings and filled her with embarrassment. She stood awry like someone waiting to be fitted.

He said, " It was your mother, not you, who invited me here. Wasn't it? "

Her blue eyes scanned immense and merciful distances while her mouth remained shut like a magistrate's listening to a bad excuse. She said nothing.

He said, " I shall go to-morrow unless you say you want me to stay. You know my feelings for you. If I've got to go I want to go while going feels possible."

It did not feel possible to go and he wondered what he would do there and then if she produced some kindly disguised " go."

Her mouth battled with her eyes. A tremor moved her head— caused by words reaching the ante-chamber of speech, before being turned back.

To wait in silence and not try to influence her answer, was beyond his powers. " Hysteria," he said, surprising himself, " is progressive because one of its symptoms is to affect surroundings in such a way as to aggravate itself. It's disgusting to witness especially in domestic, everyday form. Better in a ward or a battle-field. I'm sorry for you to have to deal with it. But from inside, Jane, you know it's worse. And the unspoken pull-yourself-together of your father's face to the world . . . and of your face to me . . . merely sows the desire to pull you, and him, apart; expose the sterility, which aggravates the hysteria. You could free me, by freeing yourself."

She said nothing but was sufficiently astonished to remain. Indeed her silence seemed propitious. He changed his tone and took her hands. " I have so much to tell you," he said gently. " Some of it might ease you as well as me. Your face, your all-but-beauty. Have you seen your face? Always so determined not to

239

fail, not to fall short. Of what? I sometimes think it is a poor advertisement for virtue. And your hands; I'm sure they could be still."

He looked at her with his soft eyes. They were insidiously sweet—he almost disowned them for their desperate efforts. But afterwards, afterwards he would make all things valid, all promises, all sentiments.

" I love you," he said. Another tremor moved her head and this time one word almost passed the ante-chamber—for her lips relaxed then tightened again.

It was like feeding a bird from the hand. When it was only one hop away the suspense of the lure was so acute that all thought was vested in the motionless come-hither of the proffered crumb, as though by the strength of willing he could influence that separate brain—to come closer, closer still.

" Obviously," he said, " my need is frantic—perhaps fashionably clinical; but less obviously I believe that when you have answered this I will love you in the level way you wish, talk of the weather for six months, and be content with kissing."

She moved her hands in his to free them.

" I love you," he said.

Somebody walked in the passage. She moved her head, looked over her shoulder, wishing to go. In a voice which seemed quite at sea as to what tone to adopt, what loudness, what words, she said, " I don't know why you should think I want you to go." And when she was in the doorway, she added, " Because I don't."

He stood by the jewel on the mantelpiece, and there, so to speak, he took out her three words, read them over and over again, and put them where he could see them.

" Let's not open our brown presents till after church, do you think, darling."

The voice—Neenie's—was that of anxiety itself. It was directed at Sir Wilfred as he appeared in a blue suit, slowly, economising in the energy which was to get him to church, and through lunch and then back to bed.

In sickness and health he was used to being called out of sober silences in order to cope with his wife's immediate problems. It was always a little like national mobilisation to put out a fire.

Gravely he gave judgment on behalf of opening the " brown " (i.e., posted) presents after church—though, considering it was a question which would only involve Jane and herself, since only they had " brown " presents, it had better be decided by them. Christopher might still be in bed after church, and John and he, so far as he knew, had no " brown " presents. He always gave every side of any question.

" But, darling, there's a big parcel for you from Aggy. I've been keeping it for weeks for you."

Sir Wilfred trusted it was not perishable.

" Oh, darling," she said flying to him, " you can have all my presents—all of them."

Sir Wilfred kissed her and referred to his watch. They would leave at two minutes to. Jane appeared in a bonnet and scarlet coat carrying an ivory-backed Prayer Book, with already a foretaste of church in her expression. Sir Wilfred said to her, " Has Christopher gone to bed yet? "

As always quick to follow her father's mood, she brightened and laughed. Yes, she thought so.

Now we are going to church—thought John—a special department of Sir Wilfred's hydro-electric establishment—almost the control chamber. And he will move from dial to dial as though there were water driving the great turbine, as though there were not in fact a hideous drought in the Vicar, in himself as well, as in us all.

Was Christopher a drop of the storm which would end it? Incoherent, ugly, clumsy, shrill—with only the eyes set deep, protesting honesty, even humility: not I, but this true feeling. What was Christopher for Sir Wilfred if not the vengeance of the profound human weather which in its average moments Sir Wilfred had learnt to canalise, mitigate, control with installations of humour, common sense, and learning—all driving the central turbine Duty, until the source was lost.

The stricken scream of the jive trumpet and belated wail of the jet engine coinciding with the welfare state professing progress is a conflict which will have its consummation, John thought, because there is only one harmony, the original harmony of the body with the coarse earth and the mind with that infinity, now a Divine vacuum, the sky. And while he thought this, Jane thought he really might have put on a suit to-day.

Sir Wilfred looked at his watch again, as though he were a company commander waiting for the barrage to lift. One minute to go. Jane sat with her Prayer Book on her lap. Lady Matlock said " finished," and rushed to get a hat.

How correct they would seem saving the noticeable absence of the son of the house. Their pew would be in front waiting empty for them. In Sir Wilfred's pocket would be a pound for the collection folded the size of a rusk. There would be three old women who always went, otherwise twenty regulars of red-letter Sundays. The choir would be the children young enough for the schoolmistress to influence. And there would be one, perhaps two, men in white who attended because they revelled confidently in the sound they made while they were singing. One tenor, perhaps, soaring like a crude horn—making the schoolmistress's mouth an inarticulate O.

Jane would not only look demure, she would feel it—also charitable. She—still—would get a mental wash from Church.

Time. Sir Wilfred rose, Jane rose, and Lady Matlock scuttled for her bag. A heavy tread sounded on the stair. Sir Wilfred perhaps hastened a little and was gone into the passage by the time Christopher in his dressing-gown reached the turn and stood above the room at the head of the last flight, where his father had stood ten hours ago, like Gandhi or a ghost come back to curse.

Jane went also, but the sight of her son stopped Lady Matlock dead, and she said, " Darling! *Merry, Merry* Christmas." And she ran up to him as though it were a play and put her arms about him and kissed him closely, taking care of her hat and veil and at the moment of the kiss, as always, lapsing into a graceful position, like a statue for a pleasaunce. Then she hurried after the others, talking both forwards to them and backwards to Christopher.

To John, Christopher said, " *Merry, Merry* Christmas." His eyes were weighted with physical pain; and he trudged towards the dining-room with an old *Daily Express*.

A Share of the World

The general smell of polished cedar, old Hymnals, and coke fumes mingled with Jane's particular composite smell beside him as he went forward till his knees found the straw-stuffed texture of the kneeler. Whispers and clanks behind the organ. Beyond Jane, Lady Matlock was going through her bag for the Afghan clip in which she kept notes, and a memorandum.

His left shoulder touched Jane's and from that touch took on the mildest ache as though it were in a draught.

She wanted him to stay. To-night, he thought, his eyes shuttered with fingers. To-night, for with her there is only one way—the way which goes by the thing which never happened, the thought that was never thought, the motive that was certainly not the motive and the refusal that was really assent. She is a large and fine ship sailing to the warm south, he thought, and on her bridge is a hidebound narrow skipper plotting a course to the angular rigid north. But the ship is at heart southward.

If Mr. Hickman, the vicar, had ever seen six-inch, wedge-shaped nails hammered into the palms of hands and the arches of feet, he certainly could not have looked out over the church as he did. He pronounced words of two syllables on two different notes—man-ger, for instance, contained a musical interval about of a third, and Bethlehem had three notes, the last two of which were the same. The difficulties he had with his thoughts might have necessitated some play for time, but that did not wholly explain the mannerism. No. It was a substitute for the feeling that clearly should have been there—it was a dress to hide the nakedness of nothing.

Before, and six feet below him, Sir Wilfred had covered his eyes with his hand. Thus, only hearing, not seeing, Mr. Hickman, perhaps the provocation to spiritual pride was halved.

John tried to pray but the attempt did not thrive in the sun of Jane's favour, and the lush-growing weather of her proximity. Besides, he had had his church—his moment of " flow," as he called it. Pews had frequently been places where he had taken stock of that morose " web of himself " by which he felt trapped in a life-long pattern of failure and futility, inherited and conditioned beyond his powers to alter. But to-day he looked forward amongst other things, to lunch.

243

A Share of the World

Returning to the house, they went to their various rooms, passing Christopher in the hall, slumped behind a book of Chagall reproductions, his head on a level with his knees.

Jane's room was near enough for John to hear her footsteps (if she were shod) when she moved about, hear when she opened her door and hear which direction she took once she was in the passage. He usually left his own door open so as to miss no opportunity of meeting her in the passage.

Whenever her door-handle unclasped, he stood still, hoping she would come his way to the hanging cupboard in the passage outside his door, or to the head of the backstairs, past his door—or even perhaps in her present mood he believed, to his door for no other purpose than to see him.

He was looking down at the now-friendly lawn upon which he had hysterically (he told himself) and melodramatically thrown the lovely brooch which her hands had put back, when her door-latch unclasped and, as always, he went through his ritual hope, now gladly, as though—if she did come this way—it could only be to be kissed till they were late for lunch.

She came his way.

He went to the door in case her course should only be to the hanging cupboard or the head of the backstairs.

But she came to his door with a puzzled face, and an opened letter.

" What *is* this? " she said.

A twinge of dread came to him as he touched the paper. The jagged script was by a child yet not by a child. Did the twinge come from that or from the way Jane handed it to him, her manner?

DEAR MISS MATLOCK,

If you knew Mr. John Grant's War effut you would not have him under your roof, any more than his platoon would have him as their offiser.

A WELL-WISHER.

Is it a flooding or draining of blood—which comes at first glimpse over a precipice, when a car like a beetle brings home to the brain in sickness the intervening nothing.

A Share of the World

And how is that feeling related, as it is, to the ache of not being able to move in a nightmare? I want to but I can't; I mustn't but I want to. The same ache.

Of course, thought John, as the feeling ebbed and flooded in him, of course. What was I thinking of. This is what was coming, what was here all the time.

Like a prisoner at the window of his cell whom a stray beam of sun has lured and held in an hour's dream, he looked over his shoulder, and took in the familiar geography, the furniture of the cell.

Of course—how could it have been otherwise?

After a minute he said, " Bright! " The contempt in his voice was extravagant, false.

" Is it? " She had clearly thought so herself, " But, why . . . ? "

It never happened of course. The whole thing as it appeared, never happened. But how conceivably could that be made clear.

He said, " Your mother didn't give him notice, did she? "

" No. At least I'm pretty sure she didn't."

" I thought this letter might be revenge—for telling you all about the blanket business—and getting him the sack." He did not think so—but it would do: there would be a time and place for telling her the truth.

" But if my mother hasn't sacked him how does he know you told us? "

" Perhaps he doesn't. On the other hand, perhaps your mother's maid told him." John's voice sounded dispassionate and puzzled as though he was as much at a loss as Jane.

" But such an extraordinary thing to write—isn't it? And why to me? "

He looked at her, honestly and satirically. " Can't you guess? It's really rather sad if you can't guess."

She thought. They both stood in silence a moment before she said, " There's something about anonymous letters which gives me the creeps: it's the sudden revelation of hatred which may be everywhere—the paint flaking off."

" Yes," he said. " There is something about them."

She took it out of his hand. " I'd better show it to Mummy—
so she can get rid of him—to-day if possible."

He said casually—but too quickly, " Oh, why show her . . .
it'll only upset her."

They talked with their eyes and he admitted he'd sooner the
letter did not become public property. She began tearing it up
slowly. " Just as you like," she said. " It's not very pleasant, is it—
—however complete the lie? No. I was only thinking he *ought*
to go . . . after this."

She stood a moment with the pieces in her hand and he felt
something more was expected from him.

She said, " I thought I ought to show it you at once."

There was something warm about her manner as though this
letter, and bringing it to him, had been a bridge in his direction—
as when she brought the jewel.

" She believes it," he thought. " And she pities me."

" Yes," he said, " I'm glad you showed it to me. Thank you.
Do you believe it?

She was astonished.

He said, " I just wondered. People's ' effut ' in far countries,
under strange and extreme conditions—always a mystery, really."

He had become solicitous of his dress—he brushed his hair,
looked for something in a drawer, moved about. He said, " Bright's
most memorable ' effut ' was to go to sleep on sentry when we were
the spearhead platoon."

This sounded wrong. He tried to cover it up. " Bright! " he
said. " Brother Bright. I'll tell you a long story about him one day.
Then you'll see."

He spoke briskly, efficiently. Like a man who knew men, the
commander of a " spearhead platoon."

He did not know who or what he was trying to be. He knew
Bright would be in the dining-room. His appetite had gone.

17

THE lights were turned out, and the exclamation of praise was unanimous. " Neenie! *Too* lovely! "

All agreed: it had never been prettier, and the frost effect never more realistic. " So realistic," Christopher insisted to several guests, and he walked about with a snuffer at the end of a pole, stepping forward with exaggerated alacrity whenever a candle wilted to " save the situation."

Only the children were unexuberant about the tree. They looked at it with wonder but critically, and gauged the quality of the presents underneath. Two who could just walk stretched up their hands, and gugged twice, before becoming reconciled to the unobtainable.

The candles picked out faces, gave bright eyes and merged bodies with furniture in an undergrowth of shadow. The servants stood solid by the far door leading to the backstairs, hugging their means of retreat. They had packed round it as they came in so that the last to enter had difficulty in opening it enough for her to get through. Helen stood in front; Bright behind.

Jane crouched to be on a level with the children in the first rank and attempted to sow enthusiasm, at which some grouped tighter for solidarity, others allowed their eyes to follow her indications of splendour and marvel.

She was in scarlet velvet, with gold at wrists and neck, and her skin, the perfect pallor for candlelight, took an apricot bloom from the two hundred flames.

John watched her.

Between the tinsel doll and the peacock in painted glass Jane did not speculate on John's military record as he imagined she must, nor did she think of him, except once. Looking for Christopher to deal with a guttering candle, she caught sight of his face and it made her think, that one's face is not only " one's own look-out " —it is also other people's, and therefore one should try and keep it companionable. By her bed in the floral-bound *Common Place* book was written:

> " There is no duty we so much under-rate as the duty of being happy." "R.L.S."

Training the deep by the superficial—or as Christopher saw it —killing the deep with the superficial; putting the cart before the horse. At such a quotation he would have made the preliminary noise of vomiting, if eloquent with drink. If sober, his eyes would have receded yet farther into their holes like the tendrils of a snail having touched something antipathetic. At most, murmured, " Christ."

He stood there now with his pole by the lighted candles paying for his point of view, his " vision," which must have been similar to the side of each silver bauble—people with gaping mouths, egg-shaped skulls, bodies like hour-glasses one moment, puffer pigeons the next, grinning, leering, and undulating in a meaningless play—none of them " existing."

Under Jane's direction the children danced and perhaps her enthusiasm was stepped up because she knew what Christopher's vision of her was, and she wouldn't disappoint him. Indeed, with his pole, he did look at her as if there was a light which needed snuffing first.

John watched her, and beyond her he felt the man with whom he had been in the dark before now.

Bright behind the Christmas tree, Bright with the children, Bright's present in the pile under the Crib scene. How could he have ever doubted the reality—that " web of himself "—with Bright at the front door saying, " It's a small world." A small world! The world was one room and Bright was in it, with his pinched skull, knowing eyes, baby mouth and exhausted troubled breathing. Where else would that face appear—in a pulpit; or perhaps under moonlight Jane would turn to him and on her shoulders would be Bright's face.

A Share of the World

"Mister John Grant's war effut." John gave him the tommy-gun magazine in the back as the big man wrote and the toy-splattering sound was of the fat bullets smashing into him as into sticks and mud—for it was Bright who killed Corporal Bowen. Bright had wanted it to happen, whereas I offered my life afterwards for it not to have happened. Stood up, didn't I, waiting for one of those red spasmodic streams of tracer to slope down to me, dwell on me till it hadn't happened, till the futility was taken away? It is our desires, John thought, more than our practice which makes us what we are. But Bright lives on my desires, digests them to excrement with a smile—of affinity.

The room got darker as more and more candles became candidates for Christopher's snuffer. He seemed to enjoy ending their last feeble flames. The activity exempted him from making conversation, and gave him a chance to be a caricature of the helpful grown-up son at the Christmas tree.

"Mind, Mummy, your dress was nearly touching one. There goes another. Oh, dash it, a drop on the floor." He darted here and there. The children returned breathless to their parents, and Jane gave out the presents.

"*Now* the presents," said Christopher.

The central heating acted on and, increased by thirty bodies, became oppressive. The Vicar, clutching red crêpe paper in one hand and a book on gardening in the other, inquired in his two— sometimes three-noted voice, about Christopher's life in Oxford.

The lights went on amid praise of a last candle that was still tall.

"Gosh," said Christopher; "look at it!"

There were murmurs by parents to their children about home, bedtime—as though it were in the children's hands—mingled with compliments for Lady Matlock. The agent was heartily, loudly knowledgeable of the geography of the house, and maintained a manner of having been able to drop in between work.

The servants left with relieved faces returning to their element. But Lady Matlock shrieked, "Tuttie, bring everybody back. We haven't done the Crib. The Crib."

Jane was standing by the mantelpiece with a lighted match.

A Share of the World

" Now," she said, and Lady Matlock turned the lights off again.

As the flame took strength and burgeoned on the wicks of ten tiny candles, the Nativity of Christ, as reconstructed by Neenie with farmyard toys and old bits of stuff, emerged there, where the light was concentrated and utterly still. All the heads of cattle, all eyes of models, all tinsel stars and one bronze tiger (" why not, darling? ") directed inflexible attention at a manger where lay a celluloid doll taken from the children's old toy cupboard.

Murmurs, little cries, compliments. " Neenie, it's too lovely." And then Christopher's voice—out of the darkness, " Mummy—*he's too pretty.*" And then—because of the way it was said, although no one knew *how* it was said—no more compliments. Nothing—for a few noticeable seconds, then the compliments began again.

If the tiger had been in the manger, perhaps Christopher would have been satisfied. Christ the Tiger.

At the front door, Christopher was loud in farewells shouted through closed car windows at huddled figures—as he directed the backing, the turning: " Yes, yes, you're all right; left hand down, mate . . . Same to you—Happy New Year."

When the last tail-light had gone he stood alone in the moonlight and looked at Jane in the front doorway, cringing and hugging herself against the cold, and at John behind her.

" Couldn't we go somewhere? " he said. " Let's go to Hatchford."

" Come in or I'll close the door."

" Let's go to London," said Christopher, his voice histrionic. He was looking up at the clear stars. " Let's go anywhere. Anywhere," he shouted, and flung out his arms.

" Or let's play ' Murder ' and really murder someone. So ' realistic,' darling."

Jane shut the front door. " I don't know why Mummy thinks he's ill," she said. " He's just bloody."

Among rugs, tennis balls, old rackets, dog leads, and two rows of wellington boots, John put his hands on her arms above the elbows.

" Will you come up early, to-night? "

" Let's see, shall we? "

A Share of the World

He kissed her. " You see," he said, " There's something I want to tell you."

It was after dinner. The others were settling in the drawing-room and he had gone to the outside door to let Sir Wilfred's dog in. He opened the door, and caught his breath because there in the sky was memory; a full moon.

Like the apex of a pair of dividers planted on the paper of time, it stood there: one point on Italy five years ago, the other on Edgeby now. Five years almost to the day.

Anniversaries are more than mere arbitrary, man-made excuses for celebration or mourning: there is that inside us which makes anniversaries real, as though, like a wireless frequency, there were the event itself—and then at regular intervals, geared to the seasons fainter and fainter, harmonics almost repetitions of the same event tapering off into time.

What was there for him to celebrate or mourn—enough to make him take three steps outward on to the grass as though at the bidding of that cold, impassive planet?

A patrol inwards, the deepest patrol inwards, up to the white walls and the comprehensive smile? Determinist smile. Determining him.

Distances, he thought, looking at the suggestion of an espalier, had been hard to judge, and things had not been what they seemed; though in another sense they had been so intensely what they seemed that it had been another childhood—tree, wall, bang, boots—each object fuel for the eternal flame of wonder.

Was the tennis hut occupied?

I go now across that diaphanous flat which might be mist, which is lawn and then there is that noise which became religious because it meant death—the spandau-purr—in the distance; close up—a noise to jam the machinery of thought, and cut the wires of will.

It was a well-made gun to have been so eloquent—even far, far away, where you could smoke in the open night—and listen: perfectly eloquent. The quiet purr under the stars.

And then nostalgia came to him—as to the very old. Oh, life—precious, precious life.

A Share of the World

Yes, really, when you approached the matter like this—the failure mattered less.

Fragments read and heard came to him. Men are of various kinds as God made them, and there are some worse than me—yes, even worse.

Life does not belong to us. A poor Indian asleep in his boat above the monstrous steep of Montmorenci. Let what is broken so remain.

You could cross your legs and fold your hands in your lap with the palms upward and just, just smile—twenty centuries in one mouth. Yet *could* you—if you couldn't cross the lawn first.

He decided not.

He suddenly thought; I would like it again—I would like to have the whole thing again—and at that moment the door began to close behind him, the light on the lawn to diminish like a slide being put in at a lecture.

He turned.

" Oh, sorry sir; I didn't see you." Bright held the door open for him as though he were an important guest just arriving. And he moved towards it as though compelled. As he stepped in Bright said, " Clear as day isn't it, sir."

John looked at the little eyes. Of course—how could he have doubted it: they knew the date.

" Did the dog come in? "

Bright said, " I think that's him beside you, isn't it, sir? " And he breathed there, sibilantly, a few feet away.

Jane did not come up early. She went to bed when her mother did, after twelve.

At the ceremonial spot on the landing where each night the members of the Matlock family had for years left each other for the night as though the nine hours ahead were nine years—with close embraces and kisses on both cheeks from Neenie, and grave gentle ones from Sir Wilfred, and murmurs meaning love and marking the end of another minute subdivision of life, so much too short even in youth and health when one was so apt to forget—there, as usual, Neenie took long leave of Jane, but not of Christopher who had stayed downstairs behind his knees—or of Sir Wilfred who was, she hoped, sleeping.

She also took leave of John with a kiss for the first time. " *Dear* John," she said. " I *did* enjoy your description of your commanding officer. You were suddenly so like Osbert."

And John hoped she would say nothing more because behind him he could hear Jane's footsteps receding towards her door which he must pass to get to his own room, but which he must get to before she went in.

He did. But having done so, it seemed remarkable that he should have made the effort, for he crowned his achievement with the words " Good night " uttered normally and in the act of passing by.

" Good night," she said pleasantly, normally.

Lady Matlock's door closed. He turned back on her as though she were a pickpocket and seized her arm.

" Are you mad? "

" What d'you mean? " Her face was blank, nothing had occurred to her.

" Don't you really know what I mean? "

" No."

" You don't come up early—and then you go to your room like that: ' Good night.' " He imitated her.

" Well *you* said good night. I had to help Mummy with her patterns. I never said I *would* come up early. Anyhow, this is quite extraordinary. Let me go."

" But you *could* have."

" I can't leave Mummy alone."

He was aware of his ludicrous sibilance in the quiet passage, but he went on:

" What *do* you mean? Think—why don't you *think* what you're saying? ' I can't leave Mummy alone.' Why can't you leave Mummy alone? The reason is because you prefer talking about Noona for three hours to . . . You *like* talking about Noona. Noona and your father's tray. Sorry objects for jealousy! "

She went into her room and closed the door gently, almost sympathetically in his face.

He went in after her. She looked round angrily from the dressing-table; then with a sort of apprehension because his face had changed. He said " You believed that letter."

" Oh, John—please, *please* don't be so silly. I haven't thought about it since. Now, good night."

When the door was shut he told himself he'd gone in to tell her about " Bright." He hadn't told her, because if he had gone in and said, " I will tell you now," and she had said, " Not now," then she would have passed the whole night prey to doubt that there was something to tell. No. Perhaps that wasn't true. Perhaps he hadn't told her because it takes two to tell the truth and one of them cannot be a person who says, " I have not thought about it since."

At three o'clock that night—when there was no witness of Jane but herself, no one to see if she were being " wonderful," and when she was too tired herself to care what she was, or what anybody thought she was—some force in her which fatigue could scarcely touch kept her beside an ill cat in an attic spoon-feeding it with Brand's essence from a saucer. It had been partly the reason why she didn't " go up early."

Anyone who objected that Jane was inclined to wear moral armour and was careful to keep it polished only so that she could see a satisfactory version of her face in it, would have relented not at the sight of her kneeling by a packing-case in the small hours preserving reluctant life by a tendril of care, but at the sight simply of her eyes.

In them now there was mercy without any trappings—mercy and affinity with that mystery of life which is often most apparent, not in great, intimately tragic moments, but like this, when somebody else's cat pauses uncertain which way to take and you hold the spoon.

This expression in her eyes John overlooked when he was jealous of her father's tray.

It was the reason too why in 1947, in spite of her Lady Bountiful's manner and speech, she was welcomed naturally at village doors, as though the people sensed a *passe-partout* of the human heart beneath the Samurai carapace.

" Come on," she said gently—with two melted drops sliding to the fore of the teaspoon.

The drying bubbles of the last fit stayed on the cat's whiskers and the tip of its tongue looked trapped in its own teeth. Jane's little finger could not get in.

Life in it seemed centred only in the lungs and trying, heaving, to get out.

She put away the spoon, finally, and stood up. She moved the paraffin lamp nearer the wood. She looked down and it is, in a sense, no exaggeration to say she looked down, not at the cat dying, but at herself dying—and at that instant the character of her eyes assumed for a tranced moment, the character of the sea.

John believed she eschewed intimacy with anything that gave her pain, but her father sometimes regretted what he saw as her instinctive gravitation towards pain, wherever she found it. He had even said to Neenie that he hoped this characteristic would not involve her *blindly* with John.

Jane put out the light so that the pattern of the paraffin lamp's slots were magnified on the ceiling like the patterns children cut in folded paper with long scissors.

Outside was the moon—low and full. She looked at the dead planet's version of the garden, so different from the sun's. And she thought of John.

Fatigue, and being awake in the small hours, she found, could make you like an actor relaxing in the wings of your own life. It did not seem to be herself who would meet him in the bright light and bustle of the next day.

18

PITY, which had brought John several times to his knees beside wounded men during his two-days' war, and which had made it easier for him to feel affinity with the numerous unknown enemy, human beings of all kinds, than with the known Bright at his side, was a purge not available so far at Edgeby, near Hatchford. Telephone, Hatchford 4.

But futility, his own, which he had seen fulfilled in the dead face of the man he shot as dawn broke, and the smile of Bright above it, had followed him into a sterile pitiless peace. For on Boxing Day, at Edgeby, when he longed to lay down—as he imagined he could—the burden of his past at Jane's feet, or (to put it differently)—to lift from between them the barrier of the present which had cropped up from the past in a letter from Bright —he found himself obstructed by little things: a shoot during daylight, the Vicar to tea, and after dinner the sit-round in the drawing-room.

None of these events would have prevented a *tête-à-tête* had it not been for Jane, for whom the major feelings of the mind and the chief delights of the body were like the hundred million miles of cubic fire in the earth's heart—indicated by a few mountains which glow at night, otherwise, there, but buried, and the hotter for that.

In fact, even if she had reciprocated his love, the shoot, the Vicar to tea, and the sit-round in the drawing-room would still have "come first." But he did not realise this.

Her day was predestined. In the morning she would make her father comfortable, wait till the doctor came, hear whether he was to get up, prepare the shooting-lunch, take it out in the van, spend the afternoon with the guns, the neighbours, return, help her mother to entertain the Vicar—till six. Then because the cook was off, do dinner—four courses—then come down to it in a long dress as if she had not cooked it, but had gone to rest at the sound of the dressing-gong two hours earlier. Finally, after doing her father's tray, bed—already half asleep.

This dutiful, trivial, programme was for John the resurrection of the white house into which he could not move—the thing he couldn't affect. Futility.

Finding his vowed " I will " powered now by theory, now by desire, obstructed by a vicar coming to tea, a little tattle about Noona, he was goaded to the familiar brink of hysteria.

At breakfast Jane worried that Christopher, who was for the first time in charge of the shoot, would go late or not at all. She made several visits to his room and once came down with moist red eyes, too angry to pretend she was not.

" Poor Jane," John said, " you're even sports manager. Can I help? "

She was at the sideboard and the back of her hair shook, the limit of her intimacy with him when it came to a serious, that is to say, family matter. Suggesting sympathy with Christopher was the one unfailing means of upsetting her, and after last night he desired to have that effect upon her rather than none.

" Are you worried we won't get the usual bag—or what the neighbours will think of Christopher? "

She transferred her anger to him.

" I don't care how many pheasants you get. My father just happens to mind when his friends are kept waiting because his son has a hangover. That's all."

So he paid for his petty power—leaving for his day's shooting with her contempt ringing in his ears, and such a claustrophobia in triviality and irrelevance that rape occurred to him as one other healthy thing he couldn't do.

Christopher was finally unexpected; he shaved instead of ate and got straight into the car cursing. They were only a few minutes late.

The tweeded and mittened neighbours were already making jokes about the morning-after in the lee of three haystacks. Their dogs investigated each other with animation and sprinkled the wheels of cars and shooting-brakes, making yellow slush in the shallow snow.

Faced by people he had played cricket with, lunched with, danced at—for whose wives and daughters he had opened gates out hunting, fetched soup and scrambled eggs at dawn suppers, cars at weddings, rugs at point-to-points, Christopher dropped one shoulder lower than ever, limped, and spoke in the urgent, quiet drawl which his family said was Paul's. "Will you take the right? Will you stay here, Joe? They'll bring it this way. Would you mind walking this time, John?"

The familiar phrases at the familiar moments—every syllable was served up carefully on a toast of derision—so far-fetched that the neighbours never noticed, but thought he was in pain from alcohol.

Particles like shooting-stars drifted and vanished before John's eyes, and were there again, silver plasms, amoebas of light—things that a proper sleep would have dissolved. The first cock pheasant exploded from firs, chirking, towering, a vigorous curve of colour into the blue, over him.

Shouts from the wood; sticks stopped. "Over."

John's first shot might have been a blank cartridge, the second made the bird adopt a different sort of flight, contract, tense its wings, glide. "Mark," shouted voices; "watch that one."

It glided far over another wood and when last seen was still in the air.

Three birds flew over Christopher and though heralded by shouts, he only fired when too late—both barrels—and then in exhibition of despair and surprise opened his arms to the sky. Only at the last stand before lunch he killed seven consecutive high birds with his first barrel, so that they dropped like handkerchiefs with a stone in them. Then he avoided his fellow guns and came on with the beaters.

Jane brought lunch to a farm and stood before the briared porch like an American advertisement for Fall gauntlets. Hair with several different shades of yellow from wire gauze to umber sable like sand on a beach, wind and health or was it rouge colour in the cheeks which neighbours knew as pale, and background of a hamper, a new car and an old rustic. Youth, colour and genial welcome—only female among six males. For a Canadian Club, thought John, or even the cover of *Life*, close up enough for the regularity and sanitary condition of the pores to show up like selected sand.

Jane, although she had made dying easier for people behind screens in big wards, had no confidence with neighbours especially when it was " up to her and Christopher."

She did not look at John. She lavished questions on her brother as though they were close friends—had the birds flown well or whatever it was they did; had there been any to fly at all—wasn't that more important still? She never knew.

Christopher opened a sandwich analytically and murmured noncommittal noises, which, decoded, said she made him sick. She understood and became more nervous, more unnatural and more platitudinous. Also more talkative. Luckily, a confident bore in the shape of Major Miller was present. Soon all shrillness was absorbed in the foggy booming of long anecdote.

They were in the farm parlour, chill with disuse, in spite of a big fire. There was a picture called " Hope " on the wall, a woman with wings, one hand on an ornamental urn, the other upraised; and another called " Farewell "—a cavalier waving from the saddle to a face at a lattice window which seemed incomplete without an advertisement for old-fashioned humbugs.

The guns would go out of the room after lunch making their jokes, and Jane's presence, though out of earshot, would add zest to Major Miller's " Well, I don't know about you, Jock, but I'm the one who goes out among the cabbages and leaks."

And when they had got their guns they would follow Christopher who would drop them off one by one, each at a peg, and Jane would have to stand somewhere, with one of the guns. John looked at her to see if she would be coming to him. But she was talking to Major Miller—and her own nerves were a ventriloquist in whose lap she sat, speaking with a voice that she did not recognise and which stilled Christopher with a slow fingering of a cartridge. Thus, even her present, let alone her future intentions, were concealed.

A Share of the World

The keeper said. " First gun here, sir."

Christopher said, " John would you stay here? "

Jane had gone on a few paces so that Christopher, indicating the peg, was behind her. She looked out over the fields as though for something specific.

There was still time for her to turn round and come back.

John let his voice be heard with a question, showing where he was, dropped off at Number One peg, behind her.

He said, " Shall I move up when the beaters reach me? "

And while the keeper answered he saw Jane's back stay still as she continued search of the field for something specific.

When joined by the group she did look back, but without meeting his eyes.

At the last drive of the day she approached and he saw that she had known—from the first to this, the last peg.

He said, " Perhaps I shall hit something now."

She was relieved, seized the lightness, in spite of the tone. " You haven't been hitting much, have you? The last one parted your hair." Keep it like this, please, she asked, looking at him.

" It has been difficult to concentrate."

" Too much turkey." .

" No, the sight of you—with other people."

He ground it into her with his farouche stare, defying her to be " light "—or to pretend that he had no claim on her to justify such a protest. She weighed the claim; admitted it existed—just. Though God knows why—four, five days.

" Don't you see I have to talk to those people who have come to shoot."

" Christopher, for instance."

She said nothing. A slow hen came over low. He got it messily. She said, " Don't you see . . . I was so pleased to see Christopher out . . . doing it all—I thought he might be enjoying something at last. You must see. This shoot—every year for years—and Christopher and I there for years, as far back as I can remember. We built a jump in that field one spring. I wanted to remind him; talk to him about it—see if there wasn't some common ground— if one went far enough back. Try and nail the lie that our life here was all false—by pointing to a place in a field where he was happy."

" Where a jump stood? "

" Yes. Where a jump stood."

" And what was the result? "

" Oh, that voice. That Ye-ee-es. How Paul talks. And then that ghastly selfconscious silence."

The proximity of her body, as always, began to wean him from the bitter suck of theory and analysis, save him from the eye of satire. Even her preoccupation with Christopher, put as she was putting it now, seemed reasonable.

He even weighed his five-days' proximity against Christopher's twenty-five years; his hysterical attachment against old consanguinity; and found it natural that though Bright's letter had filled his house of thought she had not found room for it in an attic.

She went on about Christopher, about what " it " has meant Father.

And listening to her, he suddenly felt her not so much " wonderful " as weak, worried and available. With this came a sense of power. Aggressive resolution fell away. He said, " Poor Jane."

She talked reluctantly because it was " dreadful that one should have to talk like this about one's brother." The obstinate mouth let things out as though they were lucky and the blue eyes were at the same time, tough and merciful. ¡The movements of her hands continued even in thick gloves, and the tremors and little movements in her face reminded him of the bridlings and wincings, the living on endless edge, of racehorses.

Yet, he thought, she is alkali, the warm wash of the earth, full of real blood, real tears and female ambivalence; and she is the longed-for neutralisation of the intelligence. With her I might begin to *live*—that is to say, exist with a permanent feeling of immortality and cyclic return. She's like the characterless building that marks a well or shaft.

He rambled on with her, speculating sympathetically about Christopher. He killed a high pheasant.

She said, " That was better, wasn't it? "

Her face underwent a special tremor for the directness of the remark, the intimacy it involved—and she even added a nervous laugh to modify the impact of having referred to something he had done. She had come closer.

So this was how. It had often seemed probable that no effort was most effective—as in floating; but—also as in floating—it had seldom been possible. The reflex was to fight.

The sun like a blood orange above birches, lightly sugared with snow, sank towards a house which naturally emerged from brambles and willows, like something growing. The individual noises made by different beaters reminded him of shoots at Stiley as a child when his father, a king—without effort—among keepers, and looking like them, had seemed in those days a hero in every branch of human activity, his ability to kill two high pheasants in different parts of the sky in the same second, being merely one proof.

Silence except for the tapping of the sticks. He felt a sense of peace and continuity.

A woodcock parted from the shadows, batlike, and a particular cry went up, added to by the guns because light was failing and because it was probably the last shot of the day. And because the bird was going towards a pretty girl Major Miller added a hefty " Timber."

At John's first shot it fell untidily and Major Miller shouted a hoarse, " Hurrah—don't worry, they don't run."

The bird stood up and examined the changed possibilities of movement. One wing trailed. Then slowly—as though there were all the time in the world, it began to walk back to the wood.

John went towards it and it hastened, turned to its left and fell over its wing. Then it started off again. He grabbed at it and it used its good wing to do a fluttering, saving jump.

Jane, five yards away, cried. " Oh, hurry, hurry. Oh, do it quickly."

He made another grab and when he missed again tried to put his foot on the bird. He trapped two feathers. As though only then aware of its danger, the woodcock renewed at least part of the power of flight. It fluttered and jumped twenty yards, ending tangled in snow and its own wing, and perhaps through exhaustion unable to do anything but wait.

A Share of the World

Major Miller shouted, " Tally ho! "

The blood-stained snow was like hospital cotton-wool, and its neat head was raised, watching him with an eye like a glossy bead. The marking of the feathers was something no designer could evolve in the way of complicated harmony. A last palpitation of will to live threw it lop-sided with its long beak under its breast. He swung its head like a heavy tassel against his heel and after the third swing looked to see if the intelligence had gone out of its eyes; and he flung it to a man with a game-bag.

The peace had gone out of him. Instead there was pity—warm flowing pity for life taken—and the bone-stump in the snow, and the eye with only one sight more to see: Himself. The eye which was also his eye.

Saliva in his mouth increased, was sweeter. He could at that moment have prayed, because love as usual had come to him through pity.

Yet at that moment, if another woodcock had flown out of the wood, he would have fired at it.

" Poor woodcock," said Jane. " I hate it when they're wounded."

" I shall give up shooting one day," he said.

" You? Never."

Although given up to another mood which had gone beyond her, he was surprised and interested; she had some sort of opinion about him. He wondered what.

" Perhaps you're right. Perhaps I shoot for the pleasure of contrition."

" How German. How disgusting."

" Surely the opposites are mutually indispensable, God and the Devil the same person." He smiled, " No. I shoot because there is excitement in that life up there against my skill, and satisfaction in the victory. I'm sorry when a thing is close, looks at me and reminds me of a link . . . Very sorry; sympathy is then a reflex; but when it is out of reach and self-willed—there is excitement and the desire to destroy."

He looked at her and smiled. " So come closer."

A Share of the World

Lady Matlock went from face to face, on the landing, from John to Jane to Christopher—kissing and not letting fall her arms in between each kiss, or ceasing to coo affectionately, kissing two darlings and one dear, good night.

Half an hour after the last passage light had been put out, the last door shut, John knocked on Jane's door and went in.

She was reading, hunched up by the bedside light and, as he closed the door behind him, he said quietly, " May I come in? "

Since he could so easily dispense with permission, she seemed to spare herself the bother of speech; she watched him blankly come towards her in his shabby dressing-gown.

" Darling," he said, " I've come to say good night—properly."

She wore spectacles for reading and her face was covered with grease which she took off before turning out the light, with a paper handkerchief. Her face contained no greater welcome than a suspended interest in the page.

It was a fact known only to herself that she would have enjoyed possessing beautiful slaves of both sexes to stroke her and massage her while she closed her eyes while she thought of certain imagined and actual people, and of certain objects—one of which was nothing less innocent than a large apple.

Therefore, when occasion offered the equivalent of the slaves— as it often had in the shape of doctors, medical students, sons of squires on hunt-ball balconies, and latterly John when convenient, she submitted with satisfaction and closed eyes. It was convenient now.

But John imagined himself selected, welcomed, even though she said nothing.

He took off her spectacles and soon her book slid to the floor, as he turned back the bedclothes to get in.

Some tautness came to her then and her legs remained like the legs of a chatelaine of her tomb—or like those of a cheap toy sentry, all one.

" You can't stay long," she said.

But her private dreams reasserted mastery and she enjoyed a relaxation which resolved the determined lines of her face into a childish and good-natured blank.

A Share of the World

" Your hands are asleep at last," he said.

At the sound of his voice, as though it were an unpleasant reminder of his presence, her face hardened.

" Please don't speak," she said sincerely. Then realising what she had said, added sweetly, insincerely, " It's—it's so peaceful—the silence."

Don't speak? He looked at her. Some emanation from the body beside him, from the face with shut eyes confirmed his sudden suspicion: he was, even at this moment, excluded.

" Jane," he said carefully, " It's so difficult to know with you—but there's something I must ask. Are you making a little progress—now, at least? "

" What do you mean? " she said.

" Are you any nearer being in love? "

She said nothing.

" You lie there," he said, " but . . ."

" But what? "

" It's as though . . . you were alone."

She shook her head with closed eyes.

He said, still carefully, " Don't speak? Is that it? Don't intrude? "

Her face hardened—with resentment for words, planning, reason—all that would mislead.

" Please don't spoil to-day," she whispered. " Please." This reached him with its obvious sincerity, and gentleness. But it could not stop him. " Don't speak! "

Like the first sound of a train on a quiet night, the murmur of oncoming hysteria had crept into his voice. She lay there now like the white house, like the smile of Bright, and everything that he could do was nothing. He now *knew* she had been thinking of something, perhaps *somebody* else.

" You just like being stroked and titillated? "

The resentment in her face condensed into pain, and she shook her head from side to side, meaning stop.

" You like being stroked. And you like talk—provided it's beside the point. But if we talked here—it might not be beside the point. It might be about myself—or about yourself intimately,

265

so you say, ' Don't speak.' Perhaps Christopher's right. Perhaps you not only ' don't exist '—you don't want to."

Tears burst out under her shut lids getting mixed with eyelashes and obliging her to blink and grope clumsily for a handkerchief under the woolly rabbit with a missing eye.

" You'd better go," she said. " Please."

It needs a lot of affection and sometimes a little humour to make comely and dignified the withdrawal from a bed of love where even under ideal conditions the splendid butterfly enters and the commonplace grub leaves. As it was—in tears and anger and the confusion of internal and external conflict, squalor thrived.

In his dressing-gown he said from the door:

" Yes, I'd better go. And from this house."

" I don't know," she said. " Perhaps you had."

" Then I'll go to-morrow."

He said it as though it would matter to people in China and South America, old men fishing with bamboos by the Seine, Burmans sowing rice, and Ruhr miners. Then he closed the door.

19

JOHN told Lady Matlock at breakfast with apologies for not having told her sooner, inventing some excuse, and she put her hand on his arm with an exclamation of sorrow and surprise.

" Dear John," she said. " You too! "

Christopher was going. Everyone was going—" before the decorations come down "—and Jane would " have no one." She permitted herself to hint that John " ought " to stay a bit longer; and nibbled a nail sadly comparing this to other Christmases, and in a sudden *tour d'horizon*, blurting all out, wondered whether this spring she could face running the village school play " what with poor darling Wilfred and everything." What indeed was happening, what worm now frequented the Edgeby bud which had once bloomed for four seasons annually. Instead of many happy guests staying, Osbert among them, here was the one and only face going, Osbert's son, a little dreary but *so* good looking, and adoring Jane in a clumsy way. Still; Christopher had come. One *must* be thankful for anything.

Her thoughts, like her speech and letters, were full of warm underlining. If weakly ideal in one easy, satirical sense, they were strong in another. They would have survived almost unmodified a year on the Burma-Siam Railway sleeping among cholera faeces. She would have written on the P.o.W. letter form that it was " *so* cruel, darling, it broke one's heart and tried *one's faith*." Then, she would have quite soon died like some animal in captivity, not of disease but of unhappiness, of ugliness of incongruity, she couldn't live on.

Jane came to John's room while he was packing. " My father says would you like to take some game? "

A Share of the World

" You remind me a little of Moses," he said.

She wondered what he meant.

" You are always coming down with the Tablets—from Father."

Was it meant funnily or nastily? She didn't know. She only knew she was tired of twisted young men; brothers and strangers.

" Thank you," he said. " I'd like to . . . While I'm here," he went on, closing the door, " there's something I want to say. Are you taking me to the station? "

She was taken aback: that particular argument with her mother had only been won a few minutes ago.

" No? I thought not. So this is our last opportunity of talking together."

She indicated by silence that the talking had always been his concern, and must remain so. She stood by the edge of the bed and looked curiously at his packing, as though it explained everything.

" Falling in love," he said, " is not a tap you can turn on when you like. How can it ever come to a person for whom ' there's a time and place for everything '—like you? "

Why must he always be like this at ten o'clock, when everything from bedclothes to breakfast dishes were stale. All theory bored her, and the way he spoke of love was like someone singing out of tune—a wrongness you didn't need to be musical to detect.

For a few minutes yesterday afternoon as the sun sank behind birch and snow, she had wondered if she was in love with him. That bird was now flown—but she still occasionally looked up at her sky, vaguely as though it might come back from any quarter— from his packing perhaps. He looked ill; how much better if he had been.

The discrepancy of their thoughts came home to him and his face tightened with the rage of being unable to affect that beautiful and disciplined face. Like a figurehead, he thought, on a ship called *Duty*—wooden loveliness cleaving the waves of life unflinching, always emerging bright and determined from every head-on shock. Not I, but this ship I'm part of—whose course is clear.

How stupid she must be if she thought the course of duty was clear.

A Share of the World

" Buried," he said; " you're buried. You think you help people by your example to be unselfish; on the contrary, you drive them to the opposite by your suffocating example. Intimacy is a talent. You have none."

Her face then indeed became like a figurehead, looking over far seas of paradox—which she had crossed this way and that in adolescence, the memory of which he revived. Her fingers moved, her breath went out, not smoothly, but in stages.

" Love," he said, " is not the farthest, hardest, imaginable thing, not a pin-prick in the distance for your striving; it is under you everywhere, demanding abandonment, relaxation. That is the meaning of ' Resist not Evil.' " Gospels which he did not practise suggested themselves naturally as tools with which to obtain leverage on her pure, shut character. " I love you," he said quietly, " that is the hook on which I wriggle. I try to explain to you—that you force and will force, not only me, but anyone who loves you to behave extremely—hysterically. You'd like a time-table, suitable love-affair of mutual self-denial—which, where love is concerned, is like having a service without God. Like the one you attended on Christmas Day."

She said, " This is the fifth day we have been under the same roof. I don't know what you're raving about. Is it that—that I haven't said I'll marry you? "

She flinched at the sound of the direct word " marry " from her own lips—bridled with an interior flutter of nerves necessitating a more than ever controlled expression.

To John her question conjured up a prosaic picture of herself saying " Yes." He repudiated it. No, no, he told himself—that was the smallest part of it all. She must love him. They must be like one. He imagined an intimacy which could dispense with " Yes."

" No," he said. " Not only that. To have to share your affections with father's tray would be a new and subtler department of hell. I want you all, everything. And again everything. Because that is what I will give—have given."

He imagined that he had " given " everything; and he imagined an intimacy of which the main characteristic was *no difference*. Did

he mean by this—not an intimacy at all but a duplication, reflection
—of himself?

She thought, " Father's tray." He's back to that. The incredible,
unpardonable (two of her most used words) selfishness of not seeing
what that meant, what the possible death of a parent, and death
of someone she would have loved even if he had not been her father,
someone noble, sweet and humorous, who all his life had been
nothing fashionable, and who had been there for her since the
beginning as constant and reassuring as the sky, and the earth;
someone who was now pathetic beyond belief, because suddenly
something which he had never seemed—mortal, even weak. . . what
his death would mean. And this boy said " Father's tray " like
that. Why did she linger in his room?

She lingered.

" Don't I know, Jane," he said, with a quiet look of truth-
treachery, " what this Christmas must have been for you. But
there again—had you accepted it, instead of sublimely resisting
it . . ."

" I must go," she said, " I really must. You may be right.
Perhaps I am buried. In hospital I had to do a good deal of burying
—of myself—in order to prepare other people for burial. Perhaps
it'll wear off and, like a mole, I'll come up for air—or is it exercise?
No. Please let me go."

He stood in front of her. " If you come south—you'll let me
know."

" Yes," she said, " I'll let you know."

" Then after to-day," he said, " it's not the end? "

" Haven't I just said . . ."

He took her in his arms. " No," he said. " It won't be the
end, and even if you tried to make it that—it wouldn't be."

If melodrama—boring, she thought: if meant—embarrassing.

" This Christmas " was not yet over for Neenie. The sharpest
sting was in its tail tip.

" What is it, darling? " she said, for Christopher, noiseless in
his socks, had appeared in the middle of the drawing-room without
apparently ever having been at its edge.

A Share of the World

"My shoes." He whispered it, yearned it in his special drawl. "I left them here last night."

"But darling, have you only one pair?"

"Yes."

Neenie looked sad. Wilfred gave him two hundred a year and he had the full government grant—and he had only one pair of shoes. Almost certainly he would be hungry in London. And why, WHY didn't he want to stay?

"Darling," she said, "which train are you taking?"

"The evening one."

"Not the same as John's?"

"The evening one."

"Then we'll have to leave at six."

At least she would have the drive with him, alone for fourteen miles. She might get *into* him then. Find out.

"No, Mummy, it's all right, thank you. I've got a lift."

Neenie didn't at first understand. When she did, she knew what to say. After all—there was a limit. "*Of course* I'll take you in, darling. I've never heard such nonsense."

As always when she exploded the blast was exhausted before the last words, which became querulous and interrogative, as though she were saying, Surely I'm right, aren't I, to put my foot down here, and to have spoken those first words so bluntly? Aren't I?

Then in plaintive curiosity, and apology:

"But, darling love, a lift? Who on earth with?"

"Bright."

"White? *Bright!*" Now she was again certain. "No, darling, I've never heard anything so silly. Of course I'll take you in."

She straightened her back and put three periodicals tidy with one movement.

"Mummy, I sometimes don't understand. Father wouldn't let me take the car into Hatchford the other evening because of the petrol business. Now you won't let me save you the same distance."

He was twenty-three. She wanted to cry but controlled herself. "Darling love, I too don't understand. Daddy didn't want

271

you to motor twenty-eight miles of petrol—by yourself—for a
drink, and how many drinks . . . and then back . . . by yourself. Isn't this different? A little different? " Let him, she prayed,
agree—just this once.

Blinds seemed slowly to cover Christopher's eyes. He no longer
looked at her.

" I've promised," he said. " Would you want me to ' break
my word ' ? "

He got up and resumed search, furtive, half-hearted and
short-sighted because his spectacles were upstairs.

Lady Matlock bit her lip and went hurriedly out of the room.
A moment later Wilfred was holding her in his arms, saying:

" Don't, don't. You must think of him as ill."

Wilfred came down to lunch wondering whether, if he were well,
he would go to Christopher and say, " You will do as your mother
wishes or . . ." Or what? Or never come here again, or you'll
not get another penny? The wind was already out of these sails.
His son was twenty-three. He smiled gently at the absurdity of his
thoughts. He had not raised his voice for fifty years. Nevertheless,
in health he could have coped—perhaps. But now his " sphere
of influence " did seemed suddenly constricted. For instance, he
moved in the house feeling, Yes, and this is the way to the door, on
this side of the little table, because on the other side the chair makes
the space narrow, and now along the back of the sofa, over the
carpet fringe and on to the different surface of the boards, and so
to the handle cold to touch. It was a little like childhood, the floor
a world, lunch-time an event, uncongenial effort a persecution.

He warmed his hands on his plate and looked round the table
with a dry smile. Neenie, as always, like an animal in new straw,
was arranging her place to her satisfaction, the nearest silver group
of pepper, salt and mustard, a little farther out; the knives and
forks a little more separate from her plate, the flowers a shade off
centre so she would see Wilfred without having to lean into her
neighbour's face.

Jane, having heard how Christopher was getting to the station,
sat pregnant with the unspoken piece of her mind she was giving him.

A Share of the World

Christopher's head was bowed, sparing present company the undisguisable opinion of his eyes.

Sir Wilfred said, " Are *you*, John, also going with Bright? "

Neenie sighed, and said, " It would be admirable if he took people one didn't particularly want to drive with."

Wilfred often had to pick up the bits after his wife. Even ill he was ready.

" Nasty one for you, John."

Neenie lamented: how could he have thought she meant John? She was thinking of Gladys; it would have been admirable if Bright had fetched Gladys last week.

" The admirable Brighton," said Wilfred.

Neenie said, " I may be very old fashioned, darling, but how do you reach the state of affairs in which it's possible for the butler to offer you a lift? Where did you meet him . . . to speak to."

" He lives here," said Christopher.

Neenie laughed—that had been like his old self. A spark, if only the context could have been different. She said, " But I never see you talking to him."

" We talk in the Rose and Crown."

Oh. Of course. She looked a little hurt; she didn't *mind* him going to the village pub but . . .

" What d'you talk about, darling? Is he good company? "

She tittered nervously at the idea of Bright being better company than herself, than darling Wilfred. She couldn't imagine what servants found to talk about except " us," and Bright couldn't have talked about " us " to Christopher—or could he?

" As a matter of fact, we talked a good deal about John."

The food in John's mouth became tasteless material the stomach didn't want.

" What fun for you. What did he say? "

" He seemed to think you told us he had been court-martialled for stealing blankets, without mentioning that he was acquitted."

John said, " I'm quite sure if he *was* acquitted, there must have been some mistake."

He shouldn't have spoken with so much feeling; he felt Jane's eyes on him.

A Share of the World

Sir Wilfred folded his hands in a new position looking as he did so at the wall over his wife's head. His dog moved and he turned towards it almost gratefully and stretched out a hand.

But Neenie said, " How *fascinating*, darling—do go on . . ."

Then as Bright came in, " The snow has all gone."

Bright breathed sibilantly as he bent by each of them, offering treacle tart.

When he went Wilfred said, " Shall we go on talking about the snow? "

A little laugh from Neenie faded quickly from lack of support. Silence. All Christopher's silence. His destructive stare sank to the Saxe pattern—his blight had triumphed.

Neenie said, " Or the new way of getting to the station."

Christopher's face surfaced smiling. He had once had " such a sweet smile." He had of course altered it; but without complete success. It was now half-leer, half-sympathy—with head tilted suiting the drawl, yearning for some obscure significance.

" I don't see what's wrong. I'm saving you twenty-eight miles of petrol. That's what you wanted the other night."

He never looked at his father.

Wilfred managed a spark of energy. " Then, old boy " (kindly, not heartily), " if you don't see what's wrong then that's just very sad, and we needn't waste any more breath on it."

Though still up and about when Christopher left, Sir Wilfred did not go to the front door to wish him good-bye as he climbed into the mauve Vanguard which, driven by a middle-aged artificial blonde, came for Bright.

But Neenie went out and embraced him on what she called " the perron ", bitter experience though it was, and not helped by the peculiar proprietorial smile of Bright as he stood holding the door open.

Jane watched from a landing window. She had tears of indignation and anger in her eyes; and John watched Bright holding the door open, and felt that Bright knew he was watching.

" And, darling heart," said Neenie, with tears in her eyes, " send me the poem. Promise. Otherwise I shall get John to send it."

A Share of the World

She wanted it from Christopher, from Christopher, Christopher. A tear escaped and she waved.

When the car was out of sight she went to Wilfred who was doing *The Times* crossword puzzle, with short pauses between each clue, and frequent careful markings.

She said tearfully, " If he could have said something—explained. That was all I wanted . . . . this time, a good talk."

Sir Wilfred took off his spectacles with his right, pencil hand, and placed the left round her nearest fingers. Then he looked into the fire.

" After Christmas" and " the operation ", he realised, had this moment arrived for his wife.

The logs hissed, the cyclamens bloomed, the Christmas tree decorations shone at the end of the long room, Neenie's sobs were like a puppy on the wrong side of the door, and Sir Wilfred, who had once been earmarked for highest non-political office in the service of his country, sat there, ill.

Before leaving Edgeby, John wrote a letter—to America.

Sir Wilfred, devotee of the *New Yorker*, and especially the tail-pieces, had never heard that that newspaper had once brought out a skit edition of *Punch* in the twenties, when *Punch* was still producing large carbon drawings of Charwoman and Mistress with eight lines of dialogue.

John put " airmail " and " urgent " on the envelope. This was the way that felt right: take Jane in Father, Jane in Edgeby, and go away.

She saw him off from the door and remained waving till the taxi was not only out of the gate but also till it had reappeared, as all cars leaving Edgeby did, on the road a hundred yards away.

Even more than from the friendly look in her eye as they had touched each other's hands, John took hope from this apparently reluctant last sight, this lingering on the reappearance of his car, far off.

He could not know, and for once did not pessimistically guess, that she made it a point of honour to remain on the doorstep, until the conveyance of any departing guest had disappeared for the second and last time.

20

WHEN she was no longer under the same roof, when he could not hear her footsteps on the landing above, or sit on a sofa with a space she might come to, or hear her moving in her bedroom from his bedroom, then he could not remember what she looked like or even what she was like. He got panic in the thought that he had never really known her. " Who is she? " he asked himself —as though there were an answer other than her name.

He now became frantic at the thought of her occupied with her father's illness, her brother's behaviour, and if with him at all then only through Bright's letter. He imagined her wondering why he had not told her of Bright's acquittal. Did she think he was ashamed; hiding something? At once he wanted to write to her, and left his cousin's tea-table in the middle of a conversation in which he had been taking part. He climbed over knees and went to an empty room. (As usual he was staying in somebody else's large country house—a condition into which he had been born, and which seemed to survive war and social revolution.)

After affectionate preliminaries, as pertinent as a dentist talking of the weather, he wrote, " Even allowing for your many preoccupations, you must if you have thought of me at all, have wondered at my manner when Bright's name was mentioned at lunch that last day. Darling, I said all along that in time I would tell you about that man. I will still do so . . . Meanwhile . . ."

He stopped, looking with hostility at the page. Then he tore it up and wrote instead, " I think you ought to show that letter from Bright to your mother before she goes south. He's hardly a creature to harbour under your roof if it can be avoided."

Why had he not been able to tell her?

A clear memory of her face answered him.

A Share of the World

Back at Oxford mood succeeded mood. He gave each one a chance to scrabble at that distant wall.

She wrote that her mother had enough to worry about without Bright's letter. He was relieved.

The next day his anxiety took a "literary" turn. He wrote, "You are the last wound and the cure for all wounds. You are at one and the same time what I want, and the reason why I cannot have. In fairy tales you would be guarded by a dragon, or an impossible task of counting grain before dawn; in 1946 you are no doubt in love with your father. I think I would know better how to cope with the grain."

In spite of this apparently low opinion he held of her, he continued to see her husband or lover as "a man"—in other words not himself, because he still could not imagine himself as that.

No proofs of masculinity were wanting, but they were not enough. What was he then? Less . . . and more; yes, both less, he told himself, and also more than a man.

God within me, had been the increase of which he had been conscious when listening to music and in moments of pity during the war; now, another afflatus, from some other source, but similar in sense of expansion, allowed him to inform himself with passionate conviction that if he was less, then he was also more than a man. And between the two feelings of the world filling him, and himself filling the world, he made no discrimination.

Jane answered every third letter. "Dear John," on top and, "Love, Jane," at the bottom, usually sandwiched some plea not to make things harder than they already were—for himself (she put first) and finally herself. She did not think she need feel guilty on many of the charges he made. Perhaps she was "a bit buried," as he so often insisted. She had been unhappy nursing (except when actually *nursing*) "even though my patients loved me!!!" And in the same letter, before the end, she found another niche for exclamation marks. "Perhaps I'm frightened of becoming a nurse for life!!!"

It surprised him. She seldom attempted a joke, still less the intimate contact a personal remark involved.

"Do I need a nurse?" he replied. "I at least can run a

277

temperature. Isn't the patient who can't the more seriously ill? "

He wrote to her as if her " yes " would be something apocalyptic, like death, something after which there would be nothing predictable; to all earthly intents and purposes an end. Perhaps to protect himself from such a death through achievement, he fashioned an exacting definition of " yes."

" If you were to say ' yes ' and then continue as you are now, changed only by wearing a ring and receiving a collectable number of flattering letters, then I hope I would have the strength to give you back your ' yes.' Darling, I want you but a different you—a you that could forget your father's life for a chance of laying your hand in mine."

The back number of the *New Yorker* arrived for Sir Wilfred, on the eve of departure by ambulance for a London nursing home. Jane's acknowledgment started, " Dearest John."

Was it as simple as that. He did not want to believe it. He wanted to be loved, to be known for some essence that had nothing to do with whether or not he obtained for her ill father an old journal.

At first he restrained himself, finally he must say it all. " What does dearest mean, except most dear and, if most dear, why so remote with your mental legs always as tight together as your physical? Please spare me the casual superlatives with which ' society ' supercharges its jaded talk. And please say outright soon whether this change to dearest means even half what it says. A more or less calculated kindness to your father is surely not sufficient grounds in itself for such rapid promotion. Or is it? If so he shall have a bound collection of every *New Yorker* that ever was."

Her reply started " Dear John," and said among other things, " please, please, please try and control yourself for *your own sake*." He would only make himself more and more unhappy.

He replied : " Unhappy! I see you are beginning to pity me. Be careful—out of that might come any lie; out of that might come the ' yes ' which I ought but would not have the strength to give back —the refinement and holy of holies of this particular purgatory."

He did little else but think about or write to her. " If I believed I'd get a first in you I'd go boating and be better company."

A Share of the World

Apart from letters, the only link with her was Christopher. John saw him often in the distance, in duffle-coat, loitering beside the modern poetry in Blackwell's, drinking coffee with Paul or louring drunk in corners at parties.

John always sought then regretted contact with him. Like the envelopes which contained Jane's letters, the sight of him stimulated hope of some unimagined satisfaction. In each case disappointment was acute. The letters were vacant of intimacy (of " shape " John told himself; they might have been by anyone to anyone) and Christopher had merely to say " Jane! " for blight to touch her image.

In the street one day Christopher said, " I expected to see you in London yesterday."

" In London? "

" Jane is there—with my father."

She promised, she promised, she had sworn on love's crucifix she would tell him if ever she came to London.

And was she staying on in London? Where? But that would be her hotel, where now; at the station soon but where now—this minute?

At a nursing-home.

How out of touch in its slowness the operator's voice sounded, asking for London, telling John to put in two and eightpence and press button A. The sister on duty said she would see but she thought Miss Matlock had left. John wondered whether by ringing up the loudspeaker at the station he could get her brought to the telephone. Perhaps the train stopped at Oxford.

But she hadn't left and there was her voice, happy, and when she heard who it was—still happy, but no happier.

He said, " You said you'd let me know. I could have met you."

She explained. She had come in the ambulance, she had not had a minute, she was going back now. Wasn't it wonderful? They thought the operation had been a success. Her voice was aerated with relief, almost glee. She had not noticed the tone of his protest; she could not notice anything disagreeable in the world.

A Share of the World

He said he was so pleased, and he was pleased; yes, he was pleased. He tried to imagine Sir Wilfred's kind old mandarin's face, to think of it going on for a long time yet and so feel truly, not conversationally pleased. Then he came back to the point, and soon the crescendo of his pitched voice over the long-distance wire mounted to an inhuman falsetto.

She protested, realising slowly—his incredible objection, his unpardonable lack of interest in the only thing in the world that mattered.

" I'm going to ring off John, because this is doing you no good."

Even Jane's friends found her voice unrecognisable on the telephone. The threat, spoken in the voice of someone he had never heard before, exacerbated the fear that he had never really known her, that he had merely known some invention of his own necessity.

He ceased to make sense shouting, " Jane—I must hear you. I must hear you. I must, I must." Then, torn between the desire to listen to hear if she were still there, and the desire to say something which would keep her there, he floundered between not enough words to make sense and not enough silence to hear.

At last he listened.

She had gone. " Jane," he said quietly.

" Have you finished, Oxford? " said a voice.

" I was cut off," John said. " You cut me off."

He asked for the number again. The sister answered. Miss Matlock had left for the station.

To the letter he wrote that evening and subsequent letters Jane did not reply for a week.

Then she wrote two lines.

His scout placed the letter as usual on the spot where John looked whenever he entered his room, even at midnight or after then when there was no post, and on Sundays.

DEAR JOHN,

I thought you might be interested to read this—the paragraph I have marked.

Love,

JANE

Enclosed was a letter to herself from her father. The handwriting was like a child's, only regular. Not a redundant line or flourish, either for gracefulness or out of gusto, or bombast, or style, but all regular like the printed model handwriting in a copybook set between the lines like a musical score, the lower loops of g's and y's being identical.

MY DARLING GIRL,

I wish the parents of Miss Hislop, my nurse, had been so fortunate when begetting a nurse, as Neenie and I. She comes in when I would she wouldn't—and vice versa. And she never, never smiles. Can it be me?

Your mother was under my bed looking for her spectacles when matron paid her first ceremonial visit. While I was being formally questioned about my health and comfort a voice from down under said, " There's a lot of dust here considering." And then, " I'm so sorry, nurse dear, I didn't see you." A right and left I think.

Felicity visited me yesterday and said she had met Christopher at the Gages'. She found he had " such charm." Poor chap, he really is dogged by misunderstanding.

My dear daughter, I hope you are happier about John. I have always thought these lines very true.

> *He who binds to himself a joy*
> *Doth the winged life destroy*
> *He who kisses the joy as it flies*
> *Lives in Eternity's sunrise.*

Thank you for bringing me here so competently. It is not a bad place as such places go. They moved me again and I have seventeen chimneys and two fire-escapes to look at over flowers from Edgeby. The management keep the knives out of sight. We are reading *The Heart of the Matter*, a distressing book with a misleading title which Neenie has corrected to *The Hell of it All*. Certainly it is not a Christian work, being practically uncoloured by either faith, hope, or charity as I understand those words.

Your loving
FATHER

A Share of the World

John replied that the quotation from Blake chosen by her father was one of which he must often have had need in the face of his wife's personality. Had not her real love been the stage—the profession she was never allowed to follow? Jane did not reply until he had written something else.

Lady Matlock wrote to John thanking him for the back number of the *New Yorker*—Wilfred had adored it. Now she was going to ask him for something else. Could he get her a copy of the poem which Christopher published in the Oxford paper (Isis—or Cherwell)? Had it not been for Felicity she " would never have heard of it!!! " " Why," she wrote at the end, " don't you keep Jane and Christopher company at Edgeby over Easter? Alas, I don't see us being back before the end of April. Though God knows we must not complain. Wilfred's *ticker* turned up trumps in the end!!! "

John sent the poem—was thanked again, and this time pressed to stay at Edgeby for Easter.

" Your mother," he wrote to Jane, " is pressing. Shall I come? "

" Yes, of course," she answered, " if you feel you will be happy."

He raged. He asked her if she had any definite feelings about anything.

That term was remarkable for six weeks' continuous frost and snow. A thaw came at last and in mild sunlight the male pigeons were strutting importantly on the college grass, each puffed up in endless circular pursuit of a female, but never gaining an inch, as though each he or each she were limited by clockwork. Short flights changed nothing. They went on where they left off, on new ground. The still unravished bride, John thought—and the male kissing the joy as it flew. That was all she wanted—a little circling and strutting first.

Snowdrops appeared unexpectedly in odd corners where their buds had passed for grass, and the President's wife came through the lodge with catkins from the water-meadow.

The cricket and rowing credentials of freshmen were assessed and a committee was formed for a June ball. Sir Wilfred was so much better that he looked forward to cherry if not almond blossom at Edgeby. He said he heard the matron humming as if she would soon lay, and Miss Hislop had smiled. Jane passed this information to John because she had received two letters from him, one after another which she considered " sweet and almost normal," and she felt it worth while to prove her father was none of the things Christopher thought.

Was John suddenly " sweet and almost normal? " Even the person who has only imaginary mountains to climb and aims always at their sunflushed peaks which promise impossible solution —has, like any mountaineer, periods of going down, before again going up.

In schoolmaster language John might have seemed to have " pulled himself together "; in fact, for a time through exhaustion, he was content to fall apart, cease trying to pull himself together by his own definition of that phrase.

He had felt suddenly, " Let what is broken so remain"; the godsent resolution of tension, like a musical chord sinking back to its origin as though all were accomplished. The experience was not new to him for, once when he was seventeen, after the Battle of Britain, he had applied to join the R.A.F. in order to become a fighter-pilot at the youngest possible age (it was about the same time as when he ceased getting someone to load his Brownie camera, whenever it needed a new film), and he had gone to London for physical examination and been failed because he could not blow mercury high enough. When he got back to his room at Eton he lay down on his bed, and there looking at the ceiling experienced relief, a sweet annihilating weakness which was beyond the dream of opium, and the orgasm of sex. He had been spared the transpiercing point of the impossible; but he had offered himself to it.

Jane, the impossible, was still ahead, but the mood of relief persisted and John went out and was reminded by a warm wind off the grass of all the springs that he had ever known, and all the springs that had ever been, including those in the backgrounds of primitive paintings where the green of then had lasted exactly till now.

The mild rain of true affection fertilised some corners of his remorseless, ranting letters. Pleasant sentiments cropped up. A joke—clumsy, like a patient walking for the first time—about Bright ("spending Easter with Bright and Beautiful"), and an objective account of coffee with the Dean which made Jane laugh. And two lines of the word "Darling"—repetition to eye and ear but, full of variation, set to the music of love, as words for a song.

21

AT the prospect of meeting her—in five or ten minutes—the
memory of his letters weighed heavily upon him. The neutral
day, neither spring nor winter, wet nor fine, and the grey and
hazy green normality of the landscape, the ploughed plain and
occasional spire going by, recalled him to the massive strength
of the commonplace, soon to be reinforced by Jane's " Hallo."
There would be the familiar car at the kerb, and the county town
where she could pick up parcels at " the club," before taking the
road out to Edgeby past the only traffic lights, wedged between a
Norman keep done-up and a Tudoresque café. No. " One " did
not marry either for absolution or for extrication from a hypo-
thetical web; " one " married, either as suitably as possible, for
love; or with as much love as possible, suitably.

He tried to recall the face, the " atmosphere " of the person he
had abused, entreated, and adored by every other post for three
months. But no foretaste of Jane came to him. " Who is she?" he
wondered again as he saw her as a grain of sand on the beach of
time, one of a million million Janes, yet unique, as each was unique.

Could her last letter, he wondered, be counted as having
seconded Lady Matlock's invitation? " I look forward . . ." she
had written. Was that merely another mesh of her all-embracing
politeness.

She was standing under a light labelled Hatchford, in an old
mackintosh and beret. " Hal*lo*," she said, and he remembered she
always emphasised some word or syllable in any sentence, even if
there were only one word in it.

The cordiality of the final *o* drove him back on himself. Surely,
he thought, silence on this platform would have been the only

deference to what lay between them. In fact, at that moment she could not have done right.

They started towards " Way Out," and he remembered she walked like a duck hurrying.

Darling, darling, darling—where was that relief? It was somewhere—shut in by something. He did not dare or wish to look at her face, which though beautiful would not seem so. He would keep it for when it would be more, not less, than it was.

They walked along the platform like two people who happened to be going the same way at the same pace . . .

She pulled the starter and although her hand twitched at the first pulse of the engine, she still remained pulling as though mesmerised into an extra second of possibly destructive clumsiness. And her foot was heavy on the accelerator. The subsequent unnecessary roar of the engine seemed the escape of the suppressed forces which kept her hands and head moving, her body trembling, keen on the edge of that particular moment like a racehorse in the paddock.

She might indeed have shuddered if he touched her with a word, jibbed or whinnied with nerves. He could not cope with his surgical, satirical point of view, the blight of no love, no momentum of any kind.

" How's your father? " he said, and remembered a joke on those lines: The C.O. in a battalion of the Grenadiers who never said anything but this to a new face, and so had surprised a window cleaner in Birdcage Walk.

The trot of conversation soothed her, she went quietly, drove better, went into technical details of the operation with her eyes wide and capable. She hooted aggressively at any offender against the Highway Code.

They picked up parcels in the brown porch of the club—bulbs and fish. Then they talked of Christopher.

" Mummy," she said, " counted on him to chaperon us— some hope." She laughed shortly, nervously.

They were alone—and when they entered the house, they were still alone.

" Bright's out to-day," Jane said. " Leave your case there."

A Share of the World

The house was different. Fewer things lay about in the hall. The drawing-room seemed in icy white mourning for its mistress, and Jane said behind him, " We just use this room now." Drake, the retriever, wandered listlessly, flung himself down to sleep as though anywhere did. And the wet lawn with its threatening limit of weeds was clumped with bedraggled crocuses and unopened daffodils.

She said, " Everything's late this year . . . Did Christopher say anything about coming? . . . Did you see him? "

She was still formal, pretending he had never written those letters and that she had never said she was looking forward to his coming. He turned towards her and intimated as much with a smile. She said, " I'm sure you'll be dreadfully bored here."

" I'm sure I shall." Behind her were the stairs leading to an empty landing, and empty house. They were alone. A twinge of desire proceeded from the fact as though it were a part of her body.

They had not even shaken hands, or touched each other in any way. He moved towards her and she said, " I'll get the tea. Helen's got 'flu."

The emptiness of the large house came closer to him. He looked along the line of rosy and pale-cheeked ancestors, chosen by Neenie for the colours of their doublets and their dresses, to survive the sale of the less old, but bigger home.

" She will say ' Yes.' " The statement materialised in his head from God knows what deduction, wish . . . or even fear. To explain, he added: " Otherwise she would not have let me come like this when she's alone." Though that was not the reason, he knew, for the presentiment.

Did, at this prognostication of achievement, a great Hallelujah fill John's heart? No. The satirical mood of the station platform lingered, and now the face which often seemed to say, " How could she possibly say ' No ' *to me?* " Elaborately concealed even alone in that empty room, the thought, " If she takes me it must mean she had no one else." And from there proceed to wonder if she were so very " wonderful " and if he were in love. Emotionally, his character was a house built of cards, the full pack.

Although they cooked supper together in aprons, they ate it by

A Share of the World

the light of four silver candles ten feet apart, and half hidden from each other by flowers. The things they said were as relevant as the handshake of boxers. Bedtime with the house to themselves was approaching, and gradually at that thought the sharp and arid peaks of the mind, their caves false horizons and labyrinths where John had lived painfully, sank softly down into the first waves of the physical flood which would bring annihilation to all but the succulent, tender bliss of the double nakedness; the creative writhe in the warm tide of life.

At eleven forty-five by her travelling clock, John looked through her hair so close that the lights in it were thicker than the unfocused strands, and he thought how nearly this feeling of physical well-being was to complete happiness.

How nearly—but not quite. The tide was receding and again the inimical peaks and labyrinths began to stick out. " I do not know her," he said. " Is it only ' imagination ' that I ever *could* know her, ever *could* be intimate with her. Are we all of us alone for life? Is part of my feeling of perpetual impotence rooted in a refusal to accept this? To accept . . . the furniture of the solitary confinement cell, the furniture of heredity and conditioning—and turn from the bars where some unplaceable sun lures us to hope that out there it would be different."

She was sound asleep.

Leaving the bed he woke her. He found himself tiding the transition over with facetiousness.

" Well," he said, " the walls of Jericho are not down yet."

She smiled. " No. I'm sorry. Do you mind terribly? "

" I suppose the art of the adequate *pis aller* is one of the most important in life."

" You mustn't think I thought it adequate."

" Oh, dear, I hoped it was."

" You know what I mean."

He sat on the edge of the bed and took her hand. The china horses curvetted by the Swiss chalet musical box, and on a level with her face the florally bound common-place book lay under the *Oxford Book of English Verse* and ivory Prayer Book. Beside the

288

travelling clock lay the nurse's watch, a suddenly utilitarian article with its long red counter silently indicating seconds which nobody counted.

" Are we engaged now ? "

He said it like someone asking the rules of a card game he does not know and slightly despises. And as he looked at her, he saw what he had half expected. With the sheets under her chin suddenly, like a corpse, she was cold to all this. Silent—without promise of being otherwise.

" You don't want me to go on, do you? "

" No."

He stroked her hand, thinking how unusually still it is. I have given something. Would it one day after many nights together become still all the time? Cease wrangling and twining itself with its mate. Don't I know her now? Chinese wrists and Balinese breasts, drunk conjuror's hands, private schoolboys, the ace bowler's arms, skin so smooth it's sticky, like a petal; Prima Vera Botticelli's spring belly, obstinate mouth and large pitiful eyes, and outsized ballet dancer's legs, strong ethics, strong sex, self-realisation nil. I love her. I do now love her as " one " should love. I know her. I gave. Why should she not give. Or rather, why should she not *receive*. That was it. The true receiving was the real giving. And he wanted to give and she wouldn't let him.

" Sometimes I don't understand." The feeling was coming like the aura of a fit, the spasm of the denied spoilt child and he mustn't release it—he mustn't—so he spoke more quietly and carefully, and began again.

" Sometimes I don't understand. Can't you unbury anything —*anything*. Can't you even say which way you're moving, or say if you are moving. You share your bed with me, luxuriate in all sorts of caresses which leave nothing out and you cannot even say Darling, or commit yourself to the smallest piece of interest in me— or (much more important) in yourself, which would be a beginning. Do you know—I believe as I touch you, you are thinking of something else—some*body*, perhaps? "

It had come—the claustrophobia, the thing she gave him—

rising, choking him. She said nothing, nothing, but her face was tense and her eyes huge with what would soon be tears. He went on, " I see in your books you underline passages of poetry with a pencil that goes nearly through the paper, and yet your own feelings can't even stumble out."

She said nothing.

The blood was in command of his head, thickening his head and his lips were forward and the hysterical sneer in his eyes.

" Sunsets, rainbows, Christmas, the Louvre and Charles Morgan. Is that the long and short of it? With an *Encyclopaedia of Sex* in the po cupboard."

A tear as though mysteriously geared to her faculty of speech slid out of one eye as she said, " Oh, John; *please.*"

There had been, until recently, an *Encyclopaedia of Sex* in the top left-hand drawer of the chest of drawers within reach of her bed. Her mind became a motionless audience of what he would say next. " Have you ever said ' I love you ' to anyone? You know you ought to practise—for a quarter of an hour daily—just saying it—to that frayed teddy bear; then, when the feeling eventually makes the timid suggestion, you will be able to give tongue. Otherwise you won't."

She began to cry properly, sobbing with one sob connected with the next like a combustion engine firing, turning her head and the wet distortion of her features away from him. He had never loved her as much as he did now—and as though conscious where this love was derived from, he gave another stab.

" If everybody kissed every joy as it flew—bound no joy to themselves—there might not be any babies in the world. And love affairs would be a side-line for Wykehamists—like running Youth Clubs in slums."

She shook her head and ground her teeth—at his sudden ugliness—and when he tried to draw her towards him she said, " Leave me," in that weird wail of a voice speaking between sobs, from a constricted larynx and a mouth pulled wide at the sides.

So he had affected her—through her father again—the nerve in which she was sensitive.

How he hated at this minute that kind good man with his empty copperplate handwriting, the contagious claustrophobia of his self-effacement.

"Joy in killing high pheasants," he said, " and quoting Blake are in the last resort incompatible—especially for a man devoted to consistency like your father. Gandhi in the cap of the Eton Ramblers: He's the *ne plus ultra* of Dr. Arnold's mortgage—but an end, or worse—a *cul de sac:* an end where there shouldn't be."

"Go away," she sobbed. " *I mean it.* Leave me."

" Christopher was mechanically inevitable. He is pruning for new life. Your father is a dignified undertaker of the temporal power of his country and his class. This would be good if he had in reserve for us, some spiritual compensation. But he has the poem " If," and that is not enough."

"Go AWAY." She sat up and her voice was like a slap for hysteria. He stopped and put his hand to hers.

" No, leave me now."

She had been so composed her sleep had been like a trance or a child's, without breath. Now her face was drab with tears and formally resolved. She looked for a handkerchief which she did not find at once. She was ugly, pitiful. He loved her. Why could she not understand? He brought the intolerable burden of the past, and the love he had never given, and now he had reached her he could lay down neither, because she would not let him in, but talked to him from an upper window of a house without a door. Everywhere the familiar wall, the ubiquitous wall which must be smashed.

Going, he said, " The apostles of love—you and your father—are never likely to reap a harvest in it. The temporal monk and a ' county ' nun." She blew her nose—trying quietly at first—finally forced to trumpet grotesquely.

" And I love you," he said, as though it were a resolution just carried inside himself against an almost equal vote of hate.

When his hand touched the door-knob, she turned out the light.

22

THE room was half-lighted by the drawing of curtains but wholly lighted when the drawer left the window. Wheezing breath and deferential tread, from dressing-table to chair, from chair to wardrobe; stillness and a cough to request communication, and finally " Good morning, Mr. Grant," opened John's eyes to Bright.

The big man coming closer seemed to have surfaced with the waking dreamer from the tiring world of tight and shallow images in which responsibility is heavier and control slighter, than in life awake; and in which Bright co-existed with Jane, the ugly and beautiful impediments.

First light after long dark was behind him, cutting him out in black cardboard, emphasising the strange shape of his skull which shrunk sharply inward above the level of his brows. And when his features emerged there were the eyes, fastened on John's in spinal intimacy like a stoat's teeth. They seemed to know how yesterday had ended, for they reminded John of that—and of the other eyes which should have been intimate—but which had stayed closed, evasive or remote even when she was naked in his arms.

Thinking Bright must have spoken, John mumbled what he would wear, hoping thereby to have deprived the man of his excuse for standing there, so close—and then turned to the wall affecting sleepiness.

Perhaps Bright had never spoken, but had come to have a smile, a meal; perhaps he might touch. The idea nauseated John and he at once expected it until the wheezing breath—after taking its time—stopped to say, " Very good, sir," and the deferential tread resumed.

A Share of the World

At breakfast John went behind Jane's chair and, laying his hands on the outside of her upper arms, he said, " I'm sorry, darling —about last night."

Like sending for the *New Yorker* back number, his words at that moment, his " sorry " seemed merely a means, something he privately despised. It was she who should be sorry about last night—sorry for the barriers through which she could not come half-way to meet him, the aquarium she lived in with the wonderful infinite ocean painted on the sides, lighted herself—oh, lighted, but not seeing who was looking at her, either the crowd—or the one. She made a noise which accepted the apology and, at the same time, suggested it was due.

They rode at ten. He did not like riding much but he found it relaxed Jane, as some people are relaxed in a ship or a train. She left home behind and with it some of the chains of her legalistic and " ideal " self.

The sun shone and on the verges of fields the banks gave promise of the packed stadiums of summer. Brooks were already screened and gurgled unseen. And the celandine, violet and daisy, seemed inexplicably slight representation for so much moist floral sweetness in the air.

Perhaps, only now, under the influence of all this, did Jane accept his apology, saying nothing. And John came nearer to meaning his apology, regretting conflict of any kind in Nature's good mood; the coloured quiet beauty which is the owl's symmetry and not the shadow which alights on life, the butterfly and not the ichneumon's insemination of slow death, leaf, not aphis.

Jane, in conversation, was a fanatic of all things pleasant and therefore, often, of irrelevance. She even felt it right to talk for the sake of talking, that is to say—for the sake of projecting in tone and manner (words were not important) her general desire for friendliness and, yes, frankness. Who could have denied frankness to those eager blue eyes, even if they were fixed on the horizon of absolute high principle and not on you—or to that crusading brow¿

When Jane did *not* speak for the sake of projecting friendliness; in other words, when she meant to communicate seriously, the difference was apparent from the first syllable of the first word. Her voice became tense and jerky like a car moving with the brakes still on.

And sometimes she followed what she said in this way with a little interrogative noise—" h'm? "—a cry of protective care for the nakedness and vulnerability of that which she had brought forth in pain.

This noise she now made as she said, " Bright's going, did I tell you, h'm? "

She looked nearly at John—and like a racehorse at the start, living on the edge of this keener-than-ever moment, her whole body was subject to a bridling ripple of nerves which she disguised as a proud movement to throw the hair out of her eyes.

In the past John had had many different plans how to introduce the man's name, the whole subject. He now said indifferently, " Is he? Good." And to show a more complete disdain, he said, " Any more *billets-doux* from him? "

" Yes," she said. " That's why Mummy sacked him."

His horse sneezed, bellowing towards its hooves. They were on a path and the eight muted hooves sometimes approached unison of rhythm, before breaking up, after a moment of interesting cross-accent into haphazard confusion of sound. . . .

He said with a querulous edge to it. " Why didn't you tell me? "

" Because I didn't think it important."

The hooves converged on their common rhythm and left it.

" Yet you told your mother."

" When Father was better I told her, as you suggested I should —and she said he was to have a month's notice. She thought it mainly funny. I put it so that she should."

" In other words—*you* didn't."

" Didn't what? "

" Think it funny."

" Oh, John . . . please now . . ."

" Well, if you *had* thought it funny you'd have mentioned it in your letters. You'd have shared a joke that concerned me."

" Would I? Knowing you? Would you have found it funny? You ran a temperature over less."

A Share of the World

He thought, She wants to know what really happened . . .
That's why she brought the subject up.

Hoof rhythm re-emerged with the wheezing of harness.

She said, " When you told me it was all ' nothing '—that you'd
tell me about Bright sometime—I believed you. That's all. Hm? "

He looked at her. Civil war in her face; mouth obstinately
refusing, eyes wide and mild giving more, but fixed far away at
some abstraction of the situation, some principle covering it—not
at him.

He decided she was merely torn between curiosity on the one
hand and fear of hearing something intimate, and therefore
embarrassing, on the other. Yet that voice—why suddenly unrecognisable, keyed up to brevity, and pertinence?

She said, " What *did* happen? Hm? He isn't asking for money?
Why does he do it? I don't understand."

He had often imagined her saying just this, " Why does he do
it? I don't understand." From there, he had told himself, it
would be downhill all the way.

John said, " A grudge, I suppose."

The inadequacy of his words expanded in the silence like ripples
from a stone falling in a pond. He said, " I took him on a patrol
as a punishment. We had an accident on the way back. There was
. . . confusion. And I shot one of our corporals thinking he was
a German. Bright tried to get his own back—by complaining
about me. He found some supporters among tired and frightened
men. It was my second day."

Silence.

" *Did* he . . . get his revenge? "

" He managed to make trouble. No one believed him."

And that was how John closed the subject.

In the past he had imagined himself ending, " And that I
should see, looking up from the dead man's face, above me Bright
smiling seemed the confirmation of his eternal company, and the
proof that we are atoms without responsibility—and in my own case,
arranged in a pattern I wished to escape from. But the way out
—my desires—were his meal, his excrement.

" Whether it was wholly or partly because of these feelings

295

that I came after you I don't and will never know. Certainly I desired . . . What? . . . Some extreme and final possibility of disproving that smile, of breaking the web of myself—and as you walked into the floor, and knowing a little about you—I decided you would be the talisman. Perhaps there were all sorts of other things that really explained what happened at that moment as you waited for your partner to come through the crowd; perhaps I had been in that hell which someone described as the inability to love—and perhaps I saw you as the way out, the relief. Though God knows I loved Susan in a way, and in my two days' war I loved enough for a lifetime—a lot of people, the enemy not least. My dear friends and brothers in life, I could have said, Stop, and I think I might even have walked among the bullets saying that, even though I could not go into the white house. But whatever was the reason for setting you up as the solution—I did so. And when I came here the first time and found Bright at the door, then I knew that you were indeed the appointment I sought. That is all, really."

He had imagined he would say that.

He had imagined the moment so vividly—the relief of the confessional, the relief of humility and the vessel for intimacy which her face would be. As though she knew already—like Bright.

Instead there were the hedgerows, the horses restive for home, the first beech leaves like green darts for airguns, soup of leaves in puddles, lunch-time approaching, her eyes apprehensive (he was sure) of intimacy, fixed gratefully on solid natural scenery—far away—and in himself fear. Fear of what?

" Her fault," he thought; " it's her fault that I cannot tell her."

But Jane—even if she was devoted to the tangible pleasantness of her surroundings—and apprehensive of intimacy, retained the expression on her face which went with the subject.

And she said, " Did you loathe the war, h'm? "

And she leant forward and patted her horse ; allowed herself that.

" Loathe!" Gratefully he let himself out by an honest academic door. " Loathe is hardly the word. So huge an experience involving the extreme of so many emotions—can't be ' loathed ' (' loved ' would be as true as ' loathed '). All things considered the war was the experience I most value—which, considering my record in it, might seem extraordinary."

" Your record. What was wrong with your record? "

He did not reply at once.

" Hm? " She thrust the little interrogative at him, entrusted it with full powers to ask for everything. Her eyes, had they had their way, would have put down their blue cloak of kindness for him to step down—right down from his carriage—and still feel a king, standing in the mud of himself. But her thin wide mouth with the dominant upper lip restricted the gesture to opening the door, and looking graven.

" Oh, nothing in particular. No worse than many other people perhaps."

At such a suggestion of general equality (even though it came from himself, the former officer who had yearned to walk among the bullets saying, " Oh, my dear friends and brothers in life—stop," and who had known the war was not really being fought at all,) now felt rising a heady wave of blood and experienced a sweet taste. His face became " heroic," haughty, answering Bright's smile, and thinking of the never recorded superiority of German and Indian troops to the troops of the Democratic press, he suddenly added, " Perhaps far better than many."

Jane now took in her sun-golden, tangible surroundings for the first time since she broached the name of Bright. And she looked at them with disappointment as though she had expected better. " We must hurry a bit," she said, and spurred her horse to canter.

He followed, wind like winter in his nostrils. And he imagined that she had rushed off—at that particular moment—to avoid hearing what he had still to say; that she had shut him out, and prevented him from telling the truth.

23

IF lying with her nightly provided no emulsive scabbard for his body, it did for the sharp edges of his mind. The hysterical feeling of being " shut out " diminished. He began to succumb, while touching her, to a vegetable oblivion upon which specific thought whether of her or of anything else, was as slight as a ship on the sea.

Only occasionally, when the moment was over—or when he kissed her—he wondered if such apparently self-sufficient passivity could be a common denominator of women caressed. From beginning to end she was like a ballerina, never acknowledging with a personal look the pivot of her whole movement. And when her eyes were open they were more than ever shut.

Nevertheless, while he kissed her good night and put her woollen animals beside her, put her father's photograph where it was more clearly visible—a joke she just permitted—and tucked her up, he congratulated himself on a gradual return to that mood (of " Poor Jane ") in which he felt outside her in the sense that he encompassed her—even though shut out.

Poetry made her blank-eyed—or as it is more usually called, starry-eyed, so he wrote in her common place book, " Oh, my share of the World; oh, yellow hair."

When confidence comes to a person who has little, or none, the result is as plain as alcohol in a teetotaller. John after three days had distilled a single drop of confidence—from so much beauty, so much nakedness so often in his arms—and from the aggregates and averages of the ineffable sums of encouragement and discouragement—carefully figured minute by minute from her looks, movements, occupations, tones and words.

A Share of the World

And this one drop of confidence he made into a heady vapour. He felt—and behaved—as though he had enough confidence for two. "We," he now said. And as formerly, he had believed Jane shared his preoccupation with Bright's letter, he now imagined she shared his preoccupation with their new and better relationship. She herself avoided it more than ever as a topic, but that, he told himself, is because "She's changing—she's quite different the last few days." And he was right—she was.

Long absent-minded pauses interrupted her, whatever she was doing. With the receiver of the white telephone at one ear her face would cloud and peer with the effort of remembering why she had picked it up.

She looked worried, guilty, and apparently engaged herself, while knitting, in argument. Like a sensitive listener to a good actor, her face was moved by the soundless words she heard in her own head.

John, spring sunshine within and without, assured himself that she was suffering the pains of that necessary birth—"of her true self"—from which could proceed "intimacy" and love; that awakening of which the first coherent word would be his still unuttered name. (She had never called him by his name to his face.)

Then without pertinent preliminary, one afternoon, she spoke in that quick blurt which was not the usual one but again the pure metal of her communication.

"What are you going to do, h'm?"

"Do?"

"How're you going to live?"

She tried to camouflage the blurt with a nervous laugh and a long word. "If it's not impertinent."

So we're as near as that, he thought, like a passenger looking out and seeing suburbs.

"Does it matter to you?" he said.

"Not particularly. You know what I mean. It's the sort of thing one usually knows about young men. I suddenly realised I didn't know it about you."

A Share of the World

"I expect I'll find something," he said. "You see—there was the war. Then you."

The "you" made her sheer off.

The suburbs; his confidence increased. The right, smug, childish and extrovert side of his face was dominant. Meringues for dinner, bed with Jane, job from Mary's millionaire perhaps (why not), tennis after lunch, rest in the hot hut with few clothes—her body in another covering, white—and baring her breasts in the rose-garden where the wall was high and the beds black, and no gardener ever came.

"Do you want a big family?" he said. "You look as if you might."

She was amazed. "Why on earth do you ask that?"

He sent her a look but she refused it admission. He said, "If it's not impertinent."

"I've always wanted six children—if you really want to know." And she went on knitting.

She went upstairs to fetch something and forgot what, and then sat mechanically at her dressing-table trying to remember, which led to a slumped brooding, interrupted by two looks at herself in the mirror and one adjustment of an everyday ear-ring, but without enthusiasm. And then a long look out of the window and a self-reminder to post Father's pile of pattern books, for his knitting, and her mother's Bentham and Hooker. John. Cruddock was putting the ponies out and she had asked him not to. John. She would wash her hair after tea, she had meant to do it yesterday. It had to be done. It was a perfectly legitimate withdrawal. A beginning.

Three months ago he would have been shrill in his suspicion of why she left him after tea to wash her hair. Now he read happily. At dinner he found her conversation so "made" that he felt a twinge of the familiar panic.

"Darling, I'm not the Vicar—or a neighbour," he said. "You needn't distress us both with so much effort. If you feel like it—say nothing for an hour."

The false animation of "nerves," fear of him and of the situation vanished. She went blank and stern—then slightly

A Share of the World

shook her head as though there were no reply to such unpardonable rudeness.

" *Inoui*, am I? " Like " *assommant* " and " *impayable* " this was one of the French words she used commonly. Then he tried to retrace some of these steps—but without success.

By now he took their nightly lie together for granted. But to-night more than usually he looked forward to it—to wipe out the sound of her voice at dinner, hateful because it treated him as a stranger—and the subsequent more formidable sound of her silence.

At her door she said, " Good night."

She always said this even though they were together again in half an hour.

He replied, " Good night, Jane "—also common usage. He returned to her room—in less than half an hour. She was still dressed, kneeling by a gaping drawer on one knee, using the other as a table for folded clothes.

" Not undressed! "

" I haven't rung Mummy up yet."

" But it's past eleven."

" That's nothing to her."

" But . . . you'll be ages."

She went on tidying. He sat on the edge of her chair within reach of her and put a hand on her shoulder.

" What is it? " he said.

Her face was wretched. He drew her towards him but she resisted gently and put his hand away. Before releasing it she looked up and said, having gentle hold of him all the time:

" We ought to stop. Shouldn't we, h'm? "

And then she put down his hand as she had once put down the diamond and ruby brooch—sweetly, gently, gratefully, soberly. He looked carefully at her.

" What do you mean—' stop? ' "

" Before it's too late," she said.

" What are you trying to say? "

Against resistance he took her in his arms—smothering this

301

mood in her and in himself, smothering the sick fear of the un-
thinkable, unfaceable. He closed her mouth with kisses.

" You see . . ."

" No," he said. " Don't, darling, don't."

Gradually caressing and lulling the protest and pain of her
face, he undressed her gently with honour and attention for every
exposure, and eventually restored to her the self-sufficient peace
which he was able to accept, even though it did not include
him.

And he returned to bed thinking, " My hands—my hands build
and my words destroy."

For the fourth successive day the sun shone and the news from
the nursing home was still good. Scilla, grape hyacinth and crocus
opened, and they, with the sweet warm sweat of the lawn, scented
the air which was warm and cold in patches like the sea to a bather.
Sitting still in the garden on a seat hot out of the breeze, and watching the birds bouncing from worm to grub, with quick queries
between, John succumbed to the gentle inebriation of spring,
unbearably sweet, he thought, not in the promise of what is to come,
but in the recollection of all previous promises of what was to come
—and what came, and went. Usually fierce in his forward-looking
planning or his backward-looking analysis, shrill with present
discontent or yearning, he now sat placid in the moment like the
fat thrush and found it enough.

In time, he thought, as he sat there in the sun, he would tell
Jane about Bright, about the past—gradually—as such things
should be told, if and when they seemed worth telling, and his
failure to tell her the other day was not serious. In time she would
open her eyes to him, and one day she might call by his name to
his face, the thing she had never done. That mood of last night
" shouldn't we stop? "—he would smother as he had smothered it
then—with kisses, and he would take off her clothes because, without
clothes, she seemed his.

Jane's face—in spite of the sun, the scillas, and the news from
London—seemed less happy, and her fingers, as Neenie would have
said, more than ever *mouvementés*. John attributed this to the

" breakdown " which she must be experiencing while her heart thawed, while she " lets herself go."

And on the hot seat out of the wind she joined him and she watched the bright medallion on a cart-horse's forehead go along the top of the low garden wall, and he held her hand through which went the involuntary tremors, which he had promised glibly, like a pedlar of home-made pills, to take away from her " in time."

Enough. Life was enough, and he would nurse her through these pangs of rebirth—or first birth of herself—and be there to shield the nakedness of that first sincerity, protect the vulnerability of her abandonment . . . as he had protected that of Susan when she was fourteen. Yes, he assured himself, as he would have protected that for life, had Susan required. But she hadn't.

" Oh, that none ever loved but you and I," he thought—what an odd wish . . . to sentence oneself to the incommunicable; to have one's truth set down as madness! To have this extraordinary gentleness derided.

He raised her hand and kissed the inside of her wrist where the small blue veins divided and multiplied like lines coming to a station. She looked at the place he kissed apologetically as though it were to blame. His fingernails showed like crescents of Indian ink on paper. Her conscientious blue stare was clouded by pity and distaste which together blended into doubt. A butterfly went by, a drunken erratic blob of colour in the sun and he assured her that she, too, would soon leave her chrysalis and be like that in the warmth of his love. He began to make a daisy chain, and childhood returned to him with the feel of his thumbnail splicing the first stalks. She watched him apprehensively and said nothing when he suggested, without looking up from his task, that they should go to the wood where they could dress totally in daisies, or whatever grew in the wood. He took her silence for tranquillity and when the circle was complete put it over her head. She picked up the bottom where it lay on her breast and like a shopper who wants to go out without buying, said flatly, " How sweet."

He speculated about getting a job, though " not in a town " was as far as he got. It didn't matter. She was beside him now and would be beside him in bed this evening.

A Share of the World

Like Icarus, his wings were all his own work.

When the evening post came she said, " The awful thing is "
—she looked at him with unusual directness—" Mummy wants
me to go down to London the day after to-morrow and be with
Father. She's got to go away for three days. Then we'll bring
him back together."

He signified he could wait three days. It was even possible he
might get some work done.

And then she said, " And the thing is, Bright goes to-morrow,
and there'll be no one left to look after you."

He said, " Without Bright where would I be? "

" And Mummy wants to let Helen have a few days off before
she comes back with Father . . . You could go and come back,
h'm? In a week or ten days—when we've moved Father."

" I could come to London with you."

She considered this.

" I shall be terribly tied. But why not? Do."

Then suddenly he understood. It had been on his lips to say
something facetious about being " able to face Father's tray—
especially an away match—in London." But now that he understood, the tin-pot rattle of the remark was like gramophone jazz
from a top floor after a newsboy shouted " War." How—only a
moment ago—could such a sound have been selected?

She was plunging logs into the fire, her legs astride the brass
and iron impedimenta of the hearth. He said quietly, " Do say
what you really mean."

But a log crashed, as it sent a champagne of fire up the chimney.
The other night she had said, " We must stop "—and they
hadn't stopped. Yes, this feeling would be over any moment now.
Life as it had been, would come back.

She said, " What? Would that be all right then, h'm? "

There was fear in her face.

" I said—do say what you really mean."

" H'm? "

Numerous, almost imperceptible movements, occurred in her
limbs and her face. He sometimes thought you should be able

to see her heart and her liver and her whole complex of nerves through her skin as in an angel-fish, and above it a fin spinning like a propeller, marking the pulsations of life fitted by its fragility for existence in water or air—or love, he had thought; the kindest encompassing love. Then she made that jerky little noise again, meaning pertinence.

" H'm? What do you mean? I mean I've got to go to London and I'm afraid you'll have to move out too."

The obstinate mouth and charitable eyes were on the same side now. " Be careful," they said fearfully.

The human mechanism for rejecting the truth that cannot be born is like the force that keeps a mussel tight shut; it reacts least strongly at the first prising apart, even admitting a peep of light and air, and expelling a squirt of itself; after that it is braced and solid as a stone. After a pang of fear like nausea John had felt suddenly strong and cheerful in the determination not to take her seriously.

" In a million years," he said, " your mother would not take you away from having fun, having youth—' with Osbert's son at Edgeby.' Would she? Precious, precious youth. How glorious it had been; now yours; all yours. Can't you see her eyes? No, Jane, no. Do me the kindness of killing me with a less obvious weapon. Come up behind me with a humane killer and call my attention to the swans on the mantelpiece. Tell me your mother's ill—not gone anti-social."

As a matter of fact, Lady Matlock had asked Jane to come south " if you could possibly, possibly tear yourself away, darling, for three days: I promise no longer."

She clung to his error with relief.

" Why do you think you know everything? "

He watched her, calculating.

" H'm? " she said.

" Then, Jane," he said; " give me the date I can come back— so I can look up the train now. Or better still, come and sit here and behave about this going south in such a tearful way as to make me believe it."

He listened to his theatrical verbosity. At heart he had nothing but a prayer. He took her arm and pulled her gently down beside him.

" I love you. Why d'you want to go away, Jane? "

Suddenly she began to cry and he thanked God. Every tear was a relief for him: her submission, her retraction of all she had said. As before, she never wept, as she spoke—with reserve or stilted exuberance. She wept always with abandonment and quick disfigurement. It was her moment of truth.

In his relief he was moved and bent down to kiss her but when his lips were on her head she pushed him away, and she blurted out, "This tyranny . . ." She sat up with instantly organised face. "Don't you see? What I've been trying to tell you—we must *stop*—for *your* sake. All along you've assumed things. It's such . . . claustrophobia—you. And Mummy. And the last days—you made me feel a liar."

" A liar? " He felt sick and suddenly a spectator. She said, " You made me feel I'd promised something. I haven't."

Perhaps from some internal crack of the ethical whip she obtained strength to hold her features in control and gradually regain her normal manner. Strength also to call him by his name to his face for the first time and to look at him directly and intimately, taking him in a few inches from her; him and all he was, and had been and probably would be; in fact the look he had imagined, the longed for intimacy—and she said, " John, I'm sorry for you. But that's not enough, is it? "

Sorry for . . . That half of his face which owned the eye, arched with a higher brow and dulled with the objectivity of a corpse, repudiated the words " sorry for " and took behind it, so to speak, the smithereens of the smug, childish other eye, its complete and unbearable pain, the tatters of its moment of normality, its sporting attempt. The arched eye took control now with its strange comforts and theories, its lines of defence behind which any imaginable withdrawal was and had been in the past, possible. And he said quietly, " Yes. Or rather I should say, No—that's not enough."

She said nothing and was quite still. Her tremors had ceased—as they did in bed after the last caress. She was looking away—she also trying to find something out.

"No. My . . . atmosphere," he said. "I quite understand —can't have been very reassuring." Then in a different voice, "You see . . ."

It was the note in his voice she dreaded. Rising. She took her hand out of his but he took it back.

"Oh, John—please. Now, *please*."

"I want to say that I understand, Jane—but also just to ask you one thing. Was I very ingenuous to take your body as your spokesman—since your tongue seemed to be tied?"

"I don't really know what you mean. If you mean, should I have let you into my bed . . . But what's the good of all this?"

He still held her hand. The rawness, the ugliness, of the thing that was dawning in his face obliged her to look away whenever she looked at him.

"Bright's letters," he said, quietly and contemptuously; "they didn't help, did they?"

With her free hand she separated his fingers on her wrist.

"You will believe what you want to believe—so what does it matter what I say." She got up.

"Perhaps you lapped them up. And perhaps I never told you 'everything'?"

"John, this has nothing to do with anything."

"Do you know something? It takes *two* to tell the truth. The alternative is silence. And do you know another thing—the hell of being with you was . . . *being alone*."

When she was some distance from him, collecting odds and ends to take upstairs and pack, she said, "Then you'll soon be out of hell."

24

HE noticed, in a corner between the sash and sill of the window, the single dried wing of a fly and some grey dust. When life, that is to say, desire, failed—the details of whatever was close became invested with the significance which had been drained from everything else. The wing, the dust, the grain in the cedar and the marking of it like the marking of seed-cake under his eyes seemed to have acquired all that he had lost. For in him there was nothing —nothing except the feeling that the dried wing, the dust and the scraped cedar of the sill were important, the inexpressive holders of the complete secret.

Light was failing so that when Helen put her head round the door, briskly with the faintly contemptuous assurance of old servants, she did not see him at once. Then she said, " Miss Matlock asked me to say she wouldn't be coming down to supper . . . as she isn't feeling very well."

" Yes," he said. " Thank you."

The old face took him in, how he was sitting close to the pane like a child, on a window-seat too narrow for sitting on, and no light.

" You can't see like this, sir," she said testily, and turned a switch on, partly in order to look at him. Then she thought of the undrawn curtains and that man who calls himself a butler. She waddled from window to window, pulling cords so that the rectangles of grey dusk were replaced by sweeps of yellow satin after one short swoosh.

When she had got to his window where he had leant on the garrulous going to bed of the birds, the calm change of light, the dried wing of the fly and the dust, he got out of her way like an old dog uncertain where to go next as though she might come after him wherever he went.

A Share of the World

He made an effort. " Nothing serious, I hope."

He said it mechanically as though talking about weather to a liftman, each pair of eyes escaping into the moving wall.

" No, sir, nothing."

She went, flipping at the cushions, as she had come, with a burdened urgent tread and much sighing.

At quarter to eight, when he was reading a book of which he did not know the title or author, the door behind him opened and he heard someone stand there. He did not turn round.

" Dinner is served, sir."

" Thank you."

He heard Bright standing there and saw him as clearly as though he were looking at him. Then he heard him go.

Jane's, or rather his, place had been moved so that he sat at the head of the table. Bright eased the chair into the flexing angles of his knees from behind so that he had only to lower himself. The four tall candles burned at the four corners of a mass of spring flowers like a miniature tableau of a lying-in-state. Their freshness and fragrance reminded him of Easter Sunday at Stiley during his childhood, his father reading the lesson, saying, I am Alpha and Omega, the beginning and the end, high up behind the brass snarling eagle, his head high and eyes downcast at the text or raised to affirm the meaning to the back of the church.

Alpha and Omega . . . Bright's hand he did look at—as the soup was laid down in front of him—and noticed that it was plump and small, suitable to the man's high voice and thick thighs, but not to his huge frame.

" All alone, sir? " said Bright.

" Yes," John replied.

" Beer or whisky, sir . . . Or water? "

" Whisky."

Bright went and came and went, and John never looked at him.

A person in physical pain who finds no position comfortable never settles in one because it will be as good as the next, but continues to experiment, failing where he has failed before. Since light had fallen John had examined every possible course of action, present and future, and also every alternative for the past. Satisfied

309

by none, he now went over them again desultorily while he ate. Every scene he imagined had Jane in it—yet now he had to plan scenes without Jane. He did—but they were not true. He could not see himself unstacking the accumulated editions of *British Butterflies* off the bed in his father's so-called spare room in Knightsbridge, and settling down there till the next Oxford term. He could not see himself joining one of his three or four friends for company; he could not see . . . himself.

The door would open and she would come in, wouldn't she? No, she wouldn't come in because, really, this situation in which he found himself without her was both familiar and expected. It seemed to have happened before because, in fact, in essence, it had. In essence nothing but this had ever happened.

Between courses he listened for Bright's steps after he had rung the little silver hand-bell inscribed " Neenie," and when once they didn't come but instead there was silence, no noise of himself or anyone else eating or moving, no wind, no creak of the house or night-cry from out of doors, he became aware of the blood in his ears; he continued to live.

The childhood fear that he was the only person in the world —all others in league against him, seeing what he would do next, came strong like a memory from a smell.

He rang the bell again, and Bright came with a summer pudding from which a section had been taken already. She would be eating it now from her tray beside the *Oxford Book of Verse*, and her curveting china horse.

Love had increased only as need had been satisfied. He had explained the vicious circle to her from the start. What more could he have done, what more could he have explained?

Bright's letters? She had been the white house, which he could not go into.

After dinner he moved into the hall where he and Christopher had drunk with Bright until Sir Wilfred had appeared at the stair-head. He sat in the same arm-chair as he had sat in then and listened to Bright clearing the table next door. He wondered vaguely about trains to-morrow. Would she still go to London?

A Share of the World

He began passing a strand of hair through his fingers looking at the bottom stair.

As long as the bereaved write and receive letters about their loss they almost cease to be bereaved such is the relief, the irrelevance, of trying to put sorrow into words, or thank people for sympathy. Then there is the sheer distraction in labour of writing, licking, and stamping a hundred, two hundred letters. But with a look into a wardrobe, or silence in a certain place where there should have been movement at that time of day, with some mess of work or play for ever unfinished—then comes the dry stab beside which the fluid, almost sweet-sad idea-of-it-all, is vanity.

So when John looked up the stairs and imagined her coming down them to-morrow, different, he closed his eyes. For an instant he had seen her. The idea-of-it-all gave place to the stab.

As a result he immediately got up and went up the stairs to her room door, and after a pause of fear at the sight of it, knocked. There was no reply. He turned the handle and pushed. It was locked.

From this he got a vision of himself seen through her eyes, and it hurt so much that he knocked louder.

A door opened down the passage where no light was on, and Helen said, " Miss Matlock took a sleeping-draught and put her light out early. She asked not to be disturbed, sir."

Helen's door clasped many seconds after she ceased speaking. The leaf which came out from the wall where Sir Wilfred's tray used to lie with its beaded napkin cover, was beside him hanging down. John remembered the four lines, neatly spaced and indented as though in a book, written in the copperplate adult-childish hand.

He who binds to himself a joy.

He returned to the hall chair. In the mound of old ash, a few lights burnt at different levels, like a village at dusk.

The phrase, and the variations of the phrase " I didn't know what to do next " is usually used lightly and untruthfully since it is nearly always followed by an account of what the person *did* do for which it is merely an anecdotal enhancement and aperitif.

A Share of the World

But occasionally it happens that a stream of action and of thought comes like a road to a blown bridge; or to put it differently— occasionally people in " civilised " life are like those desert guides who can go on from oasis to oasis across ten links of horizon by intuition like an ant in the deep jungle of a lawn, but who for several times in their life stop and say, " I don't know where I am," and from that moment on are less use than people who calculate or remember where the sun or the pole star roughly is.

John now did not know what to do. Jane had everything. He had given her that position theoretically; then she took it in reality.

In the past he had been capable of prayer, feeling it to be " the discipline of harmony," transferring consciousness from flower to roots, that is to say, the act of remembering the origin and destination, the common bed of all roots, in order to balance the top-heavy temporal airy feeling of personal flower and difference.

But now, clearly, the " discipline of harmony " was not in the power of the ravaged, untidy face which watched the logs as though they might suggest something, have some answer. He did not, could not pray. And didn't try to.

His right hand still had the feel of the lockedness of her door.

At this time there was quite a run of suicides among older-than-usual undergraduates—in digs—for no reason which newspapers were able to relate. Coroners claimed the balance of each mind was disturbed, but strangely it was with a feeling of inspired lucidity and balance that John realised he wished he was dead, and that, therefore, holding no clear religious or other objection—in theory— the logical thing to do was to give himself the immediate benefit and comfort of that condition.

As when he had tried to separate the " idea of " the patrol to the white house from the reality of it, when he had gone out in the imagination before he went out in fact to see if it were possible, so now he went to the right-hand, big, brass-handled, stained drawer in the gunroom, and saw that the person pulling the trigger of the old revolver was not him . . . But perhaps, he thought, where conscience and pride failed, misery will succeed.

So he stopped imagining—and went.

A Share of the World

Loose rounds of several types and nationalities rolled sonorously about the butts of their parent pistols when he pulled the drawer open. A Luger, a long barrelled Mauser, a Webley and a Belgian Browning .45 automatic offered their black, in childhood exciting, " the-idea-of-it " shapes.

He took up the Luger and a piece of Sten-gun ammunition and looked at them both.

He loaded the weapon, having difficulty with the " bridge " which once flexed up would not go down. He remembered you took out the magazine. It slacked down straight and he clapped home the magazine—and there it was, lying in his hand as faithfully as a piece of squeezed clay and as heavy as gold.

The idea of it. The reality. Here now—there afterwards in one of those extravagant attitudes, pedalling or trying to keep warm—reaching for something. " *There's no vanity.*" Being an instrument of death, the thing stimulated the feeling for life. The associations of the oil and tow smell of the gunroom were bright winter and boyhood and the feeling of immortality, of even that day being endless in time and unlimited in promise, of dogs crazed with anticipation, their yawns half-yearning yells of impatience. Then he thought of taking *British Butterflies* off the spare-room bed in his father's flat and " doing some reading "—on a level with the men and women in white coats mending furs, near pigeons bigger than buses below, and looking up from his book, waking up from his bed, seeing, hearing, tasting, touching his loss of Jane, his complete loss; and so arriving at the latest strand of the " web of himself," the shape which he must accept.

He raised the neat muzzle roughly in the direction of his temple and at once felt an ache there.

He lowered it.

He saw himself then and a qualm of nausea made him turn his head to one side, away from the pistol, as though to have picked it up had been actually to *touch* the recurring pattern of his futility.

At that moment despair was his master—and showed itself the perfect torturer in that it kept him alive.

Alive—the word occurred to him as he stood there. That was all he was—alive. Nothing more—or less.

A Share of the World

He again moved his head, but this time it was one of those blind movements which sick animals suddenly make—a sudden stare at a spot nearby—as though the pain were a phantom outside them.

And then—into this suspense of life while still alive—into the ears of this breathing nothing, there fell a sound.

Was it a quality of the sound which told him; did he decide by a rapid elimination of alternatives; or did he merely have a premonition that the person who had never failed him when it came to intimacy should now know where he was—and what he was doing—or not doing—and wish to join him?

Slowly he raised his eyes to the door as though the big man already stood there. With that smile.

Soft steps in the passage.

Affinity, he thought, with that smile of affinity.

Affinity.

And then—some dam of blood inside him seemed to break. He felt a hot rush to the head. His saliva changed taste—and the inside of his nostrils stretched. His face felt all mouth—and when a hand touched the outside of the door he called out in a high unnatural voice, " Come in, Bright."

The door which had begun to move stopped as though it had changed its mind. Then it moved again.

And although it was opening he called out again, " Come in," because there was only now. His blood was a mob in frenzy, pounding his will with one reiterated cry: Now, now, now.

Then—there stood Bright in a flashy dressing-gown—and polished shoes. He didn't look at the pistol—as though that went without saying—but he looked at John's face and his huge body seemed to expel air as he settled down to a smile. " I heard a noise, sir," he said, " in the gunroom. Seeing the hour, I thought I ought to investigate."

The thickening of John's head with blood had subjected him to an extraordinary stillness and the look in his feverish eyes was entranced as though then, at that second, he saw a car skidding towards a rock.

Bright's eyes wavered.

314

A Share of the World

He said, " Seeing as how there's valuables in here . . . I thought I ought . . ." And now Bright's voice stumbled as though the words he was really saying, the words of his second nature, were disregarded. He picked up suddenly, and said with vicious carefulness, " Make sure no one was playing with guns. Because an accident might happen even *if nothing else*."

John stood still.

Then Bright's eyes were like frantic carnivorous teeth slipping . . . slipping.

The pistol lay limp, rested, in a hammock of apparently neutral hands.

Bright blurted, " You shouldn't do yourself an injury, Mr. Grant. There'd be people sorry. Wouldn't Miss Jane be sorry? "

As though that name had been a clock striking, John's hand holding the weapon now pointed at Bright's face, the time being Now.

The big man's smile quivered—was by fits and starts, greater and less than ever before. Finally it flourished, fattened on what it saw.

" A gun! Mr. Grant," he said; " a real gun. It might go off . . . like the other did."

A sudden softness came into John's face, and Bright said sharply like a twig snapping, " Don't."

He followed frantically with the same word again and suddenly the long worm of his smile seemed to have been hooked; it turned on itself, writhed. And the third time he said " Don't " it sounded almost sleepy.

" Don't—'s . . . *loaded*."

A dog barked in the yard.

Sometimes the sleep-walker, driven by the obscure and profound compulsions of a symbolic word, comes, as it is called, to himself at a place where another step would have killed him, at a place, too, which he does not recognise. And he thinks, where am I? How did this begin?

John lowered the pistol slowly, then looked at it as though the conjuring trick which had put it in his hand without his knowledge was now over. He was a stranger to it; and he put it down on a ledge and it made a solid noise. Then he noticed the open drawer with other pistols in the bottom—so he put it with them.

A draught felt on his forehead as though it came from frost. He put up his hand—and it came away wet. He shut the drawer.

Behind him, half-exultant, half-querulous Bright said, "Playing around." And a moment later in exactly the same tones and with the same suggestion of insanity as a stuck gramophone "Playing around."

John saw the vague reflection of the man in the glass of the gun-case. He turned and walked towards the door. Half-way across he stopped.

"Pretending," Bright said, and then went back to "Playing around."

John suddenly felt, "I could touch him," and he looked at the body in front of him as though he might do just that. But like a mummy unearthed, unswaddled after millennia, there seemed every second, to be less and less of Bright to touch.

As John passed through the door a hectic intense whisper followed him, "F—— crazy. F—— hopping mad."

There is a state in which the limbs sleep, even sweat and seem furry with relaxation—while the mind floats, as it were, with idle motors, on the surface of consciousness.

It brings, like some stages of fever, a sudden bird's-eye view of life which is impersonal but reassuring—as though "I" could look upon it all without that "I"—and find the value undiminished.

John lay thus, and it seemed to him that he had passed through pain and attained a calm, which one moment seemed an unthought-of triumph, at the next—merely the aftermath of nervous strain—a *post coitus* of the mind, sweet and sad.

When he thought of it as the former, he asked himself, at what point he had used the correct initiative. The ethics then, became blurred, because it seemed to him that when he had "tried" he had spoiled. "Resist not Evil," he thought.

He drifted a bit in the current of that thought. The ceiling had a rift of pallor which he put down to the moon till a cock crowed and was copied far off.

Jane. So close in the house. Through three walls. Twenty feet away.

" I did not love her," he thought; " certainly not at first, perhaps not even later."

A cold fragrance came from the window which he could now place as an opaque square. He imagined the dew—the unexpected wetness beneath a clear sky.

The admission that he hadn't loved Jane opened up in retrospect, a landscape that did not astonish him. He followed his road across it, reserving surprise only for the place to which it had brought him. " Because now," he said, " in a way I do love her."

How strange that this should make it easier—or at any rate, *possible*—to go away from her; as though to love were to own . . .

" The world," he thought; " the whole world."

And when he left next morning, under his own early arrangements, enough of this mood remained to make the departure feel, not an end, but a beginning.

The curtains of her bedroom were still drawn, and he looked back at them as he passed under them and again from the main road.

THE END

CPSIA information can be obtained
at www.ICGtesting.com
Printed in the USA
LVHW090050280520
656702LV00022B/176

9 780992 523428